**Leabharlanna Poiblí Chathair Bhaile Átha Cliath
Dublin City Public Libraries**

Comhairle Cathrach
Bhaile Átha Cliath
Dublin City Council

Drumcondra Branch Tel: 837720u

Date Due	Date Due	Date Due

Brooke Magnanti received a Ph.D. in Forensic Pathology from the University of Sheffield, where she studied in the Medico Legal Centre and specialised in the identification of decomposed human remains. She later worked for the NHS in child health research and cancer epidemiology, before being revealed in 2009 as the anonymous author of the award-winning blog Belle de Jour and bestselling *Secret Diary of a Call Girl* series of books. She lives on the West Coast of Scotland with her husband and hardly ever sees dead people any more. Visit her website at www.brookemagnanti.com, and follow her on Twitter @belledejour_uk

THE
TURNING
TIDE

BROOKE MAGNANTI

An Orion paperback

First published in Great Britain in 2016
by Orion Books
This paperback edition published in 2017
by Orion Books,
an imprint of The Orion Publishing Group Ltd,
Carmelite House, 50 Victoria Embankment
London EC4Y 0DZ

An Hachette UK company

1 3 5 7 9 10 8 6 4 2

A CIP catalogue record for this book
is available from the British Library.

ISBN 978 1 4091 6374 9

Printed in Great Britain by Clays Ltd, St Ives plc

MIX
Paper from
responsible sources
FSC® C104740

www.orionbooks.co.uk

For Thin Lash Connolly:
we'll always have the informesa.

PROLOGUE

Of all the things that Daniel Wallace had hoped to do on holiday, finding a dead body was not one of them.

The kayak trip from Skye to Raasay was perfect. It was his girlfriend's first visit to Scotland and he wanted to make it a weekend she would never forget. Daniel had planned this leg of the trip carefully: a journey starting on Skye, going up the long east coast of the island of Raasay. Winter weather in the Highlands was tough to predict but although the water was cold, there was little wind and the only snow was on the mountaintops. They would paddle past the steep cliffs and fossil beaches with views over to the mainland and lunch on the cobble beach below castle ruins he knew well, then continue on to a romantic night at a bothy inaccessible to walkers and unlikely to be occupied at this time of year.

Maya teased him for being such a list maker, but as the day went on he was pleased at having planned it so well. There was a slight chop on the water as they left Skye and late winter light on the wavelets sparkled like sequins. It changed to perfect glass as they rounded the tip of Raasay and turned north. There was a superpod of dolphins spanning the sound between the island and Applecross on the mainland, hundreds of them leaping and squealing for the sheer fun of jumping around. He could tell Maya was nervous about the large mammals at first. She clutched the shaft of her paddle tightly, but was soon laughing with the joy of it all.

They landed on the northern tip of the island. Maya pulled her kayak above the tide line onto the shingle beach while Daniel hung back. 'Something wrong?' she asked.

'I think there's something caught in my rudder,' Daniel said, 'bit of seaweed, maybe. You go on ahead and find the bothy, I'll catch up.'

'Sure,' she smiled. Daniel watched her buttocks cased in her kayaking drysuit disappear along the path. Three years in and he still fancied this woman as if they had just met. That had never happened to him before. A good sign, right? That she was a keeper. The One.

So far, so perfect. Tonight they would watch the sunset from the beach and share a bottle of whisky. He would make them a simple meal of bacon and tuna pasta on the gas camping stove. The bothy had a fireplace to ward off the cold but there wasn't much wood on the island, so Daniel had brought peat bricks and coal in a thick blue rubble bag.

Then there was the ring, tucked safely away in his dry bags. He planned to pop the question after dinner: maybe on a moonlit walk, maybe sitting by the bothy fire later. With the day going so well he could afford to play that part by ear.

They had met on a kayaking course Daniel was teaching at a leisure centre pool in Croydon. Normally he didn't date students but Maya had caught his eye. That would have been where things ended, but to his surprise she asked him out after the course was over. It didn't take him long to realise that she was, not to put too fine a point on it, the love of his life. Even more so than kayaking.

The best part was that Maya wouldn't be expecting him to propose. It was as close as he had ever got to being spontaneous, and she knew that wasn't his usual style. She probably thought he would pop the question after a long discussion, then they would shop for rings together. She hadn't known that he figured out that the diameter of her finger was the same size as the plastic ring pull on the orange juice he always bought.

That was tonight sorted. Tomorrow? Tomorrow they would paddle around the smaller nearby isle of Rona before heading back down the other coast of Raasay and back to Skye. He had already booked a table and room at an inn that specialised in fresh local seafood and folk music, and they could toast their engagement with a pint of local ale.

He stood waist deep in the water and tugged hard on the rope deck lines. The boat would not budge. Daniel took off his gloves and felt along under the boat to the rudder. Something was caught on it, as he'd suspected. He pulled but it wouldn't give way. So it was not seaweed then. It felt a bit like rope. 'What on earth . . .' he murmured. Maybe a belt? Someone's old climbing gear? The cliffs further down the island were popular with climbers and the waters were trawled by fishing vessels. You never knew what could wash up on the beaches here.

He gave one last pull and felt something come loose. Daniel crossed to the bow and, with some difficulty, dragged the kayak up the shore. He flipped the boat on its side and saw what looked like a holdall caught underneath with one long strap that must have caught on his boat when he paddled over seaweed in the shallows. He sighed. Maybe the bag fell off a hiker on a hill somewhere. 'Someone wasn't having a great day,' he said to no one in particular. Still, stranger things had happened. He chuckled at a memory of the time Maya once left her bra on a sandy beach in Cornwall after a little al fresco romance. They were half a kilometre away by the time she realised.

Daniel unwound the strap. A sports bag, all right. He leaned over and unzipped the top. Probably there would be a wallet inside, or a tag perhaps, and they could get this back to its rightful owner. He didn't relish the thought of carrying someone else's luggage around for the next day or two, but he liked to hope someone else would at least have done the same for him.

The zip came unstuck with a little effort. Inside it looked like – well, he wasn't sure what, exactly. Something the size of a melon poked out, round. It had a slippery, translucent quality rather like a jellyfish. But it was far too early in the year for jellyfish. He poked at it with the toe of his neoprene boot. The stench hit him at the very moment he realised exactly what it was he was looking at. Not a jellyfish at all, but a head. A bald human head.

The contents of Daniel's stomach bubbled into his throat as a wave of shock ran up his body. He collapsed on the ground.

He blinked, lifted his head from the pebbles on the beach. He looked up the path where his partner had disappeared. 'Maya!' he shouted. 'Maya!' He tried to clamber to his knees, but his legs felt rubbery and uncertain.

Maya was only seconds away but to Daniel those moments felt like hours. She knelt by him and put her hand gently on his shoulder. 'Are you OK?' she said. Daniel did not often lose his cool, not even the time they went out for a routine outing that turned into force eight gale conditions off the Isle of Wight. Her paddle had snapped and he had to tow her to shore, battling wind against tide, both of them swallowing facefuls of sea foam. Maya had been in bits afterwards – it was her first open water crossing – but had never felt like Daniel wasn't in control. Even then he didn't raise his voice or anything. No, Daniel wasn't the sort who freaked out at any old thing. This had to be something serious.

Daniel closed his eyes and shook his head. He tried to raise one arm and point back to where his boat was pulled up on the beach.

'What is it?' Maya asked.

'You tell me,' he said.

Maya spotted the bag next to his kayak and crouched down to get a closer look. The sight and smell knocked her back for a moment, but she recovered quickly and leaned in to see what was in there. There was a body inside the bag. No doubt about that. Three years of a forensic science degree had prepared her, but only just, for something like this. She had seen plenty of specimens in the lab or in the morgue but that was different. Those were lifeless, static things that looked more like oversized dolls than anything else.

This however was . . . well, it was kind of great, actually. Her first cold one *in situ*. 'It's dead,' she said. She picked up Daniel's paddle and poked the remains with the end. 'Human.' There was a retching sound behind her. 'Daniel?'

He was sitting upright, head between his knees. 'Are you sure?'

'Sure it's dead, or sure it's human?' No reply; only the sound of more heaving. 'Yeah, I'm sure,' she said.

Maya frowned at the remains, trying to puzzle out what she was looking at without removing anything from the bag. The back of a head, bald. A shoulder and arm pulled back, maybe tied? A slender elbow joint poked through the grey, gelatinous scraps of flesh and connective tissue. If the body hadn't been in the bag, odds were the rest of its extremities would have fallen away from the trunk by now. Whoever this was had been in the water for some time – weeks, at least.

Daniel flopped back onto the ground above the cove. His chest rose and fell heavily. 'What now? Do we radio this in? Pull the GPS beacon?' His voice was uncharacteristically panicked. Of all the emergency situations he had prepped for over the years, this was not one of them.

Maya inspected the outside of the bag for clues. It was covered in black algae. There was no sign of ID, no nametag that she could see.

'Pulling the beacon might be going too far,' she said. 'Whoever it is, he's already dead.' If someone was dead it was a collection job, not an emergency. And the fishing boats wouldn't want to get involved. No point getting the lifeboats and helicopters out for this.

Was it an offence to leave a dead body unattended? She couldn't remember. Maya surveyed the horizon in all directions. There was the tiny island of Rona to the north and six miles of heather bog to the south; Skye on one side, mainland Scottish Highlands on the other. No place within walking distance of where they were unless she fancied a four-hour yomp to Raasay's only village in wet boots. And while under normal circumstances Daniel would have no problem going out in the kayaks again once darkness fell, Maya didn't fancy it.

Even if they wanted to go find help on their own, Daniel didn't look in any shape to do it. She popped the covers open on his kayak and rifled through his dry bags for a phone. 'Do you have reception? We could call the police station in Portree.'

'No reception here.'

'I'll get on the VHF and radio the coastguard, then,' Maya said. 'Ask them to pass it on to police. Looks like we might not be staying the night here after all.'

Daniel's five-star instructor's course had offered no guidance on what to do if you ended up having to haul a sack of decomposing human remains on a sea kayak. 'Please tell me we're not paddling this – this thing – to shore.'

'No,' Maya said. 'Best not to move it more than necessary – in case there's any evidence to be found at the site.' She sat down next to her boyfriend. 'We'll see if we can get a lift off the coastguard and grab a B&B on Skye tonight,' she said. 'It's not the end of the world.'

Daniel nodded weakly. Maya repacked his bags. She spotted a tiny jewellery box among his things and her heart skipped a beat. 'Oh my God! Daniel . . . is this what I think it is?' She tugged off her gloves to slide the half-carat sparkler on her left ring finger. 'And it's a perfect fit!'

Her fiancé rolled to one side and chucked a mouthful of foamy spittle on the grass.

: **1** :

Today. She was going to leave him today.

Erykah leaned into the catch of her oar as the low-slung rowing boat slid along the Thames. She squinted against the icy rain that raked her face and tried to concentrate on the back of the rower in front of her, synchronising her movements to Nicole's movements. There was nothing but the sound of their blades hitting the water in unison, the rush of the river underneath, and one word in her thoughts. *Today. Today.*

The rhythm of the pair was constant and strong. Catch, drive, recover. Catch: two oars dropped into the water together. Drive: the push as two pairs of long legs stretched out, the blades snapping out of the water at the finish. Recover: slide forward, square up, get ready to repeat. Catch, drive, recover. The racing shell sliced through the water like a knife. *Today, today, today.*

Early-morning outings were the best part of Erykah's day. Nothing else intruded on the physical pleasure of being competent, of getting something done. She indulged a glance at the water where the wash of their strokes bubbled up. The whirlpool puddles of her oars chased Nicole's upstream, equally deep, equally strong.

The London suburb of Molesey was always quiet at this time of morning but today it was eerily still. Sleety rain from the February sky flattened the water and dampened all outside noise. The gardens were still bare of leaves, the pleasure boats tied up on the bank still shrouded in canvas for the winter.

On one side of the river were the reservoirs and nature reserve, beginning to rustle with the first stirrings of the dawn chorus. On the other side, in the houses facing the water, a few lights flickered in Erykah's peripheral vision. The exodus of commuters from the suburbs into London was an hour or more away.

The rain soaked her clothes, ran down her arms and washed the sweat off her skin. Droplets hit the water, each sphere hopping like quicksilver before being swallowed by the river. Erykah turned her thoughts to the handbag in her locker and how much she might be able to pack into it.

She thought about the cash she had been withdrawing since last year, odd amounts here and there, so that it wouldn't raise suspicion. She had sold a few pieces of jewellery, including two Swiss watches her husband hadn't worn in years. She didn't know yet how she would tell him: Rab, we're done. Rab, I've had enough. Maybe she would walk in the door, the light framing her from behind. His face would crumple, maybe he'd wail, but he would be unable to stop her.

Today. Today was Valentine's Day.

It was Erykah Macdonald's twentieth wedding anniversary.

The anniversary was a date on the calendar, a silent odometer showing how much of her life she had wasted with her husband. Her unemployed husband, she reminded herself, not that he would admit it. He was still leaving the house and pretending to go to work in the City every morning, paying their bills on loans and credit. Credit that couldn't cover his debts for much longer. And the longer the situation went on, the more obvious it became that he was hiding things from her. His darting eyes when he left the house and when he came home, the far-too-casual questioning of how her day had been. He didn't know she knew, but she knew. She was not born yesterday.

She had watched Rab fossilise his morning routine over the course of months until it was a ritual. He prepared the same pot of coffee and soft-boiled egg every morning, cracked and ate it using the same egg cup and spoon, washed them up – he had never done his own washing-up before, not that she could remember – and left them in the draining rack. Left at the same time, to the minute, every day. She recognised the signs. He was secretly trying to keep things under control. Wasn't it what she had done, as a child, primly lining up the few possessions in her mum's flat as a talisman against future failure? Hoping that if everything on the shelf was neat, maybe everything else would be OK too? It was play-acting, a way of keeping up appearances.

Catch, drive, recover. Catch, drive, recover. Without saying a word Erykah and Nicole both fell into a longer, more languid rhythm. The boat responded and picked up in the water, raising the bow like a goose's neck in icy air.

Most club members gravitated towards the team camaraderie of rowing in an eight, or the solo achievement of bashing up and down the river in a single scull. But Erykah loved the pair. The days when their eight was broken up into fours and pairs were her favourite training sessions of all. Without the constant staccato demands of a cox sat in the front broadcasting instructions to the crew, Erykah could really lose herself in the feel of the boat.

The secret to the pair was syncing your movements perfectly with the person in front of you. Not that it wasn't important in any other crew, but in a pair there was nowhere to hide. Pull too hard or too light, or be a fraction of a second too fast or slow in the water, and the boat would pull around, throwing the rhythm off and slowing them down. Nicole kept time like a perfect metronome; it was Erykah's job to mirror her. But it was as much chemistry as physics. They knew each other, could read each other's mood in the boat, often without even having to speak.

Nicole raised one hand off her oar as they reached the landing stage. Erykah squared her blade, slowing the boat and swinging it around. Nicole tapped her oar backwards through the water, bringing them parallel to the wooden dock outside the boathouse. Erykah held on to the planks while Nicole got out and steadied the boat for her. They took the oars out of the riggers, then crouching together, lifted the boat over their heads and dropped it to their shoulders.

They were smooth; from the minute the boat was lifted off the rack to the last stroke before they came up to the landing stage. They fitted together, with the boat, with each other, like a key in a lock.

Erykah didn't want to jinx anything, but it had been a long time since a boat she was in had felt this good. Years. They had squeaked into the top twenty at the Pairs Head before Christmas. She hoped the coaches would put them together again once head season was over. There would be a few cups at the regattas to be won this summer – maybe national championships. Maybe more.

Erykah walked from the landing stage to the clubhouse of the Molesey & Hampton Anglian Boat Club, aware of the men's squad standing in the rain. Their coach, Dom, was giving the men a bollocking for almost crashing into the weir. Eight heads bowed and ducked, trying to avoid the rain spattering off the roof onto the pavement. They stood quiet and guilty in their black splash tops. Eight pairs of eyes took in surreptitious looks of her and Nicole's bodies.

Few of the men at the club ever tried it on. There was the age difference, for one thing. The top squad were fresh out of university, in their early twenties, twenty-five, max; the women were both over thirty, and Erykah was forty. Not to mention that Erykah was the one mixed-race member of the women's squad in a sport that was usually whiter than white. No, none of them would ever have dared. Eight pairs of eyes followed the women all the way to the changing room door.

'Fierce outing today,' Nicole said. She loosened her pigtail of reddish-blonde hair with one hand and squeezed Erykah's shoulder with the other. 'That was good. Passionate.' She turned on the shower and flinched as the first spurt of water came through ice cold. Nicole was once part of the USA squad and also had a few Henley medals under her belt. She might have been a decade or more off her best performances but she was still a cut above most of the other women at the club. Praise from her was praise indeed.

'It all fell into place, I suppose.' Erykah smiled and wrapped a towel around her long body. 'Have to keep warm somehow.'

'That's not the only thing . . .' Nicole peered around the corner to the lockers, but the women from the eight weren't back yet. At the rate the other boat had been lagging up at Kingston it might be twenty minutes or more before anyone else came in. Seeing they were alone, Nicole's hand strayed to Erykah's towelled waist.

They kissed and she felt Nicole's fingers tangle in the moist curls at the nape of her neck. 'Not now,' Erykah hissed, ignoring the warm lust rising inside her. She was still smiling, though, as she flicked the towel off and slipped into a pair of jeans and a soft cashmere jumper. She loosed the knot of curls from her head and combed through them lightly with her fingertips, pulling the hair back down from where it had shrunk against her scalp from sweat.

Nicole smiled and watched her lover primp. 'I have something for you.' She handed Erykah a thick, pastel-pink card envelope. 'For my valentine.' Her smile was part mocking of the silly holiday, but also part tender.

Erykah clapped a hand over her mouth. She had been so wound up, thinking about her anniversary and about leaving her husband that she'd forgotten to think of Nicole. 'I didn't get you anything!'

'It's only a little thing,' Nicole said. She traced a finger along Erykah's arm. 'And I'll see you later, anyway.'

Erykah felt Nicole's green eyes on her as she drew out the card. Affixed to the front was an antique-looking key, secured to the card with a pink ribbon. The weight of the key sat in Erykah's palm and she caught her breath. It looked like the key to Nicole's cottage along the towpath. A short walk from the boathouse, they had spent many stolen afternoons there.

'Oh my God,' she said, 'I can't take this home.' If Rab found the card she would have questions to answer. She didn't want to start a row about infidelity while she was walking out the door, and she definitely didn't need him to know where she was planning to go tonight.

'I know,' Nicole said. 'Let's not talk about him.'

'All right,' Erykah said. 'How about . . . when are you going to give me the photos from the Star Club Head Race so I can upload them to the website?' she teased.

Nicole laughed. It was a shared joke: they hadn't gone to any such race, as it had been cancelled at the last minute. But it was the excuse Erykah had given her husband to justify being away from the house. For a glorious forty-eight hours, the pair hadn't left Nicole's cottage at all. And any pictures wouldn't have been suitable for the club's website anyway.

Erykah tucked the key and card back into the envelope and wedged it in the corner of her locker door. They had talked about running away, wrapped in the afterglow of sex, so many times. You can walk away from him anytime, Nicole would say. And Erykah would make some excuse. She didn't want to put pressure on the relationship to become more than what it was. Erykah knew from bitter experience what could go wrong when things went too far, too fast.

Eventually, though, her resistance started to wear down. They stopped talking about someday and maybe, and started talking about how, and when. Erykah set a date: her anniversary. She started taking cash out and saving it, just to have a buffer until things calmed down. She would pack her bags, break the news to her husband, and walk out. She didn't want to move in with Nicole straight away, but the cottage was close and Nicole assured her she was fine to crash there while she looked for her own place.

There had been a connection from the start with Nicole. Maybe it was because they were both outsiders in Molesey. Maybe it was the way Nicole saw her, *really* saw her, after years of indifference, bordering on outright hostility, from Rab.

Erykah closed the locker door, her fingertips lingering on the cool steel. She watched Nicole dress and felt a swelling in her chest. Nicole was an ex-Radcliffe girl, one of those healthy American types with freckles and muscular thighs and tan lines that extended only as far as the edge of her Lycra shorts. Nicole was someone who had grown up with orthodontist checks, being driven to tennis lessons, and apples for a lunchbox snack. The casual confidence about her place in the world showed, from how she walked and talked, to how she treated other people. Like nothing could stand in her way, be it a powerful opposing crew, or a lover's difficult husband. Like nothing had the right to stop her.

Nicole caught her staring and smiled. 'I'll pick up the wine for tonight,' she said. 'Or whisky for you? Ring me when you're on the way.' She brushed her lips against Erykah's neck. 'I love you.'

Was what they had love? Erykah didn't know. What she did know was it was like lungs full of fresh air after being trapped inside.

Erykah walked home the long way, through Molesey village instead of along the river towpath. She felt buoyant, as light as the boat in the water. Even though it was still cold enough for there to be patches of frost in the shadows, the few shards of sunlight seemed to her like high noon in the middle of summer.

There was some work she needed to do on the club website. Members had been asking for the training schedule for the weeks leading up to the Head of the River, not to mention all the photos from recent events stacking up in her inbox. They would have to wait for now. Managing the club's site wasn't a paid position – Erykah had volunteered herself as web admin – but normally she did her best to keep it up to date and professional.

She stopped in a corner shop to pick up a post-training coffee and scrolled through some tasks on her tablet while the assistant got her drink. The website admin never ended. This morning, it could wait.

Most of the website work was just a matter of cleaning house. Like last week, when she logged in one morning to find a queue of troll comments about the club's latest blog update. Only registered commenters could post directly to the page; everything else went to her inbox for moderation and three unapproved comments claimed to be from three people. The comments used different pseudonyms, but according to the IP addresses, they were all coming from one person using a rival club's Wi-Fi. Or possibly it really was three different people all sitting in the same club at the same time, but she found that unlikely. Trolls talking to nobody but themselves. Erykah had sighed and deleted all three comments. Weren't these people bright enough to realise that she could see where they were posting from?

Erykah thanked the shop assistant for the coffee and continued home. She thought of the card from Nicole. It had been a long time since someone had made such a romantic gesture to her, and she was overwhelmed – in a good way.

Rab probably wouldn't even remember it was Valentine's, much less their anniversary. Not that she wanted him to. Even when things between them had been good he was more likely to bring her some petrol station flowers and rewrap a free mug from work than remember to buy her a real gift. Lately, he hadn't even done that much.

Even before Nicole entered her life, Erykah had spent ages trying to figure out why she had married him at all. Erykah Macdonald and her husband hadn't shared a bedroom in several years. They hadn't shared anything of substance since well before that.

It was hard to remember, but when they met she had been bowled over by who he was. Or at least, by who he appeared to be. A dashing, tall officer type, lean and handsome with slicked back blond hair and a stilted, formal way of speaking. He could have walked out of a war film, all cheekbone angles, glowing skin and snappy, smart comments. And at a time of her life when it felt as if everything was crashing down around her, he made her feel safe. As if he really could whisk her away from all the worry about the press, about money, about what other people thought of her.

Then the mask started to slip. She started to see his patterns, as if he was a computer program looping through a script. He knew a lot of general trivia, but wasn't as smart as his allusions implied. His healthy glow came from a tanning bed, not from sport. The witty comments she admired were a handful of lines and quotes he repeated thousands of times for effect. He could tell you the first four lines of *Macbeth*, but she came to doubt he had ever read it.

But that wasn't the real problem. She assumed all couples go through a stage of discovering the gulf between who you thought someone was and who they turned out to be. No, it was the lying that troubled her. He had told her he was a former Army intelligence officer, but she learned he had been kicked out of his university's Officer Training Corps for failing to turn up to training nights and hadn't even got in to Sandhurst. She discovered he was born in Norwich, not Edinburgh as he claimed. Nothing about her husband was what he said it was. Not his high-pressure job in the City as a trader on the commodities floor – it turned out he was really an insurer.

'A property underwriter actually,' he'd said, peevishly, when she found his card in the pocket of a suit she was taking to the dry cleaner and confronted him. 'Soon to be senior. Some women would be grateful to have a partner who can provide for them through honest work.'

That hurt, and he had said it knowing it would hurt her. The implication that her love life up until meeting him was populated by criminals and thugs. But what hurt even more was he had got her wrong – it wasn't the job title that mattered to her, and certainly not the money, he earned plenty whatever it was he was up to and she didn't need that much. It was the fact that he had felt the need to lie when there was no reason to. To juice things up, to make himself sound more interesting than he was, when the truth would have been fine. By then they were married and living in a nice flat paid entirely with his salary, and her mother was gone, and, as he reminded her, she had no one else; nowhere to go and lick the wounds of her humiliation.

The morning rain eased and the mist hanging over the river had lifted. It was the time of the morning when Molesey transformed from commuter-land into the Ladies Who Lunch belt, from Weetabix and coffee to long conversations over bresaola and Côtes du Rhône.

On any other day, Erykah might have joined in, but today things were different.

She could finally see her marriage through clear eyes. Gone was the frustration, anger, and guilt that usually clouded her thinking. Suddenly, being on the wrong side of forty didn't matter. Maybe she would take Nicole out to dinner, their first date as a public couple. Did people still do that? Have dates? And in a couple of weeks they would be at the training camp in Switzerland with the rest of the squad, preparing for the Women's Head. Anyway, it was a day worth celebrating. Her marriage had been seven thousand, three hundred and four days too long. Today was the first day of the rest of her life.

The snug suburb of Molesey had never seemed more unreal to her than it did today. Beyond each gravelled driveway and shiny painted door, who knew what was really going on? Couples and families playing their perfect parts, buffered from the reality of other peoples' lives by money and geography.

It was less than twenty miles from where Erykah was born but might as well have been another planet. She'd grown up in a one-bedroom flat on the third level of a council block where the lift, when it was working, only stopped at the even numbered floors. They kept a stack of pound coins inside the cupboard next to the gas meter, with a torch to find it when the meter ran out.

Sometimes as a kid Erykah felt brave enough to sneak a coin out of the stack and spend it on crosswords and second-hand books, but she always had to hide them in case her mother found out. Her mum, Rainbow, religiously switched off unused lights because, as she always said, at least sunlight is free.

Free. Now wasn't that a funny kind of word?

Erykah came in through the back door to the kitchen, knowing Rab would have left by now, kicked off the wet trainers in favour of her sheepskin slippers. The stainless steel units and granite counters she'd had installed a few years ago still looked new because they rarely ate together, and rarely anything but takeaways. She switched on a talk radio show and turned the volume all the way up. The sleekly expensive Bang & Olufsen stereo system echoed through the large empty rooms and long empty hallways.

In the front room was a small cupboard where her collection of whisky bottles sat. Erykah opened the cupboard and poured herself a shot of Glen Ord. She grimaced only slightly at the first hit of alcohol, waited for the sweet finish of spice lingering on her tongue. A fine breakfast dram.

Was there anything worth packing here? Not the wedding photos, sitting on the mantelpiece above the fire they never lit. The booze was replaceable. The polished pewter cups won over years of rowing regattas would have to wait for now. She could always come back for more things later.

She caught her reflection in the oak-framed mirror above the drinks cabinet. On a good day, in the right light, she didn't look too different from how she had looked the day she got married. With some make-up and generous backlighting, she could pass for a much younger woman. But that still didn't give her the time back.

Twenty years. How did it happen? For so much of it, it had felt as if time was dragging so slowly. Then, before she knew it, two decades were gone.

The house was as still as a museum and, she supposed, not altogether different from one. They had bought it a few years after getting married with a down payment from Rab's first big bonuses after getting a promotion. He had left any renovation and redecoration to her, and Erykah spent months poring over catalogues and magazines. What did people who lived in houses like this think looked good? Would they laugh at her for buying top end everything, or laugh at her if she didn't? In the end she dumped the pile of magazines in the hands of a decorator whose final interpretation could probably only generously be called Hotel Lobby Chic. There were nice touches, but it had no soul. Such as the double-ended jet bath for two in the master en-suite. The catalogue showed a laughing couple, bath bubbles up to their shoulders, clinking champagne glasses. Erykah couldn't recall a single time she hadn't had a bath in it all alone.

Upstairs there were banknotes in her underwear drawer, rolled inside a stocking. Erykah counted it: about five grand. That would do for a start. She threw a large, buttery leather bag on the bed and started to pack what she would need to take with her.

The bag was a memento from a trip to Milan, a rowing camp when she and Nicole had snuck away one afternoon for shopping. It was huge and chic, and she loved it. She stuffed some underwear into the bag. A dove grey silk bra and knickers Nicole said she looked good in. A make-up kit, a notebook, a jersey dress. In a jewellery box she found her diamond engagement and wedding rings. She stopped wearing them because they got in the way during rowing – or that was what she had planned to tell Rab if he asked. He had never asked.

Erykah slid the bands on her left ring finger. Might as well take them; they would be worth a few quid. She looked around the room. There ought to be more. Two decades of marriage and all it boiled down to was a half-filled handbag? But so much of what they had together was a display, for show. She felt no real emotion about any of it any more. The photos of her and Rab together: she didn't want them wherever she went next. The stacks of books on the shelves and the bedside table? Well, there were always bookshops.

She had fantasised so many times about leaving, and in her fantasies Rab always let her go. But she knew that wasn't what would really happen. He wouldn't take her at her word – he would browbeat her into submission. He would demand 'his say', ranting about how she was lazy, reliant on him, took him for granted. How no one else would put up with her. How no one else would have done what he did, how no one would want someone with her background, her history. How he was the only reason anyone in Molesey accepted her. He heard the way other people talked behind her back, he would say, things they would never dream of saying to her face. And he was her only defender, he would claim, the one thing standing between her life now and social ruin. She had heard it all so many times before.

And the threat that came up most often? How, if she left, he would tell everyone the whole truth about her. A part of her believed him when he said these things. He had said the words so many times over the years, so convincingly, that she had started to see herself as the trash he insisted she was. 'You and your Jeremy Kyle family,' he said with disgust, and she felt it was the truth. His words had become part of her own head and her own heart. Even with a new life waiting, with a bag packed and Nicole in the river cottage along the towpath, would Erykah be able to forget it all, walk away that easily, and just be fine? She wasn't sure.

Maybe she shouldn't wait until he came home. She should go now, so she didn't have to hear it all again. Leave a note. Send a text. Or just disappear.

Her finger grazed the spines of the books, organised – her own idea – by colour. Covers of black, blue, orange and red grouped together, an undulating continuum of shades. Her hand paused on an older paperback, slim, the cheap card cover yellowed with age. She felt a pang. It was the last birthday present Rainbow ever gave her, one of the few her mother could afford to give.

It was a book of puzzles and brain-teasers, the type of book that mixed up riddles with history, in the style of *Ripley's Believe It Or Not*. There was a page about the mystery of the Pyramids in Egypt, a page about Stonehenge, how to solve a Rubik's cube, how to pick a lock. It was a book Erykah would have loved when she was ten. It was an odd gift for a teenager on her way to university.

Rainbow had been trying. She knew her daughter liked maths, even if she hadn't paid much attention to what Erykah did at school for a long time. She had been hoping to make a belated connection, in her own way.

Maths was Erykah's spiritual home. Numbers had always come easily enough, but the first time she sat in an algebra class, it was like someone was finally speaking her language, thinking the way she thought.

Maths up to that point had been like any other school subject – easy and not engaging. Multiplication tables and spelling tests both were simple feats of memorisation. She could conjugate French verbs without much thought, though no matter how much vocabulary she swallowed, the knack of conversation still eluded her. But algebra was different; a puzzle to be solved. There was a map of how to get from where you were to where you wanted to be, there were logical steps, and if you happened to follow the wrong path all you had to do was retrace your work to the point where you had made a mistake, and correct it. Proofs and solutions were patient, they would wait until she found them.

She was put in the top set, but her work soon went far past even that. On parent's evening her mother had asked Mr Allinson whether he thought Erykah might go on to college. Rainbow was shocked when his reply was she would probably go on to get a Ph.D.

It hadn't quite worked out that way.

'And finally, an unidentified body was discovered in Scotland late last night on the Isle of Raasay, near Skye.' The smooth voice of Diana Stuebner oozed from the radio speakers. 'Sources close to the investigation suggest the body was found inside a bag. Circumstances of the death have not yet been confirmed by Police Scotland, as the post-mortem examination is still pending. And now back to our next caller . . .'

For some reason now the book seemed like something Erykah couldn't leave behind. She put it on top of her bag. A link to her old self, maybe? The person she had been before she met Rab and before she became . . . well, whatever it was she was now.

'. . . Sarah from Islington, you're on the Stuebner show.'

'Erykah,' said a voice behind her.

She jumped.

She hadn't heard anyone come in the room. The radio must have covered the sound of the car in the drive, of the key in the lock, of the front door closing, of the footsteps on the stairs.

'Rab,' she said. Her husband's features were arranged in a state of permanent exhaustion. Once almost handsome, now her husband most resembled a photocopy of a photocopy of a good-looking man. 'You're home early.'

'I am,' he said. 'I have news.' He glanced over the scene in the master bedroom, the open drawers with clothes pulled out, the bag on the bed.

Not good news, not bad news. Just news. 'Oh?' Erykah wasn't in the mood for news. It wasn't the way she had pictured this going.

'I found out this morning . . .' he said. He held a rolled-up newspaper in one hand, a little scrap of card in the other. 'It's hard to explain, but I – I mean *we* – we've won twenty million pounds in the lottery.'

: **2** :

Cameron Bridge was a grey town wedged in the crook of a sea loch on the west coast of Scotland. For reasons no one was able to explain, the town had been built with the backs of its streets facing the sea, so that the first impression any visitor to the area had was of a town showing the world its arse.

That was how Morag Munro saw it. She made the short walk from her hotel to her office and tried not to make eye contact with anyone on the way. Under any other circumstances she would have long since left the place and never come back. But as the region's local MP, she was obliged to pop her head in a few times a year.

The mountains that hulked above Cameron Bridge ensured that, no matter what the weather or time of year, the town was always in shadow. In winter the streets were covered with a layer of ice as fine as plastic wrap and as slippery underfoot as spilled oil. Even in summer, stubborn patches of snow on the highest mountains would chill the wind that swept through the town. Morag scowled. She hated this place.

Maybe hate was too strong a word. But she could do with fewer visits. Morag's first few trips up after Scotland's independence referendum had been the worst. Because she had been one of the public faces campaigning for No, constituents beat a path to her surgeries to debate the outcome. She had heard it all: accusations of fixing, uncounted ballots found in bins, a conspiracy that went past the BBC and all the way up to the Westminster elite. 'It's the settled will of the Scottish people,' she said over and over, a serene half-smile the most she could offer in the face of their anger and disappointment.

When the general election came and she managed to hold on to her seat with the slenderest of majorities – fewer than 200 votes between her and the SNP candidate – that hadn't helped put the conspiracy theorists down one bit.

Like most political fads this would pass; they couldn't stay angry for ever, could they? Eventually life would have to return to normal.

Though once or twice she had wished the stepped-up security that came when she was campaigning side by side with English MPs had stuck around here once those other politicians retreated south of the border.

Morag's assistant Arjun came in wearing a pink wool waistcoat and flecked brown tweeds, armed with two cups of coffee from a high street café and a copy of the *West Highland Independent* tucked under his arm. Morag arched an eyebrow. She so wished he didn't feel the need to wear hipster clobber up here. The locals would probably think he was taking the piss. 'Decided to blend in, did we,' she said dryly.

Arjun did a spin. 'You like?' Morag rolled her eyes and he laughed. 'I'm inspired to go native. The sleeper train is fabulous. Next time I take my boyfriend on holiday we're going first class all the way.'

Morag couldn't help but smile. She had long ago grown weary of the rattling old carriages chugging their way on the track, the thin blankets and soggy breakfasts, but his enthusiasm was sweet.

'And you won't believe what I found in a charity shop on the way here this morning,' he said, and pulled a package from his bag. It was a large plastic suit with a hood, bright white, and big enough for a six foot man with a thyroid problem.

'Crivens, Arj, those look like my father-in-law's cricket waterproofs. I hope you weren't planning on going out in public wearing that.'

'Brilliant, isn't it?' he grinned. 'Vintage, and only a fraction of the cost of Gore-Tex.'

'And not breathable, so you'll sweat your cods off in it.' Morag shook her head. She could imagine him gamely having a go at the local hills clad in his new white plastic suit. The locals would likely think the CSI had turned up. Or possibly a spaceman.

At least Arjun had been able to come with her on this constituency visit. Usually he stayed in London while she made her trips north, but she was short-handed this time around. Her constituency secretary had cited the barrage of abusive letters after the referendum as the source of her stress, and quit. Morag couldn't make head or tail of it. The letters had been addressed to her, after all, not to the secretary. But she could hardly object when the woman served notice. To do otherwise would be to invite a lawsuit. She supposed that was Britain now, compensation culture all the way.

'Newspaper headlines before we let the grannies in?'

'Go on then.' Morag sniffed at the cup of coffee. Any place in

London offering a drink this poor would be shut in days. She sighed, tucked her silver-streaked bob behind her ears and sipped the indifferent brew. The coffee at least tasted better than it looked, but that was hardly a ringing endorsement.

'Right, above the fold ... Council backs option 8 on the town bypass,' Arjun began. 'Local protestors turn out in force.' He looked up. 'What's "in force" around here?'

Morag considered. 'Eight, maybe ten.'

'Not twelve?'

'Don't be ridiculous, that would be a "mob". What else?'

Each time she came back to the Highlands, Morag felt more and more out of place. It wasn't helped by the local memory of her predecessor in Parliament: a heavy drinking ex-boxer and leader of the Liberals who was ousted by the party for punching the Speaker. She got the feeling people would rather have an alcoholic Auld Boy representing them than someone with ambition and drive. He had died shortly after losing his seat and the funeral procession went on for five miles. Quite an achievement in a town that hardly had five miles of tarmac in it.

Not for the first time she mused that if Scotland had gone independent, it would have spelled the end of her current tenure. At least that would have freed her from any responsibilities up here. She shook the thought out of her head. Heresy. Without that referendum success, she wouldn't have secured her place on the front bench.

Yet moving up into the Shadow Cabinet seemed to make her local detractors even angrier. What was she meant to do, aim for the middle? Settle for average? Waste time in a backwater constituency with no greater ambition than getting EU approved *terroir* status for Stornoway black pudding? That was not her style. Shadow Home Secretary was not the most glamorous brief, but she was determined to work as hard on this as she did on anything else.

Arjun kept reading while Morag checked her make-up in a hand mirror and freshened her taupe lipstick. The deep lines etched either side of her mouth gave her the look of a stern headmistress. What folks in Cameron Bridge failed to appreciate was that her rise in the party had not been easy or quick. Far from it. Sure, the odd columnist might sneer about 'uneasy alliances' during the referendum and MPs who 'sold out the voters', but whatever they thought in Scotland, London mattered more to her. Down there, which croft your granddad had worked was less important than being able to play the political game.

Not to mention looking good while doing it. Her first years in the Commons, she watched and learned. The tweed skirts and boxy dresses that had done the job at home when she sat on the town council were replaced with tailored suits that whispered good taste. She stopped trimming her own fringe and started paying hundreds for the requisite swishy bob from a salon in Covent Garden. In time her sleek style was practically Westminster legend – even if she was, as commentators never failed to note, a greyer version of the woman who had first gone down to Westminster. Funny how the men who were freshmen MPs at the same time she was elected never took any stick for having aged too.

Looking the part was only half of it. The other was never letting her schedule slow down. Morag had lost count of the times she bookended a day with breakfast radio on one end and *Newsnight* on the other, with back-to-back meetings crammed in between. If Thatcher had been the Iron Lady, then she was the Iron Maiden. She would never be caught propping up the Commons bar when there was work to be done.

It had all paid off, but at the cost of alienating the people at home. Only lack of credible opposition kept her in the seat now and she knew it. Opposing the independence campaign was a black mark against her in their eyes and being named Shadow Home Secretary hadn't helped. They knew she wasn't one of them any more – if she ever had been.

'Crikey, a murder!' Arjun rattled the paper.

'What?' Morag craned her head to get a better look.

Arjun pointed to the lower corner of an inside page. 'Well, maybe. Found off the coast of Skye. Says it was brought back here to Cameron Bridge yesterday.'

'Huh,' Morag said. The details were scant, the paper calling the remains 'as yet unidentified' and stated that police 'had not ruled out foul play'. A tingle of nerves crept up her neck. For all its craggy isolation, unidentified bodies were unusual in this part of the world, murders even more so. When killings did happen they were more often of the drunken rage variety. An unidentified body on the beach? Out of the summer season? That was . . . unusual. Worryingly so. But there were other jobs to get on with this morning. Morag made a note to herself to look into it later.

Later, as it turned out, was still a long way off. Morag's coffee went stone cold as she smiled and nodded her way through hours of a constituency surgery with all the political verve of a slug on a lettuce.

Morag nodded in time to the cadence of mumbles and squeaks emitting from the woman opposite her, her twelfth appointment of the day. She eyed the packaged cheese sandwich Arjun had brought her for lunch, but she probably wouldn't even be able to eat it until she was on the train back to London.

'It's criminal, is what it is. The access road behind the church is all but impassable.' The lady in a bobbled cardigan as dull as her dishwater hair jabbed a finger in Morag's direction. 'It's slippery and the gritters never go up there. I nearly broke my hip when I slipped on it last week. Year on year nobody does anything about it.'

Morag tapped her foot idly on the corner of the desk. She was sporting her signature navy suit and red patent kitten heels, the same ones that had caused a stir at the party conference over a decade ago when she was still one of 'Brant's Babes'. Well, not exactly the same ones. At the last count there were seventeen pairs in her closet.

Tales of parking woe were a common local preoccupation. Also popular were complaints about the state of the A road to Cameron Bridge, a single carriageway dented with potholes the entire hundred miles from Glasgow onwards.

The complainers had a point and she was mostly sympathetic. The dire state of the road was why she took the train to and from London. That, and the fact she could get a single sleeper carriage and doze through the entire wretched journey. There were still sections of the road where two cars would find it difficult to pass each other, and that was even before accounting for all the tourist caravans and coaches pootling up the way in summer. Still, none of these problems were technically her responsibility, and hearing about them was keeping her from doing anything productive with the day. 'This might be better put to the council instead of me,' Morag would gently suggest. 'Or to your MSP.'

Her suggestion was part of a well-worn script. The constituents knew as well as she did that an MP could do nothing about the roads. They were simply blowing off steam. Morag was of the opinion that things in Cameron Bridge would never improve. Shops stayed closed, the road stayed riddled with holes and the occasional badly placed patch of tarmac, and the outlook stayed as grey as the place they inhabited. The economy was always worse than expected, the jobs fewer. The prospects for anyone born and raised in Cameron Bridge, save perhaps for Morag herself, were not so bright.

This had not always been the case. Only a few decades ago Cameron Bridge was busy with shoppers, drawing people in from all over the Highlands as far away as Cape Wrath and Stornoway. The forestry plantations provided valuable jobs – jobs that many young men who entered the business assumed would be for life. As the plantations came to maturity, though, the forestry companies suddenly decided that the lumber wasn't worth the cost of cutting it down. The sawmills closed, then the paper mill. In a short time the town went from being a regional hub to a struggling backwater.

Much the same story had played out all over the Highlands, but Cameron Bridge, compared to some other towns that were quicker to adapt to the new service economy, failed to recover. The poor roads and infrequent trains were only one part of a larger problem. Chain shops that had invaded high streets elsewhere in the country caused their fair share of problems, but even they wouldn't touch Cameron Bridge. Foreign investment schemes kept rents in the empty shops as high as a tax scam, offsetting profits in more popular parts of the Highlands. The high street was a mix of boarded-up fronts and charity shops. Most people in the area did their shopping online these days.

'It's the incomers is what it is,' the woman said. 'No respect for our way of life here.' Morag nodded with feigned sympathy. Most likely by 'incomers' the lady meant families who had been in the area only two, maybe three, generations. Even those too young to have ever experienced a war talked about the Clearances and 1745 like they were yesterday.

The body found in Raasay though – now that was real news. Like many isolated Highlands towns Cameron Bridge had some local crime, though more usually drug related. The exposed West Coast was a perfect location for traffickers to smuggle in contraband, and the local police were little more than Keystone Cops in her opinion.

But a body. She was going to have to see about this.

Morag Munro drummed her fingers on the desk as her mind wandered. The drumming was a bad old habit that had started in boring lessons at school. It continued through insultingly basic lectures at university, worsened in her years on local committees and councils in the Highlands, and had since reached something of a frenzy in the tedious time-wasting that comprised ninety per cent of her working day since being elected as MP.

By now she hardly even noticed when she was doing it. The same could not be said of anyone who saw her at work or on television. Early in her career, when the political press corps had picked up on it, she laughed it off as 'nervous energy'. As opposed to what it so often was: a thinly veiled desire to throttle whomever was talking.

And while Morag had never quite been able to break herself of the habit, she did learn to not be so loud and obvious while doing it. 'The council are useless,' the old dear continued. 'All they do is send the same form letter. Impossible to get anyone on the phone to listen, much less see you in person.'

Morag bobbed her head, the smile pasted on her face. The fingers of her right hand tapped lightly, rhythmically, across the top of a folder. Arjun caught her eye and motioned for her to cut it out. She glowered, but stopped. She nodded at him to start shutting the office in the hope the woman would take the hint and finish up.

'It is an unfortunate situation,' Morag said to the scowling face on the other side of the desk. 'But it is in the Council's hands, not mine. I am sure that if you persist with them, you will get the satisfaction of an answer.' She reflected, not for the first time, that it was just as well the contents of the surgery appointments were confidential. Not because of sensitive information, much the opposite. Anyone having to read through them would likely die of boredom.

At least getting involved on the independence issue had resulted in one pay-off she'd hoped for: the front bench. Local concerns had slipped even further down her to-do list since being appointed Shadow Home Secretary. Morag checked her watch discreetly. If this didn't wrap up soon, she would have no time left to visit the morgue before the train went.

'The lottery?' Erykah said. 'Since when do we play the lottery?'

Erykah sat down on her bed – their bed – in the large room. Maybe she'd misheard. She waited for him to correct her. But he didn't. 'You never play the lottery,' she said.

Rab peeled off his suit jacket and loosened his tie. He extracted a handkerchief from his pocket and mopped the sweat from the back of his neck. 'No, I . . . It was on a whim. I saw the Big Billions Lottery in the shop, and, well . . .' He unfolded a newspaper to the page where the results were printed and laid it alongside the crumpled ticket next to her.

'Big Billions? Never even heard of it.' Erykah looked at the ticket and paper in turn. In a corner of a back page, in a small black-bordered advert, the winning numbers were printed. And they were the same ones as on the ticket she was holding. Matching six numbers from forty-nine was a one in fourteen million chance. You were more likely to get hit by an asteroid. Or struck by lightning. Playing the lottery was one of those things other people did. Desperate people. Not them.

So this was what he had come to: a man loses his job and has to pay the bills somehow. By her calculations, he was probably getting down to the end of what little buffer he had. So he might pick up a ticket in desperation. Hoping against hope. When hope was all he had left.

But while buying a ticket made some kind of sense, winning sure didn't.

'This is – this is *real*?' she said. 'Twenty million jackpot?' Rab nodded, dabbing sweat from his brow. She flipped through the paper, looking for a line or a page to let her know this was a wind-up, an anniversary prank. A specially printed edition of the paper, bought from a humour website. But there was nothing, because this was real. It was the same newspaper she had seen at the corner shop on her walk home from the boathouse.

'I don't get it,' she said. 'If there was some kind of new lottery, wouldn't there be adverts for it on all the time?'

'I don't really know,' Rab admitted. 'I think it's run from the Isle of Man, or something. Anyway. It's money. It's a lot of money.'

Twenty million pounds. Erykah felt a jolt of adrenaline that she recognised from being on the start line of a race. Her mouth went dry. It was both exciting and terrifying. She wanted to leave Rab. Scratch that, *needed* to leave. The charade of a marriage had gone on too long.

But this. *This*.

She remembered the money Mum scraped together to play the first National Lottery draw in the '90s. Pound coins, shrapnel of change, to play her 'lucky numbers'. Erykah was visiting and Rainbow had insisted they watch the programme. Her mother leaned so close to the orange flickering face of Noel Edmonds on screen that Erykah thought she might trip and fall through the television. Neon-coloured balls tumbled in a spinner like socks in a dryer and an announcer shouted the results as they appeared.

Even before the National Lottery started her mother had been a sucker for any promise of money with no strings attached. Horse races. The Irish Sweeps. Raffles in the pub, charity draws. Erykah collected up any losing tickets and flattened them out between the pages of her textbooks. She punched a hole in one corner and threaded the tickets onto a piece of string. She did this until Rainbow found the collection and went apoplectic. Erykah couldn't understand why she was so upset. Hadn't she realised how many there were? Why spend the money at all if you didn't want to know you were spending it?

But it wasn't the wasted money that bothered Erykah. Saving wasn't for people like them anyway. A few pounds each week spent on food instead of lottery tickets wasn't going to get them off the estate in Streatham. It wasn't going to make her blend in with the white kids at school or make their parents stop talking about her in hushed tones the few times she had been invited over to do homework in one of the detached houses that bordered the estate. It wasn't going to stop final notices for bills coming through the door. It wasn't going to stop the few valuables they had ending up in the pawn shop, and it certainly wasn't going to stop the times when Rainbow was looking ragged and sweaty and was pushing down a kind of hunger that food alone couldn't fix.

No, what bothered Erykah was what the lottery represented. It stood for the loss of hope for any future apart from blind luck.

What was excruciating was not that her mother kept playing these games, no matter how many times Erykah explained the statistical improbability of winning. That wasn't it. It was the look on Rainbow's face that night when each neon ball dropped, and they were all the wrong ones. The look as whatever dreams she had were snatched away, piece by piece. Then, when Rainbow had checked her numbers over once, and once again to be sure, she disappeared. Out the front door, going to do whatever it was she did out there. Erykah didn't want to think about the details of that bit very much. She promised herself that, no matter what, she would never have nothing left but blind hope. Betting on luck was a fool's game.

'So,' Rab said. He looked down at her bag, at the bits and pieces of clothing on the bed. 'Are you going somewhere?'

Erykah bit her lip. Was she going somewhere? Half of twenty million was a hell of a lot more than she had been planning to carry out of the house today. 'There's a training camp tomorrow,' she said. 'It's in Peterborough. Instead of driving up early I thought I might stay over.'

The weight of Nicole's key had felt so good in her hand, so natural. Leaving was the right thing to do. For herself. For them. But this . . .

This was money. To a girl who had grown up with her mum reeling between double shifts on a miserable wage or sick with drugs and unable to work, money was nothing to sniff at.

'Nice of you to tell me.' Rab sat on the corner of the bed and looked up at her. 'About going away.'

'Yeah, well,' she said. 'I'm not the only one who's been keeping secrets lately, am I?' She held his gaze, hard. Go on, say it! Say it. I dare you. I dare you.

Rab broke the stare first. He turned the lottery ticket over and over in his soft white hands. 'No, I suppose not,' he said. 'We . . . I mean I . . . have some, ah, unexpected debts to cover.'

'So I guess this money comes at the perfect time for you, doesn't it,' Erykah said.

'Yes, I guess it does,' Rab said. There was a pause, longer than was comfortable, shorter than it felt. 'I took out a bank loan.'

A bank loan? Was that all he would admit to? 'What about that second mortgage you didn't tell me about?'

Erykah watched her husband's mouth open and close silently and knew she had him bang to rights. 'You forged my signature on the application,' she said.

'How did you know?'

27

'Ha,' Erykah said. 'You think I don't check my own credit history? Come on.'

'Credit history?' he said. 'Credit history. When have you ever had to check your credit history?' Rab's voice raised now and creaked near its breaking point. 'When have you even had a credit history? I've always been the one who provided anything you wanted. Cars, jewellery, spending money . . . Unless this . . .' he glanced at the clothes on the bed. '. . . is really because you were planning to walk out behind my back all along.'

'Fuck you Rab, fuck you,' she said, her voice level calm. 'Don't talk to me about managing money, and don't you try to turn this around on me! I know you've missed over a year of mortgage payments and that we are less than a month away from repossession.'

'You could have done something to help,' he snarled.

'Oh, that's classic,' she said. 'Turn it around on me. But you know what? I've had it. I am done. Falling out of love with someone is hardly the same thing as committing fraud.' She hadn't even thought the word until she said it, but it felt so good to say out loud. He was a fraud. The relationship was a fraud. Everything about their life together was a fraud. It always had been.

Fraud. The word hung in the air between them. Her brown eyes bored into Rab's blue ones. She dared him to make his accusations, to say whatever he wanted to say. He probably had no idea about Nicole, but would it change anything if he did? Right now she was standing and he was sitting down. It felt good. No, it felt better than that. It felt great.

When they first married, he said he understood her need to be out of the spotlight for a while. When she tried to find work and couldn't, he said he would support her to train and try to get back into the GB rowing squad selection. When she finally accepted that the effort she was putting into that dream was never going to work out, well, that was ten years they had been together, and by then they were hardly speaking any more anyway.

'I know the truth,' Erykah said. 'I know you were fired from your job. Did you really think you could hide that from me? You drive down the street every morning, you park your car at the station, and you sit in the coffee shop – or sometimes, the library – until it's time to come home.'

'How did you find out?' Rab said.

She snorted. He wasn't half as smooth as he thought he was. Never had been. 'Two decades married to a man who works in the City, and you think I wouldn't notice when his mobile goes silent? Come on.'

Rab closed his eyes. 'I was ashamed,' he said.

'So ashamed you couldn't tell me?' she said. He didn't answer; there was no answer to give. 'Do your family know?'

He looked up. 'God, no,' he said. 'I wouldn't bother them with this.'

Typical. There was probably little they could offer apart from a scant equity in a pebbledash bungalow in Norwich. His head shrank into his shoulders. 'I knew you were a liar and a sneak, Rab, but I never imagined how far you would go.'

'Would you have understood?'

'I haven't understood a thing about you – about us – in years,' Erykah said. Once upon a time it had felt like the two of them against the world. Wasn't that exactly what he had said, over and over? She had clung so hard to that idea, even when slapped in the face with his lies and infidelity, because she had nothing else to believe in. Bit by bit, year by year, insecurity had chewed away at that. Until all that was left was what was in her bag: a roll of cash, an old book, and a change of clothes. 'At least I would have been able to make an informed decision.'

'Now this,' Rab said. The lottery ticket, and whatever else came with it, was technically as much hers as it was his.

'Yeah, this,' Erykah said. Maybe her plan could wait.

'We don't even have a prenup,' he said.

'We sure don't,' she smiled.

: **4** :

A few miles away from Morag Munro's constituency office, the Cameron Bridge mortuary was bucking local trends. Business on the high street might have fallen to all time lows, but traffic through the morgue was very good indeed.

The reason was accidents. Loads of them. Although the year-round local population was shrinking and few murders happened in town, the tourist trade in misadventure on the hillsides was booming. Keen walkers and climbers might have been giving the local shops a miss but they were falling off the mountains with a vengeance.

Thirty-six people had met their ends in the vicinity in the previous year. The bodies were duly transported to a barn-like building tucked up one end of a glen like a dirty secret. Winter brought the ice climbers, the skiers, and many more. Avalanches claimed the greatest number of winter adventurers, followed by a couple of ice-climbing accidents, and one young woman on Hogmanay who reckoned that flip-flops and board shorts were appropriate climbing gear for January. Drivers as well, unused to icy conditions, often came a cropper.

Today's mortuary excitement was neither an accident-prone tourist nor a careless driver. For the helicopter team that had collected the bagged human remains found on the beach in Raasay, the Cameron Bridge facility was nearest. It was here the decomposing body in a bag first rejoined the mainland and here it would be autopsied.

Mortuary assistant Iain Laudale opened up the post-mortem suite. The lights flickered to life one by one. Half a dozen stainless steel autopsy stations stood like monuments in the main theatre, each with an examination table, rolling cart for surgical instruments, and a tap and hose.

Iain swung open the doors of the body refrigerator with a calm born of routine. He rolled a green trolley up to the edge and tugged on a handle inside the refrigerator, pulled a tray inside onto the trolley. On the tray sat a long white body bag. Whatever was inside was distinctly not body-shaped.

The cavernous room was cool, almost too cold to work, but he was used to worse. Iain's head nodded to the rhythm of a death metal mix CD playing in the background. The overhead fluorescent lights gave his buzz cut a greenish cast. His face had the etched look of a man who grew up fast and stayed there. His skinny arms were covered in tattoos, remnants of years on the terraces as a Rangers fan and, later, in the Army. It was the service that took a teenager with no skills, apart from tanning a bottle of Buckie, and gave him a vocation. They taught him how to collect up a body, to prepare it for what came next.

But it also taught him cynicism. The hard way, looking at rows of bodies shrouded and waiting for the cargo plane. He learned that the slogans and songs on the terraces about honour and tradition were only songs and that the Army he'd idolised had an insatiable appetite for young flesh.

Iain switched on an industrial-grade bug zapper and it flickered to life. Standard operating procedure with a decomp. No matter how well the morgue was cleaned after the autopsies, inevitably a few flies would escape, and maggots were a concern. Even in winter, even in the cold of Scotland's west coast. The body had picked up a few sand-flies when it washed up on that beach and probably worse.

Iain hadn't been squeamish to start with, but the stint with the Army had turned him into a hardened pro. After fishing parts of Omagh bombing victims out of gutters, anything else was easy by comparison. When he left the service he joined a forensic recovery company and did some airline crash and mass grave work for the UN in Srebrenica and Grozny.

Yugoslavia made Omagh look like child's play. The mass graves overflowed with bodies of men who had been rounded up, their arms and legs tied together with wire, shot in the head and dumped into pits. Three generations of men in some families. Sometimes children. Iain and the others pulled the bodies out of the ground in the same clothes they had died in. They washed the clothes after the post-mortems, left them out to dry on the grass. Every day weeping women came past, hoping to recognise a T-shirt, a pair of trousers, a hat. It was terrible when they didn't. It was worse when they did.

Iain manoeuvred the trolley up to the first examination table and slid the tray across. The post-mortem team waited in the doorway outside the autopsy suite. Apart from Iain himself, the team today numbered only two. Pathologist Harriet Hitchin chatted with a ginger whip of a police photographer. The young man was looking decidedly green around the gills. Iain unzipped the bag. Inside it was another, a black sports bag.

'First day?' Harriet Hitchin asked the snapper, who nodded. 'What's your name?'

'Dougie,' he said.

'Well, welcome to the morgue, Dougie.' Harriet's cut-glass English accent was much at odds with her distracted and unkempt air. She washed and powdered her hands, selecting thick rubber gloves for herself and for the snapper. 'Has MacLean deserted you?' she asked, referring to the police sergeant who usually tagged along on these chores.

'Ali said he had a few things to get from the van,' Dougie said. His eyes darted towards the examination table, where a very wet and very smelly piece of luggage sat in the middle of the opened body bag. It did not look promising. 'And wanted a smoke before he came in.'

Harriet nodded. Alastair MacLean's extended smoke breaks were the stuff of legend. Most people reckoned he spent as little as one minute in ten on the job. Not that it seemed to have a negative outcome on his work that anyone could see.

Bit mean to leave the new kid to cover this on his own, though. 'Documenting autopsies is never a good way to follow breakfast,' she said with a brisk assurance that might have passed for sympathy. 'By the way – if you're going to vomit, make sure you do it before you get up on the stepladder to take the top shots, please?'

'Vomit?' Dougie asked.

Iain waved at the pair to let them know he was ready. Harriet showed the photographer where they kept the wellies, then how to step over the half wall blocking the doorway to the autopsy suite. On the other side was a basin on the floor filled with disinfecting solution for them to walk through.

Dougie watched Harriet roll a disposable plastic apron off a spool and tie it over her scrubs, then motion for him to do the same. 'Does everyone vomit?'

'Either that or they faint,' Iain said. 'If you don't do either then you're a sociopath.'

'Great,' Dougie said. He reached into his pocket and withdrew a small container of mentholated chest rub to ward against a wave of stench.

Iain spotted the snapper about to dab some of the gel under his nose. 'Och, you don't want to be doing that,' he said. 'That's a myth. It doesn't help with the smell.' Dougie looked at him doubtfully. 'Makes it worse,' Iain nodded. 'Instead of getting delightful overtones of corpse à la carte, you're now getting full on corpse plus noxious top notes of pine cleaner. You'll wantae boak in no time.' Iain stared hard until Dougie pocketed the chest rub.

'Not what you thought it would be is it?' The kid shook his head. 'Nah,' Iain said, half to Dougie and half to himself. He had seen enough trainee police and university students wander through, especially in the last ten years or so, hoping for something more technological, more glamorous than the reality the mortuary offered. 'Not like the television is it. Too bright in here,' he said, indicating the tube lights suspended across the length of the room. He gestured at his own faded scrubs and plastic apron. 'And none of the fit emo lasses they tell you work in all the morgues.'

Dougie laughed in spite of his churning stomach. 'No, I guess not.'

Nothing had changed at the Cameron Bridge morgue in all the time that Iain had worked there. There was no need for change. People died the same ways they always had and were autopsied in the same way it always happened. If there was lab work they sent it to the police or to a university.

Iain popped a fresh CD in the boom box and hit play. Screeching guitars and an apocalypse of drums blasted through the morgue.

'Iain, do you mind?' Harriet scowled. 'We have a guest.' She smiled at Dougie as if to apologise. 'If it gets too much, I keep earplugs in the changing room,' she said.

'Sorry,' Iain said and turned the volume down a notch.

Dougie picked up the CD case and looked at the illustration, a photo from what appeared to be the scene of a death. 'That was a belter,' Iain said. 'Rescue helicopter snagged the bloke on a tree and had to cut the line or else the Sea King would have crashed with six crew on board.'

'Jesus Christ.'

Iain nodded. 'You could say that,' he said. 'Or it might be more accurate to say gravity is the fella responsible.' He pointed at the picture with one gloved finger. 'The body bounced twice on the way down and landed next to Scouts on a camping trip. I don't know about them, but if a man fell out of the sky and landed in the middle of my campfire, Jesus is probably the last person I would be calling on.'

The photographer gulped again. 'Isn't this a little disrespectful?' he said.

'Disrespectful,' Iain considered this. He watched the young man's eyes dart from spot to spot in the morgue, unsure where to land, as if looking at anything too long might be contagious. The stainless steel counters with autoclaved instruments lined up ready for the autopsy; the worn and chipped lino on the floor; the rolls of cotton batting, the stereo blasting music. It didn't add up, he would be thinking, as they all did. What about respect? What about dignity? But there is no dignity in death, only the end, and what gets done for the living.

Iain shrugged at the young photographer. 'Depends on your definition of respect, I suppose.' He turned to Harriet. 'Speaking of which, Professor Hitchin?'

'Doctor,' she corrected him.

'Right, doctor. Not professor. My mistake. So, I was listening to the news and it seems like someone let slip to the press that our friend here was found in a bag.'

Harriet's frown seemed exaggerated, for show. 'Oh? Is that a problem?'

'It just occurs to me possibly the police would have wanted to hold that back,' he said.

Harriet nodded, but didn't meet his eyes. 'Someone should really have a word with those Coast Guard boys,' she said. 'They won't know how we normally do things around here.'

Iain nodded sceptically. 'No, probably not. I'm sure *whoever* it was won't do it again.'

'What's the deal with the press?' Dougie said.

'In a word?' Iain said. 'Don't.'

'Don't what?' The young man looked confused.

'Don't talk to them. It's always bad news. Best to say nothing at all, even if they get it wrong. Especially in your job. The police have media advisors. Let them handle how and when information is released. We're just here to do a job,' he said, and looked pointedly at Harriet. 'Not seek attention for ourselves.'

Harriet shifted nervously from one foot to the other. 'Gents? Please? Can we get on with this?' She didn't like to spend more time in the suite than she had to.

'Sorry,' Iain said.

'So we're looking for an ID here – who is this man,' Harriet stated

34

matter-of-factly. 'Then it's how did he die. And then: can we say how long he's been dead.'

Iain rubbed his gloved finger over the darkened fabric of the sports bag to reveal some kind of pattern showing through. He moistened a wad of gauze and wiped it across the surface, revealing a Union Jack print. 'So possibly not a local, then,' he said. 'Or at least not one on the right side of the independence debate.'

'Iain, give it a rest,' Harriet rolled her eyes. 'The referendum is old news.'

'Maybe to you,' he said.

'Could the bag itself lead to someone?' Dougie asked.

'Might do,' Iain said. 'I like your instinct.' He cut through the seams of the bag, careful not to nick any of the dead man's flesh. 'But could also be the kind of tat you might buy at any souvenir shop in England.' A puddle of fetid liquid pooled from the bag, some of it seawater, some of it brown purge fluid from the body itself.

Slowly the thick canvas fabric was peeled away from the skin. Iain's crablike hands moved over the surfaces gently, with great skill. In some places the skin and fabric seemed almost fused, like soft cheese stuck in a sieve. It took him half an hour to arrange what was left of the corpse onto the slab, lying on its side.

Anyone who knew the man in life would have been hard pressed to recognise him now. Even freed from the bag the body was still wrenched into unnatural angles, the legs folded up against his chest, the arms twisted behind his back. The skin had started slipping away from the underlying tissues like a badly fitting suit of clothes. Large sections of the body bore the impression of the inside of the bag, its seams and the zip. The colour of his flesh varied from waxy pale to purple-red. The bag hadn't stayed completely closed, at least not near the end of the aquatic journey, and his eyelids and lips had been eaten away by insects and fish. Something had chewed away the flesh of his penis.

The dead man's eye sockets and lipless grimace looked out at the room like a caricature of someone laughing. But with no cock, no eyelids and no lips, this fellow's laughing days were over.

'Fuck,' Dougie repeated weakly. 'How long do you think he was in?'

Harriet wrinkled her nose. 'Difficult to say.' She had no fondness for any case she couldn't swan in and out of. 'He probably stayed down for some time, then the gases built up until the bag floated.'

'Weeks,' Iain said. 'This early in the year, when the water is cold? Let's say a month or six weeks, if we were taking bets.'

The photographer winced. 'He almost looks . . . shiny.'

'Waxy,' Iain said, his gloved finger passing over the body's mid-section. 'Bit like a candle?' Dougie nodded. 'That's because he is, or would have been if he had been under the water much longer. You see here, these spots around the fat of his belly where it's smooth and pale? This is adipocere. Grave wax, they used to call it. The chemistry is complex, but in short this man was starting to turn into soap. Happens when the body isn't exposed to air. Only a little bit now, but give it another year or so and most of his soft tissue would have turned into this.'

Iain whistled low as he looked more closely at the corpse. 'It gets better,' he said. 'Or worse, if you're this poor sod.' Whoever had put the body in the bag had trussed the man up first. Iain gestured to Dougie to come over and indicated where the hands had been tied behind the back. 'What's this – some kind of jewellery?' Iain asked.

'Looks that way,' Harriet said. The photographer leaned in and started snapping away.

'Well, what do we have here,' he said and held the object up to the light. It was a braided length of leather with metal ornaments – possibly silver, though tarnished and mottled. 'Some kind of jewellery,' he said. 'That is probably more use to us than wherever the bag came from.'

'Did that happen . . . I mean, do you think he was tied up before . . . or after?' Dougie said.

'You mean was he tortured?' Iain thought for a moment. 'Could have been. Difficult to tell in this state.' Evidence of struggle might indicate that, if they were able to find defensive wounds on the body. Or if there were other signs, like broken bones that had happened perimortem – around the time of death. Damage to internal organs might be a clue – ruptured kidneys or liver sometimes pointed to extreme beating. But all of that would depend on what survived the decomposition.

Iain arranged the freed arms in a more natural position now. The wrists were marked from where they had been tied. The skin had come away from the flesh underneath, making it look as if the man was wearing a pair of thick latex gloves. 'That's his skin,' Iain said. 'Fingerprinting not impossible, but a chore.'

'How'd you do that, then?' Dougie asked. His eyes were

narrowed, as if he was trying to let as little of what he was seeing in as possible.

'Couple of ways,' Iain said. 'You need to fill out where it's gone slack to pick up the fingerprint ridges.' They sometimes had luck injecting the slipped skin with saline. 'Or we might be able to peel it off and stick it on Alastair's hand like a glove.' He laughed, his teeth bared; they were like crooked tombstones in an old cemetery ground. The photographer looked like he wished he never asked.

According to MacLean, the people who had found the body were camping out on the north end of Raasay when it was discovered. Some English couple up on a holiday. The woman was fine but the man was a shattered wreck after seeing it. 'Going tae cost us a fortune in Victim Support,' Alastair had grumbled, as if police budgetary concerns were more important than a potential murder investigation.

Harriet read over the notes from the scene and the interview with the couple. Not much information there – two kayakers, no other witnesses to the discovery. The bag was caught on the underside of a boat when they came to shore. The woman had a forensic science degree, so knew not to move or touch anything, and radioed for help straightaway. Unless it was some elaborate double bluff, they probably had nothing to do with it. She noted that no one had thought to take DNA samples from them anyway. One more thing to follow up on later . . .

'Race?' she asked Iain.

'Mmm, probably white, but let's wait and see,' Iain said. He caught the photographer's curious look. 'This far along, the skin can do all sorts of things. And what time doesn't do, water will. I've seen black men bleached white and white people so far gone you'd swear they were from Africa. Until we have an ID, no way to know, but judging on his features and where we are, probably white.'

Iain plucked a nail clipper from the rack of sterilised instruments and picked up one of the dead man's hands. He carefully trimmed the middle three nails and put the clippings in a plastic envelope, then chucked it at the kid. 'Make sure Alastair logs that and gets it to the lab,' he said.

'Bet you twenty pence you get nothing off those,' Harriet said. 'The guy was in the water for weeks. Any genetic evidence is long gone.'

'Twenty pence? You're on,' Iain said. He turned to the kid and winked. 'You never know what you might turn up. There was one time, we had a ten-year-old pit of burned bone shards in Cerska—'

'Iain, no one's interested in hearing your RNA extraction story again,' Harriet sighed. 'That was ages ago.' She turned to the photographer. 'The way he goes on you would think he judged the tribunal himself.'

Iain tipped the corpse's head back on a plastic block. 'Get some pictures of his wallies,' he said, and pointed to the teeth, exposed from the absence of lips. The teeth were big and square and mostly straight. Iain pulled gently down on the mandible and peered inside. No obvious fillings, no denture. 'Not much to go on here,' he said to Harriet, who nodded. 'Dental records probably won't help much.'

Harriet Hitchin frowned at the body. 'So, apart from the bag I don't see anything that absolutely excludes the possibility that the death was natural or self-inflicted . . .' she said.

Iain raised his eyebrows. 'You mean apart from the tie on his hands?'

Harriet glanced at it. 'Could have been an autoerotic accident,' she said. 'I've seen more extreme.'

'I don't doubt it,' he said. 'But in a bag?'

'Remember that spy?' Harriet said. 'The one who zipped himself in a locked suitcase in the bath? This guy isn't even locked in.'

'Aye, sure. But I'm betting that fellow didn't also have a cut neck,' Iain said.

'What cut neck?'

Iain ran his finger across the stiff's chin, brushing where a deep gouge spanned the neck from ear to ear. The edges were nibbled just as the lips and eyelids had been, but it was clearly a cut made by a knife. The photographer raised the camera to his face and started snapping.

Iain smirked at the doctor. 'See? Even the kid can see the cut,' he said. 'First day and all.'

'Uh, well,' Harriet said. 'Hard to tell when decomp sets in.'

'The body's in bad shape, but not that bad,' Iain said.

'It could still be self-inflicted,' she said.

Iain shook his head. 'Man ties himself up, cuts his own throat, then zips himself in a bag and throws himself in the sea. Possible? Sure. Likely? Nae chance.'

Harriet crossed her arms. 'Iain, who's the pathologist again?'

'You are, Professor,' Iain said. She wasn't a professor any more, not after an inquiry into poor record keeping in Leeds threw her expert witness statements into question. It hadn't been enough for her to lose her license, but her career would never recover. If she went back to

England, it was unlikely the Home Office would have her as one of their pathologists again.

'It's Doctor, please,' she corrected.

'Of course, Doctor,' Iain said, and smiled. He hadn't forgotten. Her reputation for sloppy work preceded her, and even if it hadn't, a simple Internet search would have revealed it. Harriet Hitchin never spotted the windup. Nae sense of humour.

'Right, enough of what we can see; now let's get to what we can't see. Will you open up?' she asked.

Iain nodded. The pathologist was meant to do this part but he didn't mind getting on with it. First he made a y-shaped cut below the neck and down the chest. He loosened the skin and fat from the abdomen by wiggling his finger underneath; the layers separated from the muscle easily. There was no need for the rib shears today. The sternum and fronts of the ribs, softer than they would have been in a fresh body, came away easily using a bread knife.

Iain's tattooed arms sunk in the opening he had created and freed the organs. He kept a large PM-40 scalpel handy to loosen the connective tissues, but it was unnecessary and they pulled free with ease. Even so, the organs were in better shape than he expected – from the cold water, probably. He took out the heart and lungs together, then the liver, stomach and kidneys in another block. It all went into a washing-up basin.

He went back to the body and prised the skin of the neck away from the muscles, slowly and carefully excising the trachea and tongue. The cause of death was clear: the deep and fatal cuts to the throat. Iain put a white plastic ruler for scale next to the cuts. He guided Dougie to the shredded trachea to make sure there was a photographic record of the damage that had gone deep into the tissue.

'Oh, now that's interesting . . .' Iain wormed his little finger under a thin arch of bone.

'What's that?' Dougie's voice grew high and thin. Iain hid a smirk. He knew the tone of voice well; by his estimation they would be mopping up vomit or peeling the newbie off the floor in five minutes' time, ten at most.

'The hyoid bone,' Iain said. 'It didn't look fractured at first, but it is.'

'Which means what?'

'Well,' Iain crossed his arms over his aproned chest, seemingly unaware of the brown fluid dripping off his gloves over his front, 'we often see them broken in strangulations. So, this could be a strangulation gone wrong.'

'Could be. Or . . . ?' Dougie gulped.

'Or, it could have happened when whoever was getting rid of the body stuffed him into the bag. Tough to tell either way.'

'Why's that?'

'It's a thin bone, and the fracture point is pretty high in post-mortems where violence is involved,' he said. 'Not being connected to anything makes it more vulnerable to breaking.'

Dougie had passed through the sweating stage to the stage where he was just clammy and shivering. Iain reckoned the lad had a minute on his feet, tops.

'Doctor, are you after the head?' Iain asked Harriet. He set up a side table with a face mask and the skull saw, but hadn't peeled back the scalp yet.

'No thanks,' she said, looking up from where she was poring over the X-rays Iain had taken earlier. 'It's brain soup in there. We have a cause of death, no point going further.'

Ian grunted his assent and unfurled a black bit of plastic from a roll.

'What's that?' Dougie asked.

'Bin bags – ten for one of your fine Scottish pounds at the supermarket in Cameron Bridge,' Iain said. 'Best deal on the high street.'

'No, I mean what's it for?' Dougie asked. His voice was as weak as a sick child's.

'This is for the organs when the examination's finished,' Iain said. He started scooping the organs from the washing up basin into the bag with his hands. In the periphery of his vision he saw the photographer pitching and rolling like a ship on the sea. 'Normally they go back in the abdomen and we pop the ribs back on. Then it's stitched up. But this one's a wee bit far gone for an open casket, wouldn't you say?' He had hardly finished the sentence when Dougie's limp body hit the floor.

'Bloody hell, not another one,' Harriet Hitchin said. 'Iain, hold his feet up while I get the smelling salts.' She strode across the room to the first aid kit by the sink. It rarely saw action apart from fainting photographers and students. Not much call for first aid in a mortuary, seeing as most of the visitors there were already dead. 'And tell Alastair to stop bringing us the newbies.'

The sound of a phone made them both jump. 'New security door-bell,' Iain said and gestured to a phone and screen on the wall. 'Bet it's Alastair. Typical of him to turn up now that all the action is finished. Go on, buzz him in.'

'It's not Alastair.' Harriet checked out the black-and-white moni-tor. 'This is going to sound odd, but . . . it looks a bit like that MP,' she said. 'You know, Morag the Moaner?'

'A real live politician?' Iain whistled. 'Must be my lucky day. Well, let her in then.'

: **5** :

Morag Munro smoothed her silver streaked bob behind her ears and checked to make sure no one was was coming up the road. She was recognisable to most of the population of Cameron Bridge and if anyone saw her at the mortuary it would surely be the talk of the pubs for days. Luckily the building was halfway up a glen and off the tourist drag. Cameron Bridge was even deader up this end than usual.

No pun intended.

She rang again. If no one answered soon she would have to go, or else risk missing the second sleeper service. She had sent Arjun down to London on an earlier train. 'I have some paperwork to finish up,' she said, assuring him she would be back at Westminster and raring to go before nine a.m. tomorrow.

The door finally cracked open. 'Good afternoon!' she said, and gave her best neighbourhood-canvassing smile. Morag offered her hand to the scarecrow-haired woman in wellies and a green plastic apron who opened the door. 'Is your supervisor here?'

'I'm Dr Hitchin.' Harriet's plummy voice revealed her irritation at being mistaken for the help. 'I'm the pathologist.'

Morag paused a moment. She should be able to recognise the UK's forensic pathologists cold; there were only about thirty of them. 'Harriet, I remember now,' she snapped her fingers. 'You were the Home Office path on the Bulgarian nanny trial in Leeds, yes?' An infant had died in the care of a nanny, with the prosecution arguing hard that it was the result of shaken baby syndrome, not cot death. Harriet's testimony had been key to getting the conviction, though that was overturned on appeal after her record-keeping scandal emerged. 'Sorry for not recognising you sooner,' Morag said.

Harriet stood aside and let Morag enter. 'Thank you. I do what I can in service of the law,' she said.

'So what brings the Shadow Home Secretary here?' Iain shouted through the open door of the post-mortem suite. 'We've already gone and voted for your precious Union, there's no one to impress now.'

'Sorry, what did you say? I couldn't hear you over the . . . I guess you call that music?' She raised her eyebrows at Harriet.

'Cannibal Coffin,' Iain said. 'Best zombie-themed band coming out of Scandinavia these days.'

Morag deployed her static smile. Christ, what a plonker. 'Lovely,' she said. She and Harriet walked to the threshold of the PM suite. 'I was passing through, on my way back to London tonight. National preparedness for mass disasters is coming up in committees and I thought that it would be good to have a chat with a manager here, to see how we're prepared in the Highlands. In case there's anything the facility needs from the Home Office to get up to scratch.'

Her eyes wandered over the walls, illuminated with flickering fluorescent lights. Outside the mortuary was nondescript, hardly discernible from the many ramshackle farm buildings on the edge of Cameron Bridge. Inside it looked like a horror set. Forget contingency plans and emergency preparedness. What the place needed was a wrecker's ball.

'Iain, turn the music off or I will,' Harriet growled. He grumbled an oath in response but the racket stopped, severing Cannibal Coffin mid-wail.

'Thank you so much,' Morag said. 'Do you think the facility would need any particular improvements to deal with a localised or regional crisis?'

'What sort of improvements?' Iain loped over to them. Morag's sharp eyes took him in one look, from the rounded shoulders and heavy fists of a pub brawler to the cynical and pinched face of a disappointed Yes voter. Her fingers started to drum lightly against her thigh. This was a variety of man she knew well. The kind who had joined the SNP in their droves after the referendum with promises to vote her out, but with any luck had forgotten to turn up on polling day. All mouth and no kilt, as her father would say.

'I think upgrading the facility is an excellent idea,' Harriet Hitchin said. 'We can never be too prepared for what might befall us.' She paused. 'If you need someone to head up a survey of the mass disaster capacity in Scotland . . .' she babbled hopefully.

Morag could hear the edge of longing in Harriet's voice, the hope for escape from this backwater, this go-nowhere post. Useful. She filed that titbit away on her mental Rolodex. She craned her head and tried to peek round the corner. 'Could I perhaps see the rest of the building, or are you in the middle of something? I mean apart from the death metal?'

'There's a PM on,' Harriet said. 'Post-mortem, I mean, not the Prime Minister, ha ha.' Morag smiled weakly. 'You're welcome to come through but it's a ripe one.' She pointed to a neatly folded lab coat. 'Put this on over your clothes and grab a pair of wellies.' She looked at Morag's shiny red heels. 'You're a braver woman than me: I wouldn't chance the pavements here in a pair of shoes like that.'

'Years of practice,' Morag said. That, and a stubborn refusal to let visiting Cameron Bridge mean she should take a day off from looking professional. No one seemed to take any pride in their appearances any more, not in her opinion. The number of people trudging up and down the high street in rigger boots and joggers was appalling. Only slightly better were the outdoor gear brigade in top-to-toe North Face all year round. Fleeces and walking trousers were for the hill, not the office.

Harriet walked back over the low divider on the floor. Morag shucked her red shoes in the corridor and slipped into a pair of rubber boots. She tiptoed over the barrier but hung back slightly as the smell hit her. She couldn't say she hadn't been warned, but this was beyond foul. Almost sweet, like shit and cake. 'You know what, I'll watch from here,' she said, putting a hand over her nose and mouth.

Iain grabbed her by the shoulders and steered her towards the hand-wash station. 'Don't be daft, lass, you're here, might as well muck in. Scrub up.' He threw a pair of gloves at Morag and she reluctantly washed her hands and followed him to the examination table.

'Is it anyone special?' Morag asked, crinkling her nose as they stood round the body. She longed for a handkerchief, some perfume, anything.

'Body from up in Raasay, by Skye,' Harriet said. 'A couple of kay-akers found it washed up on a beach.'

'I think I read about that in the paper this morning,' Morag said. 'Rum business. What a terrible tragedy.'

'All in a day's work,' Iain said. A few tissue samples had been put aside to send to the toxicology lab, but the rest was otherwise untouched.

Morag looked at the body, then looked quickly away. It was too late. The image of the black and green torso, cut open and splayed like a carved Christmas turkey, was already burned on her retinas. The head lolled back, supported by a white plastic block, displaying the cut throat and lidless, horrible eyes.

She tried not to gag, but words were slow to come. 'I'm sure the fiscal and the police will have it solved soon,' she eventually said. She looked round. 'Are you on your own? No police to witness the procedure?'

Iain looked at the clock on the wall and shook his head. 'Ali Mac-Lean was meant to be here for the PM, but I think he'll have sneaked off for his tea by now.' He clocked Morag's look, the one that said she expected no better from the local constabulary. 'He's a good man, that MacLean, you know,' Iain said. 'His dad was mates wi' yer husband's dad, as I understand it.'

'Mmm.' Morag turned back to Dr Hitchin. Obviously, with a career like hers, what was most important to the constituents was who her father-in-law had been friends with. The Highlands never changed. 'Any ideas on who the body might be? Such a terrible thing to have happened, and right on our own doorstep.' Her eyes were starting to water now – how on earth did they stand the smell?

'He's a bit of a mystery man at the moment,' Harriet said. 'His hands are in poor shape for fingerprinting, no ID on the body or the bag. With luck it won't stay that way. We'll get an approximate age off the bones and his stature and compare those against missing persons. If there's a match, we can get family DNA and confirm it. Or we might get lucky and get dental records, you never know.'

'I guess any evidence you might use for catching the murderer is probably destroyed, too?' Morag asked.

'It depends,' Iain said. 'Why, is there something you want to tell us?' He chuckled until Harriet shushed him.

'We don't know yet,' Harriet said. 'Since he was in the bag, there might be a chance of some evidence surviving under his fingernails. It's a matter of the lab trying to extract genetic material and seeing what they come up with.'

'Interesting,' Morag said. 'And this takes, what, a few hours? A few days?'

'If we're lucky, days. Could be weeks or longer.' Iain said. 'Or months, depending on what the path labs have on their schedules already. It's not like that rubbish you see on the television, with all those magical hologram databases instantly matching enhanced CCTV images to your ID cards and that nonsense, you know. Maybe as Shadow Home Secretary that is something you ought to know about—'

'Don't listen to him,' Harriet sighed and turned back to Morag. 'You know, this is refreshing. It's so nice of you to take a keen interest in our work. The details will all be in my report,' she said. 'Anyway, about the rest of the facility. Iain can give you a tour if you like?'

Morag's eyes widened. 'No, I think I've seen enough for now,' she said. 'Train to catch. Don't worry, I can let myself out.' She spun on her heel and marched towards the door, leaving star-struck Harriet trailing in her wake.

Morag Munro left so quickly that she forgot to take her shoes. And she never even noticed the photographer lying on the floor, much less the quiet click of his digital camera snapping away.

: **6** :

Erykah's mobile wouldn't stop ringing. She had set it to vibrate, but even that was distracting.

She twirled the diamond engagement and wedding rings on her finger. They felt unfamiliar there. But they were necessary for keeping up the pretence. The Big Billions Lottery publicity shoot was supposed to be a small thing, they said. A couple of hours at most. It was now taking over the entire house. 'We want to show you as approachable and normal as possible,' explained the set dresser they had sent. 'Your own home, your own clothes. An everyday couple – like any of our other players.'

'It could be anyone,' Erykah said.

He nodded. 'Exactly. Gorgeous house. We couldn't have had a better couple for our first winners, you two really look the part,' he said. 'This place is immaculate. I wouldn't change a thing.'

He started scattering primary coloured cushions and vases of flowers around the rooms. The photographer's assistant rolled out a huge Union Flag rug in shades of grey on the dining room floor and fluffed some newly purchased Keep Calm pillows. Erykah cringed.

'I feel terrible,' Erykah said. She looked over a printed sheet of talking points she had been handed when they arrived. 'I know almost nothing about the lottery, my husband bought the ticket. I have to admit, I had never heard of it before we won.'

The set dresser looked over his shoulder and chuckled. 'To tell you the truth, I hadn't either until they hired me to do this job,' he said. 'You're not the only one.'

'No, I guess not,' Erykah said. 'But you took the job anyway? For a company you had never heard of?'

'Sure, why not?' He grinned. 'So it's registered in the Channel Islands, or whatever. We're living in a global economy now, right? It all goes in my bank account just the same.'

'Sure,' Erykah said. It occurred to her that so far, she hadn't met anyone else from the Big Billions lottery. Rab assured her everything was in hand; he showed her some emails he received, and a business card from someone he said came by when she was out buying groceries. But shouldn't someone from the lottery be here right now, hovering over their first jackpot winners? Something about the arrangement felt strange to her.

'Anyway, honey,' the set dresser said. 'I think the entire point of this photo shoot is to spread the word. Get it up in the public consciousness, you know what I mean?'

'Oh, right,' Erykah said. 'Of course. Of course.'

The glass doors facing out into the garden were flung open and let in a chilly breeze. The set dresser examined Erykah's outfit, a sleek navy blue bandage dress that showed off her athletic frame, her bright coral lipstick. 'I don't suppose you have something a little less . . . severe? And maybe, I don't know, softer make-up? The press will be here any minute.'

Erykah gritted her teeth but obliged. It had been a long time since anyone had told her how to dress, when to smile, and how to do her make-up, but she wanted this over with and quickly.

By the time she came back downstairs in a prim tea dress that she hated the reporters were already waiting. The photographer shoved her outside. Pots of hothouse flowers had been dotted around the garden, and lights were set up to make it all look warmer and more spring-like than it really was.

'That's it; now pop the champagne, Rab. Erykah, if we can get you with a glass in there . . . perfect.' They were ordered this way and that. Sitting on the stone garden seat, standing by the glossy black door to their house. With the cheque, without the cheque. Standing together, standing alone. Erykah under the horse chestnut tree in the back garden, close cropped so the bare branches didn't show, trying to hide her chattering teeth. Rab put his thumb over the top of the bottle of fizz and shook it up, spraying it all over his wife. The cameras snapped away.

'She's a great looking lady,' one cameraman murmured to his assistant. 'And look at this place. This guy's got to be the luckiest slob in the world.'

Erykah had misgivings about playing house for the cameras but did her best to go along. She bared her teeth in the perfect imitation of a spontaneous laugh over and over. Meanwhile she was totting up the sums in her head. Maybe her initial reaction to the news had been over the top. Even subtracting Rab's outstanding loans, they were still going to end up with more cash than she could ever have expected to see in her life.

Her married life up until now had been only merely wealthy. This? This was *Rich* with a capital R. The kind of money that made even people in Molesey stop and stare: vulgar, shameless. The kind of rich that hip-hop songs were written about, that kids back in Streatham dreamed about. She didn't stop herself from doing the mental maths, calculating how many childhoods of growing up in poverty this would have bought. It would have paid for her first sixteen years a hundred times over. With cash to spare.

In between shots she grabbed a bile-coloured chenille throw that had been draped over the sofa and wrapped her hands around a mug of tea. 'Warming up,' she smiled at the photographer's assistant who noticed her trembling hands. 'Do you have to do an outdoor shoot in February?' He shrugged and mumbled something about the light. She fumbled with her mobile, clocking the missed calls and voicemails. She decided to ignore those for now.

Because she was scared. Really scared. How much longer? she wondered. How much longer until someone in the press figured out who she was? Before her name pinged some newspaper editor's memory bank and they dug out those photographs?

Maybe not, though. Maybe they would miss it. It was all back in the time before the Internet, and who knew for sure, maybe by now it was gone for good. Maybe no one would care. Maybe her married name would be enough to trip up anyone who went looking. The trial had been big news at the time, sure, but who would remember the girlfriend of an accused murderer from over twenty years ago?

Erykah put the mug back on the counter. What would her life be like now if things had gone differently? She might have stayed at university, never met Rab, and had a career. Or she might have stayed with Grayson and life would have been, if not much like her dreams, at least interesting. In the three years they had been together, he had never bored her.

She smoothed the ditsy flowered fabric of the dress down over her thighs and scrunched her fingers through her hair. Grayson would have liked the first outfit better, the sex kitten look, not this fake '50s housewife image.

God, it had been ages since she last thought of Grayson. Maybe other women wondered where their exes were more often. She supposed maybe it was because she didn't have to wonder. She knew exactly where he was. He was in prison, probably for the rest of his life. And unless something had changed in the last two decades, an unrepentant killer.

'Erykah, tilt your head this way. Erykah, over here.'

Photographers hadn't changed at all since the last time she was faced with a bank of flashbulbs. Ordering you to look this way and that way, parroting your name over and over, pushing for a reaction.

Grayson had been her first boyfriend. He was ten years older, already with something of a fearsome reputation, but loyal to friends and family. He was the first to look past the gangly nerd in glasses and see – well, a gangly nerd who cleaned up nicely. And was good with sums. Which, given his ambitions, was exactly what he was looking for. 'My diamond in the rough,' he used to say. And she made the effort to look more like the kind of woman he wanted her to be. Not that it was all one sided. He took a subscription to the *Financial Times*, he said, to impress her.

He always had money. She knew where it came from; his source of income was common knowledge in their neighbourhood. But Grayson assured her he was more than some go-nowhere street dealer. Some said he had big connections down the hill in Brixton, others claimed it was further afield, Manchester, even. He promised he was going to do her proud, cash out and go straight. Get into the real world of business. Invest in property. He talked about their future life together as he drove her from Harrods to Harvey Nicks to Selfridges in his 5 Series Beemer. 'Nothing's too good for my Rikki,' he would say, and squeeze the top of her thigh. 'You ask, and it's yours.'

'Don't you see, Rikki,' Rainbow would hiss as she watched Erykah get ready for a date, 'he's with you because he can control you. Why would a man like that be interested in a girl your age? Why would he be interested in a girl like you at all?'

Erykah hated her for that. Hated her mother for reducing her to an ugly duckling, to a little girl. She would show her mum, she would show them all they were wrong about him.

Rainbow put her hands on her shoulders and turned her daughter towards her. There were tears in her eyes, although that might have been the watery, unfocused look she had sometimes when she was deep in withdrawal. 'Rikki, honey,' she said, 'I don't want you to make the same mistakes I made,' she said. 'I look at you and I see a girl who doesn't know yet that the world is not going to give someone like you a lot of second chances.'

Erykah shrugged her off. What was she talking about? She got good marks, worked hard. She had never even tried drugs, and she and Grayson always used protection. She and her mother were nothing alike. She knew that with the certainty only a teenage girl knows.

It was Grayson who took her under his wing. When she was with him she saw less of the things she hated about herself. When she looked in a mirror her skinny arms and legs didn't bother her so much. Her frizzy hair, her eyes too close together, they no longer seemed so bad. He was the one who told her, no, she was long like a model and she should dress like one. She should style her hair so it fell in ringlets, emphasise her eyes with make-up. And he was right.

'Come here, baby, come here.' She would lean in and let him rub a moistened finger along her forehead, smooth her baby hairs into place. His big hands framed her jaw. He looked her over and nodded, satisfied with what he saw. When Erykah was accepted at university to study computer science, it was Grayson who bragged to all his friends and family. His girl was going to have a degree. Rainbow barely seemed to register what was happening by that point, wrapped in the layers of her worsening addiction.

'Maybe someday you gonna figure out how to hack a bank and make me a millionaire,' he had said.

'I don't think so,' she said.

Her perfectly straight response made him laugh. 'My baby's smart and beautiful.' She ducked her head and felt a flutter in her chest. No one had ever called her beautiful before.

A couple of years passed. She went to university. Still Grayson was no closer to leaving dealing like he promised. It was the money, he said. A little bit more, that was all he needed. She got impatient. How much before it was going to be enough?

'But we earned this, Rikki,' he would say, rolling down the tinted car windows so she could feel the thick, hot air of the city waft through, rustling the heaps of shopping bags in the back seat. He paid for her driving lessons, so that he could give her a new car someday. 'And this is only the beginning.'

It wasn't the beginning of anything good. But they had no way of knowing it then.

What Grayson never understood was that, for Erykah, it wasn't about the money. She loved him with that heart-rending puppy love that only happens the first time. She believed he was a good person, not the heartless criminal everyone else painted him as. And when he was torn from her life she thought – really thought – she might die.

Numb with grief through the trial, she did all she could do: told the court what had happened on that rainy night outside the stranger's house in Hampstead. Told them what she knew and when she knew it. When she was on the stand she could see him from the corner of her eye. He nodded gently as her words unfurled into the rapt courtroom. It bothered her not to be able to talk directly to him – to explain that she'd had no choice. Did he know? Did he hate her for it?

'Let's get you two on the sofa now,' Champagne glasses were pressed into Erykah and Rab's hands and they were shepherded back towards the photographers. The cameras clicked away as Erykah draped an arm around Rab. Now this was a part she had practiced to perfection.

On the outside, anyway. It was a long time before Erykah had stopped feeling like a fraud in her Molesey life. Virginia Woolf was wrong. A woman doesn't need a room of her own. What she needs is a credit card of her own.

'A second honeymoon? Well, I wouldn't say it's out of the question,' Erykah answered questions from the pre-approved list the lottery company had supplied to reporters. A buzz as her phone vibrated again. She looked at the screen and switched it off. It was time to play the part of happy and loving wife for now. And she could act, boy could she act. The brush of the lips with a man she hadn't kissed in years; her hand linked with his while they listened to the press ask the same three questions over and over again . . .

Rab wasn't handling it as well. He flinched at any direct question that came his way, his eyes darting from person to person like a prisoner facing the Inquisition. It irritated Erykah. With all the money they had won surely he would be feeling a sense of relief? It was enough to pay off his debts nearly twenty times over. If she had been in his shoes, she would have been howling at the moon with sheer delight.

She smelled the tang of anxiety in his sweat as they settled on the sofa and another journo vied for their attention, asking about holidays, homes and yachts. 'I think we should give it all to charity,' Rab mumbled.

Erykah elbowed him in the ribs and her smile didn't budge an inch.

'My husband has a wicked sense of humour,' she said. 'Obviously we'll give some of it to charity. But this opens up all kinds of opportunities for us, doesn't it, darling?'

The reporter nodded, jotting notes on a pad of paper. 'With your husband being one of the many who lost their jobs in the recession—'

'Exactly,' Erykah said, and rubbed Rab's knee. Her smile felt as if it was going to split her face in half, a parody of interest and affection. 'We know how lucky we've been.'

The reporter nodded. Keeping Rab's unemployment status a secret from the press hadn't been possible. But, if anything, it sweetened the tale for the papers. Rich people becoming even richer are hardly news – middle-class couple falls on hard times, then lands a windfall? That's the stuff tabloid dreams are made of.

Eventually the questions dried up and the press started packing their cameras away. Erykah excused herself and went upstairs. Her bag still sat in the corner of the bedroom where she had left it, a dense hole drawing her gaze in each time she came in to hang up new clothes or check her make-up. She looked away. Now was not the time.

Erykah turned the brushed steel handle of the bathroom and locked herself in the en-suite. She scrolled through the missed calls and messages. Six of them were from Nicole. Shit.

She dialled back, heart thumping. She started to walk the bathroom floor. The phone rang and rang. Please don't pick up. Please don't pick up. What was the point? There was nothing she could say to make the situation better. The black bag wasn't the only thing she was trying to avoid. Erykah had bottled it. She felt like a coward. She was about to hang up when Nicole finally answered.

'It's me,' Erykah said. She felt dumb for saying it; of course Nicole would know who had phoned.

A long sigh. 'Where have you been?'

'I can't talk,' Erykah said. Her heels clicked on the polished limestone floor as she paced the short distance over and over. She tried not to think about Valentine's night. Had Nicole been sitting at the farmhouse table in the cottage waiting, before finally blowing out the candles and going to bed alone? Had she drunk the wine she'd bought, reading and rereading Erykah's terse final text *Can't come – talk later*?

'I saw a picture of you on the news.' A pause. 'Are you coming to training tonight?'

Erykah's stomach churned. Why wasn't Nicole yelling at her? Or even asking where they stood? Nicole's even, flat American accent made it worse somehow, made Erykah feel more guilty for standing her up. 'Probably not tonight. I'm sorry.'

'Mmm.' Nicole did not sound surprised. 'Your husband looks different from how I pictured him.'

'Does that matter?' Erykah said. Nicole had been the one to always shut down discussion of her married life in the past.

'No, not really,' Nicole said. Erykah thought she could hear an echo, like she was taking the call in the club changing rooms. 'So where does this leave us?'

'Leave us? Nothing's changed. God, Nic. It's only money.'

'Only money, yeah,' Nicole said. Another extended pause. 'You looked happy.'

Erykah glanced in the mirror and watched as her lips drooped into an involuntary frown. 'It's just a photo,' she said. 'Nothing has changed between him and me. Not really.' She sounded surer than she felt. 'Don't make me feel guilty about being married, you knew this from the start,' Erykah added, and instantly regretted saying it.

Nicole did not rise to the bait. 'I hope you make it to training tomorrow.'

'I'll do my best,' Erykah said.

'Don't you always,' Nicole said.

Erykah hung up. It was unfair to make her feel bad for something that was out of her control. She should never have rung back. These were the kinds of conversations best had face-to-face, not over the phone. Why get so bent out of shape over a photo? Couldn't Nicole tell it was all fake? But she also imagined how she would feel if Nicole was splashed all over the news laughing and hugging someone else. She would feel like dirt.

Rab tapped on the toilet door. 'They've gone. The reporters are gone now,' he said.

Erykah slipped the phone away, unlocked the door and poked her head out. 'Well, that was a hell of a day,' she said. They went back down to the sitting room where the prop pillows had been left behind. Rab slumped on the sofa like a marionette with its strings cut. Erykah switched on the radio.

'Please, don't,' Rab said. 'The last thing I can take right now is more – more news voices.'

'Fine.' Erykah turned it over to a classical music station. The jazz-tinted flutes and slithering piano of Ravel spread into the corners of the room. She hated Ravel. His music sounded to her as bland as the walls and furnishings, a poor imitation of the passionate music it aped, a highly mannered pastiche of a living, breathing thing.

'There are more of them coming tomorrow afternoon, you know,' she said. 'And we haven't had the investment advisors from the lottery company yet.'

Rab nodded, but his eyes were unfocused and his mind was clearly elsewhere.

'You can do this.' She sat next to him on the sofa and crossed her legs. 'Today went well. Really well. A few days, a few photos. And then it's tomorrow's chip paper.'

It was the exact phrase he had said to her once, a long time ago, when she'd felt as though her life was spinning out of control as it was plastered all over the headlines. She wasn't sure she believed it, but she couldn't think of anything else to offer. 'And then we can talk about what to do next.'

He nodded again but said nothing. It had been years since she'd felt that he was trying. She had married him because she needed someone who made her feel safe but as soon as the ring went on, it was as though he stopped caring.

Maybe if she had been a better person, he would have behaved differently. Maybe if she had been more like his ideal. He used to talk fondly about the kind of girls he had known when he was at university, blonde medical students who loved skiing and fishing, the ones who had 'turned down better men than me.' But if that was what he'd wanted, why had he chosen her? And would girls like those have accepted his terrible memory and lack of effort, like the time he brought her back a half-eaten bar of white chocolate after a business jaunt in Mayrhofen?

No, she mused, probably not. They probably would have gone with him, and expertly plied the off-piste itineraries, charmed his clients, worn cosy socks and known what après-ski was.

When they argued, he would berate her for not being a better person. There was a Good Erykah, he would tell her, and when she was that person she was amazing, but he couldn't deal with Bad Erykah. The one who let her past and her choices weigh her down like a diving vest.

It was strange to her, his preoccupation with a ghostly, better version of herself. He talked about Good Erykah as if she was a common acquaintance of theirs, some kind of role model. Did that person even exist? He couldn't seem to accept that she had faults, and she wondered what sort of vision of her he had built up in his head before becoming disappointed with the real person he married.

And by that time she had no one else to rely on. Not her mum, not Grayson. No one but herself.

'What do you think the stories will be like,' he said. 'Will they find out. You know, about your . . .'

'Yeah,' she said. 'I don't know. Depends how curious the journalists get, I guess. As far as I know it's not on the Internet, but that doesn't mean they can't find out if they want to.'

She remembered, with bitterness, how she had been told to leave the university after the trial. Jump before you're pushed – wasn't that what the Dean had said?

And then trying to find work in IT, which was a joke. When she'd started as a student she had found that she already knew things a lot of the others on the course didn't. Little skills like setting up networks and TCP/IP protocols. She taught herself a lot of skills on top of the degree courses: database admin, web design.

With websites starting to catch on, there were still more jobs than there were people with the know-how. Not having a piece of paper should not have been an issue, people with fewer qualifications than she had were walking straight into good careers. But for some reason she wasn't as lucky. She suspected it was because too many people still recognised her. It was never openly discussed, just a feeling she got. A mood. She lost count of the number of interviews where a panel of white men sitting behind a table told her she was great but 'not quite what we're looking for'.

Rab had been sympathetic the first few times she failed to get a job. After that, he started saying it must be something she was doing, an attitude she was giving off that made them reject her. He told her she needed to work harder. Pull up her bootstraps. Screw her courage to the sticking place. Go once more unto the breach. And all the other empty lines he offered in place of understanding.

So she threw herself into training for GB squad selection. Trying to worm her way back into that world. But her moment had passed, if it ever even existed. She did well in the five kilometre trials, but struggled against bigger women in the shorter distances. One coach suggested she try to diet down to lightweight, but on her almost six-foot frame, that was a disaster. By the time Erykah was able to admit to herself that she didn't stand a chance against the younger rowers coming through, she was already old enough to be in the veteran squad.

'You're ashamed?' she said to Rab.

He shrugged. 'Curious what angle this will take.'

Erykah pursed her lips. They had made no secret of Rab's employment status to the press, so it wasn't as if his past was sparkling white either. And she could wave off her indiscretions as the actions of a young woman. His affairs over the years, or whatever else the press didn't yet know about her husband – and she included herself in that circle of ignorance – those would be tougher to explain away when they came out of the woodwork. That's what always happened when people won the lottery, right? Folks from your past came out of nowhere with their arms wide open, hoping for a piece of the windfall.

She wondered if she might hear from Rainbow. It had been years, and she had no idea if her mother was alive or dead. She hoped she wasn't dead. But she didn't fancy a family reunion, either. Not after Rainbow had sold stories to the press during Grayson's trial. There were a lot of things her mum had done over the years, a lot she could overlook and sometimes even forgive, but that, for Erykah, had been the final straw.

Rab looked at her. His blue eyes were ringed in red, the pupils like the beady pinpoints. 'I can't do this,' he said. 'The money . . . I can't do it.' His voice sounded fragile.

'Rab—'

'I don't know what to do,' he said. 'I couldn't sleep last night.'

'I couldn't sleep either,' Erykah admitted.

'I thought about coming into your room, but—'

'No.' Whatever else, she was not going to roll over this time. She knew that she couldn't trust him. 'We need to screw our courage to the sticking place, Rab. It's only for a week.'

She had meant the line to be grimly ironic, but he nodded as if it was wisdom from a hilltop guru.

When she looked at him now it was like looking at someone she had only briefly known, long, long in the past. What had she seen in him? She shouldn't have jumped into the marriage. She knew that. But she was still wounded from what had happened with Grayson when they had met. Marry in haste, regret at leisure – wasn't that what people said? Wasn't it the kind of thing Rab would have said, if it had been about anyone else but him?

Maybe he did say it, for all she knew. Behind her back. To his family and colleagues. To the interns and new hires he bedded year after year. Maybe it was another one of his scripted lines, another polished little nugget of ersatz wisdom, designed to pacify anyone who didn't scratch the surface too hard.

Too late she had realised her husband was not, as she had first believed, deep. He was many compacted layers of shallow.

Well, what could she say now? They sat parallel on the sofa like a pair of dolls. A pair of dolls holding a lottery ticket worth twenty million pounds. Rab clutched a Keep Calm pillow so hard that his knuckles turned white. The tinkling sound of piano filled the room like snakes.

'It's only eleven,' the landlord said to the silver-haired man with the handlebar moustache. He selected a pint glass and pulled the first draught of the day. The room, decorated in red tartan and polished dark oak, was empty apart from the barman and the fellow in head-to-toe Barbour leaning on the bar with a fiver in one hand and a newspaper in the other. 'You're druthy for a morn.'

'Pardon, what?' said Major Whitney Abbott.

'Thirsty,' the barman pushed the pint glass across the bar. 'You're thirsty for so early in the morning.'

'Yes,' the Major said. 'My wife would be dragging me up and down the high street otherwise.' The prospect of touring the dismal shops of Cameron Bridge, followed by stilted conversation over tea and cakes, did not appeal to the Major. Visits to their holiday abode in the Highlands rarely deviated from the same boring formula. She would likely squeeze in a visit to the town's museum as well, which as far as he could tell contained the same dull exhibits on nineteenth century tweed weaving it had contained the other two dozen times they had been inside.

Whitney Abbott had long grown to despise the company of his better half, who seemed to choose her leisure activities specifically to irritate him. 'I told her I had some work to catch up on.'

'Aye, good call,' the landlord said. 'Leave the shopping to the lasses. Scunnered of it maself.' The Major nodded. 'I was meaning to ask—'

The Major flashed his dentures in a well-practised smile. 'Am I Major Whitney Abbott? Why yes, yes, I am,' he said in an impeccably posh accent. 'Have you read my book?'

The memoirs of his time with the Royal Marines in the Falklands had been out a few years, but failed to trouble the bestseller list. Initially the publisher had hoped the book would gain some positive reviews and attention based on the fact that Abbott was the hero son of a WWII legend. What they hadn't expected was that revelations that Abbott junior was shagging his ghost writer would take over the headlines instead.

It was uncomfortable to see the allegations splashed everywhere – he still referred to them as allegations, although everything that made it into print was true, or at least true enough. The frustration was that, instead of interviews about his military career, all anyone wanted to talk about was a bit of rumpy pumpy.

Still, if that meant the average man on the street recognised him, perhaps it wasn't a bad thing. Maybe the fellow had a copy handy and would like the Major to autograph it.

The barman shook his head and pointed at the Major's crotch. 'Nah, I was sayin', do you hear that noise? Man, I think yer phone's buzzin'.'

'Oh, right. So it is,' the Major said. He fumbled inside his sporran for the mobile phone. He had managed to avoid owning one of the things for years, but had recently been convinced to keep it on hand in case of emergencies. Why people these days accepted unsolicited interruptions to their day was beyond his ken.

'Abbott here,' he barked into the handset, which rang again in response. He jabbed at it with his finger, 'Damned thing.' The Major finally found the answer button. 'Abbott here,' he said again, not as loudly.

'Whitney, it's me.' A woman's voice, Scottish accent. 'Where are you?'

That would be his darling goddaughter, then. She never had been one for pleasantries. 'Betty and I are in Cameron Bridge for a long weekend, checking up on the cottage. She wanted to see a—'

'Fascinating, I'm sure,' the woman interrupted. 'When are you back in London?'

'Tomorrow, possibly the day after,' he said. 'What's going on?' The Major wandered to the bar window. The inn overlooked the decaying town centre with its downtrodden hotels and muddy little square and clutches of visitors snapping photos of the grey waterfront. Tourist buses carried people in and out all times of year, dozens of Canadians and Americans disgorging to have a look around at the shortbread tin landscape, take a couple of photos with a bagpiper on the high street and then climb back aboard to be whisked away to Loch Ness.

'We have a situation, Whitney,' she said. 'The ... thing I had you take care of over the holidays? Three guesses what turned up on a beach in Scotland yesterday afternoon.'

The Major sucked in his breath. Suddenly a pint of ale seemed entirely insufficient for the occasion. This called for a stiff whisky. 'No,' he protested.

'Yes,' she said. 'Didn't you hear anything about it in the news up there? It was in the paper and on a couple of websites, though they haven't identified the body yet.'

'I never read the local news,' he said. 'Pointless waste of time.'

'Mmm,' she said. 'Well, try not to say that too loudly or too often, if you can manage to do so. I can't imagine your future constituents would be terribly pleased to hear it.'

'Do we know anything about the . . . package?' he asked.

'Nothing yet,' she said. 'It's in Cameron Bridge mortuary.'

'How do you know it's him? If it was only found yesterday. Don't bodies usually take, I don't know, months to identify?' The Major really did not know, although his sinking stomach felt as if he probably did.

'Maybe, maybe not. But the location. And the news is already reporting it was found in a bag,' she said. 'The body is with a pathologist, although from what I understand, she isn't top-tier.'

Whitney breathed out. 'Good. Good. Even if it is our man, there may be wiggle room yet.'

'Maybe,' she said. 'But I hope you understand it's a situation that I would sooner not be in at all. And that if this is what I fear it is, then you need to be as far away from this as humanly possible.'

'Goes without saying,' the Major said. 'But no plan survives first contact, as we say in—'

'Yes, yes, as you say in the Corps,' she finished for him. 'You've mentioned it once or twice.'

Major Whitney Abbott gritted his teeth but said nothing about her dismissive attitude. He needed her more than she needed him. The penny had dropped around the time he found himself giving an after-dinner speech at a banking conference last year. He was rehashing the Battle of Mount Harriet for the hundredth time and noticed the audience looking fidgety and bored where before they had been amused and engaged. When he described what it had been like in the middle of the night, dug into his own trench, eyes searching the dark – that was where he was accustomed to the audience falling silent, reverent, in awe. But it wasn't happening. Instead of a thousand eyes on him, he looked across the room to see heads bent over the light of a hundred mobiles. The room clinked and jangled with glasses and the sound of cutlery on dessert plates, hummed with vibrating phones replying to texts and calls.

They weren't interested in war stories. They were there for the scandal, and as soon as he refused to talk about it, they switched off. He might as well have been talking to the bathroom mirror. He looked out over the crowd and saw more than just young people who had never known war glued to their mobiles. He saw the gulf between his generation and theirs. He had committed the cardinal sin of any entertainer – good or bad, you had to hold the room. They had to love you or hate you. Indifference was poison.

Soon after that the slowdown in bookings hit. News shows stopped inviting him to be on panels. Papers sent fewer requests for interviews. He went to his publisher and begged them to reissue the paperback with a new afterword, but he could not nail them down to a deal. Major Abbott's editor suggested he might have better luck pitching a biography of his famous dad instead. The Major told him where he could stick that idea and stormed out.

So when his goddaughter approached him with a new project in mind, he was in no position to refuse. And it was a doozy.

'So what do we do now?' he said. Whatever it was, he hoped it wouldn't involve the Internet. He had a strong dislike for the Internet and, he suspected, the feeling was mutual.

'Now? We push the next stage forward.'

'The shipment, you mean?' the Major said in a stage whisper.

'Shipment?' She sounded confused.

'You know, the *shipment*,' Abbott said. They had agreed on a code for phone calls, so why wasn't she using it? 'The shipment of expenditures.'

'Oh, right, that silly code of yours,' she sighed. 'You mean the money.'

'Don't say it!' Abbott hissed. He glanced over his shoulder to where the pub landlord was polishing glasses. 'Anyone might be listening.'

'Fine, whatever. Organising the shipment. This week, if we can manage it. We'll announce your bid for Brussels straight away. Start getting coverage for the campaign.'

'May as well wrap them up into the same event,' Abbott suggested. 'Maximise media impact. If I may be permitted to make a suggestion with regards to getting the press corps on side—'

'Let me handle it,' she said. 'Your idea of media attention is reporters papping you and your totty *in flagrante*. Cheers, but I'm on top of this.'

Politics had never interested the Major, apart from an historical and, he supposed, genetic, right-leaning tendency. He had seen too many of their tribe close up to have much respect for supposedly democratically elected leaders of office. Theirs was the breed of man who sat behind a desk and commanded that troops be sent to the front, rather than leading from it.

As he saw it, though, he had few options but to go along with the scheme. His goddaughter was a smooth talker with valuable connections. And he needed a new wheeze or else it would be coach tours and Highland museums with his wife from now until the grave. His goddaughter assured him that, for the price of public representation and being the face of a new political party, he would be all but guaranteed a seat in Brussels.

Once the election was over he planned to spend more time in Brussels and London than in his proposed constituency, enjoying the perks. His mouth watered. He could taste the sweet return to fame. The news panel invites, the Eurostar. First class. He would be back in the headlines, back where it mattered. Not forgetting the women. He had always had a soft spot for the women of the Continent.

'I need you to do something else,' the woman said.

'What's that?' Whitney said.

'I don't know what the post-mortem will turn up. I hope nothing. But we need to clean up the other end. Make sure no one can draw the connection between him and us. Hit his office, his computer – whatever it takes.'

The Major scowled. 'Very well.' Yet again another task being dropped into his lap that shouldn't be his responsibility. For an uncharitable moment he suspected that his goddaughter had nothing like the resources she had claimed, and that all the people in London and Scotland whose names she had dropped in order to entice him into the scheme were not friends at all.

Outside, the stout form of his beloved wife barrelled up the path to the hotel. Betty, in her cornflower blue top and trousers, clutching a handful of pamphlets advertising local excursions, with a face like a Rottweiler that had eaten a nest of hornets.

'But get on a train today, Whitney. We need you back in London

ASAP. Leave Betty up there if you have to. In fact, it's probably better if you do.'

Whitney smiled at the thought of reprieve from his wife. 'I will do it as soon as humanly possible,' he said.

'See that you do.' The woman rang off without saying goodbye.

: **8** :

'So if I understand correctly,' Morag said. 'Brant is using the Scotland results to circle his wagons, to try to derail a leadership challenge.' She marched unhappily along the corridor. Morag despised people who made walking down a hallway together into a meeting. There was a special place in hell for this one in particular.

'Well, more or less, yes,' Delphine Barrett said. To be fair to her, Morag understood the long-time media advisor to the opposition leader was recently out of a job. Delphine would no doubt be working her remaining contacts and trying to secure a new position before security confiscated her ID cards. But with the shite-to-info ratio of her blather tipping firmly towards shite, Morag thought, it was no wonder Brant let her go.

'The concern here is whether Brant's likely to get support from the backbench, and whether someone – say, myself, would head a challenge. Is that right?' Morag said. Last year's election that followed the referendum had been a disaster, and she was the only MP her party had left in Scotland.

'That's the long and short of it.' Delphine, in a tight pencil skirt, struggled to keep up as Morag and Arjun strode down the corridor. 'The way I interpret the polls . . .'

Morag sighed. She wasn't ready to be drawn either way on the topic. But there was also an opportunity to be had by someone. Lionel Brant was considered dead wood both by the public and his own party. He should have done the right thing and stepped down after the disastrous general election result, but he hadn't. The most credible challengers – his Shadow Chancellor, and several longer-serving MPs – had all woken up the day after the poll to find themselves voted out of office. It was no secret that Brant had got the job in the first place because it was his turn, not because of an aptitude for leadership. The wrong man in the right place at the right time, as one cruel columnist put it.

While Delphine nattered on Morag thought about what she still had to get through today: two consultations, an energy committee review, and a debrief on what was likely to happen to the Scotland Bill in Lords.

They were at her office door. Arjun put his hand on the knob, an obvious cue to shove off that Delphine ignored. 'Well?' Morag asked. 'What do you have, Delphine? I don't need the full dark arts treatment, a little shade will do.'

'There is this photo from an orchard wassailing event in his constituency at the weekend—'

'Wassailing? God, how fucking grim.' Morag rolled her eyes. Grim was her new word. Mondays were grim. Not quite as grim as that body in the mortuary back in Cameron Bridge, but not a pretty sight.

'It's all about the margins right now,' Delphine said, and produced a printout from her folder. 'An online poll last Tuesday predicted his seat might be at risk if the momentum is with the protest parties. This blackface gaffe is the toehold you need, Morag. Strike while the iron is hot and all of that.'

'Blackface? Brant blacked up?' Morag was surprised. Surely even a clot-faced public schoolboy like Brant knew better than to be caught smearing shoe polish on himself.

'Not him, a group of dancers he was photographed with.' Delphine jabbed at the printout. 'Morris dancers.'

'Is that a thing they do?'

'Apparently it is.'

'Trending on Twitter?'

'Third in UK, top in London for about an hour.'

'Any columnists on it?'

'*Telegraph* has a strong piece hitting the hypocrisy angle. Otherwise no.'

'Print, or online only?'

Delphine smiled apologetically. 'Online only.'

Morag considered the picture while her fingers drummed the door frame. 'No, not good enough,' she said. Delphine and her bloody Internet polls. 'Middle England loves its twee pish. Take away their blackface Morris dancing or Imperial pints and next thing you know it's wall-to-wall nationalists banging on about building a wall to keep Romanian plumbers out.' She paused. 'If there are still thinkpieces on this a week from now, I'll reconsider.'

If only Delphine's intel was hotter. Morag knew she had what it took. She was younger than Brant, well into her forties, which in politician years was sweet sixteen. She'd also had a knack in the past for delivering cross-party support for unpopular bills.

But a woman could not make a challenge the way a man could. There was no way she would survive a failed challenge to the leadership in London, and no way she would survive a successful one back home. It had to be done softly-softly, or not at all. She could not afford to be the one holding the knife when the coup went down.

Instead, it had to look like Brant was crumbling on his own and that only she was qualified to step in. Better yet, that the party membership demanded it.

To convince the rank-and-file members, though, it would have to be a particular kind of attack. What Morag needed was something that would show the leader as out of touch and, preferably, beholden to big money. A lobbying scandal, for example, maybe with links to Europe, a backhanders-for-the-boys club, or in a pinch, a health crisis, with hints that he was covering up late-stage cancer or serious heart disease.

A cut above the usual sex-and-drugs tabloid run. Blackface was nowhere. Even an affair wouldn't be enough to knock a party leader off his roost any more. Those days were long gone. There would have to be accusations from people who were underage, preferably with some sexting, to raise even the least bit of media interest.

It was a double standard, of course. Men's lives were private, women's reputations, public. If people thought Morag was messing around on her useless husband that would end her career. A woman could never be caught cheating. Other female MPs had been done for far less. One unfortunate woman was dragged through the mill when her husband hired a soft core DVD. Since then any time the poor thing stood up in Prime Minister's Questions the Commons erupted in loud, pornographic moans and jeers.

Morag had to look whiter than white. Not that she put it around without discretion, but she had been enjoying something of a budding romance recently. Even Arjun didn't know. Couldn't. The stakes were too high.

Either way she didn't have time for this. 'Have you got something or haven't you?' Delphine's mouth opened and closed wordlessly: a no, then.

'Meet me at the Pugin later for tea,' Delphine pouted. 'We'll strategise.' No doubt she wanted to be seen meeting with Munro, to try to drive up her stock in advance of being shoved out the door. It was an odd choice though. The heavily decorated Pugin Room was favoured by lobbyists and the odd tour group and not many others. Maybe she wanted to try to slide a copy of her CV in with the menus, Morag thought uncharitably.

Morag waved her hand. 'Too busy,' she said. Which was true, but she also hated the room's overstuffed formality. It reminded her of uncomfortable visits with a despised auntie during her childhood. Even the members' tea room was rarely on her agenda, though with its faded red armchairs and burnt toast it more closely resembled the kind of hotel in Cameron Bridge where coachloads of tourists grimly munched their Scottish breakfasts before trudging around the local viewpoints.

'Please,' Delphine wheedled. That was the final nail in the coffin. Cajole or bully, lie or swindle, do a favour to get a favour. These were all standard operating procedure. But heaven help you if you begged.

Morag rolled her eyes and disappeared into her office. With luck someone would have confiscated Delphine's ID cards by tomorrow and she wouldn't be ambushed in the hallway again.

The office was tiny and dark. The room had previously been assigned to a Labour backbencher, an ex-trade union man, who, after four decades' stolid residence of the Commons bar keeled over one day in his customary lunchtime pint.

Morag kept the office as she'd found it; from the green-and-white flocked, leaf pattern curtains that looked straight from a 1970s Indian restaurant, to the upholstered green leather chairs, so old that permanent impressions of buttocks were worn into the seats. The smell of mildew permeated the entire place, especially in spring and summer, probably because the toilets on that floor were always malfunctioning. There was no air conditioning in her office, and the knocks and clanging of outdated radiator heating echoed well into the sunnier months. It was carpeted in the same forest green-on-bile print that covered most of the building, in a pattern whose main, and perhaps only, redeeming feature was that it did not show stains. This was in part because it already looked stained.

Morag had found it difficult to focus since coming back south. When she closed her eyes she could picture that corpse in Cameron Bridge as it had been laid out on the slab, the lipless smile pulled permanently into a macabre grin, with the sticky, waxy flesh that had looked like it was melting off his body and the loose, peeling skin of his hands. And the smell. Something between rotting seaweed and rotting meat with undertones of the industrial cleaner they must have to use in a place like that. A chemical smell identical to the one she sometimes detected in the toilets and stairwells here. Probably the same firm, privately contracted to supply institutions all over the country. She shuddered and opened her eyes again.

Arjun popped his head round the door. 'There's a call waiting on line one,' he said. She nodded. 'Are you OK?' he whispered. 'The heating seems to be out again today. Do you need a cardie?'

Morag smiled wearily. He was so keen. So very keen. And also irritating. 'Arj, I'm good, thank you anyway,' she said.

'Are you sure?' He gestured at his own cardigan, a vintage woollen knit under a Prince of Wales tweed jacket.

'I think I have dressing myself covered, Arj, thank you,' she said. Arjun flinched and disappeared to the outer office.

Morag's eyes scanned her desk. The saying went that the truly powerful had empty desks, but then those people probably didn't also have to campaign for re-election once every five years to an increasingly sceptical constituency. There was the combination pen holder and clock from the Highlands & Islands Rotarians, presented on the occasion of her second election win. A framed photo of her turning on the Christmas lights in Tobermory ten years ago. A squat glass block engraved with 'Most Inspiring Politician' from the Women of Alba Public Service Association.

She didn't give a fuck for any of it.

There was a faint flicker of guilt at having brushed off Delphine so abruptly. It wasn't that she didn't have ambitions to leadership of the party, quite the opposite, in fact. But even if Delphine had any useful knowledge, Morag's success was not guaranteed. The biggest problem with being Shadow Home Secretary was . . . being Shadow Home Secretary. Many regarded the post as the knacker's yard of politics, to the point where senior civil servants openly joked about Morag's bad luck after the Shadow Cabinet was announced. She had to toil there for now and bide her time, be seen to be on side – or else risk being backbenched forever.

Morag popped a couple of antacid tablets and washed them down with a swig of cold coffee. Since accepting the position she had battled crisis after crisis. Between her existing membership on the Energy and Climate Change Select Committee, soothing hurt feelings over the

Scottish referendum, and trying to keep up with her opposite number in the Cabinet, she barely had the time for any casual knife twisting these days.

The hold light of her desk phone was still blinking. Whoever it was, they were far more patient waiting for a call to be answered than she would have been. It was probably something important. No – it was probably something somebody else thought was important. 'Morag Munro. Sorry to have kept you waiting.'

'Hi! Hello,' said the woman's voice. 'It's Harriet Hitchin . . . you remember, the pathologist from the other day? You visited us in Cameron Bridge.'

'Dr Hitchin, a pleasure to hear from you,' Morag said. The unkempt English doctor and her friend the metal head mortuary gimp. Morag's free hand resumed its impatient drumming on her desk. 'How may I help you?'

'I'm afraid I have an awkward request. When you came in, we were working on a post-mortem that we weren't sure would become a murder investigation or not. Things are starting to look as if it might and we need DNA samples from anyone who was at the scene or in contact with the body.'

'Oh?' Morag wondered what would have made them think it was in any way a natural death. But then she hadn't been impressed with the professionalism of the place when she saw it. Even she knew someone found zipped up naked inside a sports bag probably didn't put himself there.

'It's a formality,' Harriet assured her. 'Everyone who works here or comes in regularly is already on the books. We do it in case of cross-contamination with any of the forensic samples.'

'You need to make sure you don't accuse someone who was in the morgue of being a potential murderer,' Morag said.

'Exactly.'

'Do you have DNA from a suspect yet?'

'Not yet, but we need to cover all our bases. Strictly between us, it would be a long shot to get anything useable,' Harriet said. 'A body exposed to the water that long . . . the chances of getting a sample are not impossible, but only if we're lucky.'

'Fifty-fifty? Less than that?'

'It's hard to put exact statistics on it,' Harriet said. Morag figured that meant she didn't know. 'The police are keen we keep trying, though. A case like this will probably stay on their roster unsolved if there aren't forensics. And putting the screws on us takes the pressure off them to spend any more time on the investigation.'

'What an awful business,' Morag said. 'I suppose it's lucky you found the body at all. I'm happy to help in any way that I can.'

'Brilliant,' Harriet said. 'I'll post down a sample tube. If you would swab your cheek and pop it back in the post? Won't take five minutes.'

'Fine,' Morag said. 'Mark it for the attention of my assistant, Arjun Lakhani; he'll see that no one handles it before it lands on my desk.' As soon as she said it, it occurred to her that it was hardly the most secure way to handle samples. Anyone could send a swab back and claim to be her – within reason, of course. But she was not keen to go back to the mortuary again, next time she was in Cameron Bridge, any more than she was to mention her thought about tampering with evidence to Harriet.

Harriet exhaled. 'Thank you so much,' she said. 'It is a bit awkward. We should have done it when you were here, but you know . . . '

'Yes, I understand. Unexpected guests can sometimes mess with your internal protocol,' Morag said. 'It happens all the time in Westminster, let me assure you.'

'And you don't even have a bunch of dead bodies hanging about,' Harriet said.

'Now that's an arguable point,' Morag said. 'But they do a good job of appearing animated enough to represent their constituents, mind.' Harriet chuckled on the other end of the line. 'If you don't mind my asking, do you know who the man is yet?'

'I shouldn't be telling you this, but this could turn out to be an interesting one,' Harriet said. 'There's a fellow who went missing in London in January, and so far all the particulars of the case match.'

'Really?' Morag's hand paused above the desktop she had been drumming.

'A researcher, some geology professor,' Harriet continued. 'The lab is working on the DNA and dental identification, but so far, a connection is looking stronger all the time. Nothing has been ruled out. Apparently the chap's disappearance was kind of a big deal. They thought a suicide at first. Did you hear of it?'

'Can't say that it rings any bells,' Morag said. 'But when I get a chance to read anything other than the news . . . well, I read anything other than the news.'

'I understand,' Harriet said. 'On which note I should mention this info is not common knowledge, for now. The forensic lab is still working through a backlog. If the press get hold of this information before police officially statement it, that could be awkward for me.'

'I'm the last person to go handing the media vultures any confidential information,' Morag said in what she hoped was her most reassuring voice. Though most people these days assumed all politicians had a handy leak on the side, or a reporter they slipped unattributed quotes to from time to time, that had never been how she operated. She liked her schemes to be a little subtler. Under the radar. 'Anyway, I do have to get to a meeting, so . . . Harriet? Thank you again for calling. Why don't we have lunch the next time I'm in Cameron Bridge.'

'I'd love to!' Harriet said eagerly, but Morag had already hung up.

: 9 :

'Erykah, Nicole, you're here.' The coach popped his head out of his office as they walked from the weights gym to the changing room. 'I was hoping to catch you. A quick word?'

This was unexpected. The head coach, Dominic de Besombes, was so seldom in his office that rowers called him 'Dom the Doorknob' behind his back on account of the fact that he never stayed on the premises long enough to let go of the door handle.

There had been a lot of excitement when he got the job, thanks to his reputation as a powerhouse in the gold medal winning Sydney Olympic eight. What quickly became clear, however, was that he was incapable of transferring any of his ability to anyone else. Unkind remarks started sprouting behind his back that he was past it.

'Everything all right?' Erykah asked. She needed a shower after a hard session on the deadlifts and squats. Nicole, after being frosty to her on the phone, had seemed fine tonight, even inviting Erykah back to hers after training. Maybe there was room for reconciliation after all. She hoped so. The atmosphere at home was unbearable. At least she had the club as an escape.

Erykah and Nicole stood in the tiny coaching office because two of Dom's mates were already sitting in the chairs, leaning back at precipitous angles. Rupert and Oliver, or whatever they were called, eyed the women with the prurient leer that men of entitlement seem to be born with.

Dom tugged at the frayed, turned-up collar of his rugby shirt. He gestured to the evening newspaper on the desk. 'I take it you've seen the news today?'

Erykah picked up the paper. Above the fold, a snap from the lottery shoot. They had cropped the shot of Rab spraying her with champagne, so only she remained. Without context her smile looked manic, almost threatening, like a snarl.

Below it, the headline 'Lottery Dame Is Pop Cop Murder Moll'.

Then in a smaller section header: 'Notorious Rikki Barnes and her rich new life in Molesey'.

'Thanks for the heads-up, Dom,' she said and threw the paper back on his desk.

'You don't want to read the rest of the story?' he said.

Erykah shook her head. 'No thanks, I'm pretty sure I know how it goes,' she said.

No doubt a curious journo had gone through old archives and found her. It was inevitable that someone would.

Grayson had been dealing to a former pop star called Rory Lovelace. Rory scored a few hits with his group Northern Boyz back in the day and a few more when he went solo, then dropped off the radar as his party lifestyle took over.

Erykah had no idea that Grayson knew Rory. A sale is a sale was Grayson's motto. Except Rory had fallen behind paying to the tune of several thousand pounds. And Grayson being Grayson, well . . . this was not going to stand.

One night they were on the way to a dinner date when Grayson made a side trip to a client's house, a quick stop, he said. He had been arguing with Erykah, again, about the amount of time she was spending with the university rowing club. 'Your studies are number one, I'm number two. You should be investing any free time in your man,' Grayson had said. He kept taking his hands off the wheel, gesticulating in the air to make his points, but his eyes were staring straight ahead. 'That coach of yours is putting nonsense in your head with this Olympic talk.' She bridled at his suggestion. Sure, Grayson had given her a lot, but she was still her own person and this was her decision. Wasn't it? Who would turn down the offer to do GB trials for the national squad?

It was a moist night, summer came early that year. The air felt as thick and close as the tension between them. He parked on double yellow lines and told Erykah to stay in the car; he wouldn't be long. She sat and waited, stewing over what he had said. Grayson came back five minutes later.

He opened the boot of the car and Erykah looked at him in the wing mirror. Was that blood on his shirt? He didn't *look* hurt. He reached in the back and pulled a fresh shirt out of a bag, unbuttoned the one covered in blood, and put the new one on. No marks on him. So it wasn't his blood.

'What happened?' she said when he got back in the driver's seat.

'Shut up, bitch,' Grayson snapped. Erykah was shocked. He had never spoken to her like that before. Had he killed someone? Would he kill her?

They sat silently through dinner that night. He dropped her home without a word, didn't even walk her to the door. She couldn't sleep. What had he done? In the past, if anyone didn't pay, Grayson turned up and waved a gun around. That was usually all it took. And if they still didn't pay, he let someone else handle enforcement. She had never wanted to think about what that meant before, but now she couldn't ignore it.

She went to her early morning training session the next day, then to uni. The police were waiting outside her Differential Equations lecture. They didn't cuff her in front of the other students, but it hardly mattered. Everyone froze where they stood, watching as she was led away to a waiting Rover.

The drive to the station was short. 'So you're Rainbow's girl,' one of the cops said. 'With a mum like that I'm surprised we haven't seen you sooner.'

The other cop smirked. 'Rainbow Barnes, yeah. I wouldn't touch that cunt with someone else's knob.' His eyes met Erykah's in the mirror. 'Guess not every man thinks that way though.'

The driver shook his head in mock sorrow. 'Trying to turn Streatham into Brixton is what they're doing,' he said. The other one nodded. It was not necessary to explain who *they* were. 'Used to be our kids could play in the streets. If we weren't in negative equity I would have moved the family out of London a long time ago.'

At the station, another cop patted her down, smiling as his hands lingered over her waist and hips. The knowing glances he exchanged with the police who had brought her in frightened her. She was led to a small room with reinforced glass on the door and told to wait there.

After three hours a couple of investigators came into the room. They sat in the two chairs opposite hers and switched on a tape recorder. 'I guess you know what this is about,' the first one said. His close-cropped hair looked plastered to his head, as if he had just been washing himself in the bathroom sink.

Erykah said nothing.

'So you're going to "ride" for your man, is that it?' He nodded.

'Come in here and give us the silent treatment, and go down for that drug-dealing murderer you think loves you?'

The other one shook his head. 'It's always the same story with these girls,' he said. 'Some gangster promises them the moon on a stick, grooms them to do his time for him.' Erykah looked away, at the spindles of the tape recorder slowly turning. 'Oh, you think your man is different, do you?' he said. 'You think you keep your mouth shut and go home to him and he's going to pat you on the head and thank you and put a diamond on that skinny finger?'

Erykah bit her bottom lip. 'Yeah, that's what she thinks,' the other one said. 'She thinks she's her man's only woman, and she's going to ride for him, and they're going to live happily ever after.'

He pulled a folder from under the table. Inside were glossy photos, taken from some distance away. He spread them out carefully on the table as a card dealer might.

'Take a good long look at this,' the first detective said. 'So here's you, last Thursday, waiting by the offie for Grayson to pick you up. Right?' Erykah didn't need to acknowledge what he said, it was clearly her. His hairy finger jabbed another photo. 'And here's you and Grayson, an hour and ten minutes later, and he's dropping you off.' The men exchanged glances. 'Short date, huh? Or just a quickie?'

Erykah stared hard at the white edge of the photograph. She would not lose it in front of these people. She would not turn him in. She would not cry.

'Now here,' said the other one. 'Here's Grayson again. About twenty minutes after you left, he's back again. Only, is that someone in the car with him? Oh yes, it most certainly is. That's Tasha Jones, isn't it?' He dipped his head and forced Erykah to look at him. 'You know Tasha, don't you? Grayson has mentioned all the time he spends with her, hasn't he? I mean if he didn't, that would be odd, right?'

Erykah swallowed. She knew Tasha a bit. They had been at school together, though not in the same year and had few friends in common. She had noticed that Grayson mentioned her lately. He said they were just friends, that Tasha was dating his cousin. 'Man, that girl just don't give a shit,' he would say, approvingly. It was his highest compliment. Someone who didn't give a shit was cool, desirable, someone like him. Erykah knew she was not someone who did not give a shit. She gave a lot of shits, all the time.

'You tell us nothing, fine, we can't arrest you.' The second detective said. He leaned back in his chair and looked around the tiny room as if he was looking at buildings up and down her street. 'You go home. And then what? You wonder. What he's doing, who he's really with. You wonder when you're going to see us again and what we're going to pick him up for. And then you won't be able to say we didn't tell you so.' He nodded as if satisfied with this scenario. 'By then you won't be so clean. You will be an accessory. From now on, you will know what he is, and what he is capable of, and you will have kept that from us. That's a crime. And guess who is going to be visiting your man, when you're in jail and so is he.' The two men nodded at each other. 'Well it's not going to be you is it?'

Erykah's shoulders started to shake. 'Ohh, I think we're going to have a crier,' the first detective said. 'Wise up girl, this man doesn't care about you any more than he cares about any of his other girlfriends. Did I say girlfriends, plural? Yes, I certainly did. We've been following Grayson for a few months now. Do you want to see the pictures?'

'No, she is a tough nut, I can tell.' The second detective collected up the photos and put them back. Now it was his turn to put a folder on the table. 'She still thinks she's the main woman. How about we show you what went down at the scene while you were waiting for your Romeo to finish taking care of business.'

Compared to the black and white surveillance shots of the corner by her house, the crime scene photos were lurid, full-colour, full of detail. Rory and his bodyguard had been gunned down in the door of his penthouse suite. Grayson hadn't even tried to hide the crime. There was so much blood at the scene, the cops said, that the first police to arrive slipped and fell on the marble floor.

'I didn't know anything.' It was the first time she had spoken since the police met her at her lecture, and the words stuck in her throat. 'I didn't.'

'Come off it,' the first detective said. 'You know more than you are telling us.'

The other one nodded. 'It doesn't matter if you don't cooperate,' he said. 'Nobody will believe we just let you walk out of here without making a deal.'

'Right now he's wondering where you are,' the first detective said. 'Why you didn't come home after your lecture. Maybe one of his boys is outside, and they know you have been in here four hours already. They already think you're grassing. You know what that means, what they are going to say about you even if you deny it. So you might as well tell us everything.'

'But everyone saw you take me away. People get arrested all the time. There's no reason for him to think that I'm going to talk to you.'

'Arrested?' The first one smiled. 'But we didn't arrest you.'

The other one shook his head. 'We just brought you in for questioning. No charges. You could have walked out of here any time. Didn't you know that?'

The first one stood up and walked to the door, opened and closed it again. 'Door wasn't even locked. Nobody forced you to stay.'

She put her forehead on the table. They were right, of course.

The first cop patted her arm. 'Good girl,' he said. 'Just tell us now and it's all over. Isn't that what you want? For the chaos to end. You can't be with your man the way you want to be if his life is like this. You're a smart girl with your whole life in front of you. You don't want to ruin that now. It will do you both good. You'll be better for it. Stronger.'

It was only during the trial she realised how easily they had played her. They didn't have to deviate from their plan one bit. They never even had to offer her anonymity, or do a deal, or promise her any kind of protection. They showed her a photo of her man with someone else, and she sang like a lark.

Erykah felt as if the murder itself was her fault. Grayson was always so careful – had arguing with her that night made him careless? Or worse, had their row sent him over the edge? It seemed so out of character. She had no other explanation for why things had happened the way they had. If she had kept quiet would he even have been caught?

The trial for the double murder occupied the front pages for months. The press ran endless promo photos of Rory from Northern Boyz's first album. Then it was the turn of Rory's bodyguard, a retired policeman from Leeds, and the tragic family of seven he left behind. Then finally Grayson himself and Erykah.

And the shirt. The shirt he had changed into, calmly, when he came back to the car. When she had told the police this detail their faces had lit up. They were not just handling a cop killer, someone who had taken down one of their own. The shirt was enough to claim he had planned it to the last detail. No crime of passion here. Premeditated.

And it didn't matter to the press that she had cooperated with the investigation, that she was a witness for the Crown case, that she had done what she thought was the right thing. That she dressed well, spoke well, had never been in trouble in her life. That she was a student, and a good one too. All that mattered was where she was from, the colour of her skin, and what that stood for in the narrow minds of the editors. Her boyfriend was a cop killer. Her boyfriend was a drug dealer. She was only trash.

In her bed, night after night, she stared at the ceiling for hours, unable to sleep. I did the right thing, she told herself over and over. But no matter how many times she said it she never quite believed it was true.

And she was sure she could never go home again. She had broken the first rule of the streets. The most important one.

The last time she had seen her first love was in the dock as he was sentenced. She had never known him to be scared of anything. When the judge read his whole life sentence, the barest quiver of fear started to darken his eyes. He looked at her and he mouthed something silently, but she had no idea what he was trying to tell her.

Then the court officers crowded round. They bundled him out to a van while paparazzi tried to throw themselves in its path. Erykah wrote him three letters in that first week. All three were returned, unopened.

On the first day back at uni after the trial she was called up to the Dean's office for an academic review. Her sinking heart told her something was up. The pink-faced Dean waved his hands in the air, talking around what he was trying to say. It was all academic integrity this, reputation of the university that. In other words: you are not worth protecting. We don't see you as one of us. She felt the expectation, the assumption, even, that she would do what he felt was the right thing.

The right thing being: jump before you're pushed.

Fine then. She showed them by running away faster than they could throw her out. Would a white student have faced the same pressure? She couldn't say. Did it matter? By the time the lightweight four she had been training with rowed in the Games in Atlanta, Erykah was already married and settled down with Rab.

The group of rowing coaches was as pale and male as the Dean's office had been that day. Erykah searched Dom's face for a sign. 'This isn't going to be a problem, is it?'

Dom frowned, the gurning of a man who was trying gravitas on to see if it fitted. His finger rested on the front page as if it might draw some wisdom from there. The headline was so clunky, ugly. Spelling out a final judgment in large bold type to readers whose only interest in the news was finding out who was being torn down today.

'Erykah, you have to try to see this from my point of view,' he said. 'More importantly, from the club's. The association has already been on the phone. They suggested mandatory testing. As head coach, this puts me in a bad position. I don't want to lose the respect of my crews over this, and certainly not the association's.'

So he had no idea how people already saw him. The truth was that the club succeeded in spite of, not because of, Dom's leadership. Every year the number of high performance rowers dropped as talented oarsmen defected to other clubs. One junior had left rowing altogether for track cycling, and was already being tipped for the next Olympics. The more he stuffed the club's coaching staff with school chums and college mates, the worse things got.

'This isn't just old news, Dom, it's archaeology,' she said.

'I can't believe it.' Dom shook his head. 'All this time, living under a pseudonym, right under our own noses—'

'Pseudonym? Are you joking? It's not like I went out and bought a fake passport or something. I got married. Rikki is an old nickname. Surely even you understand that, *Dominic*.'

His long face was still pulled into the kind of sorry-not-sorry look beloved of late night news interviewers and public schoolboys who were secretly gleeful that they were about to ruin your day. 'I'm meant to be the face of this club, Erykah. How do you think this makes me look?'

Who the fuck cares how you look, you polished turd. 'I'm no criminal, Dom, which you would know if you read the article.'

'It must be a terrible situation for you, yes,' Dom said and spread his palms open. A gesture of trust. He'd probably read it in a book somewhere. 'Having your past brought up like this. But that doesn't mean it should become our problem at the club. At the least, you should have told us about your dark secret before it came out.'

'She *is* a fucking dark secret, chum,' one of Dom's friends offered in a stage whisper.

'Oh, you did not just say that,' Erykah growled.

The young man looked at her, red patches rising on his milky cheeks. 'Excuse me?' It was confrontational, not apologetic.

'You heard me,' Erykah said. 'Cretinous toad.'

'There's no need to be so aggressive,' Dom said.

It took Erykah a moment to parse that he was talking to her, not his friend in the rugby top. 'Aggressive?' Erykah said. '*I'm* the one who is being aggressive? Anyone else would have turned this room upside down after a crack like that. Any of the men's squad marched in here for twenty-year-old tabloid stories, you'd hear the shouting all the way down to the Tideway.'

'Enough,' Dom said. 'We have to think about the club here.'

Erykah set her jaw. 'If a statement of court records is what they want, then fine,' she said. 'I don't want to jeopardise our boat.'

'It's, um, beyond that point now,' Dom said. 'If it was a matter of you supplying some documentation, sure, fine . . . but it's not just the crime angle. You are associated with known drug dealers. That starts to bring all kinds of questions to the table.'

'*Was* associated,' Erykah said. 'Twenty years ago. Dom, do you really think I'm on drugs? As my coach, seriously, do you think that? You want a piss test?' She could hear her own voice, the anger in it. And it was still only a fraction of the anger she was feeling. 'Fine, I'll do it here. Now. He was dealing cocaine, for God's sake. It isn't even a performance-enhancing drug,' she said. 'If you tested the whole squad you would pick up loads of people who wouldn't pass. And you know what? I would not be one of them.'

'Yes, well, that's the problem. We don't want the whole squad tested. The men's eight are aiming at Nat Champs this year, and the men's lightweight pair are in the middle of squad trials. If we aren't seen to be strong on this, it could affect everyone.'

'Are you saying . . . ? Wait, no, I don't want to know,' she said. If the squad were juicing that was none of her business.

Dom's expression revealed nothing. 'Twelve months. Consider it a sabbatical. We'll review your case and decide if you can rejoin the club next year.'

'You have to be fucking kidding me.'

'There's no need for that kind of language,' Dom said, as if he was a schoolteacher and she a child. 'Hand over the admin details for the website and your membership card before this gets ugly.'

Erykah turned towards Nicole, who cut her eyes away. So she wasn't going to stick up for her either. Probably hoping to distance herself and try to save the rest of her season, whether she had Erykah in her boat or not.

An image flashed behind her eyes. The key in the locker. Her heart lurched in her chest.

Erykah took a deep, deliberate breath. Do not lose it in front of these jerks. They are not worth it. 'You do know, I assume,' she said, throwing her voice as low as she could, 'that I could get out a chequebook and buy this entire club right now?' She watched the expressions on their faces turn to shock. 'Fire all of you.' She looked around the room, as if assessing the club's value. 'Turn it into a fitness studio. Or better yet, a women only rowing club.'

Their mouths opened and closed like fish gasping on the beach. It had never crossed their minds before that not only could she have power over them, but that she might use it.

'But I'm not going to do that,' she said. *Jump before you're pushed.* Her arms dropped to her side and she raised her chin. 'We're done here. Take your year suspension and shove it up your arse.' She turned and reached for the door.

'Don't be difficult.' Dom's voice struggled to regain some of its former haughtiness. 'Are you sure you want to burn this bridge?'

Erykah looked back over her shoulder. 'Who needs bridges?' she said. 'Baby, I can swim.'

She walked along the river towpath slowly, in case anyone came after her. No one did. Not Nicole, not anyone. The river was quiet, all the rowers and clubs were off the water for the night. Spiders wove slow webs in the gaps between iron fence posts, setting their traps for insects drawn by artificial night-time light.

The reaction of Dom and his friends to finding out about her past upset her, but it didn't surprise her. She had learned a long time ago that people had an infinite capacity for judging others based on little – or even no – information. Of course people like them would not want her anywhere near the club, they hardly tolerated people like her under normal circumstances. This was just a convenient excuse to do something they probably wanted to do all along.

She felt bad about indulging this bitter line of thought, but then she remembered how even Nicole hadn't stood up to them, and felt a whole lot worse. The same woman who, less than a week ago, was begging her to run away and start a new life. When it really mattered, even she could not tell those pricks where to get off. Not that it would have changed much, but Nicole could have risked it, and probably not been thrown out of the club. She could have said something and didn't. Maybe that was payback for not turning up on Valentine's Night.

Erykah unlatched the garden gate and came in through the French doors. The sound of the shutting door was muffled by noise from the television. Rab was in the front room eating a Chinese takeaway and watching television.

She shed her jacket and bag on a chair. Rab's eyes detached from the television screen and followed her progress around the house like a dog watching its owner. She didn't trust this. She preferred the silent stand-off, the cool silence they had achieved after many unhappy years together, weaving their separate corridors through the house like ant tunnels that never crossed. This time last year it would have been her eating a takeaway and watching trash TV. This time last week, even.

She leaned in the doorway of the front room until he turned to the television again. Those fucking men. Those stupid, privileged, fucking men. Why did she have to explain herself to them? And why hadn't Nicole said something? Fuck it. Fuck them.

But at least she had walked. They wanted her to beg, to simper and whine and plead for a place next year. She wasn't going to be that woman. She had the satisfaction of having done that much. Except she was still coming home to Rab, who was, if anything, a poor imitation of those twats at the club. They were – she shuddered to think, but it was true – the kind of person he aspired to be.

'How was your day,' she said finally.

'Good,' he said. The old reliable lie.

So she was stuck with him for now. There were so many moments when she should have left her husband but hadn't. She would argue with herself, beat herself up about it, but she never walked. Even after she found out about the cheating.

It wasn't anything obvious. Working in the City, it was easy for Rab to explain away late drinks with clients, or claim he had pulled an all-nighter and slept at his desk. No evidence as such and lying had always come as easily to his lips – easier, even – than the truth. Rather, it was a way he would be with her. More irritable, shorter. She could imagine who they might be: a parade of interns, ripe with red-brick freshness. The affairs always ended quickly enough, probably whoever he charmed into an affair wouldn't fall for his lies for long. And she would know it was over when he bought home flowers 'no reason, just because I love my wife.' Always red roses. The closest he would come to an apology.

It hurt. And a divorce would have been easy enough with no children. But she weighed the pain and embarrassment against what Rab had done for her. He'd taken her out of the spotlight as he promised. He'd put a roof over her head, one that wasn't conditional on benefits cheques arriving on time or hustling cash on the streets. If he didn't make her feel loved, she at least felt looked after.

Maybe that was why she had never wanted children. Because it could all have come crumbling down at any time. That was what she told herself. And it was an adequate explanation. But families raised children happily and successfully even without money. Perhaps closer to the truth, something she would only have admitted quietly and when no one else was in danger of hearing, she feared she wouldn't have known the right way for a mother to love a child. And over the years, as Rab's love slipped away, she knew that whatever she could muster would not have been enough.

Instead, she poured her passion into the club. It became the centre of her life. After a few years she probably could have tried to find work, but there was always some reason not to, because of training, because of Nat Champs, because of head season, because of Henley. A few more years after that and the gap in her CV started to look more as if it was planned than accidental. In snug little Molesey, plenty of wives were doing much the same.

So many nights in bed she would lay a hand on the middle of his back, hoping for him, willing him to turn around and hold her and tell her that her loved her. For him to say that they would start trying to work things out again. That he would start trying full stop. That the lies would stop. He didn't do any of those things. He did nothing at all.

A week ago all she wanted was to leave that sterile, passionless existence behind. Now she would give anything for it to be back the way it was before. Erykah thought about the key Nicole had given her for Valentine's Day, still tucked away at the boathouse. She hadn't even had time to empty her locker. There was a feeling in her chest like heartburn.

Erykah crossed to the walnut drinks cupboard. The soft click of a hidden catch was such a comforting sound. She reached to the back for the 1991 single cask Glendronach. She loosened the cork stopper from the bottle and breathed in a heady mixed aroma like coffee beans, dried fruit and something darker, almost like rubber. It was a drop not to be fucked with. She poured two fat glugs of the reddish liquor into heavy bottomed crystal glasses. Erykah swallowed hers in a single gulp, waved the other glass in her husband's direction. He shook his head. She swirled the second and took a sip.

Rab watched her put the stopper back in the bottle and shut the cupboard. 'Are you OK?'

Erykah sat down. The square crystal glass rested in the palm of her hand, heavy and solid. 'Not really,' she said. 'I've quit the boat club.' Another mouthful. She let the liquid sit on her tongue, fill her nose and head with the effervescent alcohol lightness.

'Oh,' he said. 'Why?' She shook her head. There was only ever going to be one reason why. 'Wow. I'm sorry,' he said.

'Thanks.' She thought: if he follows this up with some shit about working harder or bootstraps I am straight up going to walk out.

'I've been thinking we should talk about things,' he said. 'I was thinking . . . hoping . . . you might want to give us a second chance.'

Erykah turned to look at her husband. His face was expectant – he was not joking. Second chance? He expected her to forget about years of seething, of wretched disappointment, just because he asked?

'I know it sounds crazy,' he said. 'And we've had our ups and downs.'

She snorted and looked down at the traces of golden liquid clinging to the glass in her hand. What a pat phrase to use for what for her had amounted to half a lifetime of anxiety and regret. 'But maybe we can make this into something good,' he went on. 'Maybe we got this money for a reason. I mean, what's to stop us leaving this behind? We could be on a plane tomorrow. Or a cruise ship. We could go anywhere – we should.'

She held his look for a long time. In his shallow way, he meant this. It wasn't a joke. But so many years after she had given up hope? Far too little, much too late. 'Rab, this is all too much for one week. We'll talk another time. When the dust has settled,' she said.

A look of surprise crossed his face. 'Oh,' he said. Deflated. She had never been the one to put him off before. They turned back to the dating programme. Bubbly girls giggled and pouted for the stubble-bearded man-boys in skinny jeans who crossed the stage. 'Do you remember how we met?'

'How could I forget,' she said. 'I'd been kicked out of uni and some friends dragged me to a singles night in Vauxhall to get my mind off things.'

'I was working the bar,' he said. 'Still wondering whether I should take that job offer in the City or not—'

'Wearing that stupid toga! Oh God,' she said. She remembered the Gladiators theme bar and laughed. 'I didn't talk to anyone else all night.' She was still smarting from the trial, not to mention the letters Grayson had returned. He asked her name, and she told him it was Erykah, not Rikki. Just in case he ran to the tabloids later. Apart from that taking the barman home hadn't seemed like the worst decision in the world. He told her she was beautiful, she thought he was cute. He had to do the walk of shame in the same white sheet and gold sandals he had worn to work the night before.

Rab prised the whisky glass away from her and set it on the floor. He leaned forward and held her slim hands in his clammy ones. 'Erykah, you've hardly changed in twenty years,' he said. 'You're still as beautiful as you were the first time I saw you.'

'Yeah, well,' Erykah said. With little else to do in most of the last years, she had taken care of her looks. Most of the women at the rowing club were surprised she was old enough to be a veteran. She ate up their unspoken envy like it was lobster and caviar. After years of chewing over the remains of choices she wished she had taken and regretting the ones she did, this at least was some consolation.

'I never regretted going home with you,' he said.

Erykah cast an eye over her greyer, tired husband. She wasn't sure she believed him. He'd taken her opening up about who she was and the trial in his stride, and for years, she was convinced that it didn't matter to him at all. But later, over time, when the cracks started to show, she was less convinced. 'Not so sure I would have stopped to talk to this guy here.'

She knew it was a lie even as she said it, though. For all his many faults he still had something she wanted. She could never put her finger on it exactly. His privilege, maybe? How easy things seemed to be for him without ever excelling? Looking back she couldn't have said whether it was that she wanted him, or wanted to *be* him.

'You have to stay with me. Jesus, Erykah – you know I would be lost without you.' His hands gripped hers tighter. 'I know you've been unhappy. You're not thinking –you haven't engaged a solicitor yet, have you?'

'No, not yet,' she said. Erykah felt the old conciliation welling up in spite of herself. And underneath it, something else, something new. It felt like maybe she was getting some kind of upper hand. Like maybe he needed her more than she needed him this time. 'Rab, I need a fresh start. I have to get away from . . .' she looked around the room, the sterile house that had been decorated in the best, blandest taste. 'From all of this, money or no money. What we have now, this is killing me.'

'Yes . . . yes,' he said. His hands, still clamped over hers, were squeezing tight now. They slipped down to her wrists, holding her fast. 'I can change,' Rab said. 'We can pack up and leave. Go for a year, for the rest of our lives. Please. We can leave tomorrow. Say you will.'

That bag in her room was still in the corner and half full of the clothes she had been going to run away with to Nicole's. Erykah tried to wiggle her hands out of his, but he clutched harder.

'Please, Rab,' she said. 'You're hurting me.'

'Just say we'll leave tomorrow,' he said. His eyes were intent, the irises a pinpoint. His hands cinched around the slender bones of her wrist. The pressure was too much to bear.

Erykah twisted her arms and tried to free herself but the more she twisted, the tighter he held her. 'Stop it, Rab,' she said. 'I told you I need time to think.' Her mouth went suddenly dry. This was not a conversation: this was . . . something else.

'*Say it.*'

She was strong, as tall as he was, and in better shape. But almost all of her strength was in her lower body, and with him holding her arms what could she do? Standing up, maybe, she would have a chance in a fair fight against a man his size, or at least a chance to hit hard and then run away. The look in his eyes scared her. A fair fight was one thing; a crazed attack quite another. 'Let me go,' she said. 'You're frightening me.'

'You're my wife,' he said. A look came over his face she had never seen before. It sent shivers down her spine. Rab stood up and hauled her body into a standing position. 'And you are going to do what I say now.'

'Let me go!' Erykah shouted. She pulled the weight of his body in towards hers, sending him off balance and falling forward, then used the full weight of her body to push him away again as hard as she could.

The force of the push was enough to break his hold. He let go of her arms and flailed, toppling back onto the sofa. For a moment he lay there with his mouth open and said nothing. 'Fuck's sake Rab,' she said, and rubbed the skin of each wrist in turn. The indentions left by his fingers were pink and white; they would bruise. But he was the one who started to cry. Rab turned his face in to the sofa and howled like a baby.

A Golf GTi undertook Seminole Billy on the M4 westbound and swerved across the lanes. Billy slammed on the brakes and felt the tyres struggle to grip at the wet surface. The banging in the boot started again. Billy's passenger was not pleased with being thrown around in the back of the Merc in traffic, he guessed. Well, tough tits.

'Next caller, Mia from Harpenden, you're on the Stuebner Show – what's your take on the grassroots boycotts taking hold in response to the Scottish referendum outcome?'

Seminole Billy steered a hard left as the GTi swung across the lanes again. Silver pendants dangling from his leather bracelets chimed against the steering wheel. There was a bump that sounded like someone kicking the back of the seat from the boot, and a rattle that might have been his passenger attempting to unlock it from the inside. Billy chuckled. Go ahead and try it, friend.

'The thing is, I'm a mother, blessed with three darling children,' a voice crackled over the radio. A kid screamed in the background. 'If boycotting Scottish businesses shows our support for the Union, then so be it. What would my seven-year-old daughter want us to do? That's what really matters.'

'What about the businesses that say the boycott is ineffective and racist?'

'I don't know about racist, but I know what I feel. Coco, Jojo, be quiet! Your daddy is going to hear about this when he gets home . . . as a businessperson myself I know what I'm talking about.'

'What business are you in, Mia?'

'I run a blog from home, so I know about small business. They have to learn to take the rough with the smooth.'

'Not retail, then?' Diana Stuebner asked. 'Blogging is not like the pressures of retail, wouldn't you say?'

'My site is a forum for mothers, much more than a business. It's a community,' Mia sniffed. 'Real big society stuff. Can Scottish shop owners say that? They are a small fraction of the population and I feel they've been overrepresented in this debate. Mothers, on the other hand . . .'

The pounding in the back continued. Billy aimed the Merc at a pothole and gave his passenger a shake. A muffled protest emitted from behind the back seat. A smile creased Billy's thin lips.

Seminole Billy's mobile buzzed on the dashboard. He looped a hands-free set over his ear and answered the phone in his slow Florida drawl. 'Speak.'

It was from his associate, travelling container class in the back. 'Do you mind turning that down?' Buster said from the boot. 'I can't hear myself think here. It's all, wah wah my children this, wah wah Scotland that. That woman sounds like her fanny is lined with Cath Kidston.'

'No can do, friend,' Seminole Billy said. He loved talk radio and especially loved Diana Stuebner's show. He made a point never to miss it. Her soothing voice was an oasis of calm in an otherwise fucked up world.

'Aw c'mon. Can't you put on an audiobook or something?' Buster whined. 'Tired of listening to this rubbish every d—' Seminole Billy ended the call and turned the radio volume up to full. The phone started ringing again, so he switched it off.

Billy turned off the motorway. The battered Merc slowed to a crawl. His reptilian gaze crawled over each house in turn, the manicured green lawns and gravel drives. The house he was looking for had been all over the twenty-four-hour news channels during the weekend. It shouldn't be hard to recognise. And yet every one of these places looked the same: big, rich, empty. Adverts for future break-ins.

Seminole Billy wouldn't have lived in a place like that for anything in the world. They reminded him of the gated communities at home that had started cropping up about the time he moved away. People fell in love with Florida, with its beaches and weather, then put up walls to keep everyone else out of their space. Especially poor people. Those were the kind of places where a vigilante neighbourhood watch could shoot a black kid and straight up get away with it, just because someone thought he looked suspicious.

People were a mystery to him. If you lived in an area like this, it was because you already had money. Late model Beemers and Volvos littered the drives. Why would any of them be playing the lottery with money like that?

More to the point, why would any of them have made the deal they did with the folks who hired Seminole Billy? Must be some real debt beating down their shiny door. Maybe a gambling addiction, or an investment that hadn't paid off. He had met a good few over the years, people who thought the charmed lives they led were the result of more than dumb luck, then blamed others when things started to go wrong. The kind of folks who were born on third base and thought they hit a triple. They never knew how to quit when they were ahead.

That was fine with Billy. It was people like that who kept him in a job.

He spotted the house at the end of a cul-de-sac by the river. Exactly as it had looked on the news, apart from the press that had been hovering around a few days ago. No sign of the vultures now. Good.

Seminole Billy backed the Merc into the driveway and checked the coast was clear before popping the boot open.

'Cheers, drive, I thought we'd never get here,' Buster said. He unfolded his long limbs and climbed out, wiping sweat from his brow. Even with the friendly Bristolian accent, Buster came across as someone not to be fucked with. He was tall, with black ink tattoos covering much of his dark skin. Dreadlocks and a scar across his face – remnant of a prison fight – completed the look.

Seminole Billy, meanwhile, was a wiry middle-aged man with a weather-beaten face and deep creases around his eyes. His hair was greased back and he was dressed all in black like a preacher, with the custom silver tipped Tony Lama footwear he called his Getting Paid boots. 'You complaining about the transport options?'

'I swear you must have hit every pothole from Hammersmith on,' Buster said.

'You don't say?' Billy smirked. He took a last drag on his cigarette, burning it down to the filter, and stubbed the butt out under his heel. 'And here I was trying to avoid them.' Buster kissed his teeth and Billy recoiled. 'Jesus, man. What did you have for breakfast this morning? You got breath that would knock a buzzard off a gut wagon.'

'Goat roti,' Buster said. 'Place on Clapham High Street.' He ran his tongue over his teeth and rolled his eyes in bliss. 'Nowhere near as good as granny's, but short of a ticket to Trini it'll do.'

'How's she doin'?'

'She's doin',' Buster said. 'Complains about the weather. Says T and T must have got hotter while she was away.'

'More like she got used to the cold over here,' Seminole Billy said.

'Right?' Buster said. 'Told her she's got thick blood now, but she says naw, it's that global warming.'

'I miss that lady,' Seminole Billy said. 'Next time you talk tell her life ain't the same without her yellow chilli sauce.'

'Oh, I tell her,' Buster said. 'I do. When we're done with this job, I'll take you over to the roti place. The food's not bad.'

'Nah, thanks,' Billy shook his head. 'But if you know a good fried chicken . . .'

Buster laughed. 'Man, what is it with you and fried chicken? I never met someone so obsessed.'

'Y'all don't get it,' Billy said. 'You've never had the real thing in this country. Correction – you think KFC is the real thing. Or worse, Nando's. There's only one decent fried chicken in London, and it's the one I make at home.'

Buster laughed. 'Yeah, OK.' He looked at the garden, the faux classical pillars on either side of the front door. 'Where in fuck are we anyway?'

'Who gives a shit. You want to buy a house or something?' Seminole Billy said.

Buster did a low whistle. 'Not likely. You'd have to be a millionaire to afford a place like this.'

'They are millionaires, dumbass,' Billy said. 'Or will be for another . . .' he looked at his watch 'half hour at most. Anyway, the house is only worth eight-nine-five according to the Land Reg calculator.'

'Not as if folks'd be welcoming a brother into the neighbourhood with open arms,' Buster said and smoothed his dreadlocks.

'Especially not one with a warrant out,' Billy added. It was Buster's own fault he had to travel in the boot since that failed bomb job at the Thatcher funeral. As usual, he had no idea who was behind the job. As long as he got paid he didn't ask too many questions. In this business, questions had a way of being hazardous to your health.

Seminole Billy had been handed plans to hit Aldwych tube station. It was supposed to be so simple. It was on the cortege route and the bomb had to go off the moment the hearse went by. It should have been a no brainer to work out.

What Seminole Billy had not counted on was his accomplice's ignorance of the London public transport network and a certain – it had to be admitted – inattention to detail. In other words Buster had gone and fucked it all up. So when Seminole Billy texted a message to the phone controller that was meant to trigger the explosion at Aldwych, the fuse tripped exactly as planned – at Archway. Miles north of the target. Not only had he got the station wrong, Buster hadn't even managed to plant the bomb in Zone 1. Instead of blowing Maggie's bones to smithereens on international television the only casualties were an empty café and the windows of a halal butcher over the road.

Even with most public services diverted to the funeral, the boys in blue were on the scene in next to no time. Cameras had got Buster at every conceivable angle and there were alerts out across the city by sundown. It was going to be tough to disguise an almost seven-foot tall black man with dreadlocks and a scar running down the side of one eye.

In any other scenario Billy would have let an accomplice take the heat for the mistake, but he wasn't about to desert his partner. He knew Buster. They had been cellmates. And Buster, it had to be said, did not have the mindset for going back to the pen. Some people could get their heads right for the long haul – all told, Billy had done nine years inside, here and there, and it wasn't a thing. But Buster was not wired like that. Another serious spell in pokey would be the end of him. Loath as Billy was to admit it, he liked having the kid around.

After the Archway bomb there was no way to guarantee a speed camera or security guard wouldn't recognise Buster. 'Boot from now on or nothing,' Seminole Billy insisted. Buster knew well enough that the 'or nothing' didn't constitute shaking hands and amicably dissolving their business relationship. So he grumbled a bit, but the boot it was.

Buster patted down his pockets and checked his shoulder holster. 'Let's get this party started.'

Seminole Billy clocked the flick of the front curtains as a man's face disappeared behind the glass. Someone was home. More to the point, someone didn't want anyone to know they were home. Billy strolled over to the door and knocked.

He heard the chain being done up on the other side. The door opened a crack. Billy put his face right up to the opening. The man behind the door flinched. 'I'm sorry, we're not doing any more interviews,' he said. 'Lottery company advised no more publicity until we get things settled with the investment advisers.'

'You Rab Macdonald? About those investments,' Seminole Billy started, 'wanted to talk to you about those.'

Rab nodded. 'You're from America, aren't you? You know, we spoke to US press already. You should contact the lottery company first if you want to arrange an interview,' he said. He fumbled in his pocket for a business card and passed it through the gap.

Seminole Billy accepted the card. Looked legit. Office address in raised letterpress print, heavy stock. He had to hand it to them, this outfit knew how to make a scam look good. Not that he had met the people who were running it. Nor was he likely to – his involvement came cloaked in plenty of layers of late-night meetings in empty caffs and conversations on pay-as-you-go phones. He doubted the address and phone number on the card led to anything more than an answer-phone in an empty room in Jersey.

Rab gulped. 'I have to go . . .' He started to close the door.

'Buster, explain for the nice man, please?' Seminole Billy said.

'We're not here about a story.' Buster thrust his trunk of a leg through the doorway gap and kicked his ankle to one side, breaking the chain off. He kicked it the other way and the door swung fully open. Rab yelped and jumped back.

Billy smiled, a thin, bloodless sneer. 'We're here about the other thing. The investment advisers you're expecting?' Rab nodded nervously. Billy pointed to his chest. 'That would be us.'

'Is this your – your colleague?' Rab said, looking up at Buster.

'No, it's my fucking twin brother,' Seminole Billy said. 'Now let us in before we have to make a scene, yeah?' He stepped inside and moved into a room off the hall that was sprinkled with the junk that middle-class people liked to scatter around a place. French candles, a ball made of sticks. That kind of shit. 'Nice joint you got here.'

It was the kind of place most people would be grateful to have. Gratitude, however, was not a default setting on humans. If life had taught Seminole Billy one thing, it was that people had an infinite capacity for greed. That much was a given. But if it had taught him anything else, it was that greed brought its own kind of craziness.

He called it the money blinders. Once the money blinders were on, you wouldn't believe what people could talk themselves into. Like this guy. No doubt once the cash landed in his bank account, he forgot all about the consequences of the deal he had made. Maybe thought he could pack up and bail out. Skip town with the millions, and no one would be the wiser.

Money blinders made you believe the hype. Everything in the

world was set up to convince you that money was power. That once you had money, you could buy your way out of anything, talk your way out of anything. That a luxury yacht in the Med was out of reach of everything that had put it there.

Seminole Billy knew better. Money wasn't power. He had seen too many millionaires die in a pool of their own blood to believe that. Like they used to say at the rodeo, you got to dance with the one who brung you. No, real power was freedom from needing money. Not the same thing.

He looked Rab over carefully. Yet again Billy had to give credit to whoever was running the lottery scam. The guy was a good choice for a public patsy. Good-looking enough. Average plus. Forgettable. They had done their job well. In a year no one would remember who this loser even was.

Much less miss him, if it came to that.

Billy stepped forward, pointing his finger. It came to rest in the middle of Rab's chest. He gave a little push and the frightened man fell backwards into the sofa. 'Have a seat.'

'Sure, sure . . .' Rab clutched at the upholstery. Seminole Billy saw him assessing the situation then deciding not to push it further for now. Good. It made life a lot simpler when people could weigh up their choices and choose not to do anything stupid.

That was one reason he had retired from knocking over small-time drug dealers for their stash and cash: fewer occupational hazards. Civilians were so much easier to manage. In general they perceived going to prison as an actual threat rather than a potential career move. Give or take the odd have-a-go-hero he hardly ever had to kerb anyone any more. These days he ended up torturing only three, maybe four people a year, max.

'Do you want something to drink?' Rab asked. 'A tea or coffee?'

Billy looked over at Buster, eyebrows raised in amusement. 'Do we want a hot drink?' Buster shrugged. 'Why not. Get us a drink.'

'Erykah, can you put on the kettle?' Rab yelled through to the kitchen. 'We have visitors.'

And then the woman walked into the room.

For Billy it was as though a moment in time had slowed down. The light through the windows caught her curls in a glowing corona. She plucked a pair of reading glasses off her nose and hooked them in the front of her jumper. The glasses pulled the neck down to reveal a hint of cleavage. This chick may have been a vintage model, and Seminole Billy was not easily impressed, but she was a grade-A, prime cut, head turner.

There was something else about the woman. Her body said *fuck me* and her eyes said *screw you*. He knew that look well. It was the look of someone who was done putting up with shit. He had seen that look in the eyes of men doing hard time. The anticipation of a big cat waiting for its minder to get sloppy one day and leave the lock off the cage. A little wary, sure, but ready to leap.

The look of a woman whose compliance with the scheme, unlike her husband's, was not to be taken for granted.

Seminole Billy had a feeling this job was about to get a lot more interesting.

: **11** :

Erykah had been at the kitchen table looking out the French doors to the back garden. A potted hothouse plant left behind by the photographers in an attempt to cheer the scene was giving up its last shrivelled petals to the cold. Was it too early for whisky? Rab was knocking around in the front, talking to someone at the door. More reporters? At this hour? No, it wasn't too early for a drink.

She flipped through the pages of the book her mum had given her for her birthday all those years ago. *Magic And Wonder!* the cover promised, *99 real tricks, brain teasers, and mysteries of the Ancient World.* The black-and-white photos illustrating the book were dated even back then. The magic tricks featured men with beards and women with winged and frosted hair, in shiny lamé costumes evoking Egyptian dress, eyes outlined in thick kohl. With fixed smiles they demonstrated the steps for making a penny disappear, picking a simple lock, a card trick that relied on memorising a grid of numbers. It reminded Erykah of a saying her old professor Leonie Mandelkern was fond of: any sufficiently advanced technology is indistinguishable from magic. Leonie's speciality was code breaking. A discipline based on simple principles, with intensely complicated iterations. It looked like magic to many but was in fact a rigorous process of testing weaknesses in a code. All it took was time, patience, and the right tools. If someone is able to do something most others can't, they are viewed with a mix of wonder and suspicion.

When Erykah was small her mum would march her in front of guests to spell words and do sums. Such a charming, clever daughter. Rainbow became less and less interested in Erykah as she got older and the sums turned into computer code and other feats not easily explained. She wasn't a dog doing tricks any more. She was a teenager splicing outside phone lines so she could get dial-up Internet access when their landline was disconnected for non-payment, online typing messages to people about who knew what all day. She was a problem.

It doesn't take much to tip from wonder into horror. Make a rabbit disappear and you're a hero; bring a ghost into the room and you're a monster.

Erykah watched the branches overhanging the garden shifting in the breeze and rubbed at her wrists where Rab had grabbed her. As she suspected they had come up with bruises, but the long sleeves of her clinging cashmere jumper covered the marks.

Rab's voice, pitched high, cut through her thoughts. 'Erykah? We have guests,' he called from the front room.

'I thought you said no more reporters?' Erykah called back. 'And we're out of tea.' She popped her head out to see who was there. Her hackles went up immediately: two men, one black and one white, neither of whom looked like they had working familiarity with interview notebooks or shorthand.

There was something about the incongruity of the pair that made her instantly suspicious. The black man was standing by the door and blocked the exit. He had a scar across his face, the kind one might acquire in prison, or from being bottled in a club. From the height and heft of him she had no doubt that whoever had done it had got off worse.

But it was the other man who was far more menacing. His old jeans had a razor-sharp crease, the kind that might have been ironed in over a decade or longer. His eyes had the flat, impenetrable sheen of someone who was not simply tough, but who genuinely did not care about his or anyone else's safety. It was an expression that was burned on her nervous system and made the hair of her neck stand on end. Her old self Rikki Barnes nodded in recognition. She knew these men were here to commit a crime, plain and simple.

'S'all right, Buster here is more of a coffee man.' The white guy stood up and pulled his face into a grotesque smile. 'I'm Seminole Billy. And you are . . . ?'

Erykah looked at the hand he extended in her direction. Seminole? He didn't much look it. 'I am Mrs Macdonald.'

'I see,' Seminole Billy said. 'And what is it you do? Apart from brighten up the place considerably.'

'What do I do?' Erykah said. 'I manage the household.'

'Like a housewife?' Buster asked.

She squinted at Buster. He looked familiar, but she couldn't place the face. Old neighbourhood? No, he was too young. 'Don't be silly. Housewives hoover. I'm more . . . semi-retired.'

Seminole Billy nodded. 'You look well on it,' he said. 'Why don't you sit down?' His accent stretched the words in some places and chopped them up in others, so the sentence sounded more to her like *Whaa down choo sit dawn*.

Erykah sat next to her husband, careful to leave space between them. She tucked her wrists between her knees without thinking about it. Billy planted his skinny arse in an oversized chair across from them. Buster remained standing by the door.

'You're American, aren't you,' she said.

'You're observant.'

He had some sort of mark on his hand, maybe a tattoo. Erykah's eyes caught the glinting charms on his jewellery. 'Is that bracelet Indian?'

'Sure is. Seminole. Florida, not Oklahoma.'

'Like Burt Reynolds.'

'Burt's family were Cherokee,' Billy said. 'Not that anyone's keeping track.'

'You don't look Indian,' Rab said.

'What are you, the tribal police?' Billy said.

Buster rolled his eyes and blew out his bottom lip. 'Anyway, thing is, we was coming by to congratulate you on your lottery win,' Buster said. Seminole Billy nodded in agreement. 'And to discuss how your payment will be distributed.'

Erykah narrowed her eyes. 'Is this some kind of robbery?'

'No-o-o-o,' Seminole Billy said. When he crossed his legs at the knee she noticed the cowboy boots: black snakeskin, with shiny tips. She had the sudden mental image of the tips of those boots covered in blood. 'Robbery implies we're taking something off you without your permission,' he said. 'What we got is more of a . . . gentleman's agreement, if you will. We're here for the cut your husband promised to hand over.'

'What cut?' Erykah said.

'He didn't tell you?' Seminole Billy sucked in air in feigned surprise. 'You see, what your husband may not have let on is the amazing windfall you won wasn't as much a matter of pure luck as it may have seemed. You see, Mrs Macdonald – mind if I call you Erykah?' She nodded. 'Erykah, your husband agreed to win this so-called lottery in exchange for a generous donation to some very motivated investors who need to make sure the cash looks like a gift from the goodness of your hearts.'

'It's a fix,' Buster added, in case Erykah was unclear as to the nature of the Big Billions Lottery.

Erykah closed her eyes and sighed, rubbing her forehead with her long fingers. She felt her face flushing with anger. 'Of course it is,' she said to no one in particular. Now things made sense. 'You need to launder some money, and we're the fronts.'

'Smart girl,' Seminole Billy said.

Erykah pursed her lips. 'I turned forty years old last month,' she said. 'You can call me a smart woman.'

'Fair enough,' Billy said. 'Woman. Me and Buster, we're here to remind your husband of the contract he agreed and to make sure our mutual friends are able to collect.'

'I should have known,' she said. She turned to Rab. 'And no bloody wonder you begged me to stay. If I had got that solicitor, you would be screwed in more ways than one.' The sleeves of her jumper pulled back as she talked, revealing the fresh bruises around her wrists.

Rab avoided his wife's glare. Instead he fixed his eyes on a blank part of the wall over Buster's shoulder and tried to change the subject. 'He's the muscle, I take it?' he asked.

'I'm the muscle,' Seminole Billy said. He looked at the marks on Erykah's arms. His thin lips barely parted as he spoke. 'Buster here's just along for the ride.'

'I can see his gun,' Rab said, gesturing at Buster's shoulder holster. 'Where's yours?'

Billy extracted a folding knife from the front pocket of his jeans. He flipped open the short, serrated blade and picked at the corners of his cuticles, working the tip under his short nails. 'I do things to men that makes them wish I had been carrying a gun,' he said.

'You said something about a contract,' Erykah said. 'Did he sign anything?' She turned to Rab. 'Did you sign anything?'

'It was a verbal contract,' Seminole Billy said. He snapped the knife closed and pocketed it. 'Equally as binding, I assure you.'

'Enough,' she said. Erykah pulled the reading glasses off her collar and perched them on the end of her nose. She stood up, brushed her hands down the front of her narrow trousers, and walked over to the liquor cabinet. 'I hope you gentleman don't mind, but this calls for something a little stronger than tea,' she said. Her fingers lit on the tops of a dozen bottles before she selected the Ardbeg Uigeadail, smoky and sweet. She nodded at the two strangers. 'Have one if you like.'

'No thanks,' Billy said. 'Used to be a bourbon man, back in the day. Expensive stuff like you got would be wasted on me anyway.'

Buster started to get up but Billy shook a finger at him. 'Not on working hours.' Buster grumbled.

Erykah poured a belt of amber liquid into a crystal glass. 'Breakfast of champions,' she muttered and held the tumbler to eye level. The tidelines of where she swirled the liquor retreated slowly, like ocean tide from the sand. She swirled the glass again, releasing a fresh wave of subtly spicy aroma. 'How the hell do you rig a lottery draw?' She shook her head. 'Weighted balls, something like that?'

'Something like that,' Seminole Billy said.

'He's that one who set the bomb off in Archway last year! I knew I recognised him,' Rab blurted. Erykah shot him a look that she hoped he would – for the first time in their marriage – correctly interpret as meaning Shut Up, You Idiot.

'How much are we talking about?' Erykah asked. 'I need numbers.' Maybe there would be enough left to cover his debts and a divorce. The bag in the bedroom was still packed. She would be fine without Nicole, she was sure, though her stomach twisted at the thought. Whatever there had been between them was in the past tense now.

Seminole Billy smiled. Good, now here was someone who knew how to move a business deal forward. He reached into his jacket and extracted a cloth bag, folded over at the top with a lock. He slowly opened it and pulled out the contents. Bank books, jointly in their names, registered with an offshore bank. 'Put simply, your husband and yourself are going to make a donation to a timely social and political campaign we have already nominated, as per his initial agreement. A one-off gift, photographs of your good selves handing over a giant cheque, and you won't ever have to see us again.'

'How much?' Erykah said.

'Let's just say, if you were hoping to spend the rest of your days commuting between tropical islands in a private jet, you might be disappointed.'

'I guess that's just something I'll have to learn to live without,' she said. 'Give me the bad news. No point beating around the bush.'

'Nineteen mil. More, if the spirit so moves you.'

'I'm sure I said eighteen,' Rab mumbled.

Erykah was momentarily breathless. She picked up one of the bank books and flipped through the pristine pages. They were from a bank in the Caymans. So the money wouldn't even be touching their accounts here, then.

'And I'm sure if you search your no doubt flawless memory you'll recall that wasn't the deal,' Seminole Billy said to Rab, and balled one hand inside the other. The skin over his knuckles was puckered with scars from countless fights.

Rab eyed the fists, but continued talking anyway. 'Is there any chance we could renegotiate?'

'Renegotiation is above my pay grade,' Billy shook his head. 'You made a deal, my associate and I are tasked with enforcing it.'

'But this is a lot of money, and—'

Billy held up his hand, his scarred palm facing Rab. 'Careful now,' he said. 'You appear to have mistaken me for somebody who gives a shit.'

'There may be something in it for you,' Rab said.

'That so? Well, you've been warned.' Seminole Billy reached out, lightning fast, and grabbed the wrist of the soft man's right hand. Rab yelped. 'Not so much fun when someone does it to you, is it?' he said. 'Been taking out some of that stress on the wife, son?'

'It was only one time!' Rab objected. 'Erykah, tell them.' He expected her to cover for him as usual. She said nothing.

'So you admit it,' Billy said, and looked at Buster. 'Buster, you ever break a man's wrist?'

Buster shrugged. 'Only once. Not on purpose. It was incidental to the rest of the things I did to him.'

Billy nodded. 'Yeah. It ain't that easy to do, not without a lot of pressure,' he said, and twisted Rab's arm slightly. 'A lot of pressure and maybe some breaking force.'

Rab looked at Billy, pleading. 'Please, let me go. I can make a deal. I can make whatever deal you want.'

'I'd say the chances of that happening are slim to none,' Billy said. His other hand moved up, and held Rab's fingers. 'And Slim's on a fucking diet. Fingers, now, that's a lot easier than a wrist—'

'Stop. Please! Erykah, do something!' Rab shouted.

'Shhhh,' Billy said. 'Now's not the time to ask your wife for help.' He twisted a little and there was an audible crack. A scream. Seminole Billy released his fingers and Rab dropped to the floor and writhed in pain.

Erykah's eyes watered. But she didn't leap to help her husband either. 'You got something to say about this?' Seminole Billy asked.

She shook her head. Rab was still moaning. Her mind was spinning with unanswered questions. Would they try to hurt her next? Would there be any money left? Could she get Nicole to take her back? Was there any way to turn the situation around – or at the very least, come out of it unharmed?

Billy nodded. 'Good. In addition, me and Buster are gonna have to take our pay from your cut, not the charity's. No offence. Helps to keep their paperwork clean. I'm sure you understand. We'll be needing, oh, about fifty grand each as it happens. More, if we have to keep coming round here.' He looked at Rab, who was curled up like a kicked puppy. 'To keep up enforcement.'

Rab whimpered. 'Jesus fuck, someone shut him up,' Billy said. Buster started to reach for his holster. 'Nah man, I mean keep him quiet. Don't kill him. Yet.'

Buster grabbed Rab's shoulder and shook him until the smaller man met his eyes. ''Ere, mate, it's only a broken finger,' Buster said. 'And if you keep up like that I'll give yer something to cry about.' Rab choked down a sob and nodded.

'So that leaves us with nine hundred thousand,' Erykah calculated. 'After the divorce, four-fifty for me, plus whatever we get when the house goes, though with his mortgage arrears, who even knows.'

'Divorce?' Rab looked up at her with puffy, red eyes. 'But I thought we could give it a go – give us six months . . .'

'This buys out that second mortgage you forged my signature on, am I right? Right?' Rab said nothing, just looked down at his fingers.

Rab hunched forward, still cradling the bent hand. His face twisted with pain and bitterness. 'Fine time to start acting like you're some kind of innocent,' he spat. 'I'm not the one whose photo has been splashed all over the news this week.'

Anger rose up like bile in her throat. 'Darling husband, and I mean this most sincerely: fuck you very much. You're lucky I don't take it all and alert the mortgage company to your fraud,' she said, rubbing her wrists. Her voice dropped to a whisper. 'You're lucky I don't phone the police.'

'Erykah, you can't do this,' Rab said, switching back to pleading. 'You said when it all blew over we would talk about us . . .'

In spite of everything that had happened that old button was still just about functional, the one he pressed knowing how desperately she wanted stability, to belong. She swallowed and it felt like a rock hitting her stomach. 'How dare you get on me about the press finding that photo. If it bothers you so much, why didn't you think of that before agreeing to front a scam?'

As she said it Erykah realised that in marrying Rab she had, in a way, married her mother. He might not have been an addict, but – no, that wasn't right, he might not have used drugs but that didn't mean he wasn't an addict. He was sneaky and mercurial, ran cold and hot. And she had become conciliatory over the years, the peacemaker, just as she had as a child. She had learned to avoid him when things were at their worst. She knew from the sound of his key in the door whether it was a good day or a bad day. She turned down her own reactions, muted every feeling and conversation until, bit by bit, she became a ghost in her own life.

'Hey, folks, we're still here,' Seminole Billy said. 'Now, are you gonna cut these cheques or am I gonna have to let Buster do his thing?'

Erykah turned to her husband. 'Face it, Rab, you've been an extreme disappointment. First as a husband, and now as a publicity prop,' Erykah said. It came out far cooler than she felt.

She turned to the men. 'Gentlemen, you deal with me from now on. Rab, why don't you fix a pot of coffee while the grown-ups have a chat?'

: **12** :

Diana Stuebner perused the headlines of the free paper that littered every available surface in London, from the trains to coffee shops. She turned through the four thin pages before holding it over her head as she ventured from the Tube into the street.

A cold sleet that had been hanging over the city was turning to wet snow. Patches of black ice lurked on every street and pavement. The city was a blur of slow-moving humans who had the bad luck to be outside. Black taxis and white vans jammed up the narrow Soho streets. She was late for work, but not by very long. Still – when you had to be on air, it mattered.

The radio station was housed in a building over four floors off of Soho Square. Rumour had it the place had been built as a Georgian brothel, but if that was true, it had had a lot of renovation since. Diana doubted the rumour herself. It was all part of the station's legend. The public were also told that the station itself had originated as a pirate radio outfit on a Norwegian ferry anchored off Margate, but that was a myth too.

Diana juggled the wet paper with her overflowing handbag outside the front doors of LCC 97.5 FM – 'London Chat Central,' as the tube and bus adverts put it. A crowd of God-botherers and Bible thumpers clustered outside the doorway, preparing for a day of harassing passers-by and handing out leaflets. Even the poor weather didn't seem to deter them. Early evangeliser gets the worm, perhaps.

Huge images of some of the star DJs adorned the windows flanking the front entrance. The one of Diana had her looking straight on, eyebrow crooked and arms folded across her chest. *The Daily Edition*, screamed tall red letters over her head. *Bringing you the new before it's news*, screeched yellow script below.

The station traded on her youth but also on her reputation for being solid, calm, measured. And her voice: a voice which had been described as crushed gravel filtered through a silk stocking and sounded as if it belonged to a forty-something chain-smoking MILF.

People were often surprised to learn she was only twenty-five and had been working there since she was a graduate of twenty-two. Three years since the job interview when she more or less blagged her way into the position, hands clenched so tightly that her nails had cut into the skin of her palms. 'LCC is in danger of turning into a legacy brand,' she had said in the interview. 'I did some research and your core audience is ten years younger than your presenters' average age. If you don't bring in new blood, you're going to lose share.' She had gone in intending to audition as a continuity announcer but she knew she could handle the real stuff; she just needed a chance to show them. To her surprise, they put her straight in as a newsreader.

Diana wove her way through the group of happy clappers. One of them, a man in a rumpled suit who was out there every morning, shoved a pamphlet into her hand. She smiled and nodded robotically. Same old same old. Station security had called the police a few times, but since it was a public pavement, there wasn't much that could be done.

Barrington at the security desk buzzed Diana in. 'All right D,' he nodded, his eyes glued to a B-grade vampire flick he was watching instead of the camera feeds. Barrington was many things as a security manager, but being attentive with the CCTV was not one of them. 'Why bother,' he would shrug. 'By the time you notice something's wrong they're already inside. Now you're distracted from what's going on.' If pressed further he might also admit to being tired of watching the Bible-bashers from multiple angles all day long. On the other hand, in the event of a sudden zombie apocalypse outside the station, he was exactly the sort of person you would want on the door.

She glanced past his desk at the back doors where a tattered OUT OF ORDER sign had been taped up some months ago. On second thoughts, maybe he wasn't.

'Is he in yet?' Diana asked. She shrugged out of her coat and shook the droplets of ice out of her hair.

Barrington chuckled, nodding his shiny bald head. 'Yeah, ten minutes ago,' he said. 'Shouting at some poor girl about his dry cleaning. I told him you had already been in and gone back out.'

'Thank you,' Diana said. Her producer, Jonathan, was always cracking the whip. He was domineering in the way only short men can be: not at ease with himself or anyone else. It wasn't enough for him to be top dog; he also had to make sure you knew about it. Even if he came in thirty seconds before she did he acted like he had been kept waiting for an eternity.

Barrington waved his hand and turned back to his console. On the screen, four screaming co-eds were being engulfed by clouds of blood-hungry bats. 'You know I got your back,' he said.

Up on the third floor, a series of meeting rooms and glass-walled studios carved up the space. The building was listed, so nothing could be done about replacing the thin, wobbly-paned windows that looked out over Soho, and the station had spent a bomb installing soundproof inner rooms.

Strict rules about how the buildings looked couldn't stop Soho from changing. Once media moved in, attracted by large offices in central London at knock-down prices, the rest weren't far behind. Trendy restaurants that catered to the new professionals, all exposed brickwork and tables that looked like they were built from construction offcuts but cost more than a month's wages. The people who worked in these places were women in nipped-waist frocks with flicks of black eyeliner and the put-upon world weariness of the very young. Skinny men with tattoos who used to stand on street corners waiting for trouble were replaced by a different kind of skinny men with tattoos, the kind who oiled their beards and turned up the sleeves of their lumberjack shirts just so. Diana felt confused around men like that, ones who were her own age but dressed like Depression-era hoboes. She wondered how long it would be until the fashion world turned again and men went back to looking like 1950s professors or 1980s cokeheads.

The restaurants did well, though. She liked being able to get gluten-free bangers and mash for lunch. In the restaurants, urbanites could coo over hacked pieces of pheasant served on slates while sneering out the windows at what little remained of Soho's sex trade. More money was flowing in now, more policing, more of a land grab to seize the old walkups and turn them into *desirable city centre living*. And yet Diana had the feeling that, too, was only temporary. The fashionably retro style nodding to a time of good, honest Victorian sweat and sweatshops was not entirely truthful. The real culture of Soho was made on the back of sex workers and when the slick of gentrification moved elsewhere, they would come back out from the wings to reclaim what was rightfully theirs.

Diana dumped her coat and bag on her office desk. She glanced at the pamphlet the pavement evangelist had given her. *Are You Ready*

To Receive Ultimate Love? A smiling, bearded Jesus stretched his arms wide as kaleidoscopic rays of light emerged from behind him. Could be heaven, could be the entrance to a cabaret. She wondered if it ever occurred to the fanatics that, give or take a robe or two, the handouts they distributed looked like a poster from one of Soho's nightclubs more than anything else. Or maybe that was the effect they were after – entrap the sinners and hope they stay? Ultimate Love indeed. She crumpled the paper into a neat ball and threw it into the bin.

The producer poked his head around the corner of Diana's office. Jonathan, wearing his usual uniform of steel rimmed frames and mock turtleneck. He probably thought it made him look like Steve Jobs. Attractive enough for a middle-aged guy, if you ignored his habit of shouting at staff. 'Morning, D,' he said and perched on the corner of her desk. 'So, headlines.'

'Weather?'

'Weather is done to death,' he said. Jonathan rifled through a collection of press releases, printouts from news sites, and emails. 'People are sick of hearing about how wet it is. If it's wet where they are, they'll ring in to complain about it. If it's not wet where they are, they'll ring in to complain we're devoting too much time to it.'

'Not our fault. It's not like we're responsible,' Diana said. He nodded agreement. 'But I take your point. Politics?'

'Rumours of an opposition leadership coup still ongoing,' Jonathan said. 'Talk of removing Scottish MPs from some votes in Commons is causing a wedge, a few are speculating there will be defections to the SNP or Green parties. We're expecting a statement from the Shadow Home Secretary later on to tamp down any rumoured splits in the party.'

'Morag the Moaner,' Diana said. 'Can't wait.'

'Even if she knew what you thought of her, my guess is she wouldn't care,' he said.

'True. What's the take online? Are the defections a rumour that's trending, or are we in danger of putting the denial in front of the horse?'

Jonathan adjusted his wire rims. 'Fuck online,' he said. 'Said it before and I'll say it as many times as it needs to be said. We're news media, not bloody Facebook.' So maybe not so much like Steve Jobs after all.

Diana pretended this was the first time she'd had the pleasure of being subjected to this particular rant. Or the first time she had trolled him into it. 'Well, Jonathan, it seems to me that our presence out there is looking a little bit thin, compared to the rest of the news media these days. Just saying.' He wasn't the one who had to deal with the callers, she was. 'We're missing out on large audiences if we can't connect with people online in any meaningful way.'

'Twitter this and blogging that,' Jonathan fumed and pounded the desk. 'You know, I'm sick of hearing about it. Ten years from now no one will even remember what it was, much less why we cared.'

'Maybe so,' Diana said. 'Or maybe ten years from now we'll be looking at the scorch marks on our arses and wondering how the hell we ended up getting ripped a new one by teenagers and their vlogs. Everyone who's anyone is out there, you know, J,' she continued. 'All the main editors, give or take a broadsheet. Every last head journalist, and don't get me started on the columnists. They're getting their content out minutes after news breaks. I know it's not your favourite topic, but news is happening all over social media, and we're missing out.'

Jonathan's face scrunched up. It was a look Diana knew too well, and if she wasn't pulling such good ratings, she knew he would be screaming his head off at her for even questioning his decisions. 'Fuck's sake, D,' he said. He stabbed the pile of papers with his pencil. 'Nothing of value, and I mean nothing, ever came from the Internet. Not when it comes to news.'

'Would you have said the same thing about *Huffington Post? Slate?* People are breaking news online, we should be right there with them,' she said coolly. Yes, winding Jonathan up was one of the subtler perks of her job.

Diana watched him gurning and chewing his cheek, trying to find a way to put words into sentences without throttling her. Finally he spoke. 'When you say breaking news, what you mean is mean spreading libel and pictures of cats. We should be leaving that sort of nonsense to the New Politician and their ilk,' he said. 'I will not let the station stoop to clickbait. It's undignified.'

Jonathan stood up, well into his flow now, and punched the air. 'No, what the world needs more of now is quality analysis, not dodgy opinions and worse grammar. This is what we made our name on.' He jabbed a finger in her direction. Diana smirked behind her hand. 'The in depth debate. The whole conversation, not the sound bites. Real content. You don't get that in 140 characters or less.'

Or fewer, Diana thought. Jonathan's features sank together like a handful of dried currants dropped into a steamed pudding. She knew the look well. It meant he was about to shout at someone, or break something. She was enjoying this, but it probably wasn't good for his blood pressure to keep it going. Not to mention the rest of the staff, who would bear the brunt of his temper. 'Sooo, today's headlines. What else are you looking at?'

Jonathan, panting and overheated from his screed, scanned the rest of the printouts. 'Scotland Liberal Unionist Party sent through a release, looks like a good one,' he said and sat down again.

'Scotland Liberal Unionist Party?' Diana asked. 'Some anti-independence thing? Never heard of it.'

'Not just anti-independence, but anti-devolution as well,' Jonathan said. 'They claim to be resurrecting the spirit of a party that existed until 1912 and then was merged in to the Conservatives.'

'1912, huh? Well, that's sure to grab the imagination of young voters.' Though given the hipster aesthetic, perhaps they weren't far wrong.

His face unclenched slightly. 'You know, I like this. Protest voting is still hot. Even people who voted for the current government are starting to turn their opinions. We should get on top of this before anyone else gets the story.'

Diana shrugged. 'What, more English votes for English parliament stuff?' she said. 'We've done that topic to death.'

Jonathan shook his head. 'Beyond that. Returning Parliament to the pre-1999 settlements, they say. Capitalising on the mood post-referendum. Not broken big yet. My hunch is it's going to explode this week. There's a tip that those lottery winners are giving a big chunk away for the party to fund a run on the European Parliament.'

'Not how I would have chosen to spend it,' Diana said. The couple had been all over the papers a few days before: good-looking, riches-to-rags-to-riches story. Wife had a bit of a past, nothing serious, just tittle-tattle. Husband was some City prat who'd lost his job in the recession. Seemed a bit odd for them to turn round and hand it all away. But if news had taught her anything it was that the one predictable thing about people was their unpredictability. 'What's their angle?'

'Blah blah Scottish heritage stuff, taking the fight to Brussels, et cetera. Who knows? Maybe they like the lottery spotlight so much they decided to stay in it for a while.'

'I guess.' Diana frowned. Plenty of celebs had made their careers on less, but still . . . They had seemed smarter than that to her. Then again, most lottery winners never went public about their wins at all, so maybe publicity seeking was on the cards all along.

A runner came into the room and put a cup of tea and plate of biscuits by Jonathan's elbow. She had a coffee as well for Diana. Diana noted that the producer neither acknowledged nor thanked the girl. Diana recalled that she might have been named Kerry. Or possibly Kirsty. Even after several months of the girl working there, they had never been introduced. She would have asked Jonathan but he made a point of not knowing the name of anyone less important than him. Which, in his mind, amounted to very nearly everyone.

'Do we know who the party's MEP candidates are going to be? Anyone credible? Or is it a load of brigadiers in fake family tartans and frothing racists?'

'No candidates announced as yet, it's an announcement of an announcement,' he said.

An announcement of an announcement? What was that when it was at home? She looked over the press release. 'Sounds a bit suspect,' Diana said. 'Are you sure this isn't a practical joke?'

'Looks legit enough.' Jonathan sniffed his tea and slammed the mug on the desk. 'This is stewed. You squeezed the bag, didn't you? What, are you trying to poison me?' he snarled at the runner. She flinched and mumbled an apology. He turned back to Diana, a false smile on his face. 'Anyway, they're over in Molesey so easy for us to get out there, or do a phone link. Then we can get a call-in after, get people to talk about how they would spend lottery money if they had it, or something.'

'Fine, we'll do that,' Diana nodded. 'So . . . any plans for the weekend?' she asked.

Jonathan's head shot up. 'What's that supposed to mean?'

Diana smiled innocently. 'Just making conversation, Jonathan. You know, talking to people. It's kind of what you pay me to do.'

He pursed his lips. 'Usual things,' he said.

'Ah.' She'd noticed he was careful not to reveal anything about his private life. Now that she thought about it, Diana didn't even know where he lived. Not that she fancied hanging out. It just seemed odd, somehow. You usually knew personal things about the people you worked with even if you didn't like them or see them socially. But Jonathan gave every impression of not even existing outside of the station. There was a rumour going round that he had a new squeeze, but from what she could tell, he was the same as he always was: a sour, middle-aged hack with a chip on his shoulder the size of Essex.

Diana turned back to her own notes. 'What about that missing geologist?'

'The Schofield case?' Jonathan said. 'Has there been anything new on that?'

'No, but it's a month now since he disappeared. I thought we could get the family down the line for a fresh appeal, ask if anyone saw anything. . .'

'Forget it,' Jonathan said. 'The guy's probably dead. And the story definitely is.'

Diana frowned. Most news stories didn't affect her either way, but for some reason this one had stuck in her head. Mild mannered geologist Damian Schofield disappears, a few days later police find an unconvincing suicide note at the house saying he was going to Scotland to end it all in the hills he loved. His wife said it wasn't even his handwriting. No leads, no sightings, no body.

Police seemed convinced it was a suicide, end of story. And in any other circumstances it would be news that came and went. An eminent professor's tragic death, one family's tragedy, and that was all.

Diana had a feeling there was more to the story than anyone was saying. Schofield had been scheduled to appear before a Select Committee on energy policy a week after he disappeared. The details of his testimony had not been released widely but rumour had it he was going to imply, if not outright state, that the official numbers on oil and fracking in Scotland had been misrepresented. Or possibly, as some conspiracy theory websites speculated, he was going to say they were altogether wrong. If that was the case, could that have been a reason for him to disappear? For him to commit suicide? Or worse – for someone to kill him, as some Internet sites suggested had happened? Already a few blogs were referring to him as the new Dr David Kelly. Maybe the committee timing was only coincidence. And maybe, Diana thought, it wasn't.

If it had been a suicide, why wasn't he on any camera footage, why was there no train ticket to Scotland if he was going there, why were his hiking boots still in the cupboard according to his wife, why were there no witnesses? Sure, people went missing all the time. The story might have happened exactly the way the police assumed it had. It was equally possible it happened some other way. Maybe he had disappeared on purpose, or had a tragic accident. But something about the story didn't make sense to her, didn't add up.

She thought about the image the family released after he had disappeared. The grainy old photo of a man in a corduroy jacket standing on a mountain path. It reminded her of a holiday by Loch Lomond with her father when she was small. Somewhere there was a family missing him, a daughter who might never know what became of her father, a wife who could only sit and wait. What must it be like to know someone for decades then, without warning, they're gone? This was about more than one man – it was a story about grief. Diana would have killed to nab the first solo interview with his wife but the family had stuck to communicating anything they wanted to say through lawyers and press releases.

'I hear you,' Diana said. 'But someone must know something. A neighbour, maybe? Did anyone ever interview his co-workers?'

The runner was still there, hopping from foot to foot, holding the mug of rejected tea. 'Um, can I like, go make a new one?' she asked. Jonathan waved his hand in the air and she darted out the door.

Diana watched the girl bolt like a frightened kitten. Jonathan had that effect on people. It never seemed to occur to him that the high turnover in station staff was probably as much a result of his general attitude as the pressure of the work itself. Only being on the public side of the microphone earned her any leeway with him, she knew. And it was an advantage she didn't mind pressing when she could. 'Come on, let's be on the right side of the story for once,' she said. 'It beats regurgitating tabloid pap twelve hours after everyone's already sick to death of it.'

'That case is police business, not ours,' Jonathan said. 'When the body turns up we'll be there. Till then no one cares.'

'Whatever happened to, "if it bleeds, it leads"?' Diana said.

Jonathan puffed out his cheeks. 'We got nothing new here, D. Come on.'

'Or what about, "if they're dead, we're live"?' Diana said.

He scoffed. 'Live where? At the family's house? Don't you think they've been through enough already?'

'I suppose,' Diana said. She had seen it many times before, but it never failed to surprise her. It all seemed to happen so quickly. How the news could go from full saturation over someone's disappearance, to . . . nothing, no interest. Overnight.

'Christ, D,' Jonathan said. 'You're still cutting your teeth. These kinds of stories can be highly emotive. Remember the *News of the World* fiasco? You can't chase every mystery down the rabbit hole. We're living in a post-Leveson world, let's not forget that. Get it wrong and we're the baddies.' he said. 'My hunch – my experience – says leave it. We'll be first out when they find him. I promise.'

Diana didn't agree, but she knew Jonathan wouldn't budge. How was raising a largely forgotten unsolved mystery that might benefit from having its profile raised the same thing as phone hacking? But that seemed to be the stock answer to anything he didn't want to do: Leveson. Libel. Meanwhile they were getting their arses toasted in the ratings. Her show did well enough, but the drop-off in numbers for the presenters on after her was shocking, and she had a feeling she could only hold on to her success for so long before listeners would start going elsewhere. 'Got it.'

Jonathan stood up. 'So it's cabinet and headlines before the break, traffic and weather, live to Molesey for Scotland donation and call-in. We're on in ten. Throw that coffee down your neck and get in the tank,' he said.

Erykah slipped out the French doors in a coat and wellie boots. She wanted a walk along the towpath before anyone turned up at the house. She needed time to think, away from Rab and his sullen looks, away from her phone and the radio and the television news.

The clouds that had brought sleet overnight were just starting to lift. The river was swollen with rain from an earlier snow, and even at the ebb of the tide patterns and eddies swirled on the surface like ripples in satin.

Even without the alarm set for early morning outings, Erykah's eyes still snapped open at half five every morning, her legs still kicked the blankets away with pent-up energy. In the bath just that morning she had looked down at her hands and seen the peeling skin on her palms starting to soften and come away from the callouses that had been a constant feature for so long.

What was she going to do?

Since her anniversary, every day had been worse than the last. If she tried to stop and put the events of the last ten days in order in her mind, she simply couldn't. It was like being back at Grayson's trial. Something was happening, and while she had no control over it, she couldn't simply opt out of being involved, either.

She needed something to hold on to. Not her husband – Rab had proved himself more of an anchor than a lifejacket. In less than an hour, the money she thought they had won would be gone too. She had lost her precious anonymity, the security of blending in to Molesey life, just another middle class wife, thanks to the papers. The club was gone. And Nicole . . .

A clutch of women from the boat club jogged in the opposite direction, warming up before their water outing, their trainers crunching the gravel. Probably one of their last before they went away on training camp, she guessed. Erykah raised one hand in greeting. The group brushed past without a word or a look – save for Nicole, at the back, whose green eyes met hers for a painful fraction of a second before she turned her head and ran on.

The syncopated rhythm of their feet on the path grew fainter and disappeared. So that was it, then. She searched her feelings and found a distinct lack of surprise. Hadn't she only ever been passing for one of them anyway? Accepted into the fold conditional on her husband's job, or her usefulness in a boat? Now she was just another topic of conversation to them, gossip fodder until something better came along. A familiar tension rose up in her neck. The way these people regarded anyone who was not the same as them. The way they talked about London, like it was a sack full of rubbish to be held at arm's length, not the city they profited from and were connected to.

At some point over the years she had stopped counting the number of times women in Molesey would catch themselves in the middle of a conversation about politics, about what was in the papers, and reassure her that of course, when they talked about immigrants or inner-city people or black people or whatever else, they didn't mean *her*. And then, still later, at some other point, they stopped apologising altogether.

'Fuck it,' she said. Maybe what she should be doing instead is making the most of the situation. Use them before they use you. She had been the only one holding things together when the press first came to their house, Rab had been a wreck. She had managed to deal with Seminole Billy and Buster and – apart from Rab's broken finger – without getting them into any more trouble. Maybe she could come out on top.

Erykah turned on the path and rounded back towards the house. The reporters and photographers were right on time. There were also about twice as many as she had expected and the crowd spilled over the edges of the garden and into the street. 'Arse,' she murmured. She felt a chill that had only something to do with the cold weather.

The last time the media had come to the house was to get the obligatory shots of the celebrating couple. This time she sensed a hungrier, meaner edge to the crowd. Erykah went in through the back door and upstairs to change her clothes.

Sitting at her own dressing table, slowly applying makeup, all she could think about was Grayson's trial and what the press had been like back then. For weeks they had hounded her. What better to decorate stories about a drug-related slaying with than photos of the accused's photogenic girlfriend? Almost overnight she had watched as her status in the papers went from 'key witness in a murder trial' to 'spoiled, haughty gangster princess'. As a witness she was gagged during the trial itself, unable to defend herself or even explain. Meanwhile her every movement was dissected for the delight of the tabloids, every fleeting expression or gesture presumed to have some sinister significance.

While the court found her a credible witness to the events of that night, the damage from the media was already done – such as her mother's addictions triumphantly announced on the cover of a Sunday paper. The exclusive four-page interview inside was presented as the key to Erykah's personality that, in the absence of her being able to speak for herself, they had already crafted as 'aloof' and 'detached'. Erykah read the interview with horror, cringing at the shot of Rainbow holding a baby photo of Erykah, begging her daughter to get help.

So cheap. So manipulative. So very popular with the paper-buying public.

By the end of the trial there was only one person Erykah felt she could still trust, and he was going to prison. The spare details of her life had been padded out by hacks fluent in boilerplate phrases and tinned motivations, written on spec to fit tabloid pre-decided agendas. *Gangster's Girl Rikki Protects Her Man. Leggy Rikki B Flashes Her Pins In Designer Frock. Good Girl Gone Bad.* Whatever or whoever she had thought herself to be was lost in the noise of public disapproval. Nobody wanted the truth because that would be boring.

Then one day the cameras were gone. No more reporters knocking on the neighbours' doors, no more suspicious-sounding clicks on the line any time she used the phone. Fresh scandals obsessed the news cycle and the vultures went elsewhere.

To her surprise, it felt like another loss. Without the constant stress of avoiding reporters or feeling battered by whatever new claim they were making, now there was nothing to distract from the wasteland of what was left. Her first love behind bars, her mother below contempt. No degree, no job. Her life in tatters and the feeling that she might be the only person left in the world who did not think she was evil.

Erykah unravelled the braid she had plaited to protect her hair from the rain, and gently pulled a wide comb through the curls. *We can pack up and leave. Go for a year, for the rest of our lives.* Wasn't that what Rab had said only a few days ago? But then she remembered what he had done and why this was happening at all. She had no choice but to go through with the plan as agreed with Billy and Buster. And maybe, just maybe, she could try to turn it to her advantage this time.

Deep breath. Hold it. Exhale. Her heart rate began to drop and the tingling pressure crawling up her neck started to ease off. Erykah went downstairs to face the music.

A beat-up Mercedes was parked halfway up the street, past the notice of any curious members of the press. There was no sign of Buster this time – too many people with cameras hanging about the place. Just Seminole Billy. He nodded at Erykah as she wove through the crowd to where cameramen were setting up lights. He stood on the edge of the garden, legs planted apart, arms folded across his chest. He was wearing those black cowboy boots again, the ones with the gleaming metal toes.

A young woman pulled Erykah to one side. She introduced herself as Heather Matthews, general secretary of the SLU. Erykah smiled and shook her hand. She felt an instant flash of dislike for the woman, though she couldn't put a finger on why. Maybe it was the air of confidence that seemed to come so naturally – a product of public schools, no doubt. Or was it that she had the flippy blonde hair and jolly-hockey-sticks attitude of the sort of woman her husband idolised? 'I wanted to say before everyone arrives, Mrs Macdonald, how very grateful we are that you and your husband agreed to do this,' she said. 'Not only the donation, but agreeing to have the press conference here as well. It's not every day we get a helping hand from a lottery in the Isle of Man!'

'Channel Islands, I heard,' Erykah said.

'Whatever.' Heather waved her hand and beamed an orthodontically perfect smile. 'The details don't matter now. What matters is this will be priceless promotion for the SLU campaign.'

'Yes, of course,' Erykah said. Details wouldn't matter to someone like Heather, would they? The soft cooing and butter-wouldn't-melt countenance of girls like her was surely a product of the fact that she was probably doing this for a lark, had taken a prominent internship to ease her way into politics or business or whatever birthright job had been hers from the cradle. But she could put aside her judgment of Heather for the moment; with luck she wouldn't see her again. 'With my husband having Scottish roots this is an issue we feel so passionately about. As I'm sure you can imagine,' she said.

'Your husband is going to join us, isn't he?'

'Absolutely.' Rab's face peered out from behind the curtain. Erykah looked over the crowd and her eyes met Billy's. An almost imperceptible nod.

'How do I look?' Erykah asked Heather, and adjusted the front of her jacket, a grey-and-purple flecked Harris tweed. Just enough cleavage, not too much, and a hint of a cream-coloured silk blouse peeking out. A loop of purple-and-white satin pinned to one lapel – the Scotland Liberal Unionist campaign's official ribbon.

'Good,' Heather said without looking. She clutched a clipboard and a stack of glossy leaflets advertising the party's policies. On the front, the SLU insignia: a purple-and-white saltire rippling in the breeze, barely different from a clip art logo. Erykah thought it looked amateurish. But maybe that was the angle they were going for – appealing to people sick of slick career statesmen and politics as usual in Westminster. 'And don't worry, it won't just be you and Mr Macdonald today,' she said, dropping her voice. 'We have a celebrity joining us.'

Erykah smiled. 'Oh?' This was unexpected.

'In fact,' Heather said as a black private hire car pulled up to the kerb, 'it looks like our headliner is here. I didn't want to say, because his train down from Scotland was running behind, and I was worried he wouldn't make it at all.'

A man with a green kilt and luxurious moustache emerged and stepped through the crowd. He took a last drag of his half-smoked cigarette, crushed it out on the bark of a tree, and turned to wave at the people shouting his name. Heather grabbed his arm and guided him to the group in the middle of the garden. 'Erykah, this is Major Whitney Abbott. He will be accepting your donation on behalf of Scotland Liberal Unionists. He's also agreed to be our Edinburgh candidate for the European Parliament in the next election.'

'I know who Major Abbott is.' Erykah smiled at the barrel-chested officer. 'I'm a huge fan,' she purred. 'Your book about the Falklands War was so inspiring. I couldn't wait to snuggle up with it every bedtime.'

Major Whitney Abbott smiled and shook her hand. 'Always a pleasure to meet a fan,' he said.

'You know, I have the book, I wonder if you wouldn't mind . . .' Erykah said.

The Major smiled as she darted inside. He exchanged glances with Heather. 'Autograph,' he said. 'They always want one.'

The crowd was growing restless. Heather tried to hand out some of the flyers, but most waved her off and asked about the website instead. 'It's still under construction,' she objected, but they were already on their phones browsing the address.

Erykah returned with the Major's memoirs and also a copy of one of his father's books of collected columns. He clenched his jaw but signed them both anyway. 'Where are you from?' he asked as he wrote.

'London,' she said. 'Born and grew up in Streatham, we moved here after we married.'

'No, I mean,' the Major said, 'where are your people from?'

Erykah's smile stiffened. She knew what he was asking. Racist old fuck. 'London,' she said sternly.

'Let's check the social media coverage,' Heather interrupted, tapping at a smartphone. 'Scotland Liberal Unionist Party is trending. We're number three nationwide!' She looked at the Major as if to say, *I told you so*.

Erykah leaned over for a closer look. No mention of the details yet, but that would come. Heather had advised her and Rab to keep the exact amount of the donation a secret so it would have more impact on the day.

But what impact would there be now? With the money about to leave their hands and someone else's star dazzling the media, the most Erykah could expect from this was an expedited divorce. She kept smiling, but her teeth clenched in anger. All Rab had managed to do was buy enough time to get himself out of hot water. She had already lost the few things that made her life bearable because of this. Her past being served up for the papers all over again hadn't occurred to him as a potential risk, because it hadn't mattered to him.

Because he didn't care.

The Major cleared his throat. Rab skulked out of the house and joined the small group. He looked grey and unwell. Erykah foisted her handbag on him and he winced as the strap snagged on his broken fingers, still taped together. Erykah hissed, 'Smile.' He smiled.

'Ladies, gentlemen!' the Major bellowed. 'And journalists.' A titter of polite laughter rippled through the audience. 'Welcome. And thank you for coming today. I know you all have vital dirt digging – I mean news gathering – to get back to, so I'll keep this brief.'

'Smooth, isn't he,' Rab scowled. Erykah jabbed her elbow in her husband's side.

'Today is an extraordinary day for the Scotland Liberal Unionists,' the Major continued. 'We all know Britain's military, not to mention its business, is far stronger together than split apart. It turned out the electorate agreed. With the bedrock of our rich tradition as both a family of nations and a nation of families upheld, it is now time to look to the future. A future where the SLU will be leading the way.'

'Says nothing at all in as many words possible,' Rab muttered.

'Oh, fuck off Rab,' Erykah whispered, her smile unwavering.

'You are no doubt wondering why we've asked you to meet us at the home of some of the UK's newest-minted millionaires,' the Major continued. 'Not only do most people agree that Scotland should be part of Great Britain, but this couple . . .' the Major turned and smiled at Erykah and Rab with the dazzling hundred-watt gleam of expensive dentures, 'have donated no less than nineteen million pounds to the Scotland Liberal Unionist Party.'

A sharp intake of breath from the press corps. A few mumbles as reporters did the sums. Wasn't that almost their entire lottery win? That was a ridiculous amount, unheard of. Was it even legal? 'That's a lot,' supplied one voice from the crowd. The EuroMillions winners who had given a million each to the Yes campaign and to the SNP a few years back had definitely been outplayed.

'Yes, it is a lot of money, and yes, it is an unprecedented gesture of generosity from a private donor,' the Major continued. 'But I think I speak for all of us involved with the Scotland Liberal Unionist Party when I assure Mr and Mrs Macdonald that it will go to the best cause possible – seeing that the SLU is represented in Brussels, mounting a challenge to the nationalist stranglehold on Scotland, and ensuring a stable future for our British children and our children's children.'

The Major paused to smile. Brussels would be a most welcome change. He had had it with London, with the backstabbing media who promised six-figure deals but delivered royalty statements that would have embarrassed a church mouse. Becoming an MEP would mean expense accounts, reimbursed travel, and crucially – time far, far away from the beady eyes of his wife.

'My dear Mr and Mrs Macdonald,' the Major said. 'I speak on behalf of the Scotland Liberal Unionist Party, and I hope on behalf of the future of Britain, when I say we cannot thank you enough.'

Erykah beamed as a dozen flashes went off just inches from her face. She'd practiced the smile for hours beforehand, trying to get the right balance of pleased and modest. She knew how to work a look. 'No, thank *you* Major, for giving us the opportunity to contribute in such a meaningful way to the debate,' she said. Rab, meanwhile, looked as though he would rather be anywhere else. 'I understand this has kicked off the discussion on the Internet, and I hope it encourages even more people to get involved with the cause of repairing the Union and healing the scars caused by that unfortunate and divisive referendum.'

Seminole Billy watched from the back. The woman was doing well. Not much could be said about the husband, which was for the best. No chance now the man might go to the police instead of holding up his end of the bargain. If anything did go sour a follow-up visit would discourage the idiot from breaking rank.

'We're the top trend in the country right now,' Heather murmured to the Major. 'Number two in the world trends. Let's open it up to questions.'

Erykah nodded and clapped as the Major dispatched expected questions with well-rehearsed answers. 'It's scaremongering, it's the very opposite of the truth,' he rumbled in response to claims that English MPs were plotting to prevent Scotland recovering from the recession. 'A narrow nationalism that makes cosy deals with media and prays for more recession to convince the Scottish people to support an independence they have told us they do not want.' The Major was getting into his stride. 'The evidence was never on the side of independence. The nationalists have not won hearts and they have not won minds,' he bellowed. 'Now is the time to talk about a constitutional settlement for all of the United Kingdom.'

Erykah exhaled slowly. She noted none of the questions were being directed towards her and Rab. Weren't they the ones making the donation after all?

'So why the need for the SLU?' asked one reporter. 'If most people are, as you say, on the side of staying with the Union, can't they do that through the existing parties?'

'It gives a unified voice to us in the silent majority,' Erykah interjected. There was a flash of cameras when she spoke. She positioned herself behind and to the side of Heather and the Major so that they both had to turn away from the audience in order to hear her. A classic upstage.

'For people like my husband, whose family left Scotland in bad economic times, and now, one or two generations later, are facing active discrimination from independence supporters for being proud to be British as well as Scottish.' She stopped and smiled to make sure the reporters were able to get every word. 'As his Glaswegian grandfather used to say,' she paused to frown slightly, as if remembering halcyon days soaking up the wisdom of the long-dead alcoholic widower she had never met, 'They may take our land, but they can never take our . . .' No, no, that was too much, too *Braveheart*. 'Um, they can never take our heritage.'

'And the independence propagandists would do exactly that,' Heather blurted, 'take away your heritage.' She smiled and swivelled back to face the crowd.

A reporter up at the front waved. According to his press card he was from one of those magazines that was given away free on the Tube and in railway stations. Not the lowest of the low by any means – but not far off the bottom of the totem pole either. Heather, feeling generous, gestured to him. He took a deep breath. 'In an economy when most charities are struggling to get donations, considering the SLU has only existed for a short time, doesn't the timing of this donation seem a little suspicious?'

The Major and Heather exchanged glances. What was this fellow on about? Heather hesitated. 'Excuse me?' she said.

'Isn't it odd that a group that . . .' He scrolled down on his smartphone for information. 'Registered only last month is already getting a larger donation than any political party to date? That's the most effective fundraising I've ever heard about and many, many people are asking questions. I'm sure other groups would love to know your secret.' The reporter smirked at Major Abbott. 'We can assume it isn't because of the quality of your up-and-coming political candidates.'

The Major glared at the weedy man. He'd been told the press conference was going to be straightforward. He didn't have the time or patience to go off-piste. 'Where are you getting this nonsense from?'

'It's all over the web,' he said, turning the smartphone towards the rest of the press corps so they could see. Some were already looking it up themselves. 'An anonymous account tweeted the link to your foundation at Companies House a few minutes ago; it's already been retweeted over a thousand times already. Someone calling themselves Media Mouse,' the man said. 'Also, Mrs Macdonald? Your top button's just come undone.' Erykah clapped a hand to her chest.

'Shut this down and get me out of here!' the Major spat at Heather. But his eyes were glued to Erykah's breasts. A dozen cameras managed to catch the moment, his moustachioed face poised between lust and hate as the SLU's secretary cowered in fear. The picture was on the web in moments.

Erykah looked out over the group of reporters and spotted Seminole Billy by the rhododendrons. She raised her eyebrows almost imperceptibly. He shrugged and shook his head – no idea. The media monkeys were typing like mad on their phones. The virtual appearance of some unknown third party was going to take over the story instead of Scotland Liberal Unionists having the final word. This was a surprise, and Seminole Billy didn't like surprises. The people who hired him usually didn't either. This anonymous tweeter – whoever it turned out to be – was on his radar now.

All the reporters had their phones out now, either tweeting the events or hoping to catch a photo that might go viral. It was time to bail. 'I'm very sorry, the Major has a prior appointment elsewhere this afternoon so we have to finish here,' Heather said, and grabbed the Major's sleeve to guide him to the waiting car. 'Thank you all for coming today.'

: 14 :

The Major lay in bed as still as a soldier on sentry. As still as a man in his grave. It was quiet, too quiet, with his wife Betty still in Cameron Bridge. Usually he had her steady breathing to mark the seconds, and the dark room slowly brightening to mark the hours as morning entered their London home. The sheet draped over his legs like a clammy shroud.

The press conference. The money. The scam. What had he got himself involved in? What if the media found out? What then? Yes, he could try to weasel out of it. Deny any insider knowledge; distance himself from the key players. And hope that was enough to keep the police from his door. It probably wasn't.

Nineteen million. No one had told him it was all coming from one donor. It smelled dodgy. No wonder the press had gone wild. He wouldn't have believed a word of it either, if he wasn't involved.

It was all his goddaughter's fault; she was the one who had roped him into fronting the SLU in the first place. She couldn't be the forward face, she said. We need someone with right wing credibility, she said. And he had lapped it up. Eager to believe the work would be as easy as she said it would be rewarding.

Why had he trusted her without question? All along she kept assuring him she had control of the media, that she knew what she was doing, that they were in her pocket. That she would do the hard work behind the scenes and the SLU staff would walk him through the rest. Then the disastrous press conference happened and everyone there looked foolish. Especially him. She wasn't the one who was risking her image on this, he was. She was behind the curtain pulling the strings. He should have demanded more skin in the game from her. He should have anticipated that any negative outcome was going to fall on his shoulders.

And the press conference wasn't the half of it. If the full story were to come out it would make them look like monsters.

The Major stayed in his bed until daylight, eyes wide open, waiting.

Mornings were the worst. His insomnia was back with a vengeance. It was more exhausting than the speed marches in formation that they had cranked out during training. He was getting by these days on a diet of booze, instant coffee, and old-fashioned stubbornness. But for how much longer?

He rose the second the alarm sounded, showered and dressed in his kilt and tweeds. He patted the bed next to him to say goodbye to Betty for the day, forgetting for a moment that he was alone in the house.

The Major took a black cab to his office, the converted pied-a-terre in a South Kensington mews where he had written his memoirs. Years ago it had also doubled as a crash pad for the mistresses and escorts who might or might not have made the Major's acquaintance. Once, many an afternoon had been whiled away over cocktails and sweaty sheets and where the receptionist now sat had been a bouncy king-sized bed and drinks cupboard. Good times.

These days his office was a hideout from his wife's barely suppressed rage. After his affair was exposed in the tabloids she had supervised the conversion of the flat into a proper office, her mouth a tight white line as she watched removal men carry the bed down three flights of stairs. 'Make sure that lot goes right to the tip,' she said as they drove away.

Other marriages might have crumbled after what happened, but he was not the right generation for that, nor was his wife. Divorce was not in either of their vocabularies. His wife had made stony-faced endurance of her husband's career into her vocation. Betty Abbott was far from ready to retire that particular commission.

'Any messages?' he asked the secretary, a battleaxe of a woman selected for reception duties by his wife.

Wilma shook her head. 'Nothing,' she said, her hands pounding away at a Cold War-era Selectric typewriter. 'Maybe later.' They rarely exchanged anything but essential information. Flirting with the help was verboten these days: the secretary was as fat as a butcher's dog and old enough to be his mother. On paper he was her employer. He was under no illusions as to who Wilma's real boss was.

With the coming political race, as well, he'd had to take on more help. A couple of interns dropped in most days, fresh young fellows with cheeks like slapped arses and thin shoulders in awkward suits, to help with the workload. Hugo and Oscar were identical apart from Hugo's cowlick and Oscar's mild stammer. Wilma had planted Oscar at a desk facing the wall to frank three hundred envelopes for posting in key swing vote areas. Whatever the young Oxbridge graduates had imagined life held for them after a 2:2 in PPE, this most likely was not it.

Whitney shut himself into the inner sanctum, a box room that had once served as a makeshift kitchen and storage. The old fittings had been removed. Blocked off ends of pipes jutted from the walls. When the office reshuffle happened, Betty had put him in the smallest room. He had no doubt it was on purpose.

She had been in last month for redecorating again. A power move to underline who was in charge, like a bulldog pissing in a bed of daisies. The room still smelled of fresh paint. The Major perused boxes of memorabilia collected over the years that he had yet to put back on the walls. Clippings of favourable book reviews. A photo of the Major shaking hands with Jimmy Savile when they met at a dinner at Lympstone – might be better to leave that one off the wall. A small walnut box with hand-cut dovetail joins that contained one of his father's pistols.

He was gazing at the box when Wilma announced a call from a Mrs Macdonald waiting on line two.

'Major,' Erykah purred when he picked up the call.

'Mrs Macdonald,' the Major said. 'To what do I owe the pleasure?'

'I thought we could meet soon. I have a feeling we might have some . . . mutual interests to discuss.'

'Is that so?' the Major asked. He doubted all she wanted was a chat over a latte, but he was pleased for the distraction. 'And remind me again what it is you have that I want?'

'I think you know what that is,' Erykah said. Her voice dipped just low enough to hint what that might be. If she was going to play the game, she was determined to play it right. 'If the news stories were anything to go by.'

'Ah yes, I remember, the famous chest,' he said. Perhaps his day was picking up after all, the cheeky minx. 'A cheap ploy.'

'Cheap but effective. It had your attention,' Erykah said. 'So let's meet. Talk. Out of the office.'

'Let's,' he said, already imagining what might happen next. He was glad she hadn't suggested dropping by. 'Sooner rather than later. Today.'

'Perfect,' Erykah said.

'What time suits you?'

'Any time. As soon as you're finished at the office.' She suggested a café near Westminster.

'I'm leaving now,' the Major said, and rang off.

Thank the gods for womankind. He'd had enough of the office for one day. An afternooner sounded like just the thing. Although a drink would have been better than coffee. With any luck, maybe she would keep him out late enough for one of those too.

'I've always wondered something,' Wilma said as he made his way to the door.

'What's that?' the Major paused to ask.

'Does that really work with men?' Her hands did not even slow as she continued to type at a violent speed. The Selectric crashed and clattered like a tractor on a country road. Hugo, or was it Oscar, paused his work, the better to eavesdrop.

'Does what work?'

The Major's secretary looked up and smiled. 'The bedroom voice. She sounded like a bitch on heat.' No doubt Wilma would be on the phone to his better half as soon as he was gone.

Crusted hag. 'Well, if it does, I certainly don't know who with,' the Major said, and left.

The café Erykah had suggested was one of a chain that had seen better days. While a steady stream of tourist traffic still wandered in and out, these days they were as often asking for directions or looking for the toilets as ordering a drink. Flyers for local events were affixed to the community noticeboard, most of them out of date.

Whitney waited to order, tapping on the counter while the baristas busied themselves with emptying coffee grounds into an overflowing bin and laughing at each other's small talk. Finally, after almost a quarter of an hour, one of them deigned to pour him a filter coffee. A tinny thump thump thump of music emanated from somewhere in the corner of the room.

Though with the prospect of hooking up with the lovely Mrs Macdonald on the cards, who could complain? The Major brushed his moustache with a knotted finger. His mind wandered to hotels he knew close by where they might remember his visits in past years. Maybe somewhere that could give him a room on account, discreetly.

The Major picked up a newspaper left by some previous customer.

He turned the pages with almost no interest – there was no news, really, just scraps of distracting entertainment served up as journalism and press releases disguised as investigations. His eye landed on the society column. *News reaches us that everyone's favourite goggle-eyed perv and erstwhile war hero, Major Abbott, has become an Internet meme.* Ugh. The Major crushed the tabloid in his paw and threw it onto the floor.

He checked his watch. It was half an hour since he'd arrived. Erykah had said she was coming straight away. He contemplated ordering another coffee but the teenagers behind the counter were still occupied with ignoring the customers. The Major began to wonder if he was being stood up. His jaw tightened. Well then, fine. At least it had got him out of the office.

Or maybe this wasn't a date after all. He wouldn't have put it past his wife to try to set him up. That was it. She was leading him on to make him look the fool. Maybe his wife was going to be the one who came through the door. Or maybe the Erykah woman would be wearing a wire while he propositioned her. Yes, that had to be it. He drank the cold dregs of his coffee in one mouthful and stood up to go.

'I am so, so sorry,' Erykah trilled as she came through the door, hands held up in apology, heels clicking on the scuffed linoleum floor. 'Tube lines down all over and the taxi queue was insane.' He sat down again.

'No sneaky wire in there, I hope,' he said and nodded towards her enormous designer handbag.

'Hello to you too,' she said as she shed several layers of outerwear and pulled off a frankly kinky looking pair of gloves. She dusted crumbs off a chair and perched on its edge.

'Apologies,' he said. 'But you can never be too careful. After the last time and all.' He searched her face for some kind of sign. There was a sheen of sweat on her brow, but that could as easily have been from running to make the meeting as from nerves. Underneath that, though, he thought he detected something else. Skittishness. As if she was trying to make her mind up about going one way or another.

If there was one thing he knew from experience, it was that uncertainty was the worst thing in the field. Be right, be wrong, whichever. But don't be uncertain. Pick a line and stick with it. Anyone who didn't? Those were the ones you had to watch the closest.

'Oh, but we're on the same team really, aren't we?' She laid her hand on his and he softened. 'You want to know if you can trust me. Tell you what. As a sign of trust, you can look through my bag if I can look through yours.' She pointed at the sporran on his lap. 'Deal?' The Major crossed his legs. 'Didn't think so,' Erykah smiled. 'Neither of us has much to gain from being exposed, am I right?'

The Major chewed this over and found it acceptable. 'So, what can I do you for?' he said.

'I was hoping you could tell me,' Erykah said. 'You see, I have a feeling you might like to make sure your side – *our* side – whatever it is, that I stay on it.'

'I hope this isn't some sort of attempt at blackmail.'

Erykah opened her mouth, a hand fluttered to her chest. 'Blackmail? Me? Far from it,' she said. Was that the dark shadow of a lie he saw pass her face? Or was she genuine? 'What I have in mind is more of a mutually beneficial arrangement. You'll find I can be very discreet.'

'You've been the model of discretion so far,' the Major said. 'Or did I imagine that smile on your face when you realised the entire press corps could see down your top?'

'I'm more than window dressing,' she said, looking him in the eyes. 'You know what it's like to be taken for granted, looked over. You never made colonel; why is that?'

His eye twitched – she had hit the mark. She had done her research. He was hungry for credibility.

'What I want is to be more than a name and face for people to use.' Erykah leaned forward and brushed the sleeve of his tweed jacket with her fingertips. 'You know how that feels, don't you?' she said.

The Major straightened his posture and inhaled deeply. He stayed silent as she continued, 'I bet I know what they say when you leave a room.' Her voice dropped and she looked up through her lashes. 'You're on the way out. Washed up. How many years can you live off the memory of a war that happened when half the country wasn't even born? Off a book that hardly shifted any copies?' She leaned back. 'I know it's not the money you want. Otherwise, why would you bother with this SLU nonsense? There are easier pay cheques to be had. No,' she said, 'it's not about money for you. It's about being in the thick of it again.'

She looked at him. 'Don't be offended. I know because that's how I feel too. You have to understand, a week ago I had a marriage, I had rowing, and I had the lottery ticket. Now I have nothing.' She looked away and tried to hold back tears. That much, he felt sure, was genuine.

The Major shrugged. 'And?'

'I know the lottery was a scam,' she said. She told him that she knew the Scotland Liberal Unionist Party was involved. She suggested that two men who had turned up at her house, and one later at the press conference, knew him. He couldn't disagree.

'The question is, what do we do about this?' she concluded. 'I am not interested in exposing your friends or the original deal – they made it clear what would happen, and in any case, I'm not the sort of woman who goes back on her word.' Her diamond eternity band glinted as a shard of light broke through the window of the café. 'Usually. But at the same time I do require some assurance that I won't be cast aside.'

'You can take your continued good health as a positive sign,' the Major offered.

'Touché,' Erykah smiled. 'But I want more than that. Like I said, I have nothing. A month from now I'll probably be divorced. So I need security of some kind. And what I want is a leg up in the organisation.'

'What makes you think it's an organisation?' the Major asked. 'For all you know it could be me and a couple of associates—'

'You don't have that kind of money,' Erykah interrupted, ticking off points on her fingers. 'And you don't have that kind of influence. No, your value is your media profile, which as we agreed, is something of a waning commodity. So it's someone else's gig, only they don't show their face. And it's someone you know well, otherwise you wouldn't be involved in the first place.' The Major's eye twitched again. Another hit. 'Who?'

Major Abbott shook his head. 'No can do,' he said.

Erykah narrowed her eyes. 'Whoever it is has your loyalty. Is it a woman?' The Major switched his eyes away. 'What kind of woman?' Erykah said. 'Not your wife. A lover? An ex?'

'It's none of your business. You won't get that information out of me. I'll give you anything but that.'

'Then I want your help,' she said. 'You have the MEP slot to aim for, and if you fail, no huge loss really, it will have done the job of raising your profile and you have more time for hitting the media pundit circuit. But me? Whichever way this goes, I have nothing.' She spun the ring round on her finger. 'No lottery win. No marriage, not a real one, anyway. And since the press release went down like a lead balloon . . .'

'You want a job,' the Major said.

'What's your staff situation?'

'I have a secretary and sufficient interns to handle the admin if that's what you're asking.'

'You have,' she said. 'But no one you can confide in, is there? A secretary is not going to be the kind of person you trust, a secretary who sounded like she would have reached through the telephone and wrung my neck if she could have done.' The Major tipped his head in concession. 'Her loyalty extends no further than office hours. With me you could have something more.'

'I presume that when you say "something more", you don't mean stuffing envelopes and answering the phone.'

'I have skills,' Erykah said. 'We haven't even scratched the surface here.'

'Is that so?' the Major said. He could see that whatever she was thinking, she was growing bolder. Maybe she hadn't walked in uncertain of what she was going to do after all. Maybe she had simply been trying to screw up the courage to do it.

'Sure,' she said. 'In the last day we've had calls from all the glossies, and several broadsheets wanting photo shoots and one on one interviews. They all want the human face of your party, and why not? It beats having rings run round your media strategy by some anonymous troll. You and me co-fronting this. A double act. For now.'

'It's not solely a matter of getting media attention,' he said. 'There is a lot more going on behind the scenes than some press conferences and a nifty campaign ribbon.'

Erykah nodded. 'I have no problems getting my hands dirty. I want what you have.'

The Major barked a laugh. 'What I have? More trouble than you can imagine.'

'I can imagine plenty,' she said.

'Lady Livia won't be pleased,' he said.

'Who?'

The Major's faced blanched. 'Who what?'

The Major was many things, but he was not a good liar. 'The name you just mentioned. Lady Livia. Who is she and why won't she be pleased? Is she the one funding this?'

'I don't know what you're talking about,' he said and frowned. But she had something he didn't want her to know now, and she knew it.

'Tell me about these skills.' He looked her up and down. 'Apart from the obvious.'

'Let's start with technology,' she said. 'I know a thing or two about computers. I may not be a social media genius, but seems to me neither is that – what's her name?'

'Heather.'

'Right. Heather.' Erykah ticked off the point on her fingers. 'She's what, a glorified intern? I'm resourceful. Loyal. And I look bloody great in a paparazzi shot,' she said. 'But then, you already knew that.'

The Major chewed the inside of his cheek as he thought. He finally stopped gurning and spoke. 'You wanted a deal, fine, we can discuss a deal. But before we go on, so you know – this would be a carte blanche. My help for your silence,' he said. 'And there is going to be a hell of a lot of silence.' He rapped his knuckles on the table as he said it, for emphasis.

'Oh?' Her mouth was a perfect lipstick circle of false surprise. 'There's more than the money laundering?'

'There may be. As I said, my help, your silence.'

'So it's agreed then.'

'Yes, fine,' he said. 'You are right. Strength in numbers. Consider this a deal.'

'Good.' She put out her hand to him, which he took, briefly.

'I suppose,' the Major said. He still had an odd feeling about her, but couldn't put his finger on it.

'Fair exchange is no theft. Isn't that one of your favourite sayings? It was in your book, three times.' She paused. She was thinking something over, he was sure of it. But what?

Erykah bit her lip. She reached in her bag and pulled out her phone. 'By the way? You should trust your instincts next time.'

The Major stiffened. 'What's that?' She set the smartphone on the table between them. A little smile played on her lips, like a schoolgirl who had done something especially clever. 'I am recording this and it's uploading to a cloud site as we speak.' The Major's face fell as he watched a zigzag line recording their voices weave across the screen. When he'd thought she might be trying to set him up, he should have held on to that thought a little while longer. Like a schoolboy, he had been distracted by a nice body and a pretty smile. 'Don't worry, it's for my own use,' she said. 'And it's encrypted, so only I can retrieve it. Unless something happens to me.' She picked up the phone again, tapped at the screen, and dropped it back into her handbag. 'In which case it goes directly to the press. Amazing all the apps they have these days, isn't it?' she smiled.

'Bitch,' he spat.

'There's no need for that sort of language. We're not in the field. You should be thanking your lucky stars,' she said. 'That it was me and not, say, a journalist.'

He looked at her hands, at the sparkling wedding bands. She noticed his glance and the implied threat that maybe she shouldn't be so cavalier with someone else's safety potentially at stake. 'Oh, by all means, take care of my ball and chain. Do me the favour,' she said. 'Relieving me of Rab would be a bonus.' She rubbed her wrists reflexively. He noticed marks that looked like fading bruises. 'And the life insurance is, how shall I put this? Comprehensive. You wouldn't just have my permission. You would have my blessing.'

'What's to prevent me telling the press you set me up? You're not exactly a clean slate, yourself,' he said.

'No?' she said. 'Just imagine how it would play out – me, a desperate woman with a past, taken for a fool by a ruthless ex-Marine and politician. You think this street goes only one way, but I can assure you that a damsel in distress is still as popular a storyline as ever.'

The Major ground his jaw.

'Listen,' she said. 'I didn't come here to threaten you. I came here to do business. But like I said, I went from twenty million to a lot less overnight. I need something to go forward with or . . .' She looked away again. 'I don't even know what. But if I have to spin this? I will.'

She wasn't wrong. He knew it wouldn't take much more than an accusation of sexual impropriety – amply supported by the viral snapshot, as well – to turn sympathy her way. He would become another casualty of the political correctness wars. 'Is there anything else?' he said.

Erykah frowned and thought a moment. 'I guess that's it.'

The Major looked out the window. He knew when he had been outplayed. And outplayed by someone who wasn't even committed to the game in the same way he was, at that. The noise of city traffic ebbed and flowed. The constant sound of footfall in the café underpinned their conversation like the ticking second hand of his bedroom clock.

'Before I forget,' Erykah added, 'I'll need cash for this. If you're sending me out on errands, then there are going to be expenses.'

'You can't have it.'

'Can't I? Let's call it a tax. For not doing due diligence.' She offered her hand. He made no move to shake it but they both knew the deal was done. 'We'll iron out the particulars another time, shall we?' Erykah raised the coffee cup to her lips and slurped down the last of her drink, holding the stare. The flicker of doubt he had seen on her face when she came in was gone, for now. Whitney was the first one to look away.

: 15 :

A constant traffic of pedestrians poured along the Victoria Embankment. The grey and drizzle did not stop tourists from snapping endless, unremarkable photos of the Thames. If anything they seemed to think it was better when it was raining, more like the London of their imaginations. Picturesque. Major Abbott found that he too was part of the scenery. Every few minutes or so someone would stop and do a double take, sniggering to their companions and pointing in his direction. The Major tried his best to look nonchalant, which, as a silver-haired man with a moustache and a kilt alone on a park bench in the middle of the afternoon, was a challenge. This was not Scotland, after all. And if they did recognise him, what was he to them? A joke of a would-be politician? A washed-up memoirist and soldier? Or notable only as the son of a bona fide hero?

The Major's father might have landed in Normandy in 1944, wet behind the ears with a new commission and no field experience, but he got his baptism of fire by surviving the beach and liberating a French village along with the rest of Four-Five Commando. The next January he was deployed in Europe again. This time heavy shelling took out every member of the company apart from himself and two seventeen-year-old privates who still went on to complete the task they had been assigned, unbelievably holding a crucial crossroads open until Allied tanks arrived seventy-two hours later, on their way to Montforterbeek and Germany.

Lieutenant Abbott and the two privates found themselves the toast of the media when they returned. They were dubbed the Good Guys by the press and newsmen fell over themselves to profile the group, and in particular the young officer, now swiftly promoted to captain. A bestselling book soon followed. The Good Guys' exploits were optioned for a film starring Anthony Steel and a university lectureship in military history and a column in the *Sunday Telegraph* for Abbott Senior was inevitable.

There was no one who could compare to the public's image of

Captain George Abbott. Least of all his son Whitney. Growing up as the only son of a war hero was objectively not the worst upbringing in the world, but it was never going to be easy.

George Abbott was not an attentive father and his wife was more concerned with gardening than with parenting, so they sent their boy away to school early. Whitney saw his parents on school holidays and often not even then.

After university he floated around in a few jobs, was set up in promising appointments by friends of the family. But though he stayed in work, he never excelled. Half-hearted attempts at teaching and a diploma in law fell by the wayside. There had to be something more, some arena in which his natural superiority would surely shine through?

Eventually, and with only six months left before he would have been too old to qualify, he drifted to Lympstone for Marine training. It was there he realised the real legacy of being who he was: everyone knew who his father was, and for once this was not a good thing. They more than loved the elder Abbott there; they revered him. Whitney couldn't help but disappoint everyone he met by comparison. Even after the Falklands, even after writing a book, he always knew that in the eyes of most there was no way he could measure up.

The Major thought about the encounter in the coffee shop. His left eye twitched uncontrollably. How dare she. How very dare she. That bloody woman had got the better of him.

Though perhaps, on reflection, she had a point? They needed more faces in the press and hers would do as well as any. Better, in fact.

At least he was out of the office. There he would be withering under the glare of his secretary or fearing the inevitable afternoon check-in call with his wife. There was no way of getting work done, no peace to be found indoors, if you were being overlooked by women.

The Major ground his teeth, 'Cunts,' he muttered, and kicked dirt in the direction of a hobbling pigeon that was circling his feet. A group of old women in plastic rain hats looked up at him, startled by the sudden outburst. He smiled and nodded, looked away and hoped they hadn't recognised him.

At last, his appointment turned up. Over the road he spotted a woman's figure in a parka and oversized black sunglasses standing at the foot of Cleopatra's Needle. She gazed up at the monument's point and looked down at what might have been a London guidebook grasped in her hands. The worn hieroglyphs on the granite obelisk made no impression on the capital's modern skyline. A monument to a time when the engineering achievements of men were both more impressive, and less so.

The furry otter skin sporran around the Major's waist started vibrating. It was her. He fumbled with the clasp and extracted a cheap pay-as-you-go phone. 'I see you, hen harrier,' he said.

'And I see you, Whitney,' the woman said. Between them lanes of traffic crawled past.

The Major harrumphed. 'Have you forgotten to use the code name?' Sightline confirmation was no reason to let protocol slip.

She heaved a sigh. 'I see you, golden eagle. And by that I mean I really do see you. You're not exactly blending in, are you? Is it too much to at least try to be a little less conspicuous?'

'I am dressed in my normal workday attire,' the Major grumbled. 'You on the other hand appear to have come out wrapped up for Everest base camp.' His vision was not as sharp as it used to be, and he had to admit it wasn't warm, but she had clearly put on a far larger coat than her correct size, and what appeared to be two hats. Perhaps it was to disguise her figure with layers of extra clothing underneath. The overall effect was of a misassembled mannequin lurching along the Embankment.

'Well then, next time we'll dress each other,' she snapped. 'If there is a next time. Which I doubt. I have news, and it's not good. At this rate we'll be finished by the end of the month.'

A double-decker tourist bus crept through the road traffic, obscuring his view of her while its tannoy blared random facts about the sights on the Thames. Evidently the needle was not Cleopatra's at all, but rather had been carved for some obscure pharaoh he had never heard of. At least New Labour and that crew hadn't seen fit to redub it the 'Tesco Extra Needle' in return for an all-expenses holiday in Tuscany, he mused.

'What news?' he said. 'Has the kitten seen the kibble?'

'Eh? What?' The woman's voice grew even more irritable.

'You know – has the bucket been in the well. Are the ducks on the pond yet?' Another bloody group of tourists paused to snap his picture. Whitney waved them off impatiently.

'Fuck's sake, Whitney, enough with that stupid code,' she said. 'I've managed to get a sneak peek of the post-mortem results.'

'Good or bad?'

'Terrible. Either the pathologist wasn't as much of an idiot as we were led to believe, or someone else has been having a word with the police. Either way it doesn't matter. Bottom line is that this business with the corpse refuses to lie down and die. You said you had a fixer,' she hissed. 'You said this was under control.'

'You were asking for a miracle,' the Major said. 'Even the best fixer couldn't put Humpty Dumpty back together again.'

'Whoever your boys were, they ballsed up this job. Rather spectacularly so.'

The Major snorted. 'If the police had anything we wouldn't be having this conversation, we would be in a cell somewhere waiting for our solicitors. There is no evidence connecting us. Without evidence, there will never be a trial. Even if there was there would never be a conviction.'

'Now it's a trial, is it?' the woman squeaked. 'How about we rewind to the bit where you and your mates guaranteed the body would never be found? And then, when it was, that it would look like a natural death?'

'Nobody guaranteed anything,' the Major said, flashing a pearly smile at a pack of giggling teenaged girls who stopped to take a picture of him on their pink smartphones. 'The deal was they got the thing far away from London, no questions asked. They held up their end of the bargain. The situation developed because your goods were in poor condition. Even the thickest doctor in the land wouldn't have missed a slit throat.'

'I had no control over that. The puppy was over the wall . . . arse, you know what I mean. There was no way to make it look clean. What was I meant to do, wait for him to poison himself on a bottle of water he never opened? You said you would take care of this. And you dropped the ball.'

The Major's smile was as rigid as his military bearing. He spoke through clenched teeth. 'It was not my fault, but you are making it my responsibility,' he said. An understatement if ever there was one. Anyone else faced with the conundrum she was up against would have slandered their enemies, or at least tried to buy their silence. His darling goddaughter had opted instead for murder. He had always known that she was ambitious, but he had not expected her to go so far as bumping someone off. 'I did my best to come to your aid. Many wouldn't have done.'

He remembered the night well: a panicked call, late, at his office. She refused to say what had happened over the phone – repeating that he should come to her house straight away and tell no one.

The Major was familiar with the good and the evil that people are capable of. Even so, nothing had prepared him for what he witnessed that night.

When he arrived he listened at the door: a voice somewhere deep inside, but no one coming to answer. He let himself in with the spare key. Inside the rooms were dark, the radiators cold, as if whoever was there had come home in a hurry. Only one light was on, the downstairs bathroom in the back hallway.

The scene in the bathroom was like something from a horror film. The Major had walked in to find her leaning over the bath, a kitchen knife in one hand, her arms covered up to her elbows in bright arterial blood. A body was slumped half in and half out of the bath and there was as much blood pooling on the floor as there was going down the drain.

The worst part was the man wasn't even dead yet.

He had seen plenty of gore in his time but the sheer impulsive violence of it shook him. He had her pegged as a stone-hearted calculator, not physically violent. He didn't ask the details and she didn't look as if she could have told him anyway. He barred the bathroom door, guided her to the living room with a couple of Valium and a bottle of whisky, then got on the hooter to the boys. When he flipped on the flat's other lights, he could see that the blood started in the front room and went the whole length of the ground floor.

It was the right thing to do, he told himself. If you botched a shot on a grouse, you were the one who had to finish the job and break its neck – end it quickly, don't let them suffer. Anything else was torture. Anything else was unacceptable.

That was what he told himself, but it didn't stop him feeling tainted with the stain of murder.

To attack a man was one thing. There were many times when it was, if not justifiable in the eyes of the law, at least understandable. In war. In self-defence. But to go after someone in cold blood, that was something else. The kind of people who did things like that were the ones you stayed far away from on the battlefield. Only in this instance he had no choice but to try to make it right.

'You know I'll always be grateful for what you've done,' she said. 'I thought we had a plan. The story put around was that the Professor was suicidal. You get a corpse in a bag washed up on a beach, this starts to look a little unlikely, no?'

A less patient man would have walked away from the situation long before now, but the Major had a lot of time for his goddaughter. Not to mention common business interests these days. 'There was nothing we could do about those kayakers,' he said. 'It was on a remote island off Scotland where there isn't even a road. You have to understand. There was a million to one chance of it being found.'

'Yeah, and the one in a million happened. You could at least have taken the head.'

'And then what? Heads don't simply evaporate you know.' The Major sighed. The situation with the body was neither here nor there. There was nothing they could do about it now, so why not move on? As they said in the corps: mag to grid, get rid. Next problem. 'Now about the Internet – the tweeter, or whatever it is.'

'I know,' she sighed. The headlines had been mortifying. The entire situation was less than ideal, but that picture – the Major caught ogling Erykah's cleavage at the moment the press conference fell apart – was devastating. If it had been one or the other they could have weathered it. Without that picture, the tweet might well have faded out as quickly as it surfaced. Without that tweet, the picture would have been brushed off as unimportant. Both together, though. Sex plus dodgy money equals irresistible scandal. 'I hope you're not putting the same men on that job too,' she said.

'Obviously not,' the Major fibbed. 'This requires a far more subtle touch.' And where subtlety was unavailable, Seminole Billy would have to do. 'I have a computer expert hunting them down, we'll have a name before the week is out.' He was lying through his teeth. But she was so wrapped up in her own cocoon of half-truths he wagered she would never detect it.

'I should hope so,' the woman snapped. 'You're still on for Cameron Bridge at the weekend, but if this sinks any lower we'll have to call it off.'

'Remind me – that was the long march idea, was it?'

'Highlands to Holyrood, we're branding it,' she said. 'Over the hills and glens. Real march of the people sort of thing.'

'Christ,' he sighed. 'I'm not as young as I used to be, you know . . .'

'Whitney, calm yourself,' she said. 'No tents involved. You will be on the trails only for photo ops. I've had someone book luxury B&Bs. But there's no sense doing it if you're going to be accosted by Internet trolls the entire way.'

'It would be a pity not to go,' the Major said. 'It would look bad to never even campaign in the country I am proposing to represent.'

'We'll cross that bridge as and when. This is the more pressing problem. If this situation gets any more out of control you're as ruined as I am.'

'What about asking that woman from the press conference to come to Cameron Bridge?' he said. He hoped it sounded casual. 'What was her name?'

'Erykah,' the woman said. 'Why?'

'Oh, you know,' The Major said. 'Young face, diversity, all of that fashionable yikyak.' Not to mention she was now in possession of a recording of him admitting the lottery was a fraud connected to the SLU. He thought it best not to mention this part for now.

His goddaughter sighed. 'She was hardly a credit at the press conference,' she said. 'All that *Braveheart* nonsense, and then her shirt pops open. Not to mention the tabloid headlines about that murder.'

'Sex sells, doesn't it?'

'Dear Whitney, you're so predictable,' the woman said. 'You want to fuck her.'

'Now now, vulgar,' he said. 'It simply occurred to me because with the amount of negative attention she has had, she's still willing to play along.' And indeed, he observed, the lady was unflappable. 'Maybe put her on the payroll. Her husband's a sad sack, but she could be the sort of person we need to stay on side.'

'Payroll, I see,' the woman said. He could see her pacing on the other side of the road, impatient. But even without seeing her he would have heard the irritation in her voice. 'I take it her cooperation comes with strings attached.'

'She wants money, yes. Not unreasonable given the risks of further involvement.' Not that he had seen much of the money yet. He was taking it on trust for now. In any case, their lives were too intertwined for her to get away with not paying him.

'Washed up fortysomething with no career to speak of and a murder scandal in her past?' she said. 'You'll have to excuse me if I don't see this as a PR win.'

'That might be one way to look at it. Or, you could say, Teflon woman takes life on the chin and keeps going,' he said. 'You must admit she looks great on camera. Not many of those to the pound. What was it you said me once? All publicity is good publicity.'

The more he talked, the better she sounded, in fact. Might want to watch that – in case Erykah had ambitions beyond her station. Wouldn't want to find himself turfed out in favour of an uppity woman with ideas. 'With a bit of guidance from myself, naturally,' he added. 'She is nowhere near ready to fly on her own as yet.'

'Mister Moral High Ground telling me how it's done, now?' she said. 'Apologies – *Major* Moral High Ground.' She paused. 'Fine. Talk to her, feel out the lay of the land.'

'We have a morning meeting tomorrow,' he said.

'Morning meeting,' she snorted. 'Is that what you're calling it these days?' She thought a moment. 'Could work. She does have a certain appeal. If you like that sort of thing. Let me know how it goes.' She rang off, no pleasantries. Business as usual then.

The Major watched from over the road as she strode away from Cleopatra's Needle. She didn't look in his direction for even a moment, and seemed to be already talking to someone else on her mobile.

What must it be like for her? he wondered. At least his public and private personas were roughly in accord with each other. She, on the other hand, had to play a very careful game. Her public face had to be carefully maintained, painstakingly constructed. The puppetmaster had to stay behind the curtain. Given a choice between soft power and hard glory, he would not have chosen the former, himself. But then she was nothing like him and never had been.

He had known her almost her entire life, and she was a fiercely determined woman. One who almost always got what she wanted. And for the first time in a long time it seemed as if things might not go her way.

: **16** :

'What are you doing the rest of the day?' the Major asked.

'Shopping, seeing as I'm in town already.' Erykah snapped her bra behind her back and eased the straps up over her shoulders. Had she just done this? The sticky sweat of morning sex assured her that, yes, she had.

The diamond rings caught her eye. Her hands seemed to belong to someone else. Was she the same woman, with everything that had happened in the last few days? And after what had happened with Nicole. Doing it for love hadn't turned out so well. Maybe it was fine to be having sex for all the wrong reasons for once.

So far, though, the thrill of checking in to a hotel first thing in the morning for an illicit rendezvous had turned out to be the best part of the experience. Erykah was disappointed to find the Major's skills in bed were not at all what his image promised. She had imagined old world romance, a man who knew his way around a woman, a slow hand. Not erection pills and emptying the minibar at nine a.m. Whatever genuine passion might have once ignited the man was long gone.

To be fair, it had been a long time since she'd slept with a man. Grayson had been . . . well, he had been her first, and she supposed it was all right. Things in the beginning had been passionate with Rab, with quickies in restaurants, and one memorable time on a picnic table in a park at night in winter. But after marriage they settled into a routine: oral sex for her orgasm, intercourse for his. Then it happened less and less frequently until it didn't happen at all. Not with her, anyway. And maybe being with Nicole had altered her expectations considerably.

The Major approached sex like someone ticking a grim but necessary chore off a list. A couple of times she caught his unfocused eyes gazing out of the window. Probably revisiting the mental highlight reel of his earlier conquests.

'Remarkable,' he said when the deed was done, and fell back on the sheets. For a frightening fraction of a second she had worried he had keeled over dead.

She looked at her hands again. Same hands. Same woman. If doing this was supposed to mark a kind of passing over from a good woman to a bad one, she certainly didn't feel any different.

There had been a moment in the café when she wasn't sure. When it could have gone either way. Walk out, not tell him about the recording, see the job through as things stood. Divorce. Go back to square one, if there was such a thing. What she was really looking at looked more like a black hole.

The sleet against the window there had been so thick that, looking out from the café to the street, it was like a dull mirror. She had turned away from the Major for a second, afraid she might cry.

In the glass, though, it hadn't been her own reflection she saw. It was Grayson's. The last seconds in the courtroom after the sentence and before they took him away. His eyes locked on hers, his lips moving. What was he saying? What had he been trying to tell her then?

'Good. I have a job for you,' the Major said. He flipped a business card in her direction. 'Check out this man. He won't be in his office today. Get in and see what you can find, and bring it back to me.'

Erykah leaned over from getting dressed and picked up the card from the floor. The print was small and raised, the card stock stamped with university insignia. Her alma mater. She knew the building. 'Are they expecting me?'

'The opposite,' the Major said. He leaned and checked his reflection in a mirror. The skin of his back was mottled with freckles and moles, hanging like a wet bed sheet over what had once been a broad pair of shoulders. 'Use those,' he gestured at her in the reflection, 'feminine wiles to get in.'

She watched his face for some kind of sign of what he was thinking. Who was he protecting, really? And as much as he was an old blowhard hustling for a last scrap at fame, he also had discretion etched deep in his psyche. Whoever had this much control over him must be very important indeed.

'You haven't told me much about yourself,' Erykah said. She looked up in what she hoped was a seductive manner. 'Why did you decide to switch from the service to politics?'

He caught her eyes in the mirror. 'I thought you said you had read my book.'

'Oh right, yes, of course I did.' She giggled, and tried not to cringe at how false it sounded. The paperback was Rab's, and she wouldn't have known they had a copy of it at all, had she not been looking at their bookshelves only days earlier. 'But that's not the same thing as getting it from the horse's mouth, is it?'

'Mmmph,' the Major grunted. 'Another time. Right now you have a job to do,' he said, and cinched the kilt straps around his waist. 'I clearly can't go in there without someone noticing me. As for the two gentlemen I would normally call on, they wouldn't get past the door of a flophouse without raising suspicion. I need someone who can pass in public crowds. Someone who blends in.'

'How will I know when I find what I'm looking for?' she said.

'You won't,' the Major sighed as he rushed her out the door. 'None of us do. If it were that easy we would have done it already.'

She walked down the street, Googling the name on the card. So it was that missing geologist. She slightly recalled the story from over a month ago. Something to do with a disputed suicide note, or similar. Though as far as she knew he hadn't been found.

Erykah stood in the end of a Tube carriage and turned the whole situation over again and again in her mind. It didn't make sense: The Major and a couple of guys straight out of prison? The scheme had all the subtlety and complexity of a middle-school shoplifting ring. No way was that all that was going on, no way were they the only people involved. And where was the money coming from?

In spite of being missing, the university website still listed Damian Schofield's office location and open hours as if nothing was amiss. Not the sort of glamorous assignment she thought she was signing up for. She had envisioned herself rubbing elbows with the media elite, not trying to break in to an academic office.

Erykah got off a stop early and decided to walk over the river. Without really thinking about it she found herself on a towpath on the north side of the Thames. Across the water, the Tideway rowing clubs clustered on the bank. Once upon a time this was her patch: the Barn Elms boathouse, where an afternoon taster session organised for underprivileged teens first caught her imagination. A couple of years later she was rowing from the university boathouse only a few hundred metres away, one of the best student clubs in the country. Better even, to those in the know, than Oxford or Cambridge.

On the shore was a group of boats all trying to launch at the same time. Belligerent geese snapped at the ankles of the rowers, while a coach on a rib shouted at them through a loudhailer. It was a scene as familiar to her as the back of her own hand; one she had been part of for years.

The Tideway section of the river was miles downstream from Molesey and it was, as its name indicated, the tidal part of the Thames. The difference between low water and high water was huge – not to mention the stream of the tide when it was running at its fastest. Nearly all new rowers here found themselves in trouble at some point, either from trying to turn a boat too close to the pylons of the bridges, or running into the infamous Black Buoy.

It had been decades since Erykah trained on the Tideway. It had a reputation, and not a good one. The first outing was nothing like she had ever experienced. Thrown into a wooden boat with seven other shivering and frightened novice girls, wondering how long it would be before the tiny narrow craft dumped them in the river. And yet, miraculously, it didn't. The cox steered them downstream, then patiently explained to them how to turn the boat around, then they came back on the eddy.

Erykah was instantly hooked. It was amazing to realise the power of the water, how it could take you where it wanted you to go. Even the strongest crews, at best, were only working with what the water was already doing.

It was also where she first saw the city in a new way. Not from the streets, buses, and parks where she grew up. From the water, as Londoners must have navigated it for thousands of years, it whispered an ancient history, the meandering river carving out the fate of a city before the proliferation of bridges and tunnels that crossed it now.

One of her first times in a pair had been here, too. It wasn't a good outing. The tide had turned during the outing, but Erykah, not realising it, steered the boat in the wrong direction when they stopped to turn and go back to the club. Other crews had been shouting at them from downstream, but it wasn't until the stream grabbed the bow of the boat and tries to push them under a moored catamaran that she realised her mistake. The girl in the stroke seat screamed and lost control of her oar. The boat wobbled dangerously, and the gate of Erykah's rigger was crushed against the catamaran's hull. The angle of the turn meant that while crews already on the water had been able to see their disaster before it happened, the larger boat blocked the sight line to shore.

The water rushing under their boat was speeding up, tugging them further under the moored cat. Erykah reached out with one arm and tried to push them off, but it was like pushing against a brick wall. Underneath, the rush of water going through the catamaran's two hulls was like a giant, sucking drain.

Her crew mate started undoing her feet from the blocks. She was going to swim for it. 'What are you doing?' Erykah said. 'If you jump the stream will carry you under the boat. You'll die!'

'I have a stage nine swimming certificate!' she said. 'It's only a few metres away!'

Nothing at that moment seemed less relevant to Erykah than a swimming certificate, but the look in the girl's wide blue eyes brooked no argument. It was obvious she would be pulled between the hulls and not calmly swimming to shore. Erykah was stunned at the confidence, even though it was clearly foolish and dangerous to leave the boat, even though they had been told never to abandon a boat if you went in, unless it was sinking.

Luckily for them it never came to that. The shouting crews on the water must have attracted attention, and two coaching launches sped out from the bank of the Thames to rescue them. Erykah and the other girl were hurried back to shore in one rib while a second one dragged the empty pair behind it. The river going from slack to a turn was subtle and easy to get wrong. Making that choice could have killed her and her partner, and it tore a hole in their boat the size of her hand.

But everyone in the Tideway had a near-miss story just like that one. The Tideway produced a different breed of rower to anywhere else. The rougher the water, the more satisfying the outing. Were the waves high? Tap your oar down harder and get on with it. Was the wind hard? Lean against it and push your weight in. Big wash coming off a motor boat? Row across it, hard. If you almost drown? Laugh it off.

Rowing clubs from Putney to Chiswick trained every day on the same stretch of the river that the Boat Race crews of Oxford and Cambridge only dared touch once a year. Molesey rowers complained about the unpredictable streams and vicious steering down here. 'More bumper cars that real rowing,' some sneered. 'Bring a sick bag.' But the fact was that, compared to the Tideway, the upper Thames was a broken beast, a glorified millpond.

The water was glinting and furious and ready to swallow all comers. In the twenty years since she last trained there Erykah had forgotten how much she loved it. She had thought rowing at Molesey & Hampton Anglian would make her into a more refined rower, a better competitor. Maybe a champion. But for all the cups and points won over the years, she was no closer now than she had been then.

The walk from the boathouses to the university was exactly as she remembered it. Students crowded the lobby of the university's main building, rushing to get to morning lectures on time. A security guard stood by the door and checked ID cards. She didn't have one and shrugged apologetically. The guard's eyes caught hers then slipped down to her chest as he stepped back to let her pass anyway. Erykah smiled and swished past the checkpoint.

The Internet hadn't revealed much about the target that she didn't already know. Apart from some news coverage right after his disappearance there wasn't a lot else to go on. He had a number of papers in scientific journals, most on oil survey techniques. The departmental website had a brief sketch of his career to date. Nothing unusual she could see there. Some work in Argentina, Ecuador, and the North Atlantic for industry, before moving into academia. One site had scans of an old magazine profile, complete with a photo showing Schofield leaning on the desk in his office, its top piled high with papers and notebooks. He was wearing a shirt open at the neck and a pair of corduroy trousers, and had the lean and rangy look of a man who spent a lot of time outdoors. There was not much else, at least not online. She would have to wing it.

It seemed the breast inspector in security at the main entrance might be her only human obstacle. The fourth floor of the environmental sciences building was restricted to card entry only. No guards to charm, but a swipe pad that needed a staff card to unlock the door. No security camera that she could see. Erykah hovered by the doors, walking up and down a few steps, trying to look as though she had just arrived. After a few minutes a group of students exiting the department held the door open for her. 'Cheers,' she said, and slipped inside.

No secretarial staff in sight. Her luck was holding. The room she wanted was around the corner on the right. Damian Schofield's office had a brass nameplate on it, the little black plastic In/Out slider below set permanently to Out.

She jiggled the door handle. Locked.

There was that book her mother had bought her. Lock picking was in it, although not in any great detail. What did it say? That picking a lock wasn't done at all the way they do it in films and television. That you needed two tools, not one. One to keep the tension and start turning it round, another to feel for locations of the tumblers.

Deep breath. In the bottom of her bag was a multitool for rigging rowing boats. She had never picked a lock before, but it couldn't be that hard, surely?

Erykah flicked out the mini nail file on the multitool and jammed it in the slot. It turned slightly, but the tumblers were still stuck fast. She needed something to tease them out. She reached into her hair and extracted a slender hairpin. Straightened, it slid in above the mini file. The tip of the hairpin raked across a series of what felt like bumps. Now what? She was trying to figure out what to do next when she heard footsteps coming round the corner.

'Hello?' the man asked as he approached. 'Can I help you?' He pushed a pair of wire frame glasses up his nose.

Erykah spun round and backed up against the doorknob. She smiled widely, hoping to distract him while getting her tools out of the lock behind her back. 'Hi! I'm here to meet Professor Schofield,' she trilled. The file was stuck fast in there now – she pried at the multitool, but the angle was awkward and it wouldn't pull free.

'Schofield?' the man said with an odd look on his face. He might have been mid-thirties, possibly, but dressed like a pensioner. His sloped shoulders and squinted eyes spoke of someone who had spent most hours of his adult life staring at a computer screen. The sort of man who, if a book fell off a shelf and landed on him, would have apologised to the book.

She put on her most cooperative smile. 'This is his office, right? It says he's out? Maybe I could . . . harummmccckkkkk . . .' Erykah coughed to try to cover the noise, tugging rather hard now on the file. '. . . leave him a message?'

'You have an appointment with him?'

'I'm an old colleague . . . Hraaaackkkk . . .' She coughed again, a deep, alveoli-wracking rattle to cover the sound of shaking the handle as hard as she could. To her great relief, the file slid free. She palmed the multitool and hairpin with one hand and smoothed her hair with the other. 'I mean, an old friend. I'm an old friend.'

'And you didn't hear? About his disappearance.'

Erykah held a hand to her chest in mock surprise. 'What? Damian?' she said. 'God, I hope Sheila and the kids are OK.'

The man gulped. 'I'm Peter Graves. Interim head of the department since – since the incident.' His hand fluttered out in the direction of her shoulder, failed to land, and retreated back his pocket. 'Can I help you?'

'Oh my God,' Erykah said and dabbed at the corners of her eyes. 'I was in town for the day and thought I might drop in, that's all. It's been years . . .' She took a deep breath. 'When did it happen?'

'Last month,' Peter said. 'It was all over the papers.'

'I was away,' Erykah said. 'At the Weybridge Head.' It was a pointless lie, but she felt she had to say something.

Peter nodded. He had no idea what the Weybridge Head was. 'What did you say your name was?'

'I didn't say. It's – it's Sarah,' she said and held out her hand. 'Sarah Miller.' His handshake was limp and clammy.

'I'll be sure to pass on your regards, Mrs Miller.'

'Thank you so much,' she sighed. 'I don't suppose . . . I mean, do you mind telling me what happened?'

'He just disappeared, according to his family,' Peter lowered his voice. 'Met police are speculating it was a suicide. Been in all the papers.'

Erykah clapped a hand to her mouth. 'My God,' she said. 'But why?'

'The pressure, maybe,' Peter said. 'There had been a sexual harassment accusation.' His low voice and shrug told Erykah that Peter did not believe that to be a serious claim. 'Or maybe it was that he hadn't had anything published in years. He had been hinting he was working on something big, and then . . . well, nothing. You're only as good as your last work, you know.'

'How dreadful,' Erykah said. If the press had already been and gone, though, there might not be anything in the office left worth finding. 'You must have had reporters all over.'

'They tried,' Peter said. 'We had one girl from the *Mail* removed from the premises by police. They caught her trying to crawl in a window. Unfortunately for her, it was the window of the building's security director.'

'Horrors!' She was aware of how fake her expressions were now, but Peter didn't seem to have caught on. 'How dare they. What a pack of jackals.'

'Some of them, sure,' Peter said. 'Although, there was a radio journalist I used to see around the department quite a bit, but she didn't come by after he disappeared and I think she was working on something with Damian. Livvy, Livia, something like that. She knew how to keep respectful limits. London Chat, I think it was? Can't say the same of her profession in general.'

'And the police have already been?'

Peter nodded. 'They interviewed everyone in the department. None of us had much to tell them.'

'Wow, how terrible for you,' she simpered. 'I bet they turned the place upside down.'

'Oh no, they only took a few interviews then left,' Peter said. 'Schofield was very secretive about his work, and had been working from home after the accusations surfaced. That was how they found the suicide note a few days later.'

'This must be a difficult time for you as well.'

'A little,' Peter said. 'Though I wouldn't have said we were close. We're poles apart, really; Schofield is an applied geology man whereas I run with the planetary soil composition crew.' He cleared his throat. 'None of the department is involved, naturally.'

'No, of course not,' Erykah said. She checked her watch. What would be perfect now was a distraction, some pretext for moving Dr Dull out of her way. She might not have another chance to get in the office. 'Anyway, I should go. I'm so sorry. Sorry to bother you.'

Peter nodded. 'No, I'm sorry, you couldn't have known.'

She spun on her heel and took a step. She slipped her phone out of a pocket and dialled the department number, then turned back. Down the hall, a muffled phone started ringing. Erykah snuck her mobile back in her bag and smiled, turning back to Peter. 'You know, this may sound awkward but I loaned Damian a book ages ago. Could I just pop my head in and have a look?'

Peter's eyes, panicked, looked down the hall towards the sound of the ringing phone and back at Erykah. 'Ah, that's my office phone,' he said.

'You should get that before they hang up.' She snuck a look down into her bag where her phone, set to silent, kept dialling the number.

He looked panicked. 'Sorry, yes,' Peter said. 'I'll be a minute.'

'Can I just grab the book while you do that? It'll only take a moment and I have a train to catch,' Erykah said.

'Yes, yes.' Peter pulled a keychain from his pocket. He tried a couple of keys before jiggling the handle open. 'I'll only be a minute,' he said. Erykah smiled and watched as he disappeared down the hallway.

The office smelled of dust and old paper, a warm and not unpleasant odour, like a library. As far as she could see it looked untouched, only the slight disorganisation of someone in their own office, not the massive mess that surely would have been left if the police had been in searching for clues.

She poked around the shelves and tables. There were a few framed photographs of Professor Schofield in decades past, when he was a keen mountain climber. He didn't look the kind to prey on young students – but then, it was always the ones you least suspected, wasn't it? Odd that detail hadn't made it into the press. One photo was much more recent, of Schofield receiving an award from Lionel Brant. And a map of an offshore region of Argentina, where Schofield had started his career in oil exploration.

The desk was a jumble of papers. Stacks of folders and notes were piled up and in disarray. There were a couple of word-search puzzle books, the kind you picked up in train stations to pass the time, turned over to mark the page he had been working on. Erykah smiled as she recognised a fellow puzzle fiend.

If Schofield had an appointment book, there was no sign of one. But on a whiteboard next to the door she spotted a fresh-looking scribble. There was a date and a time, next to the initials LL. Could that be Lady Livia, the name the Major had accidentally revealed? Peter had mentioned Schofield was working with a journalist on a project, so maybe this was the same person. If they kept that meeting, she had been to see him only two days before he disappeared. During the winter break when the building would have been deserted. So Peter was wrong – Schofield had been in his office, but was probably trying to avoid others in the department knowing that he was there. There was no way to take the board with her, so she snapped a photo of it with her phone. Good. It was a start.

There was also an ancient computer – one of those big cream-coloured boxes from the '90s. Sitting on top of the keyboard were three red notebooks and a folder stuffed with printouts. Was this the last thing he had been writing? A pencil rested on top of the papers and a thin film of dust had settled over the lot.

She shook the computer mouse a couple of times and was surprised to see the monitor flicker back on. It went straight to a password screen. Might as well try and guess it, right? She typed in 'password'. No luck. Then 'Schofield'. Nothing.

She looked around the room. What would be memorable to this man? His wife's name? A child? Did he have a dog, or a favourite band? Her eyes alighted on a silver-framed photo collage. Pictures of llamas on rocky outcrops, the broad bay of some unknown city with jagged mountains behind. One photo tucked in the corner. Schofield smiled into the camera from a snowy mountain path in Argentina. The summit ridge behind him was steep with bare rock showing through. Coils of rope hung over one shoulder and an ice axe rested on the ground next to his boots and crampons. At the bottom was a caption picked out in white lettering: Guanaco.

Erykah tapped it in and watched the screen kick back to life.

The Internet browser window was still on the department's homepage. She clicked down the menu and found the browsing history – completely empty. Odd. As if it had been emptied, in fact. There was no time to go through his locally stored files, but the dates showed nothing being accessed in the month before his disappearance. Which meant either what she was after had never been here, or someone else had been in weeks ago and already cleaned it out.

She had the strangest feeling, as if she was standing in someone's tomb. Nothing she had seen explained why the Major would be interested in this man, or why he would need to get into this office. Was Schofield someone who also tried to make a deal with the SLU somehow, and then . . . Erykah swallowed uncomfortably. Would someone else be doing this to her, in a few weeks' time? She needed to know what it was she was getting for the Major before she handed anything over to him. The recording she had made in the coffee shop was some insurance, but not enough. And if he wouldn't tell her what was really going on she would have to figure it out herself.

She shook her head. There was no time to think about that, not right now.

Erykah's gaze settled on the desk phone. If no one had been in, could his last call be connected to the disappearance? She picked up the receiver and dialled 1471 to find out what the last incoming number was. An outside number – she scribbled it on the top of the papers before stuffing the whole lot into her handbag. An unopened bottle of water was next to it. She grabbed that for later. Spying was thirsty work.

Footsteps sounded in the hallway behind her. She switched off the monitor so it wouldn't be obvious she had just been using the computer.

'Was it anything important?' she said when Peter reappeared with a coffee cup in his hand.

'Was what important?' he said, a bit confused. 'Oh, the phone! No one there. Must have seen one of those telesales calls,' he said. 'Find what you needed?' Peter tried to casually lean against the doorway, but his stiffly affected manner was of someone who never leaned against anything, casually or otherwise.

She grabbed a volume off the nearest shelf. 'Here it is,' she said. 'I'll be heading off now.'

'You read Russian?' he asked.

Erykah looked at the paperback she had grabbed. 'Oh, uh, yes,' she said. The writing was entirely in Cyrillic script. Great. It looked like some sort of conference proceedings, though for all she knew it could have been the Book of Mormon. 'I mean, da. I mean I have to go now,' she smiled, and squeezed past him in the doorway.

'Do svidaniya!' Peter said. 'Goodbye!'

Erykah looked back and half waved. 'Yeah, sure. I mean, da! I mean byeeeee!' she trilled. She headed straight downstairs and out of the building as fast as she could.

At the bottom of the stairs she turned and walked out of the double glass doors. She paused. There was an old Mercedes, engine running, in a bay clearly marked LOADING AND TAXIS ONLY. She should have figured the Major would put those two goons on her tail.

Erykah fingered the edge of the files stashed in her bag. If she was going to try to figure out what was going on herself, she needed some time to look through the papers. But how?

Erykah hung back on the edge of a group of students milling by the doors and pretended to peruse flyers and announcements pinned to a notice board outside. She stole glances over to where the car was standing. Seminole Billy's lips were moving but she was too far away to hear what was going on. Probably talking to Buster in the boot. He didn't seem to have seen her, not yet.

The building had to have a back exit somewhere. Erykah followed a group of students back inside where the friendly security guard waved her through again. She stopped and put a hand gently on his forearm. 'Is there a loo on this floor?' she asked.

'Through the fire doors, by the stairwell,' he smiled.

'Thank you.' Erykah walked away as quickly as she could. Through the double doors a corridor went two ways. One side to the men's and women's toilets, another to a door marked *Deliveries: Authorised Personnel Only*. She was relieved to see that no lock picking would be required; someone had left it propped open.

Erykah walked through and found herself in a bare concrete room strewn with trolleys and pallets. The doors on the far side exited out into a loading bay. She broke into a run, clutching the bag to her chest. If she crossed the university quad and out the other side, she could be on the Tube before Billy and Buster realised she was gone.

: **17** :

Erykah looked up from the pavement on the Euston Road to the brutal slabs of the British Library. It would do as well as anywhere. Better, even.

She put her handbag into a locker and slipped the files from Schofield's office into a clear plastic bag with a fresh notebook and pencil bought in the gift shop. The plastic bag was meant to prevent thieves making off with any priceless books – and it was also a subtle badge of honour that marked out cardholding users of the Library from mere tourists.

Erykah gazed up at the vast column of books encased in panels of glass that rose like a spine from the lower basements through the atrium and onward to the highest floors. Its reassuring solidity seemed to bear up the whole building, and everything that took place within it.

She loved to watch the hushed scholars meandering thoughtfully from reading room to reading room. Her own reader's card, gleaned from the Library back when she was a student, was dutifully renewed every year. There hadn't been many times in the last two decades that she had a need for the Library, but it was comforting to know it was still there.

She winkled the card out of her wallet as she approached the reading room. It reminded her of the time Rab had seen one of the renewal notices in the post and laughed at her. 'What's that, for reading your women's magazines?' he had said. He said it in that way where it was impossible to react correctly: if she pointed out he had been mean, he would laugh and tell her he was only kidding. Banter. So she said nothing, but knew that he really meant it.

As far as she could tell, Seminole Billy and Buster hadn't come back to follow her, nor had they tailed her here. And even if they had, well, so what? She doubted they would be able to get in the building, much less find her inside.

Erykah entered the Humanities II room. It was a large room with row upon row of old wooden desks. Users who needed a book from the counter could submit requests on computer terminals, along with the number of the desk they were at, and a little light would pop on there when the order was ready to collect. It was a wonderfully antique system, crashing up against modern designs, much like the building itself.

Erykah found a desk in a quiet corner and spread out the files and Schofield's notebooks and her own in front of her. She took a deep breath and tried to compose her thoughts. First, the questions: why was the Major so interested in this Schofield person's disappearance? Maybe he held the key to who was behind the SLU. If she could figure out what the connection was, maybe she could turn the tables firmly in her favour.

The notebooks from Schofield's office were bound in heavy, glued canvas and card. Inside, each page had a number stamped in the upper corner – the kind of lab notebooks that were once commonplace in university departments. These days students and staff alike avoided them in favour of computer records. With notebooks like these ones, though, you couldn't just rip out a page or delete an email and pretend nothing had happened. She flipped through to check; no pages seemed to be missing.

Erykah carefully dated the upper right corner of the first page of her fresh notebook. Job one: find out what he had been working on when he disappeared.

Professor Schofield had been a thorough and careful note taker, but the contents of his notebooks were as dry as a lecture: summaries of papers he was reading, notes from meetings with postgrads – and nothing dated past when he disappeared.

There were scratches in the margin that looked as if he'd been trying out missing letters from crossword clues. She smiled at the familiar habit and even recognised one or two from the Christmas papers. She noted with satisfaction that he was also a pen user, rather than scribbling tentatively in pencil. There were little grids of letters that seemed to spell nothing, maybe trying out other clues, or anagrams? He was someone who was good at puzzles. Better even than she was.

As she flipped through one of Schofield's magazines, a single paper floated out.

Erykah snatched it up from the floor. It was a solid grid of letters, carefully written in neat capitals, covering one side of an A4 sheet. Another word search? But no obvious phrases or patterns jumped out – maybe something he was working on in his spare time, a challenge to himself.

The rest of the papers were free of any useful details. Three note-books, and all she had found so far was a phone number and that the guy liked crosswords. It wasn't much to go on. It was hardly anything.

Fresh air. She needed something to clear her mind. She collected her bag from the locker room and went out to the courtyard, where other readers took their breaks.

The brick quadrangle was marked up with pale stone grid lines like a sheet of graph paper, like a crossword square. She paced back and forth and tried to think of what to do next.

Erykah switched her phone on and browsed the news. *Media Mouse Unmasked!* shouted a headline. She tapped to read more. According to a commentator, a 'linguistic analysis' of Media Mouse's tweets proved it was not run by a single person, but was a group account – most likely shared between staffers of the SLU, he claimed.

Erykah looked at the black-and-white photo of the writer. The long face and designer stubble of a middle-aged man wearing an incongru-ous leather bomber scowled back. She laughed out loud. Now here was a public schoolboy trying to act the tough man, probably with visions of James Bond dancing in his head. According to his bio he was a writer as well. She scrolled down to find out what books he had written, but none of the names were familiar. She couldn't have said whether his so-called linguistic analysis was legit or not. But she knew enough about his kind by now to spot a fake a mile away. Leather jacket or no leather jacket, he wouldn't have lasted five minutes where she grew up.

It didn't matter whether he was right, anyway. The papers didn't care. Something had to fill the news cycle. Comment writers weren't reporters; they could fill their columns with half-baked opinions and pure speculation. She recognised the formula from when Grayson was on trial. If they had no new leads, they would run old ones. If they didn't have old leads, they would just make it up. If the press were ever proved wrong all they would have to do – at most – was print a tiny apology on a back page months later.

And it was a reassuring theory for the media class – that the anony-mous person they sought was a prank, and possibly even one of their own. If this guy's Media Mouse theory was right, well, no big deal. But if it was wrong, then there was probably a person somewhere, reading the same made-up claim. A person who was possibly just starting to realise how opportunistic and venal the press could be once they got their claws into a story.

Her hunch, though, was that he was wrong, and that the press were following the wrong strand of the story entirely. She thought about the number from Schofield's phone. Was that LL's number? Or someone else's? She did a quick reverse search on the number but nothing came up in the listings. Probably best not to ring it until she knew more. She would leave that until she was more certain of who – or what – might be waiting on the other end.

Erykah tried a quick Internet search for the words Livia, journalist, and LCC but came up blank. No sign of her on social media any-where, either. Bit unusual for a journalist these days. Especially if, as Peter had said, she was young. Maybe she should call the station and probe gently?

A man answered the call. 'London Chat Central,' he said.

'Hello, could you put me through to Livia's department please?' She put on her most harassed voice and hoped that would make the absence of a surname less obvious.

'No one by that name here,' the man said.

'Are you sure?' Erykah said. 'She's a journalist with LCC.'

The man on the other end chuckled. 'I've been head of security for ten years,' he said. 'If there was anyone by that name in the building, I'd know 'em.'

'Ah. I'm sorry. Just . . . are you sure? Maybe a freelancer?'

'Sorry,' he said. 'Sounds to me like someone's given you a fake name as a wind-up.'

'Oh. Sorry to bother you, then.'

'No problem,' the man said, and Erykah rang off.

There was a coffee kiosk at the far side of the quadrangle. Maybe a drink would help. It was frustrating – so far, she could see no con-nection to Scotland Liberal Unionists or the Major, and in fact no connection between Schofield and anything important at all. The papers he was reading contained a few titbits on Scottish oil field ex-ploration but nothing to suggest an ongoing or significant interest on Schofield's part. As far as Erykah could see the man had nothing else of interest going in in his life. Nothing to hide, apart from the harass-ment allegations. But she knew there was no point trying to chase that up; no amount of sweet-talking in the world should be able to prise the name of the alleged victim out of the university offices. The phone number, the one piece of information she had, came to nothing. And the Major would want the files off her as soon as possible.

The barista behind the counter looked up from her notebook and nodded at Erykah. 'Coffee?' she said. A nametag said the barista's name was Chloe.

'Mmm, maybe something a little lighter on the caffeine,' Erykah said. 'How about a pot of tea? Earl Grey.'

'Coming right up,' Chloe said. The whoosh, whoosh of a rapid-boil tap pierced the hush of the library courtyard. Erykah watched her sprinkle out a careful measure of loose leaves into a strainer, balance it on a ceramic pot, and pour the hot water. The citrus scent of bergamot wafted over. The barista carefully arranged the pot and teacup on a small tray, with a little cup of heated milk. Erykah paid and dropped her change into the tip jar.

'What are you working on?' she asked Chloe, who had been poring over what looked like a Valentine card.

'Oh, this,' she said and rolled her eyes. 'My girlfriend sent me a card on Valentine's Day. Only she's written it in a language I don't understand and I've checked out every book on languages I can find but it's in none of them.'

'Let me see,' Erykah said, and Chloe turned the card and notebook towards her and squinted at the squiggly script. 'I bet that's not a different language at all,' she said. 'It's not a real alphabet.'

'What do you mean?'

'It looks like it's written in English, but she's made up her own symbols instead of letters,' she said. 'Each one of these corresponds to a letter of the alphabet, so all you have to do is replace symbols with the appropriate letters.'

'Easy for you to say,' Chloe smiled. 'I've been trying to figure it out for days and so far nothing.'

'Well, you try to find a word that you think could be something you recognise. That should get you started decoding it.' Erykah scanned the content of the card inscription. 'Like here,' she said, and pointed to two words written in code right at the end. 'There's a four-letter word, a comma, and then a six-letter word. She's probably signed the message, so the four-letter word could be "love", and the six-letter word – is your girlfriend's name six letters long?'

Chloe paused a moment then nodded enthusiastically. 'Yes, it's Alicia,' she said.

'A-L-I-C-I-A?' Erykah asked. Chloe nodded. 'Then look – on the six-letter word, the symbol for the third and fifth letters is the same.'

'That means it must be an I,' Chloe said. 'So if the first position in the four-letter word and the second in the six-letter word are the same . . .'

'Which they are,' Erykah nodded.

'That means that symbol is an L! Cool! Now I get it. Thank you.' She grinned and started subbing in the letters I and L elsewhere in the message. 'Here, have a ginger biscuit,' she said. Erykah started to refuse, but Chloe insisted she have it for free.

'Happy to help,' Erykah said and started walking off with the tea. Suddenly, she stopped. A Valentine in code? That was it! How could she have missed it?

If you had secrets to keep and didn't want to get your family involved, you would keep everything at your office.

If you thought someone might go looking for those secrets, you would write them in a code.

If you were the sort of person who preferred notebooks to computers, you would write it on paper.

And if you were the sort of person who enjoyed figuring out puzzles – you would make the code yourself.

That was why there had been nothing on his computer. It wasn't wiped at all. There was nothing there because there never had been. She hurried back to the reading room. At the desk she snatched the handwritten block of text off the top of the papers. These were no random letters, no idle pastime lurking among more important work notes and papers. It was a message in code. Only there were no word breaks, so there were no obvious keys to use. Still, this was a breakthrough. Now she had her way in.

Erykah checked her watch. Damn. It had been three hours already. No doubt Billy would have reported her disappearance to the Major. She decided to walk: it wasn't raining, and anyway, she needed some time in the fresh air. The solid rhythm of mornings on the river at Molesey had once provided the ideal metronome for getting into a flow. Without it, she needed something else to stretch her legs and gather her thoughts.

She arrived at the Major's door and was buzzed up. Heart pounding, she mounted the stairs two at a time, ready to make excuses for her late arrival. Erykah burst into the front room of the tiny office where she was curtly informed by his secretary that he wasn't there. 'He's out all afternoon on business,' Wilma said, clattering away on her typewriter.

'What kind of business?'

'Personal business.' The contempt dripping from her voice told Erykah all she needed to know.

'*Personal* business?' Erykah smiled. This was better than she had expected. Perfect, in fact.

'I can leave him a message if you like,' Wilma said. 'Mrs Macdonald.'

'Do you know what? It's fine, I don't need to see him. Just be sure to let him know I came by to drop off a few things,' Erykah said, and indicated her bag. 'You know . . . personal things.'

Wilma nodded at the second door. 'It's through there.'

'Ta,' Erykah said. So this is where it all goes down, she thought. A few cardboard boxes sat on the kind of stacking chairs you might see in a school assembly hall. She rifled through the contents. A few old photos and awards, nothing interesting. A framed page from the best-seller list when his book cracked the top ten.

At the bottom was a little wooden box. She picked it up and opened the catch. Inside was a snub-nosed gun nestled in the velvet box lining. It looked old, ornate letters H and S embossed in the grip.

Erykah took the pistol out of the box and felt its weight in her hand. Engraved on the side of the barrel was *C. G. Haenel Suhl Schmeisser's Patent*. Was it the Major's? Or his father's? Did it work? It had been a long time since she had seen anything like this in real life.

Grayson had always carried a pistol tucked under the front waist-band of his jeans. A Hechler and Koch .45 semi-automatic. It had been smaller than she thought guns would be. And matte black – not a cowboy gun. When she said so she was afraid he would be offended, but he laughed. 'I carry a piece,' he said, 'for protection only. I don't need to go round advertising the fact I could use it, y'know?'

The clattering typewriter next door was still going, the rat-a-tat like a machine gun. She slid open the top drawer of the desk – a few old issues of *Jane's Defence Weekly* and a mouldering apple core. The other drawers were empty.

Job done, but best to hand off in person, she wrote. She taped the note to the cover of the Cyrillic journal filched from Schofield's office and left it in the middle of the desk.

: **18** :

'Erykah?' A voice called from the front room. 'Erykah?' More urgent now. 'Those – those men are back again.' Her husband darted upstairs as fast as a cockroach caught when the lights came on.

Not even home for two minutes and Rab needed babysitting. 'Sorry, Rab, I'll take care of it,' she said.

Erykah shepherded Seminole Billy and Buster back to the kitchen. 'Smells good in here,' Buster said. 'Like curry goat or something.'

'Just some food I picked up,' Erykah said. 'Thought I'd treat myself to a takeaway.'

'Is cooking not among your many talents?' Seminole Billy said.

Erykah smiled. 'What my mother couldn't teach me about cookery would fill a library.' She pulled an array of containers from a carrier bag and spread them on the table. 'I was in London today running errands anyway.' She glanced at the pair, but no response. So they wouldn't admit they had followed her. 'Jerk chicken, rice and peas, veg patties. There's more here than Rab and I could finish on our own,' she said. Not that Rab was the intended diner. She had bought twice as much as she needed, expecting she might have company before too long. 'Please, help yourselves.'

Buster heaved himself down into a dining chair. He picked up a foil bag with patties inside and sniffed deeply, poked at the chicken with a plastic fork. 'Not bad,' he said. He proffered the bag at his partner. 'Having some?'

Seminole Billy waved his hand, his silver-charmed bracelets swinging. 'I'm good, thanks. If it was fried chicken, then maybe.'

She could see the mark on his hand more clearly now. Definitely a tattoo, between his thumb and forefinger. A faded letter B that might once have been black, but now was blurred and blue-grey. 'Prison?' she said.

'Sorry?' Billy said.

She pointed at his hand. 'Did you get that in prison?'

Billy's face twisted in a smile and he rubbed the spot on his hand absently. 'No, my stepdad did that,' he said. 'Held me down and did it with a permanent marker and a sharpened bicycle spoke.' He held Erykah's gaze as he said it, and when she shivered his eyes sparkled like someone sipping an especially fine dram.

'Is the B for Billy?' she said.

'No,' he said. 'The B's for bastard.'

'That's horrible,' she said.

'You ever have a stepdad?'

Erykah shook her head. Rainbow had done a lot of things, but she never brought her men, whoever they were, home. It had never occurred to Erykah that that might have been on purpose, or even a good thing. At the time all she had wanted was a normal family and a normal mother, like in television and books. A father, or in lieu of that, a father figure. Maybe it wouldn't have been such a good idea after all.

'Beers, guys?' Erykah stood up quickly and gestured at the enormous stainless steel American-style fridge. 'I put a few Red Stripes in the freezer for speed but they might not be cold yet.'

'I'll wait,' Buster said and tore into a fat, juicy chicken thigh.

Seminole Billy shook his head. 'You got a mineral water?' Erykah brought him a bottle. It was a glass one, all the writing in French. He cracked the twist cap and poured some into a tumbler. 'I hear you're doing a little work for the Major now.'

'He's asked me to look into a couple of things.'

'Yeah? Like what?'

Erykah pursed her lips. She didn't want to be more specific until it was clear what they did or did not know. 'Going on a charm offensive. The usual.'

'Good,' Seminole Billy said. 'Cos we got a favour to ask.'

Erykah retrieved a can of beer from the freezer for herself and popped the tab. She slid into the seat opposite Buster. 'Go on.'

'I understand you might have a talent for breaking into things,' he said. 'And for spotting when you've been spotted.'

Erykah took a swig of her beer. So they had seen her back at the university, then. 'I don't know about breaking in. Getting in isn't the same as breaking in, now is it?'

'Gaining access by fraud,' Billy said. 'Whatever semantics you want to use.'

'Am I being lectured on the nuances of breaking and entering by – no offence – you guys?'

'None taken,' Billy said. 'Only an observation. A door was locked; you got in. Nice one.'

'I talked the key off of someone,' she said. 'It's not breaking in if he gave it to me.'

'What's that got to do with the price of peas in Tobago?' Buster said. 'I bet you didn't tell him who you really are.'

'Obviously not. But it's not breaking in,' she said. 'Technically.'

'Oh, now that's an ethical conundrum,' Buster said. His brow creased as he thought aloud. 'Trust gained by fraudulent means is not consent.'

'That's still different from taking it by force,' Erykah said.

'Maybe,' Buster said. 'You have to consider, security can never protect against all motivated individuals. Even if you can't pick a lock, for instance, you can always kick in a door. Locks are not force-proof; they're there to keep honest people honest.'

Billy turned to his colleague. 'I get that, but if that's the case then why not leave everything unlocked as a sign of trust?' he asked. 'Like people do out in the country.'

'Well, how I see it's like this,' Buster said. He wiped the crumbs from his face with a paper napkin and leaned back from the table, stretching his long body. 'An unlocked door is representative of nothing but an unused lock. If folks out in the country want to make a statement about their willingness to keep their belongings unsecured and how much they trust people, then they should remove the lock from the door.'

'How you see it?' Erykah raised her eyebrows. She hadn't heard Buster say more than a sentence or two, much less anything like this.

'Yeah.' He paused, gazing at the ceiling like a man working out the meaning of life from the vantage point of a bed in a cell. 'Few people would dream of getting rid of locks, because the lock itself is symbolic. It's all about signalling public and private spaces in society. If you have a lock to it, it's yours. You own it. Like in the joint, you don't get a key to your cell. That's the punishment. You have no more private space.'

'Also to keep you in,' Erykah said.

'Sure, that too,' Buster said. 'But it's a kind of a – what's the phrase Hobbes used? A social contract.'

Erykah smiled. 'Hobbes? Isn't that a bit—'

'Esoteric for a con?' Buster said. 'You're not the only one who read their way out of the estate, yeah? With that much time on my hands

I read every book I could get,' he said. 'Technically nowhere is un-breakable, not even prison. And people on the inside outnumber the guards, so what keeps us in? We're conditioned to accept punishment. Especially if you're, you know, black. We stand where they tell us to stand.' Buster looked back at his plate. 'Breaking in and out has noth-ing to do with the locks themselves. It's a message about something else. Power.'

'You got a point,' Seminole Billy had to concur. He speared a piece of chicken with a plastic fork. 'Not to mention, you don't get less time in the lockup if you hit a house with a shitty lock.' He popped the food in his mouth, chewed briefly, then swallowed. 'You know, this chicken isn't too bad. For England.'

Erykah considered. What if Peter hadn't been there, or hadn't given her the key? She shook her head. 'Anyway, houses are a bad analogy. It's a personal crime, breaking into a home. The individual has no moral responsibility to treat an office in the same way they treat a house.'

'Well, whatever,' Seminole Billy said. 'If you want to chat about what-ifs all day, then we can stay here and do nothing until the police find out about us. Then we'll have all the time in the world for talk-ing.' He crossed his left boot over his right knee. The tops of the boots might have been polished, but underneath the soles were scratched and old, the heels pocked and worn. He turned to Erykah. 'Point is, what we need is for you to find someone for us online. Can you do that?'

'Maybe,' Erykah said. 'Who is it?'

'Remember the tweet at your press conference?' Seminole Billy said. Erykah nodded. The Media Mouse story was not something she was going to forget in a hurry. 'Them.'

'I thought someone already figured that out?' Erykah said. 'Some blogger said it was a setup from inside the SLU to drum up publicity. Sock puppets, I think he called it.'

Billy and Buster exchanged glances. 'What, that washed up ex-nov-elist trying to restyle himself as some kind of investigative journalist?' Billy sneered. 'He's about as likely to stumble over a real story as Buster here is to pass for Jeremy Paxman.'

'True.' She read the blog post herself and while the guy seemed to think his evidence was a lock, he was missing a lot – like IP addresses and email receipts. Even the tabloids qualified his claims as "only a theory". All he had was a wild imagination and a lot of conjecture. 'What happens when I find them? We're talking about probably some kid here, some online troll who—'

'We're paying you to put up and shut up.' Billy said. 'What they did and what happens next is not your concern.'

'The Major never mentioned anything about hacking.'

'And you never mentioned your computer science degree, so we're even.'

'I didn't graduate,' Erykah shrugged. 'I spend a bit of time online but it's not what you would call my base skill set.' She could see they weren't convinced. 'I mean, we get some trolls leaving nasty comments on the club website, but it's a piece of piss to track them down.'

'See? You're already more of an expert than any of us.'

She took a deep swig at the can. The beer tasted good, very good. It had been a long day.

'I thought you might need some inspiration,' Seminole Billy said. 'Which is why we brought a little financial incentive. Let's call it a down payment. For services to be rendered.'

She was glad they had mentioned money. 'How much?' Erykah asked. 'Is it, like, I'm-going-to-buy-a-car money, or are we talking, I'm-going-to-buy-an-island money?'

Seminole Billy considered. 'Middle of that. Let's call it you're-going-to-buy-a-yacht money.'

Erykah stroked the condensation on the side of the beer can with one long finger. 'That sounds lowball to me. An extra zero on that would buy a whole lot of silence.'

'You're not dealing with the Major now. If I wanted to guarantee your silence,' Seminole Billy lowered his gaze to the level of her face, 'that wouldn't cost me nothing.'

Erykah gulped. 'Yacht money is perfect,' she said.

'Good,' Seminole Billy said, and flashed the corner of a fat envelope tucked inside his leather jacket. 'And we need a positive ID, not a shortlist of candidates. I don't do interviews.'

'No, no, clearly not,' Erykah said. She stole a look down at Seminole Billy's boots. He slid the envelope onto the table. Erykah did not pick it up, did not open it. Counting the money would be something she did later, after they were gone.

'Any way you can lure them?' Buster asked.

'Maybe,' Erykah said. She pulled a tablet out of her bag. 'First thing is getting someone in a conversation. Getting them to let their guard down. I'll have to make a new account so it doesn't come back to me.' She started tapping away. 'Done.'

'Is that it?' Billy asked.

'No, that's just the start. I need some time to think this through. I have to figure out where they are, then who they are. I assume the tabloids have already tried.' Her fingers flew as she downloaded a generic webcam face shot from a random person on the Web, then uploaded it to the new account. Every secret identity needs a face. She followed the first twenty accounts Twitter suggested, mainly football players and television presenters. 'Whoever is doing this would spot a journalist a mile off. You have to ingratiate. Establish a relationship.' She filled in a short bio to complete the profile. *MSc history & romcom lover. Coventry. Will work for G&T's!!*

'You need some followers, so you don't look too new.' Erykah navigated to a page that claimed to sell Twitter followers for money. Best to choose a modest number, and an odd one – tapping in her card number from memory, it was only moments before she had 127 followers. Good.

Billy and Buster watched over her shoulder as she worked. Erykah scrolled back in the accounts she was following to tweets from a few weeks earlier. She retweeted those old messages, to give the impression the account had been live for longer. She sent a couple of tweets of her own complaining about having to write an essay. Then she followed Media Mouse and tapped out a message complimenting the tweeter for their success.

'Jesus, woman, are you baiting a hook or setting up a dating profile?' Billy said.

'Be patient. The trap has to look like it isn't a trap,' she said. 'If Media Mouse is being cautious, they probably won't reply to an account with no details.'

'So how long is it gonna take?' Buster asked.

'How long is a piece of string? All depends on if they're still active on the site and looking at their replies or not. No way to tell unless you send them something.' She typed another message, asking if Media Mouse could follow her back.

'And then?'

'And then, I try to get something out of them. An email, maybe, where I can use the headers to trace back to a location. Or maybe they click on a link and I get the ISP. It could be days though. For now we wait.' Seminole Billy looked unconvinced. 'Trust me, it's the rare person who can stay away from making a repeat performance once they've had a taste of media interest,' Erykah said. 'Especially if they're now famous – or at least, Internet famous. Tens of thousands of followers wanting to know what comes next? It's only a matter of time before they bite.'

Seminole Billy nodded, satisfied. She talked the talk even if he didn't know exactly what the talk meant.

Erykah paused. Can you ask mercenary thugs if they would please leave now? She had taken the job, what else did they want? Was this some kind of test to see how she would react?

'Didn't you say something about a beer in the freezer?' Buster finally asked.

'Oh! Right. Sure,' Erykah said. Nervous sweat had soaked through her jeans, and she could feel them sticking to her thighs. 'Here you are.' Billy helped himself to another water.

They sat in uncomfortable silence for several more minutes while Buster and Seminole Billy sipped their drinks. 'You got a radio in here?' Billy said, looking around the kitchen. 'Only we're missing the end of something I was listening to on LCC.'

'Stuebner show?' Erykah said, and ran her fingers over the tablet screen to bring up the Internet radio stations. 'I love her.' The dulcet tones of Diana Stuebner reading the headlines at the top of the hour poured out of the surround sound into the whole house.

Buster let out a low, appreciative whistle. 'Well, I'll be damned,' he said. 'Nice system you got. Sounds a lot better than that piece of shite you call a car stereo, Billy.'

Seminole Billy pushed his empty mineral water bottle in Erykah's direction. 'Missed the last of the call-in though,' he said. 'My favourite thing on the radio. That woman can talk a wasp out of its sting. We're out. Buster, come on.'

'Aww, I was getting used to this,' Buster said, looking longingly at the rest of the food.

'Don't make me have to persuade you, mate,' Seminole Billy said in his low voice. Buster sprang off the chair in record time. 'Be in touch,' Seminole Billy said, and gave Erykah an offhand salute. 'And give your husband our regards.'

Erykah smiled and nodded until they were gone, then let out

a ragged sigh. What a day. She tore open the brown envelope Billy had given here and found a stack of odd-looking cash. Crisply ironed fifty-pound notes, but green instead of pink? Instead of the familiar image of Her Majesty the Queen, the stippled head of a man in a ridiculous wig looked back at her. She turned the notes over – Royal Bank of Scotland. Surprise, surprise. Counted it up. Just shy of twenty grand. Not as much as she had hoped. So maybe a used yacht. Or a new rowing boat.

Diana's voice danced over the headlines. 'The whistle-blower known only as Media Mouse has resurfaced today with allegations of a senior woman politician trading sex for positive press,' the smooth voice purred from the radio. 'The claims came to light in the last hour from the now notorious anonymous social media account. Number 10 have released a statement categorically denying any of the cabinet are the target of the blind item. Opposition parties have not yet responded.'

Was that . . . ? Yes. Erykah clicked rapidly back to Twitter to find Media Mouse at the top of trending topics already.

@MediaMouse One way to get good press: front bench woman having affair with news producer. The future of hands on journalism? #blinditem

'Posted only fifteen minutes ago.' Erykah's breathing went short and shallow with excitement and her fingers flew over the tablet screen. The game was most definitely on.

: **19** :

'Morag?' Arjun tapped on the door between their offices, opening it a crack. 'Call still on hold,' he whispered.

Morag Munro was not feeling entirely herself. The tailored suit jacket hanging off the back of her chair could do with a dry clean. She had woken up with dry eyes so was wearing her spectacles, which made her look older. Her shoes were a new pair, not yet broken in, and pinched at the toes. She kicked off the patent red heels under the desk. On top of that Delphine had been bombarding her with emails about new rumours that had popped up overnight, that someone on the front benches was shagging a journalist. Morag was not interested in taking any calls just now.

'Are you feeling all right?' Arjun asked. He slid a mug of tea across the desk to her alongside a folder of selected clippings from political websites that morning, issues that were tipped to become the day's talking points.

Her superfood chia porridge and yoghurt smoothie sat on her desk, both untouched. All of her meals were delivered these days, the better to fit in between meetings. It suited her. She ate for fuel only.

'I'm fine,' Morag nodded. 'Thank you,' she said. She nodded at the folder. 'Sit down. What's the takeaway from the press this morning? Apart from the obvious.'

'More European elections nonsense,' he said, making the exaggerated shrug that indicated he knew she had no interest in the topic, but that he thought she should pay more attention to it. 'Anti-devolution candidates are starting to campaign north of the border, one of them mentioned you.'

'Really?' She raised her eyebrows above her glasses, which made her look like a startled owl. 'Good or bad?'

'Let's see, shall we?' Arj rifled through the clippings and held up a printout from a site known for its parliamentary gossip. 'Quote from Major Whitney Abbott, the SLU candidate,' Arj said. 'You know of him?'

'Yes. Old goat with a tenuous claim on heroism,' Morag said. Arj wasn't even old enough to have been alive during the Falklands War, much less remember it. 'Go on.'

'Says he thinks you should join his party and bring the fight for a, quote, Re-United Kingdom, unquote, to Westminster.'

Morag took off her glasses and massaged the crease in the middle of her forehead. 'You know I can't touch that. Next.'

'A-level student in Cheltenham overstayed her visa and is making an asylum claim. Home Office are moving to deport so a good chance to come out on the right side, a solid social media win? There's an online petition. Emma Watson tweeted support.'

'State school student?'

'Cheltenham Ladies' College.'

This did not sound hopeful. 'Is she black? Or Muslim? Any FGM risk?'

Arjun shook his head. 'Canadian. White as the driven snow.'

'Really? Canadians can claim asylum now?'

'Her solicitors are angling for a domestic violence exception. Parents divorced, but the court records are sealed. She's being sent back to her dad.'

'Deadbeat redneck? Trailer park? Give me something to work with here,' Morag said.

'I wish. On-paper billionaire with oil sands extraction patents and Russian oligarch friends.'

Morag sighed. 'Ten thousand forced removals every year, and no one gets exercised until it's some . . .' She flipped open the folder. She replaced her glasses and examined the grainy photo. 'Pom-pom girl from Alberta. I despair.'

'Tabloids are likely to jump on this one,' Arjun said. 'You know how they love blondes in distress.'

'Yes, well,' Morag said. 'Pull a neutral response from the archive – rule of law applies equally to all, support a sensible and sustainable policy . . . you know the rest.'

Arjun nodded and withdrew.

Morag grimaced as soon as the door shut. On any given weekday, Westminster was teeming with people, everyone living in everyone else's pockets. She was accustomed to the loss of privacy, but his keenness was beginning to get on her nerves. She slurped the tea and scowled. It was perfect even by her specifications: strong, dash of milk. His careful study of her habits, her moods, her likes and dislikes, infuriated her. She didn't care for people who were too observant. More to the point, she didn't trust them.

The light on her office phone blinked twice, then went dark, then blinked again. Over and over, indicating a call that was on hold and had been for a quarter of an hour.

Morag placed a hand on the phone. She supposed she would have to answer it sometime. She picked up the receiver and hadn't even said a word when a breathless man blurted, 'Have you seen the fucking tweet?'

'Hello to you too, Jonathan,' she said coolly. 'I have heard about yesterday's tweet.' There was no avoiding the developing scandal about the rumour of a politician sleeping her way to good press. She had feigned ignorance when Arjun mentioned it in the lift, but wondered if perhaps she had played her surprise too strongly. What was the saying – the lady doth protest too much? Her name was coming up no more frequently than that of any other female MP's. The problem was: with few women to choose from, she did not feel safe from suspicion.

'Fucking disaster,' Jonathan said. 'Christ. What do we do now?'

Morag frowned. He was meant to be the media professional. Last thing she needed was for him to lose the plot. 'No one suspects us yet,' Morag hissed into the phone. 'Emphasis on *yet*. Speaking of which, what part of "don't ring me at the office" was so difficult to understand?'

'Like I had a fucking choice,' Jonathan said. 'I couldn't reach your mobile and didn't want to leave a voicemail in case someone hacked it.'

'Yes. I turned it off because there's someone I'm trying to avoid.'

'You mean that Media Mouse twat?'

'I meant you.' Morag said acidly. Her fingers started drumming the desk. 'So instead of waiting for me to ring back, you decided to make a call to a landline that will no doubt be logged in official records. Thank you for that,' she said, her Scottish accent unfurling luxuriously over the syllables.

'Fuck sake . . .' Jonathan grasped for words. 'Why can't you tell your staff it was an interview request?'

'And then when they ask why it didn't go in the bookings diary?'

she said. 'You have no idea what it is like here. I can't fart in Westminster without someone finding out about it. If Arjun was any further up my backside right now he would be chewing last night's dinner.'

'Well, that's your fucking problem, not mine,' Jonathan said. 'I have to talk to you. Now. We need to get our stories straight in case anything does surface.'

She hated when he spoke to her like that. As if she wasn't the older of the two of them, as if she wasn't who she was. She suspected most of his previous relationships had involved junior researchers at the station, maybe some Internet dating. Places where his bad temper read as impressive, not unhinged. Places where the short-fused Alpha Male act was expected or perhaps tolerated. But she had seen enough silverbacks in the wild to know Jonathan was not quite the thirty-stone gorilla he pretended to be.

They had first hooked up at the last party conference. She was coming off the high of delivering a speech that she knew would guarantee her ascendance to the Shadow Cabinet. He was simply high. It had seemed like a permissible, illicit thrill at the time, taking him back to her hotel suite. But after he'd slunk out in the morning, dressed in the same clothes he had been wearing the night before, she realised what a risk she was running. And yet, it was she who called him first after conference season was over.

'I just came out of an editorial meeting,' he said. 'Diana is pushing hard for these rumours to be today's call-in. News updates are already covering it, but she wants to strike while it's trending.'

'A call-in?'

'I talked her down, the stupid bitch,' he said. 'Said it was too much of a libel risk if we open the switchboards.'

'Aren't you the white knight,' Morag said. 'Tell me Media Mouse isn't someone inside the station,' she said.

She heard Jonathan swallow. His answer was a few moments coming. It was clear to her he had never even considered the possibility. 'Fuck off. It isn't someone inside the station.'

'Are you sure about that?'

'No one here has seen us together, they don't . . . I mean, for all we know it's a wind-up. It might not even be about us,' he said. 'It's a nasty rumour. Just some twat fucking with people.'

Morag had to admit – obscenities aside – that this was not only possible, but likely. It wouldn't be the first time she had spent days in fear of what the media might be onto, only to find the darkly hinted scandals that had been occupying her thoughts never made waves at all. But that was no reason to be complacent.

'Are we OK?' he said.

Morag sighed. 'OK as in how?'

'You know . . . are we still on,' he said. 'Last week you said you wanted more time to think about us, about where we were going . . .'

'Listen. Jonathan, thank you for the call, but no, we are not OK, and no, I don't need more time to think about it.'

'You can't fucking do this now! Morag—'

'In fact, while I'm having another think, I think I feel very differently about you,' she said. 'This is not working for me. Calling my office, the indiscretion of it—'

There was a noise that might have been the sound of him punching his desk. 'You're being unreasonable, Morag.'

' . . . the standing assumption that us – this – whatever we have, is some sort of direct line to me and my office, then no, I think I'm having second thoughts about you. And I should have done this weeks ago,' she said. 'Jonathan, take your stupid glasses and your silly turtlenecks and your anger-management problems and fuck the fuck off out of my life.' She hung up the phone with a finality that startled even her.

Morag breathed deeply and went to her office door. 'Arjun, you are not to put through any more calls this morning,' she said.

She decided to check her email instead. One in particular caught her eye. It was flagged urgent, with the mysterious subject line Heads-Up.

Forget that. She'd had enough of rumours for one day, and it wasn't even ten o'clock yet. Morag marked the email as spam and deleted it.

Erykah kept the radio on the morning news while she worked online. She nibbled absentmindedly at a plate of cold leftovers from the night before. Rab had refused to come downstairs even after Seminole Billy and Buster left, saying he wasn't hungry. She hadn't heard a peep from him this morning either. The rice might be a bit dried out now, but the chicken was still succulent and the goat lovely and spicy. His loss.

One of the courses she had loved at university was codebreaking. The history was fascinating. Over and over again, mankind had invented unbreakable codes that were broken. And almost always not because of some mathematical prowess, although that did contribute to breaking codes sometimes. But the reality was usually far simpler than that. People did not use codes in the way they were intended to be used and gave up crucial clues that allowed others to find their way in.

The principle didn't only apply to codes, but anything to do with privacy and security. Technology was only perfect if it was used perfectly. In theory, an environment where people interacted only electronically should have the best chance of maintaining security. But people weren't online simply to transmit data; they sought out community, connections. The only way to guarantee total anonymity was to have no contact with anyone else – but that would go against the point of being on social media in the first place.

Media Mouse was back and tweeting. She had the foothold she needed. If she could lure Media Mouse into revealing more than they ought, she could catch them.

Her ears perked briefly at the mention of a murder on the radio. Diana Stuebner's honeyed voice poured out of the speakers. 'I'm joined on the line now by Harriet Hitchin, the Home Office pathologist in Cameron Bridge, Scotland, who has been dealing with this case.'

'Hello,' Harriet said over what sounded like a crackling phone connection.

'Dr Hitchin, thank you for joining us,' Diana said. 'Is there anything you can tell us? Something that might help any potential witnesses who decide to come forward?' Diana asked.

'Obviously, there are some details we can't discuss while the investigation is ongoing,' Harriet said in her nasal voice. 'But we can advise that further to reports putting the remains in a container, that the body was discovered tied up in a sports bag.'

'A sports bag. Interesting,' Diana repeated. 'Any special make or type? Maybe a particular club?'

'The police haven't been able to identify its origin yet,' Harriet said. 'But I can say that it was printed with a Union Jack motif on a blue background. The sort of bag you might see in tourist shops throughout London.'

'Very interesting,' Diana said. 'Blue sports bag, Union Jacks. So if there are any potential witnesses out there – perhaps you were out late in London on January 15th and saw someone, perhaps carrying a Union Jack sports bag – please be sure to contact police as soon as possible.' She tapped the table with her pen. 'Some sources have hinted that Professor Schofield may have been tortured before he was killed. Can you confirm or deny these rumours?'

Schofield? Erykah's blood ran cold. She had been in his office only yesterday. He was supposed to be missing, presumed dead. Now they were saying he was identified?

'Um! Well,' Harriet was taken aback. 'I can't clarify exact details of the post-mortem. No one from our office would have released such information,' she said, but there was a note of uncertainty in her voice.

Erykah bit her lip. With a body identified, the Met would probably go back in to check his office more carefully now. Or worse – maybe that Peter might remember seeing her photograph in the newspaper, put two and two together, and tell the police.

Her prints would still be on file from when Grayson killed Rory Lovelace. They would surely dust everything in Schofield's office for fingerprints and find she had been at the computer keyboard.

'Is there anything else we can say that might help listeners at home with information pertaining to the crime?' Diana said.

'The police will be following all leads,' Harriet said. 'And we want to reassure the family of Professor Schofield, his friends and colleagues that everything possible will be done to bring his killer to justice.'

If this was the same body found on a beach that she had heard about, could the tide really have carried it all that way? Erykah quickly looked up a map of tidal flows online. No, that didn't seem likely – anything coming out of the Thames would end up on the east coast or even Europe, not the west coast of Scotland. So either he had been taken there alive then killed, or someone had gone all the way to Scotland to try to make sure the body was never found. Whoever did it was trying to cover their tracks completely. Otherwise why not throw him in the Thames?

'And can we remind any callers,' Diana said. 'If you have information pertaining to the investigation, please ring the police – not us! Thank you for joining us today, Dr Hitchin.'

'Thank you for having me.'

Erykah nibbled a cold patty and put the murder out of her head while she tried to draw Media Mouse into more conversation.

The thing was, Media Mouse was more receptive to chatting than she hoped. Enjoying the renewed notoriety, most likely. And with the press as yet unable to discover who it was – well, they probably put their guard down after the first wave of attention passed.

So far Erykah had sent them several private messages, all of which contained links to news stories. But what most people would not have noticed was that before landing on the stories, whoever clicked the shortened link was forwarded via another server before their final destination. An old domain that Erykah had used to back up the rowing website, but had never hosted any content. By checking the logs she could collect the IP address of whoever clicked the links.

<3 the account! What gave you the idea?

I had a housemate who was really into twitter, Media Mouse typed. *Never saw a use for it until now! LOL*

As yet no links had been clicked, but the conversation was flowing and that was a start. What she needed was to build trust with Media Mouse and keep sending messages until they accessed their account from a place she could easily trace, such as their home, or where they worked. And then from there, well, she would figure that bit out when it happened.

Meanwhile she tried to get more information about the woman the Major and Peter both mentioned. Livia. She was proving equally difficult to identify. Public paperwork on the SLU showed no one by that name, or any similar name. And without a surname straight searches would be a problem. Where would Lady Livia be? No mention of anyone by that name on the *Tatler* website. Announcements in the *Telegraph* and *London Gazette* came up empty as well. She flicked through websites with photos from last summer at Henley where the Stewards' enclosure was heaving with potentials of all ages. Society blondes bared their whitened teeth for the cameras, each one richer or more aristocratic than the last. But no one seemed to fit the bill.

As long as Mouse was still on the hook, though, things were looking up.

Don't you worry about being found? Erykah typed in a private message.

shrug, Media Mouse typed back. *Mostly I don't think about it . . . killing time at work.*

So they were at work. Good. Success was so close Erykah could almost taste it. She sent Media Mouse another link by direct message, this time to a gossip site.

Media mouse messaged back almost immediately.

That's just tittle tattle. Wait til you see what I have coming next. Double trouble.

Are you sure? This is interesting stuff. Jobless figures being manipulated, could be juicy.

Ha, no. Read it. No one cares about statistics. I mean big time. As in corruption investigation big time.

Interesting. Erykah wondered what that could mean, and whether it might have anything to do with the SLU. But more importantly, they had finally clicked through on a link and she had an IP address for Media Mouse.

She copied the IP numbers into a website search form and hit return. When the result came up, it was a moment before she realised what exactly she was looking at.

Whoever it was, was tweeting from inside the LCC radio station studio. Right now.

It was so obvious in hindsight. Who knows better how to manipulate the news cycle, how to get a so-so story to trend, than someone already in that world? She got a shiver looking at it. Who could it be? A guest? A presenter?

What if it was Diana Stuebner herself?

Erykah's lips curled up into a smile. So what if she wasn't getting yacht money for this, she could certainly afford a holiday. She thought about how a drink on a boat moored up in the sunny Caribbean might taste right now. The soft lapping of warm, gentle waves on the bow. The hot sun on her arms and legs.

This was better than good; this was amazing. But she needed to be sure before she let anyone know.

Hey, is your work Internet an open network or sign in only?

Sign in. Why?

I know your IP address. I know the radio station where you work.

Who are you?

Was it too early in the day for a beer? Who cared? There were still three Red Stripes in the fridge. Erykah sipped from the cold can. It tasted glorious.

No one of consequence, she typed. *Meet me.*

Forget it. All you have is one building where hundreds of people work. You don't know who I am.

Erykah chuckled. Ah, bravado. She had done enough of it herself. But it was true, in a way: she didn't know exactly who Media Mouse was. Not yet. She was getting there though. The legwork might take a day or two, maybe more. It would mean some early starts to get into town, but with the money literally on the table it was definitely worth it.

Then I'll stand outside the station every day til I find you. Meet me.

No response.

Meet me.

Meet me, or I'll come find you.

: **21** :

The midday train to London was empty save for a group of teenage boys standing by the doors. Erykah worked a quick crossword and watched them over the edge of the paper. They self-consciously adjusted their trousers and caps, bobbing their heads to music played from one of their phones and aping the street style that so many middle-class kids aspired to.

Class was a funny thing. Fake it til you make it, Grayson used to say. It was one of his favourite mottos. But no matter how well or how long she passed, there were some things that could never be faked.

It reminded her of the first and only time she went to Henley Royal Regatta as a spectator, the summer before. Nicole was keen to see what 'a real English summer season' was like. So Erykah got tickets to one of the enclosures from a Steward.

She had been up and down that piece of water loads of times for the women's regatta and the winter head. Down there, it was just a stretch of river, no more intimidating than any other race. Less than most, even. But Henley-on-Thames looked very different at water level. As soon as she was on the other side of the enclosure gates, she didn't feel as though she belonged any more.

The throng of spectators was unlike anything she had seen before. Erykah had looked on as old school chums clapped each other on the back, or reminisced about Oxford. Nobody even watched the races. She stood by the bar nursing an overpriced Pimm's and lemonade. The drink had been mixed badly, so sickly sweet that it coated her throat like the cough medicine Rainbow used to give her as a child. She felt unable to talk to anyone. What would they talk about? Suddenly the people she saw at the club every day were strangers, just because of a few dresses and hats.

'What's wrong with you?' Nicole had been the only one to notice. She had pulled her aside, concern in her eyes. 'Why are you hiding?'

Erykah made some excuse about food poisoning and went to hide in the toilets. She didn't know how to answer. When she was no longer in

Lycra, the difference between who she was and who these people were could not be avoided.

'Don't be intimidated, you have as much of a right to be here as any of them,' Nicole said. 'More than most of them.' But that wasn't the problem. As an American, it didn't matter where Nicole came from, she read as classless to rahs like Dom in their striped club blazers. Nicole couldn't see how they would sooner welcome a white American to their ranks, than a black woman from a few miles down the road. No matter what Erykah did or how well she did it.

Now Erykah looked out of the window at the blur of shrubs and river. The bag was heavy on her shoulder, packed for a couple of days away. When the Major suggested she accompany him to Cameron Bridge she couldn't say no. Not only because she was supposed to be helping him front the campaign: there was someone up there who might be able to help her in a different way, someone from long in her past. If Erykah was lucky, it might be the one opportunity to figure out what was in the Schofield files before she had to give up on it and hand them over. It could be the key she was looking for. But there was some business to take care of in London first.

She phoned his mobile and it went through to voicemail. 'Hey, Whitney, it's me,' she said. 'Something came up, I can't meet you on the train today.' She paused. He'd demand more of an explanation than that. 'My husband isn't well. Nothing serious, don't worry – there's the late sleeper train changing at Glasgow. I'll meet you in Cameron Bridge first thing.'

The carriages slowed, then stopped. An announcement crackled over the speakers, signalling trouble at Wimbledon. A sliver of the river peeked through the trees. She missed rowing. She closed her eyes and imagined herself sat behind Nicole, leaning, catching and pulling.

The train jolted to life again. It crept at slow speed the rest of the journey into Waterloo. Enormous screens in the station shouted down snippets of headlines and car adverts. Thick streams of people flowed to the Underground entrance and the station exits. It was two stops to Leicester Square on the Tube but felt much longer, crushed against commuter armpits and tourist rucksacks. A chill wind whipped through the vents. How was it possible for the carriages to be so crowded and yet still freezing cold?

She looked at the faces of the passengers on the Tube. A couple of young men, chatting in French. A woman who seemed to have come out in her slippers. A man in a suit, scowling at the newspaper crossword, stuck on a clue. She could see he had got one of the Across clues wrong.

Any one of them could be the person she was looking for. She didn't know this Media Mouse person at all and, whatever they were mixed up in, it was better for her continued good health that she didn't ask questions. But the more she thought about it, the more she couldn't see how what they had done was different to what she would have done. And she knew for a fact that Seminole Billy and Buster were not the sort of people who wanted someone's details so they could go round for a nice cup of tea.

Outside the LCC building a group of evangelicals were gathered, flyers in hand for some Jesus thing or other. Erykah looked down at her own clothes – jeans and flat boots, a heavy pea coat buttoned against the cold. If she pulled her hair back and cleaned off her make-up she might pass for one of them. She tucked herself into a phone booth. Two minutes with a baby wipe, a few hairpins, and the transformation was done.

Erykah sidled up to a happy clapper and smiled. 'Hello,' she said. 'Mind if I have a few of your pamphlets? I haven't had the orientation yet.'

'Sure,' the baggy-suited man handed over a stack of leaflets. 'Good luck with this lot. It's all secular music and worldly politics in there. We've been posting here three, four weeks and not one turn.'

'Wow,' Erykah nodded. 'Bet it makes it all the sweeter when you get one, am I right?'

The man smiled and tapped the fish pin on his lapel. 'You love the fishing too,' he said. 'It's the only way to fly.'

'With Jesus as my co-pilot,' she said, and edged away before he could ask her any questions. The pavement was crowded with people hurrying back to work. What was she looking for? She wasn't sure. It wasn't as if Media Mouse would be advertising the fact. She didn't even know if she was looking for a man or a woman, yet.

Erykah held out a handful of leaflets and glued a fake smile to her face. Her eyes, meanwhile, were watching the door of the radio station. It was only a hunch that the person she was looking for would have gone out for lunch. Maybe they always brought a sandwich, and ate at their desk. Maybe they were inside, afraid to come out.

But she had to start somewhere. At least she could see who came and went, the rhythms and patterns of the place. The few people she saw going in all looked confident, purposeful. No, it wasn't any of these.

The she saw her. A woman with blondish hair dithered by the doors, peering at her smartphone, then over her shoulder, then back to her phone. Her stooped posture and worried looks were like a silent film caricature of someone trying to sneak through a crowd. Or even, like her online namesake, a mouse. Was it her?

There was only one way to find out. Erykah walked over to the woman, leaflets in hand.

'Not interested,' the girl said out of the corner of her mouth and waved her away with a bobbled mitten.

'I'm here to talk to you about something else entirely—'

'Not. Interested,' the woman said firmly, and their gazes met.

Well, well, well. She wasn't what Erykah was expecting at all. Young. Mid-twenties, maybe even younger than that. An intern maybe, or a graduate hire. She had a smattering of freckles across her nose and a crocheted hat pulled low on her forehead. Little more than a child.

She wore woolly tights and a pair of clunky, thick-soled shoes. She could see the girl had been chewing at her nails. Maybe it was because she was anxious about something?

'I'm not here to talk to you about Jesus,' Erykah said, her voice low. 'I'm here to talk about Media Mouse.'

The look on the girl's face was answer enough. It was her! Erykah felt a little wobble in her stomach. Was that her conscience piping up again? She thought she had talked it down, explained that principles were all fine and well, but there was this thing called money, and if she didn't want to end up stuffed in a bag and thrown in the ocean, she needed some of it to get away.

Another wobble. Yes, but this person was someone just like her. Caught up in a situation that was bigger than either of them had counted on. She punched it down with thoughts of relaxing on a tropical beach sipping a cocktail.

The young woman's face went ashen. 'You're the one who was messaging me?' she squeaked. 'For real?'

Erykah nodded. 'What's your name?' she said.

'Kerry,' she said and flashed her ID on the lanyard. 'You're not a reporter, are you,' she said as she looked over Erykah's outfit. It was more a statement than a question. 'And you're not police.'

'No,' she admitted.

'So what is this all about? Why did you follow me?'

'I think you may be in trouble,' Erykah said. 'I don't mean with your job – I mean real trouble. Is there somewhere we can go? Private? To talk?'

Kerry looked uncertain. 'My boss will explode if I'm not back from my break on time.' She started to head for the door again. 'And I've got a lot of emails to answer, my twitter account is going crazy, you know . . .'

Erykah grabbed Kerry's coat sleeve. 'Please,' she said. 'Listen to me. You're going to have a lot more to worry about than your boss and some twitter followers if you walk in there like nothing is happening.'

Kerry bit her lip. 'All right, fine. I'll say my bus is caught in traffic. Gives me twenty minutes, tops. There's a coffee shop around the corner.'

From the corner of her eye, Erykah saw the man in the rumpled suit give them a nod. Erykah gave him a thumbs up. One more saved, though this time not for Jesus.

The coffee shop was part of the same chain as the one Erykah had met the Major in not so long ago. The layout was the same; the shuffling queues of people looking at their phones instead of each other, grabbing their takeaway cups, looked identical. Kerry was already on her phone, scrolling and tapping away, entertaining her online crowd. Erykah manoeuvred her downstairs and brought down two pots of tea.

'No phone reception down here, no windows,' Kerry said when she returned.

'I wanted to talk in private,' Erykah said. 'Phones off.'

'What are you, a private investigator?' Kerry said. She tapped the corner of her phone against her front teeth.

'You have a South London accent,' Erykah said. 'Where are you from?'

'Croydon, actually,' Kerry said. 'You too?'

'Streatham.'

'Yeah, thought so. Neither of us is going to be reading news for the BBC anytime soon,' she said. 'And you're here trying to stitch me up, right?'

'I am not here to stitch you up. I mean, I was sent here to stitch you up, but I don't think I can do it.'

'Because, if I'm going to be outed, I want to talk about money first.'

'This isn't about outing.' The girl didn't seem to understand what level of trouble she had got herself into. 'I was hired by men who are looking for you. And when they find you . . . these men mean you harm.'

Kerry rolled her eyes. 'This is about the email to Morag Munro, isn't it?' she asked. 'I mean, I thought at the time that emailing it to her was going too far, but I guess part of me wanted to see what she did. If she came clean, or – or what.'

'Email to Morag Munro? *The* Morag Munro?' Erykah said and the girl nodded. 'I don't know anything about that. What does she have to come clean about?'

'You're not here because of Munro?'

'No, I'm not here because of the Shadow Home Secretary,' Erykah said. Although, now she had said it aloud, she wasn't so sure of that. 'At least, I don't think I am. The people who paid me to find you aren't exactly forthcoming about who sets their agenda, or where their money is coming from.'

'Huh.' Kerry turned away and gnawed at the end of one of her fingers. Erykah couldn't get a read on her. Was she scared? Or disappointed? She was putting up a tough front, but that was all it was – a front.

'Whatever it is, I think you had better tell me what's going on,' Erykah said. 'Maybe I can help you figure it out. Or at least get you to a safe place.'

Kerry snorted, but she didn't get up and leave. The corner of her lip wobbled.

'Listen, I know what this is like,' Erykah said.

Kerry sneered. 'Yeah? No, actually, you don't,' she said.

'No, I do,' Erykah said. 'When I was your age I got mixed up in something. It wasn't my fault, but try telling the press that.'

Now and then over the years Erykah had wondered what she would tell her younger self if she could. Stay away from Grayson? From university? From Rab? Don't call the police? In the end, none of those were satisfying answers. Who can predict which choices and moments will change your life for ever?

Kerry looked at Erykah. 'I thought I recognised you. You're the woman who won the lottery, aren't you?' Erykah nodded. 'So what do you need money so badly for that someone paid you to come after me? You should be off on a private jet somewhere. You didn't give all of it away, right?'

'I'll tell you something,' Erykah said, 'so you know you can trust me. Then I know something about you, and you know something about me, so I can't sell you out, right?'

'Whatever,' Kerry said. Erykah figured that was a yes.

'The lottery is a fake. The money's not real. I mean, it is real, but I'm not going to get any of it. We were set up to launder that money. Forced to donate it away.'

'To the SLU,' Kerry said.

'That's right.'

'Funny,' Kerry said. Erykah could all but see the gears turning. 'And it seems to me, Morag is from Scotland, so . . .'

'You think she's involved in this?' Erykah said. It seemed unlikely that someone so high up the political food chain would dirty her hands with such an obviously criminal enterprise. Then again, stranger things had happened. And she still didn't know who Livia really was. If it was Morag, then her reasons for staying out of the spotlight made sense.

The more she thought about it, the more the pieces dropped into place. The Scottish notes. Running a candidate north of the border. Morag was always rumoured to want the top job in her party, but it had never happened. With the total collapse of their support north of the border at the general election, no one would blame her for jumping ship. No one would be overly surprised if a new party came out of nowhere and she defected to it.

And it was her own constituency that the body had been found in.

'Right, so what you don't know is that a couple of days ago someone tipped me off to something. Someone who I was chatting with online, like you,' Kerry said, leaning in.

'Go on,' Erykah said, leaning over the table so her forehead was inches from Kerry's.

'It was a picture of Morag Munro. She was up in Scotland the day the Schofield body was autopsied and she was there – at the post-mortem. The photographer didn't know who the body was at the time. It was no big deal, then that body was identified and he thought, well this is a strange coincidence. So he sends it to me, right? And I thought maybe this is more than a coincidence. But no one else has seen it, yet.'

'Morag's in the photo.'

'That's right,' Kerry said. 'He tells me to check something called the Exif data on the photo – it's the metadata that tells you when and where it was taken? Just so I know it's real and not a trap.'

'Right. Good. And?'

'And, it was taken in Cameron Bridge, right? So I call up the morgue to check because why not? I guess the staff there are not too concerned about security, because the woman I talked to basically confirmed that Damian Schofield was the only post-mortem that day.'

Erykah nodded. She had expected something like this, but it was incredible to have it confirmed. 'My God.'

Kerry continued. 'The thing about Morag is, well, she's not at all what she pretends to be. She has this public image of being whiter than white, you know, like a schoolteacher or a nun? Meanwhile, she's screwing my boss, one of our producers – and in return he adjusts the headlines to suit her.'

Morag Munro having an affair and planting headlines? It sounded so unlikely, it had to be true. 'Are you sure about that?'

'Well . . .' Kerry said. 'Pretty sure. I mean, I heard him tell one of our presenters not to cover the Schofield case when the guy was still missing. Why would he do that? Usually we're all over dead bodies like flies.' Kerry stopped and took a sip of her tea. 'Figuratively speaking, I mean.'

'And the blind item you posted, about the senior politician – that was them?' Morag seemed a little long in the tooth to be indulging in affairs, but that had never stopped any male MPs from chasing down extracurricular excitement.

Kerry nodded and poured tea from the steaming pot. 'Exactly. I was maybe too subtle because nobody put it together.'

'You think she has something to do with the SLU?'

'It makes sense, doesn't it?' Kerry said. 'Jonathan – that's the producer – he was all over your donation story. Really bigging it up. Like, before anyone else was. Almost like someone told him to make something out of it. And I mean, the SLU wasn't even really on the map, news wise, until we did that.'

Erykah nodded. But if that was the case, then Kerry would be one of the first people they suspected.

'So you sent her an email.'

'Yeah. From the Media Mouse account. Just said "heads-up".'

'But you didn't tweet it.'

'No, it felt like too much about her all in one go. I wanted to sit on it a while first,' Kerry said. 'And I wanted to see if she would do something. I thought I was being safe . . .' Kerry went to pick up her tea, but her hand was trembling. She set it down again. 'I didn't even think of the IP address. When you found me, it was like, oh shit. That same IP would have been on the email I sent to Morag, even though I used a throwaway email. I should have taken precautions and I didn't. I didn't think until it was too late.'

'I'm sure she gets a lot of strange emails. She's not going to pass it on to the police, is she?' Erykah said.

'No, I don't think she will,' Kerry said. 'But she might pass it on to someone else, which is why I thought, when you found me . . .'

'Yeah. No, I see what you mean.' Erykah sipped her tea but what she needed right now was a whisky. 'And I can't tell you for sure whether that's the case or not, because I don't even know who's behind all of this. All I know about are the people I've met.'

'Who are?'

'Major Abbott, and two guns for hire.'

'Well it's not Abbott. He's worse than useless. I saw him give a talk when I was at university.' Kerry frowned, remembering. 'I mean, the guy was so wasted he could barely stand up straight, much less give his speech. And he ditched right after, didn't stay to sign books or anything. Everyone else was so off their faces they didn't notice. But he's, like, a joke.'

Erykah nodded. 'That was my thinking as well. It can't be him; he doesn't have the clout to pull it off.'

'And the others?'

Erykah waved a hand. 'Usual criminals. They're in it for the money, not the conspiracy. Can't be them. There's someone else, but I've never seen her. I don't even have a name, not a full one anyway. A woman. I heard the Major call her Livia. That's all I know.'

'So it could be . . .'

Erykah nodded. She could imagine what Kerry was going to say. 'Morag.'

'Yeah.' Kerry checked her watch. 'I should go. My boss is going to kill me.'

Erykah reached for her arm. 'Is there some way you can call in sick? Until this all blows over.'

'Not go in?' Kerry snorted. 'Unless you're going to pay my rent and bills, it's not exactly an option.'

'You don't seem to appreciate,' Erykah said, 'the danger you're in. Losing your job is bad, sure. But if this goes the way I think it's going you're going to end up dead.'

'So I'll play it cool.' Her eyes darted around. Erykah could tell she wasn't as calm as she was pretending to be.

'Play it cool? When the whole world is looking for you and there are people out there trying to kill you?'

'What else can I do,' Kerry said. 'If it is Munro, what point would there be in going to the police? I mean, the Shadow Home Secretary of all people. And we have no evidence. Nothing solid.'

'I know, I know,' Erykah said.

'But as long as I keep tweeting, they can't really do anything, can they? I mean, it's not like they're going to take out someone in the public eye.'

'You saw a mortuary photo so you know what they're prepared to do. I found you in less than a day. It's just a matter of time before someone else figures out who you are, and then . . .' Her voice tailed off. 'Isn't there somewhere you can go for a few days? Family?'

'The editors of all the papers are following me now,' Kerry waved her hand in the air. The more she said, the more she seemed convinced of the truth of what she was saying. 'Chief reporters, columnists, everyone. The entire world would notice if something happened to me. Right?'

'You think those editors are following you because they wish you well?' Erykah grabbed the sleeve of Kerry's coat. 'All you are to them is a story. If you end up in a box those people won't be leaping to your defence. They'll be dancing on your grave in 36-point type, all the papers, above the fold. You're not a human to them – you're content.'

'Are you going to keep me safe?' Kerry shook off Erykah's arm. 'Right now, I have a boss who's breathing fire because I was supposed to be back half an hour ago, a dozen mentions to answer, and a thousand new followers. Unless you have a better idea, I'm going to keep doing this my way.'

Erykah was aghast. How did the girl not seem to realise what could happen? But was it really so different from when she was thrown into the public spotlight herself all those years ago, naïve and unprepared? 'I have to go to the Highlands tonight, but I promise you, I will be trying to find a way to get you out of this,' Erykah said. Kerry wasn't listening. She was checking her phone for tweets and mentions.

Erykah watched as Kerry disappeared up the stairs and out the door. She hoped for the girl's sake it wasn't the last time they saw each other. It was only after the door swung shut that Erykah noticed that Kerry had left her black and yellow scarf on the chair. She picked it up and stuffed in into her bag.

: **22** :

'Where's he gone?'

'Quick, this way!'

The noise of the approaching enemy grew louder. The Major's heart was beating hard. He felt the blood coursing all the way to his fingertips and he hunched near the ground. The drills, the training, the fight-or-flight responses he had practiced over and again as a young officer. They should have switched into automatic. They did not. He had cowered and run like a fool down the alley at the back of the pub.

This wasn't the Falklands, and the shouts of the advancing mob weren't coming from Argentinians. He was in Cameron Bridge, hiding behind the bins in a back alley. It was, or at least was meant to be, his first public appearance north of the border, bringing the European Parliament campaign direct to the Scottish public.

Erykah had made some excuse about coming up on an overnight train, giving him no choice but to stay at the cottage with his wife. At least she let him sleep alone in the guest bedroom – he told her that the ongoing building work was too much of a distraction, and no, she wasn't required to come to the kick-off event tomorrow either. He wasn't sure if he had imagined the look of relief that crossed her face.

It had to go well today. Had to. There had been yet another sideswipe insult in the newspapers the night before: he was in danger of becoming a national punchline.

It was only a little thing. Hardly worth a moment's notice. An aside in a society column comparing the Major's recent forays into public life to his father's. 'He may be an Abbott, but By George he's no George,' to put it precisely. The judgment stung.

He had run the water hot in the downstairs shower and checked his voicemail while the room filled up with steam: sure enough, that familiar Scottish accent was the sole occupant of his inbox. He deleted the messages one by one and wondered why, apart from misplaced loyalty, he had ever signed up to be involved in the charade in the first place.

Ah yes, the money. That was it. He swigged from an emergency whisky flask and climbed into the shower.

The water had rolled down his back, releasing a whiff of sweat and stale alcohol. Whitney was something of a connoisseur of showers, having been shuttled between boarding schools and sports clubs in his youth, then moving on to barracks and hotels as an adult. Of these, hotels were by far the best: endless water, ample clean white towels and slick, tiled walls that he never tired of. But he had to admit that his wife's endless renovations were paying off. Finally, he had a decent shower in the Highlands.

The Major had turned off the taps and flung the shower curtain open. A ghost of his own form stood in the mirror before him, the features slowly becoming recognisable as the steam cleared. The barrel-shaped body, the skin slack over his chest and belly, the white hairs. He realised with a dull shock that he was older now than his father had ever been.

What would George have been doing with old age? Not chasing women or fannying about with European politics, that was for certain. But in Cameron Bridge, in the heart of the Commandos' historic training ground, Whitney at least looked the part.

He had cleared his throat and made eye contact with the old man in the mirror, trying to remember the key talking points to focus on. 'The spectacular failure of the Yes campaign shows us its supporters should not be awarded the consolation prize of additional powers for Holyrood,' he intoned. 'We must not give in on a fully reunited Britain. The dream consequence of this loss should be a steady erosion of Holyrood's powers until it can be abolished.'

Whatever George Abbott's reaction to his son's career might have been, the Major would never know. He had died of a stroke three days before Whitney's passing out ceremony. The papers printed long obituaries, extolling the elder Abbott's bravery – yet another of the old guard gone. Whitney had stood at the funeral in full dress uniform, his face stony and tearless at the graveside as the gunmetal coffin was lowered into the ground. 'A Hero's Farewell,' screamed the *Mail on Sunday*. 'Last of the Good Guys,' harrumphed the *Telegraph*.

A great man, perhaps, Whitney thought. But George Abbott was never a good guy.

The way things were going, the Major doubted very much that anyone would remember him except as a footnote to his father's legacy. Much less as either great or good. Especially now, this afternoon, cowering as he was in the alley with angry protestors coming after him.

'I saw him go this way!' More shouts, then the footsteps went off in another direction.

The plan had been simple and designed for maximum impact. They would start at the top of the High Street, next to the war memorial, in the shadow of Ben Nevis, metres from where the seventeenth century fort had been established to hold back the savage clans and roving barbarians of the Highlands. He would announce the SLU's manifesto to the crowd and to the press with a backdrop of rugged mountains and white-water burns. The Major would mass his supporters at the start of the West Highland Way, getting them ready for the march to Holyrood which he would join at appropriate times. 'The speeches should be over in about an hour,' Heather promised. 'And the forecast is sunshine and no rain. You couldn't ask for a better start.'

He had stood in the square in the centre of town, as arranged. The Major's feet were planted a shoulder's width apart, his kilt waving in the breeze. Heather was there, and she minded the table where she piled neat stacks of pamphlets. She set up a large cardboard cut-out of the Commando Memorial on one side of the table and a photo of Abbott Senior on the other, to remind passers-by who the Major was. Several dozen Keep Scotland United signs on wooden sticks were stacked nearby.

A few people milled around, but it was hard to tell who was there for the rally in the crowd of the shoppers and tourists. Several kept stealing glances at the Major. He kept a broad grin glued to his face but started to wonder: where were all the supporters?

They must be waiting for a signal to advance. He raised one hand and bellowed to indicate that the rally had begun. No sooner had he done so than one scruffy onlooker unrolled a makeshift banner made from a bed sheet. On it was spray painted Go Home London Elite. Within a minute, dozens more were shouting the slogan.

Whitney looked back at Heather. She was offering placards to the growing crowd but finding no takers. 'Call the police!' Whitney growled. But she didn't hear him because a bearded Scottish nationalist with a tattered Yes saltire knotted over his shoulders was arguing with her. The Major couldn't make out what they were saying – it seemed to be something about permits and regulations. Trust a filthy Nat to be banging on about health and safety at a time like this.

A pair of men started pushing their way towards him. A few of the protestors were arguing with them and holding them back. Could these be his belated supporters? He didn't like the look of them, but any port in a storm. 'Let them through!' he bellowed, and the Nationalists fell back.

The pair of men ran up to him. The Major opened his arms in a welcome and smiled broadly. At that exact moment one of the men coughed up a ball of spit and hurled it at his face.

'Get tae fuck,' the man said as Whitney wiped the frothing glob off his moustache with his jacket sleeve. 'Get yersel oot of Cameron Bridge or we'll set about ye.'

'You disgusting nationalists have held Scotland to ransom too long!' The blood rose in the Major's face and he went beet purple. 'I am here to make sure you never soil the memory of the Union again!'

The men laughed. 'You got us all wrong,' the spitter smirked. The Major glowered and puffed out his chest, but the skinny man did not flinch. 'We're not SNP,' the weedy fellow behind him said. 'Spineless cunts with their votes and referendums. We just hate all you English.' The spitter hocked up again and deposited a spatter of saliva, this time on the toes of the Major's shoes.

Whitney clenched his hands tight and brought them up to his shoulders. 'I demand you face me in a fair fight!' he said. 'Marquis of Queensberry rules!' It had been decades since he'd learned to box in the corps, but by God and country, if a man wasn't prepared to engage in fisticuffs defending the honour of the Union and all it stood for, then when would he be?

The two men looked at each other and laughed. 'Oooh, Marquis of Raspberry,' said the first one. 'Never heard of him, or his rules.'

'Lay off him,' the bearded man with the Yes cape pulled at the shoulder of the spitter. 'This is a peaceful protest. You two were banned from the High Street for kicking off outside the Maryburgh Inn. Just go home and no one has to call the police.' He turned to the Major. 'This lot aren't with us, they're—'

'Ah, fuck that,' the spitter said. His own fist whipped out at high speed, connected with Yes man's temple and sent him straight to the ground. He wheeled back to face Major Abbott, his hands balled loosely, his jaw tucked in. 'Six times junior Muay Thai champion, all

Scotland,' he said and spat on the ground again. 'Come and have a go, old man. And bring yer Marquis of Elderberry.'

A few more people had pushed through. They peeled off to Heather's table and picked up the signs. Not, as Whitney hoped, to come to his defence. He watched in horror as they ripped the signs off the placards to use the sticks as makeshift weapons. The crowd, which had been patchy at first, was now spilling from the square onto the High Street. The Major turned and ran.

It had not been his finest hour – that much was certain.

And now here he was, shivering in an alley while the enemy galloped by.

The back door of the pub creaked open. Heather looked up and down the alley in a panic. The Major, doubled over in his kilt, scurried to the safety of the building.

She closed the heavy door behind them and double-locked it. 'The police are on the way,' she said.

'Tell me this was not part of your plan?' The Major brushed dirt from his knees and straightened up. 'Because with all due respect—'

'I know that really means, fuck you,' Heather said.

'*With all due respect*,' the Major repeated, 'I am not convinced the media strategy of this campaign has been successful to date.'

Heather sighed. 'You don't have to tell me twice.' The SLU secretary had watched in horror as yet again the campaign shot to the top of trending topics for all the wrong reasons. The launch in Cameron Bridge had been weeks in the making. There had been websites to design, flyers and signs to print. She had got the word out all over social media and press releases. 'The thing is,' she looked at the floor. 'Those other guys were my idea. I told them there was twenty quid in it if they turned up and ruffled the crowd a bit.'

Whitney's jaw dropped. 'You . . . you paid those yobs?'

Heather shook the hair out of eyes and looked up defiantly. 'I thought if it looked like some bitter Nats had come out to threaten us, it would play better to the media,' she said. 'Peaceful protests never get coverage. We need people to understand how the silent majority has been bullied throughout this process.'

'Good God,' Whitney said.

The pub landlord and his wife smiled uncomfortably from behind the bar. A grainy black-and-white CCTV monitor showed the scene outside: from the few dozen who had been chasing the Major to begin with, about fifty people had come down from the square and now gathered around the pub. Most looked to be harmless and a few were foreign backpackers who didn't realise what was going on, but among those with placards were a hard-core few holding bottles and sticks and one with what looked unnervingly like a crowbar. A group of reporters and television cameras ringed the protestors.

'Fuck's sake,' Heather mumbled. She gripped the shoulder strap of her bag so tightly her knuckles went white.

'Is the bar open?' the Major said.

The landlady rolled her eyes. 'I thought all you needed was the phone,' she said. 'I don't want any trouble in here.'

'Please. . . . Eilidh,' Heather glanced down at the landlady's nametag. Her accent shifted subtly, from regionless public schoolgirl to the faintest lilt of Scottish tones. 'We may be here some time.'

Eilidh narrowed her eyes as she registered the change in Heather's voice. But she said nothing, just turned and plucked a full bottle of Whyte & Mackay from behind the counter and set it on the bar alongside a grimy shot glass.

'Pour it yersel' then,' she said. The Major reached eagerly for the bottle but Eilidh blocked his hand with her gnarled paw. 'Ten pounds per single measure,' she said.

'Disgraceful,' Heather said. Her voice had returned to its former haughty register.

'Don't be ungrateful,' the Major said as he reached into his sporran. 'We're guests.' He slapped a roll of fifty-pound notes on the counter and nodded at Eilidh. 'I'll have the lot,' he said.

Eilidh's eyes were still narrowed, but she nodded approval as she counted up the green Scottish notes and tucked them into her apron.

'What are they shouting out there?' The Major looked back at the CCTV.

'Not sure.' Heather scrolled down her smartphone. 'Oh.' A video, shot by a news team outside, looked even more threatening than it had only minutes ago. 'They're chanting, "go home you English fucks".'

'Bit racist that, isn't it?' the Major said and downed his drink. The landlady topped up the glass straightaway. 'I would get the solicitor on the blower if I were you.' Not that he set any particular stock by political correctness, but it would be some satisfaction to see the Left's own rhetoric used against them.

The Major downed the next drink as well. It hit the back of his throat like liquid fire. He looked over to see Heather still ogling that infernal phone, the muscles in her jaw jumping as she ground her teeth. Whitney thought about London. What he wouldn't give to be there now, having a quiet drink alone. Or perhaps rolling around in the sheets with someone fragrant and firm, then having a quiet drink alone. Anywhere but here.

Heather glowered at her smartphone, unable to do anything but watch as the situation went from bad to worse. Now the town's Yes Coalition organiser was talking to reporters. The media coverage that should have been the SLU's had been hijacked by a bunch of beardy do-gooders and neds steaming on Buckfast.

A loud knock at the pub door made her jump. 'Police!' a woman shouted through the post slot. 'We're here about the disturbance.'

'Fucking finally,' Heather blurted. She bounded to the door and slid the lock open. 'Thank you so much for getting here so quickly, thank you, thank you,' she gushed. Two figures in high-vis jackets over black police uniforms led her and the Major outside. She was reassured to note they had come prepared with helmets, batons and shields.

'They sent one man and one girl?' the Major scoffed. 'Political correctness isn't going to help us at a time like this. We need the real constabulary, not a brace of community officers.'

'Charming,' the woman officer addressed Heather. 'Is he always like this?'

Heather shrugged. 'Are you here to help or what?'

The woman sighed and turned round. The police formed a barrier in front of Heather and the Major and opened the back door, using their riot shields to push back the jeering crowd that had gathered there. The publicans smiled and waved the unwelcome visitors off, then closed and locked the door behind them.

Newshounds and citizen journalists jostled with each other to get the best footage on their smartphones and the Major took a deep breath. He put on the thousand-yard stare and gazed out over the crowd. If the buggers were going to try to attack him a second time, well it wouldn't work. This time he was ready.

The protestors, meanwhile, seemed uncertain about the police presence and the chants died away. Even the reporters appeared to be holding their breath, waiting to see what happened next. 'Awright, you English wanker,' a voice said from inside the crowd.

'Racist Jock scum!' the Major yelled back. He scanned the assembled faces for the culprit, but couldn't tell who had said it. One of the police officers turned his head and shot the Major a warning look. Heather laid her hand on his sleeve.

'Whitney,' she said under her breath, 'leave it.' Her face returned to its usual, composed countenance. It was as if the presence of television reporters had a pacifying effect.

The Major shrugged her off. 'No, woman, damn it,' he said. 'Anti-British sentiment is the last socially acceptable bigotry, and I've had it with this ridiculous double standard.'

'There are cameras,' she hissed. The crowd started to inch them closer and closer against the locked door. The police appeared to be getting instructions through earphones. They nodded silently, but Whitney couldn't tell what was going on.

'Forget the cameras,' he said. She might have the ability to run hot and cold on demand, and switch off her anger for the benefit of the media, but he was not about to take it lying down. 'This is about principles!' the Major roared, and shook a huge, knobbly fist at the crowd. Someone grabbed his arm and jerked it back. He attempted to twist his body away. Too late, they were on him now. 'Police!' he yelled, appealing to the officers for help.

'We are the police,' said a woman's voice in his ear. The grip on his arm wrenched back further. 'And we're taking you in for disturbance of the peace.' Her partner, with a good six inches and two stone on the Major, tightened the cold bracelets of handcuffs onto his wrists.

He and Heather were bundled through the alley to a car park then into the back of a van and the double doors were slammed shut. The jeering crowd followed. A few kicks bashed the side of the van and the sound of muffled laughter echoed in the alley. Sirens on, the vehicle zoomed away through the narrow streets.

The Major was sat on a hard bench opposite Heather, struggling against the tight handcuffs. 'Oh, would you pull yourself together?' she said.

'That's fine for you to say, you're not the one whose very reputation is at stake.' His high forehead glistened with sweat and was almost as red as his eyes. 'I should have known better than to leave this event to someone so—'

Heather scowled. 'So what?'

'Two-faced,' the Major said.

Heather huffed and turned away.

After a couple of minutes the van came to a stop. The policewoman who had cuffed the Major popped open the back door and led them out into an unfamiliar street. Unlocking the cuffs, she told them they were free to go.

'We're not being arrested?' Heather said. The policewoman shook her head.

'The danger has passed,' the policewoman said. 'Provided you agree to leave the Highlands in peace and not organise such a demonstration again, you are welcome to depart the area without any further police involvement.'

'Wait! What?' Whitney spluttered. 'Anyone with eyes can see that the demonstration was against us, not the other way round.'

'Whitney, come on,' Heather tugged at his sleeve. They were in the car park of Whitney's hotel on the edge of town, some two miles from the High Street. 'I'll call a cab and we'll get the next train back.' She turned to the policewoman. 'We've had enough of this rubbish little town anyway.'

'No, damn it!' Whitney snatched his arm back from Heather's grasp and turned to the policewoman, whose colleague had now emerged from the front of the van and was watching with interest. 'I know my rights. As a veteran and a public servant, this is a gross infringement of my free speech.'

The policewoman laughed like a schoolteacher indulging a child's tantrum. 'You are the ones who came to Cameron Bridge with the intent of causing a scene. You organised a public political event, opposite the council building, without a permit, much less completing the relevant health and safety assessments,' she said.

'Health and safety?' Whitney bellowed. 'Health and safety? This is about freedom of speech, damn it!'

The policewoman exchanged glances with her colleague. The large man slipped a baton out of his belt. 'All things considered, you are lucky we don't take you both in. We had a quick chat with Mickey and Duncan,' she said. Whitney shrugged. 'Don't you remember? The men your assistant paid to kick things off. Or didn't she ask their names?' she said. 'They're regulars at the station, records long as your arm.'

Her fellow officer nodded gravely. 'Long as your arm,' he repeated. His enormous hands slowly extended and retracted the baton.

Whitney's head whipped round to look at Heather. 'Is that true?'

'I have friends in high places,' Heather leaned forward and jabbed her finger in the middle of the policewoman's protective vest. 'Your superiors will hear about this.'

The two police exchanged glances. 'Is that so?' she said. 'Only you happen to be already speaking to the ranking officer in Cameron Bridge.' She nodded at her colleague. The policeman leant across and tapped Heather's knuckles with the end of the baton. She barked and snatched her hand away, rubbing it with her other hand.

'How dare you attack a lady!' the Major leapt in. His voice wobbled, breathless, at the scratchy height of its range. 'This is nothing short of police brutality! I will call my solicitor and ensure you are out of a job immediately!'

The police pair smirked at each other and the man slipped the baton back into his belt. 'You do that, by all means,' the policewoman nodded. 'Police Scotland appreciates your input on our quality of public service provision.' The van door slammed. She waved at them as the van drove off. 'Have a good day.'

The small ferry chugged its way across Loch Linnhe and a sharp wind pulled at Erykah's coat. To the north, the mountains behind Cameron Bridge caught the bits of afternoon sunshine; to the south, the outlines of Lismore and Mull jutted into the water in gradations of indigo blue. The ride across the narrows was a short one and she walked off the boat straight into the village of Ardgour. She double-checked a slip of paper, but really, it was not necessary: there were only a handful of bungalows facing the water. One small garden was decorated gaily with scraps of colourful rope and old fishing floats wound through the links of the fence. On a buzzer by the door was a label with letters scratched out in formal, old-fashioned block capitals. *L. MAN-DELKERN.* She pressed the button next to the nameplate.

She wondered how the demo in town was going. She had expected the Major to be upset when she told him she couldn't go, but he didn't even ask her why. Ordinarily she would have been keen – any chance to make herself more useful – but with one day in Cameron Bridge, there wasn't time to do everything.

A figure appeared behind the glass door. Wisps of white hair topped a familiar face, older now, but still recognisable. 'You made it,' Leonie said, and held out her arms. The tiny woman clasped Erykah in a strong embrace and stood back to look at her. 'Rikki Barnes,' she said. 'It's been a long time.'

'It's Erykah Macdonald now,' she said, and winced, thinking that was one more thing she would have to get used to again: her old name, once she and Rab split up. 'For a short time anyway.'

'My eyes aren't very good,' Leonie said, and raised a pair of bifocals hanging on the chain. 'You haven't changed one bit.'

'As you said, your eyes aren't very good.'

Leonie laughed, a rich chuckle broken by a lung-wrenching cough. 'Please, come in. Before the wind blows you in.'

'You're looking well,' Erykah said, and followed her into the front room. The wide front window looked out over the ferry slipway and loch. The side tables and ledges were crowded with stacks of books, and plant pots with cacti and succulents of all kinds and sizes, including a jade plant as big as a person.

Leonie smiled. 'Kind of you to say. I feel like rubbish,' she said. She eased herself into a green armchair with a crocheted cushion. 'Though judging by the general health of my contemporaries, feeling rubbish is something of a privilege these days.'

Erykah wasn't certain, but Leonie must have been near ninety by now. University rumour had it that the emeritus professor was a child chess prodigy, smuggled out of Poland at the start of the German occupation in 1939. Sometimes the story claimed she had been hidden in the back of an ox cart for three weeks across central Europe until reaching the Pyrenees, then hiked alone over the border to Spain, where she joined a ship leaving for Britain. Others said she travelled across the continent disguised as a German national, using the papers of a child of the same age who had died at birth, stolen from an orphanage and paid for with her mother's own gold teeth. Whichever version, it always ended up with Leonie in Britain and supposedly cracking codes at Bletchley Park when she was still in her teens.

Whether or not it was true was something Leonie herself never confirmed. What she would acknowledge was that she was alone among her immediate family in escaping the Lodz ghetto. And that the Mandelkerns, being among the first residents of the ghetto, were also some of the first moved on to the death camps at Chelmno. This grim count included the death of her father, a mathematician and member of the Polish Cipher Bureau. The Biuro Szyfrów had done much to advance cryptography between the wars, including early steps towards the cracking of the Enigma code. And Leonie had arrived in Britain during the winter, early in 1940. That much was a matter of record.

Leonie arranged the fabric of her shawl around her shoulders. 'So,' she said, her eyes bright and curious. 'What are you doing in the Highlands?'

'A bit of a side job,' Erykah said. 'When I realised I was going to be up in your part of the world anyway, I thought I might as well drop in to talk about those emails I sent.'

'Well, that's wonderful. It's always better to put heads together in person, saves so much time.' Leonie looked over the top of her glasses. 'I assume this other side job of yours has nothing to do with academics.'

Erykah shook her head. 'Even if I had wanted to return to university I'm not sure that door would have been open to me.'

'You should have stayed in contact,' Leonie said. 'I asked the dean what became of you, but he said you left no forwarding address.'

'I wanted to disappear,' Erykah said. 'So I got married instead.'

Leonie eyed the large rings Erykah was wearing. 'So you did. You were always one of my best,' she said. 'So much ahead of you. I wished you had come back.'

What even did that mean now? Maybe, as Rab had always said, what Erykah had needed to do was pick herself up, dust herself off, and start all over again. Doing so seemed like an impossible task. Maybe accepting her fate and slinking off to lick her wounds in the suburbs was the same as defeat. She should have tried again. Worse things had happened to better people and all of that.

But searching Leonie's face she saw no judgment, no points being scored. Only a statement of fact. *I wished you had come back.* No one, so far as she could remember, had ever said such a simple thing to her. 'Maybe I should ask, what are you doing up here?' she asked. 'Why Scotland?'

'Why anywhere?' Leonie said and looked around the room with its bookshelves leaning under the weight of books and plants. 'London life didn't suit me any longer. This is about as far away from London as you can get, in more ways than one.'

Erykah looked out the window. The village was hardly even that: an inn by the ferry terminal, a few houses, a small shop with only the basics, then sheep farms as far as the eye could see. 'I couldn't imagine living in a place like this.'

'No?' Leonie said. 'I think you could get used to anything. There's one bus a day to Cameron Bridge, and that is enough. It's quiet. Quiet is sometimes a good thing.'

'But you loved the students,' Erykah said. 'And the students loved you.' If circumstances had made Leonie's existence a solitary one, it was the students in London who became her second family. Most professors would have found ways to wiggle out of lecturing first year undergraduates, but Leonie relished it. She often said that there was nothing to match the thrill of seeing a light go on in someone's eyes when they mastered a skill they thought was beyond their ability. As a result the students were loyal to a fault to her. And she to them.

'I know, I know.' Leonie raised both hands in a gesture of surrender.

'It's too much work. I'm too old. I was already old when you were there, already being pushed out of the department,' she said. 'Here, I have a view of the loch, some trees. It's a short walk to the inn for a drink. I grow things. Did you know if you take a clipping of a succulent, it will root itself? In rocks, in sand, with nothing to sustain it.'

Erykah looked at the plants jostling for space on the windowsills, the sharp points of aloe, the spotted serpentine patterns on the gasterias, the Mother-of-Thousands dropping its tiny plantlets into other pots and on the floor. 'I didn't know that. It's amazing they grow here.'

'They wouldn't last long outside.' Leonie unfolded herself from the chair. 'Nor would I, for that matter,' she said. 'But it's comfortable here, and homely.' Leonie smiled, her lips drawn thin over her yellow teeth. 'Especially these last few years with so many bakers and grocers coming to the Highlands from Poland. Finally, I can buy a loaf of bread in this country that I don't feel ashamed to eat.'

'You never wanted to move back? After you retired? Everything must have changed for the better by now.'

'No. And that's why. There is a saying, what is it? You can never go home again.' Leonie shook her silver head. 'Visiting a memorial to the people I knew, to those who died in the ghetto, that is not the place I want to see.' Her voice dropped to a whisper. 'People of my generation are already history. My memories of it should stay as they are.' Her face was drawn now, the lines in her skin pulled vertical. 'The home of my childhood is a fragrance I catch sometimes on the wind. A piece of a song being played far away, a reflection in glass. It doesn't exist in life.' Leonie drew the shawl close around her shoulders and smiled again, though it did not quite reach her eyes.

She stayed that way for several minutes, Leonie with her back to the window, the early spring light concentrated by the windows.

'Anyway,' Leonie said. 'Have you brought the rest of the files?'

'I need them back before tonight though, or else there might be trouble,' Erykah said.

'Ah. Pity about that, but not crucial,' Leonie set out a pot of jasmine tea and two tiny cups on a table. 'So, with the pages you faxed me, I've found something very interesting.'

Erykah sat down. 'You cracked it?'

'Not yet. But nearly. If what I'm thinking is right, it's a straightforward code. I'll show you how,' Leonie said. 'My first thought when I saw how it was laid out – the solid block of text – was that it's a variation of the Caesar cipher.'

'A stands for B, B stands for C, and so on?' Erykah said.

'Exactly,' Leonie said. 'There are twenty-six letters in the alphabet, so you can offset the letters using one of twenty-five different Caesar ciphers to come up with a substitution code. But using the same alphabet throughout would be very easy to crack, and I'm sure you will have tried that already.' Erykah nodded.

'But there's a variation you may not know about. It's called the Vigenère cipher, and what I'm missing is the key.'

Erykah hadn't heard of a Vigenère cipher before. 'The key?'

'A message encoded with the Vigenère cipher uses a key word over a grid of letters. Each letter in the key indicates a different offset cipher alphabet. So you take your grid of letters here, and write the key over the top of each column.' She turned a copy of the text around to show Erykah. 'It just repeats across all the columns.' Leonie wrote the letters K EY, K EY, repeating, at the top of each column until she reached the edge of the page. 'The longer the key, the harder it is to break.'

She pulled out another paper. On this was the alphabet written out over and over again in her handwriting, but each time, offset by one letter. 'Each line here is one alphabet,' she explained. 'This is called the Vigenère square, and as long as you have the keyword, deciphering the message is child's play.'

Erykah examined the Vigenère square. It was an elegant idea, so simple really. 'So the Ks mean all the letters underneath a column with K are offset by ten letters, all the ones under Es are offset by four letters, and all the ones under Ys are offset by twenty-four letters?'

'Exactly right,' Leonie said. 'But what I don't have is the real key in this puzzle, and without that?' She laughed. 'Well, there's a reason the French called it the *chiffre indéchiffrable* for three hundred years,' Leonie said. 'Because it's easy to understand, but hard to crack.'

'But you said it was indecipherable for three hundred years, so someone did figure out how to do it.'

'Yes, they did,' Leonie said. 'Brute force can work if you have the processing power. But I am retired; I have no access to the programs I used to use, or the computers. And it was a very unusual cipher, seldom used. So doing this by hand takes considerable effort. If the key was only five or six letters, then with frequency analysis I might have cracked it by now,' Leonie said. 'The one thing we do have, though, is that when people choose the keys themselves for a private code, instead of keys assigned at random for security, they will choose something easy for them to remember. Which could mean a name or other word they associate with. Something that is meaningful to them.' She paused and sipped the jasmine tea.

'A key word?' Erykah said. Her gaze lit on the surfaces of the room, the profusion of plants, the stacks of books. Framed awards and photographs that seemed familiar, that she recognised from Leonie's old office. A watercolour of a street scene in Lodz between the wars.

'Your cup is going to go cold,' Leonie said. 'Shall I warm it up for you?'

'Oh, that's very kind,' Erykah said. 'It's lovely. I'm just not in the mood for tea right now, it seems a little bit . . .'

'Weak?' Leonie winked. 'I have just the thing. Stay right here.' She disappeared into the kitchen and came back with a small glass bottle filled with pale pink liquid. Leonie set two tiny sherry glasses on the table, decorated with delicate pinks and gold leaf scrolls. She unstoppered the bottle and poured two measures of the liquid. 'Rhubarb spirits,' she said. 'Now that I can buy Polish rectified spirits, I can make my own liqueur.' Erykah sniffed at the glass. 'Please, try it. It's delicious. *Na zdrowie!*'

'Cheers!' Erykah quaffed the drink in one swallow, breathed deeply, and coughed. 'Wow. Wow. That's . . . certainly strong.' Leonie laughed.

'Now, the key word. The question for us is what would have been meaningful to him. I tried his name. First and last, then both together – none of them worked. His wife's name and his children's. The name of the university, a few other keywords that come up commonly. No luck.'

Erykah closed her eyes and tried to remember Schofield's office. The things people carry with them from place to place, continent to continent, over decades of their lives. What meant the most to someone who had travelled the world for his work? 'I think I know what it could be,' she said.

Leonie raised a thin white eyebrow. 'Do tell.'

'When I went to his office, I tried to get into his terminal. There was a password, but it wasn't hard to figure out. There's a photo of him next to his desk with a place that seems to have meant a lot to him.' The words poured out of Erykah as Leonie nodded slowly. It made sense now. The password was easy to guess, not because it was guarding anything on his computer – that would have been too obvious – but because it was guarding something not on his computer at all. No wonder his email and browsing histories looked completely clean. They didn't need to be wiped of information because he had never kept anything important there in the first place.

'So the question,' Leonie said. 'What was the password?'

'Guanaco,' Erykah said. She spelled it out letter by letter. 'It's a mountain near Ushuaia, where he lived in Argentina.'

'Let's try it,' Leonie murmured, inscribing the letters across the top of the code grid in square, only slightly shaky capitals.

Erykah watched as, bit by bit, her old mentor started to decode the grid onto a new sheet. The letters began to join up across the page. But after a few lines there were still no clear words emerging.

'No,' Leonie said. 'A good guess, but this is not it.'

Erykah wasn't willing to let it go. 'No, I think we're on the right track,' she said. 'It's too good a connection not to have some part in the puzzle.'

Leonie smiled. 'Be careful of fits that seems too good to be true,' she warned, tapping her finger on the sheet. 'Because they often are.'

'You don't need to tell me that,' Erykah said. 'Thing is, I don't think this guy was a master of codes. He was smart, sure, but if he was that good, he probably would have been good enough to evade whoever wanted to kill him.'

She closed her eyes and pictured the inside of Schofield's office again. The smell of books and papers, the motes of dust in the shards of sunlight filtering through the windows. The notebooks. The old computer. The crossword puzzle books. The word finds.

The word finds.

'Here's an idea,' Erykah said, turning the sheet back towards her and started to write out the next line of translated code. 'Let's say Damian Schofield loved puzzles, because I know he did. In fact when I first found this piece of paper that's what I thought it was – I thought he was making a word find for his students. Only I couldn't see words in it.'

'I'm listening,' Leonie said, raising her glasses again to her nose to watch what Erykah was doing.

'It's another layer. He left us all the clues we needed, because he thought someone was coming for him. The password was easy to find because he wanted the key to be discoverable. And he left puzzles and word games all over his desk because that was just his way. It's what I would have done.' A puzzle fiend can spot another puzzle fiend. He had scratched the other groups of letters in the margins of his notes, the ones that didn't seems to relate to crossword clues at all. Erykah put her pen down. With several more lines of the grid translated, in diagonal letters, a recognisable word was starting to emerge.

Leonie picked up her pencil and circled the word Density crossing the page in diagonal letters. A few more, going in a different direction, that when complete might spell Shale. Leonie's clapped her hands and rubbed them together. 'Now we're cooking with gas!' she said. 'No doubt the rest of what he's trying to direct us to will be in this pile. How long do we have?'

Erykah checked her watch. 'When's the last ferry?' she asked.

'We have a few hours,' Leonie said. 'But we need to get cracking.'

: **24** :

A wood fire crackled in the corner of the pub over the road from Cameron Bridge station. Winter walkers and climbers gathered around the open fireplace. Steam rose off their damp Gore-Tex layers as they quaffed pints of local ale. Erykah stayed by the bar and sipped a glass of whisky.

There was work to do back in London. Or so the Major said when he rang her. The Highlands to Holyrood tour was cancelled, they were booked on the sleeper train back to London. Heather was driving ahead on the route to cancel reservations and make apologies. The Major didn't say why things had so suddenly changed, and Erykah didn't ask.

Erykah smoothed her hands over her thighs, cased in a long sleeved grey jersey dress. A travel standby, a dress that could stay crumpled in the bottom of a bag for a long weekend and emerge, wrinkle-free and appropriate for most situations. Give or take a statement necklace here or a strappy sandal there.

She had put it in her bag the day she had planned to walk out on Rab and run away with Nicole. It seemed like years ago now.

The thoughts about 'what if' would have to wait until later. She wasn't looking forward to twelve hours of being shut up in a sleeper with the Major because she couldn't stay silent about what she had learned for much longer.

Once she and Leonie had the keyword, everything fell into place. Erykah had finished the decoding and the message was spelled out in words travelling diagonally, back and forth, and up and down through a sea of letters.

If what they put together was true, then it explained why someone might have wanted Schofield to die. He was poised to expose a cover-up that, had it been known before the Scottish referendum, could have affected the outcome. Not to mention proving the government had a stake in keeping the truth of Scotland's energy future secret.

And if this was what was going on behind the SLU, then no wonder there was so much money sloshing about. The thought chilled her to the bone.

Billy and Buster doing a bit of dirty work? That was only scratching the surface. In a pinch you might, if you were lucky, get the police to keep them from your door. When the rot goes right to the core, though, nowhere is safe. Not the police. Not the press. Nowhere.

Her mobile beeped, a text from the Major. *Am running late*, it said. *Check in without me. If anyone asks, you're my wife.*

Erykah ordered another whisky. The barman poured a generous double. She was going to need some liquid courage first.

The station was tiny, the ticket counter and kiosk were already closed for the night. A conductor walked up and down the short platform holding a clipboard. He squinted at the passenger list as Erykah approached. 'Name?' he asked.

'Mrs Whitney Abbott,' Erykah said. She realised she didn't know the Major's wife's name. 'My husband will be along shortly.'

The conductor nodded and crossed a name off the list. He didn't meet her eyes. In a small place like this, her lie probably stood out a mile. But then, the Major had probably been taking this train for years – doubtless it wasn't the first time the staff would have had to look the other way when someone claiming to be his wife came aboard. 'Coffee or tea in the morning?' he asked.

'Coffee for me, thank you,' she said.

'It's another half hour till we depart,' the conductor said. 'Go on and make yourself comfortable. It's a quiet train tonight, so catch the dining car early if you want anything. We'll come by to wake everyone up about an hour before we arrive at Euston.'

'Cheers.' Erykah glided down the narrow corridor and found the tiny room. It had been a sleeper seat she booked on the way up, with a change in Glasgow, so she hadn't even seen the compartments. This train was direct all the way to Euston. The two single beds were arranged bunk style. A neatly folded tartan blanket, hand towel, and single use bar of soap were arranged at the foot of both beds. The heat was turned all the way up, and she fiddled with the mysterious controls to try to get it off. The room smelled like a camping cabin, equal parts wool blanket and industrial cleaner.

'It may not be five-star, but it's clean and comfortable,' the Major said behind her. She jumped, startled, and turned around. His eyes darted around the cabin. Erykah noticed a sheen of sweat across his forehead.

'How did it go?' she asked.

'Long day,' he snapped. 'I need a drink.'

'Just let me touch up my make-up,' she said. 'Wouldn't mind seeing the dining car for myself.' She hoped it would be less stifling than the compartment.

The Major planted a hand on her chest and pushed her back. Erykah stumbled onto the lower bunk. 'No, you wait here,' he said. She couldn't put a finger on it, but something was up with him. His eyes had a strange, watery sheen. Maybe he was sick and that was why they had to cancel the tour?

'Are you OK?' she said.

'Fine, fine,' he mumbled. 'I suppose you'll be wanting to get your head down as soon as possible.'

Erykah didn't want anything of the kind, but it was obvious he wasn't going to let her leave the cabin. He checked his sporran for his wallet and phone, then snapped it shut. He went to the door. 'I'll be back soon,' he said. Erykah smiled until he left.

The mobile in her bag beeped. It was a text from Seminole Billy saying he would meet them at Euston in the morning. Not the person she wanted to see. Right now, though, she had other things on her mind. Such as what she and Leonie had discovered.

Schofield had been an oilman; working out the location and volume of untapped reserves was his bread and butter. So if, for example, there was a project to survey the possibility of fracking in Britain, you would have expected him to be involved. Which he was. Yet when the final report was released in the weeks before the referendum, his name had been dropped from the panel of government advisors.

The surveys reported, unexpectedly, that the highest volume of available gas was not in Scotland. It was in England. Under the Home Counties no less. And according to the reports, Scotland's potential was less than a tenth of what had been predicted in the early days of fracking technology development – a prediction that had been made by Professor Damian Schofield.

According to Schofield's original figures, Scotland would have been viable as an independent country and potentially a player in northern European affairs, with enough energy reserves to rival Norway. There was the possibility that an independent Scotland might gain back a measure of production and population while England sank further into a wholly service-and-tourism industry.

The updated surveys released in the run up to the vote, however, put paid to Schofield's old predictions. And the fact that the Government decided to hold back awarding new oil and gas licenses until after the referendum? It added up to a very suspicious whole.

Schofield's workmate had mentioned a sexual harassment allegation. Plausible? Sure. Plausible enough to put him on probation while the university investigated. Plausible enough to keep him from going to the press with allegations that the oil books were being cooked to look less promising than they really were.

According to Schofield's code the fracking report was a lie. Someone involved with the final report had tweaked the results, swapped the densities for sand and shale, and, hey presto, England looks like the winner and Scotland looks like the loser. Once that was done it was easy to pass off the results to the press, who reprinted the claims without looking any deeper into the data. Only someone with an eagle eye for detail would have had a chance of catching the swap, and even then it had passed plenty of experts by. Farewell to dreams of petroleum trusts and social safety nets. Scotland stays a dependent little fiefdom, good for no more than blasted hunting estates and tins of shortbread.

Until after the referendum, when all of a sudden fracking licenses were being awarded where only months before the official line was there was no oil to be profitably extracted.

But so what? Did the outcome of the referendum rest on that one issue? 'You might be surprised,' Leonie had said. 'The Scottish government supports alternatives to fossil fuel, but they're no fools. They need that short-term oil income to fund upgrades all over the grid so that renewables can feed in where the wind and water power are strongest.'

Leonie gestured to the window. 'A lot of people don't remember, but some parts of Scotland weren't on the grid until recently. This village came on in the '60s, and some of the villages west of here? Not until the '80s. There are still only two lines running in to the peninsula even now. It's not cheap getting infrastructure to the Highlands and Islands.'

She helped herself to another drink of rhubarb liqueur before continuing. 'Storms take out the peninsula's power lines all the time.

People with home turbines will be watching them spin and spin with no way to get the power to the grid. If government can't manage it reliably on that level, what hope is there for wind farms?'

'Sounds like a cop-out to me,' Erykah said. 'Promise renewables, but it's really all about the oil.'

'Yes and no,' Leonie said. 'The oil will run out eventually – or be too expensive to extract, or the price will fall. The question is, who gets the revenues until then, and what do they do with them?'

'Why anyone would trust a politician to do the right thing is beyond me,' Erykah said.

'I know, and I agree,' Leonie said. 'But it's about accountability. As soon as Scotland can't produce any more, it will be offered independence again. And no new infrastructure between now and then.' She looked out at the ferry, still ploughing the few hundred metres of water between the crumbling Cameron Bridge road and the Ardgour peninsula. 'You see that ferry? Most expensive in the country, by the metre. How do they expect young working families to cope with that? And those of us on fixed incomes?'

'But didn't this all come up in the campaign?' Erykah had said. 'The potential new oil fields?'

'A bit, yes,' Leonie said. 'But the media was complicit with the No campaign, and unwilling to join the dots. It was easy to bury positive stories and play up the negative ones.'

'Or distract the media with personal stories and non-existent scandals,' Erykah said. 'I know how that one works.'

'Correct,' Leonie said. 'Energy policy doesn't exist in a political vacuum.'

'So the SLU realised what Schofield knew and tried to guarantee his silence,' Erykah said. But money would not have been enough. The outdated furniture and old computer in his office told her as much as she needed to know: money was not important to him. He was not someone who could be bought off.

She tapped her teeth with a teaspoon. It still didn't quite add up to her. 'But the voters went for No, and no one from the Yes campaign picked up on the errors at the time. Why kill him now, when it doesn't matter?'

Leonie had chuckled. 'Oh, it matters, it always matters, when powerful interests have secrets to keep,' she said. 'Like elephants, they move slowly and they never forget. Once the SLU knew what he knew, he was a marked man. Could you imagine if the general population found out they had been lied to so close to the referendum? People would be demanding a new vote. Especially because it went No. Especially because it was closer than anyone predicted.'

'So they – what's the term?' Erykah asked. 'They sexed it up. Only the opposite of that.'

Leonie nodded. 'They *de*-sexed the report. They put a negative spin on it, buried the real numbers, and got exactly what they wanted. And when the coast was clear and no one would make the connection, they got rid of the weakest link in the chain.'

Erykah felt very out of her depth. Why hadn't she played dumb, let the thugs push Rab around a little, handed over the money and then said goodbye? Why couldn't she have stamped her curiosity down a while longer?

She had played her hand blackmailing the Major and had nothing left to bargain with. This wasn't some common or garden cover-up. This conspiracy had a body count.

She wondered why they had taken her on. Why bother bringing a casual into the fold, if the stakes were so high? Maybe it was because they had thought the danger had passed. Until his body was found, whoever did it probably thought they had got away with it. Sending Erykah in was just a formality. Insurance. Tidying up loose ends.

And if the body was discovered, maybe they needed someone like her to take the fall.

Erykah heard the sound of footsteps in the corridor. The train shook as it started to pull out of the station. There was nowhere to go.

Surely the Major wouldn't kill her himself? The footsteps grew closer. Maybe he was, as he said, tired from a long day. But the signs all pointed to something fishy. The changed plans. Making it so they didn't board together. At such a small station running a skeleton staff, there might not even be CCTV. She hadn't gone to his event during the day. He was the only person who knew she was here. Apart from Leonie, that is.

Her heart sped up. If there were cameras on the train itself, she hadn't noticed. Rab was not expecting her at home tonight. She didn't have the rowing schedule to keep to any more. If she did disappear no one would raise the alarm for a few days. Maybe longer.

There was a tap at the door. Erykah didn't move. A second tap, more urgent. She had no choice but to open the door. The Major was holding two glasses of whisky in his hands.

She could read nothing in his face. 'As requested,' he said, and handed her a plastic cup. She bent her face to the drink, trying to sniff it for poison. Did poison have a smell? All she could detect was a smoky aroma, one of the Islay malts. The carriage jolted hard as it sped up on the tracks. A splash of the drink went down the front of her dress.

'I think a toast is in order,' he said. 'When in Scotland . . .'

'Or when leaving it,' Erykah said. He raised his tumbler to hers, touching the edge, before taking a drink. She mimed a ladylike sip, the amber liquid not quite reaching her lips.

'Phew, that's bracing!' the Major exclaimed. 'I asked for a peated malt, but wasn't expecting a full on campfire.' He leaned towards Erykah and grinned. She shrank back and found herself cornered in the end of the sleeping compartment. His arm reached out past her towards her bag. He must be going for her phone. He was definitely on to her.

The Major, dentured smile still firmly intact, grabbed a bottle of water sticking out of Erykah's handbag instead. 'Water for your whisky?'

'No thanks,' she said and shook her head. The sound of blood was pumping in her ears now like a drumbeat.

'Your choice,' he said, and added a tot of water to his drink. He sipped it and grimaced. 'Bit strong for my taste,' he said, and poured a few more glugs of water in his glass. 'Always been more of a Speyside man myself.' He kicked off his shoes and undid his sporran, and leaned back on the sleeper bed. 'You look like you want to tell me something,' he said.

Erykah was stunned. In all the ways she had imagined the conversation playing out, him starting it was not one of them.

The Major downed his drink and tipped the water bottle to his mouth. He finished off half of it in a single gulp, then wiped his moustache with two fingers. 'You get your words together, honey,' he said. 'I'm going to drain the main vein.' He stumbled into the corridor in search of the toilet.

Erykah exhaled as the door slammed shut and poured her whisky down the sink. There had to be some way out. Jumping off the train was out of the question and there were no scheduled stops for passengers to alight until tomorrow morning at Euston. There were hardly any staff on board, and none who would take on the Major if she called for help.

Maybe she could go to the dining car and scope out who was in there. Maybe somebody she could get talking to, and pass the time in public. Although that depended not only on staying up all night, but convincing someone else – a total stranger – to do it too. And while she knew her powers of persuasion were good, that was a very big ask.

She had gone some way down this route of thinking before it occurred to her that the Major had been gone for a long time.

There was no noise outside, apart from the rhythmic clatter of the train. Several minutes passed. If someone was lying in wait for her outside the door she would have heard them by now. Especially a creaky old goat like the Major.

She turned the door handle and looked out. Not a soul. She tiptoed past the closed doors of the other compartments to the toilets at the end of the carriage. The window on the door at the end of the carriage was open a couple of inches, and the faint smell of cigarette smoke hung in the air. But it was only very faint, and might not even have been his. The women's loo was open; the men's was locked.

Odd. Maybe he was still in there.

'Whitney?' Erykah whispered, and tapped on the toilet door. 'Whitney?' A little louder this time. Still no response. She pressed her ear to the flimsy divide. Nothing. No gasping, no breathing – nothing.

She slipped into the women's toilet and listened through the wall. Still nothing. No farting, no sighing, no tinkle of piss in the toilet or the crumpling of paper. Nothing. She tapped harder, but again, no answer.

Ten minutes passed. She heard someone come up and try the door, then give up and walk away. No response from inside the loo where Whitney was.

Which meant he was probably asleep. Or dead.

She shook her head. No, that would be ridiculous. He could be in another carriage, she thought. Or maybe he had gone to the bar. She wandered in back to the sleeping compartment and sat on the bed. Her eyes rested on the half-empty bottle of water.

The bottle of water that she had taken off Schofield's desk the day she broke into his office. Erykah had forgotten about the bottle. It had been rolling around in the bottom of her bag for almost a week, until the Major found it tonight and added some of the water to his whisky.

When the penny dropped, it clanged. The bottle was poisoned.

'Fuck!' Erykah hurried back to the end of the carriage and tapped at the lavatory door: still locked, still no answer. But she couldn't stay out here waiting forever, someone would see her.

She went to the room, dazed, and locked herself in. It should have been obvious. Cutting Schofield's throat and dumping the body off the coast of Scotland wasn't the first time they had tried to off him. It was the backup plan.

Which meant that whoever planned it probably had to call in some muscle to finish the job.

Such as Billy. Who was going to be waiting when the sleeper arrived in London. She took out her phone. But they were already out of range of a mobile signal and would be for most of the night.

What now? It was an accident, or at least she wasn't the one who had intended to poison anyone. But would the police believe her? What were the chances? 'Slim to none, and Slim's on a diet,' she said out loud, and laughed. That was one of Billy's phrases, the one he said just before breaking her husband's fingers.

She grabbed the Major's sporran off the bed and snapped it open. Inside was his wallet and the cheap little phone he always guarded so jealously. It was switched off. She jabbed at the power button but it appeared to be dead. Shit. She replaced the wallet, dropped the phone into her bag and closed his sporran, careful to wipe her prints from the leather and the metal clasp.

There was the question of being able to sleep in one of the beds. She didn't know much about forensic evidence, but there was probably too much chance of leaving traces behind. Erykah gently transferred herself and her bag from the bottom bunk to the floor.

She stared at the wall of the little room. She wasn't on the passenger register, but had she been caught on camera at the station? Maybe, maybe not. Either way, there was nothing she could do now. She pulled a packet of make-up wipes from her bag and started frantically wiping the hard surfaces in the cabin: the doorknob, the counter, the bottle and cups, the edge of the bed. Eight more hours of sitting and waiting. And then what would happen when she got to Euston?

: **25** :

Shards of morning light criss-crossed the platform at Euston. It was early yet, the hum and buzz of the busy station day was only starting to click into place. Erykah rubbed her eyes. She had managed to doze off for part of the journey, sitting up, but her eyes felt gritty and tired anyway. Every time the train had sped up or slowed down, or came to a stop, she woke. Every set of footsteps down the hall gripped her with panic until long after they passed. She had heard the soft knock at the door of the carriage attendants leaving two cups of coffee outside the compartment; she didn't even open the door to look.

Erykah dug around in her leather bag until she found Kerry's black and yellow print scarf. She pulled it over her hair and flung the ends round her neck to approximate a hijab. Her dark coat was buttoned up, covering most of the long dress. She popped a pair of expensive sunglasses on and checked herself in the mirror above the sink. It wasn't much of a disguise, but it would do, as long as no one was looking too closely. She would have to brazen it out.

The section of the train that had started in Cameron Bridge had joined other trains on the way, and her carriage was now at the far end of a long platform. Erykah walked up the train corridors five, ten, a dozen carriages before getting out. A greater chance of being spotted and remembered by other passengers, maybe – but she was more worried about CCTV in Euston Station. Only a handful of people had boarded with her and the Major. If she happened to be identified on video getting off a Cameron Bridge part of the train it wouldn't take much to put two and two together.

Erykah stepped off the train. Just like in Cameron Bridge, there were no ticket barriers on the sleeper platform. She took a deep breath and counted her steps: stay moving forward, don't look suspicious, and don't look over your shoulder.

Once in the station proper she was folded back into the comforting chaos of rush hour London. There was no rhyme or reason to the crowds in Euston, as early commuters and eager tourists rubbed shoulders. A busker by the front entrance was trying to sing his way out of being moved on by security staff.

Erykah peeled off to join the Tube queue but changed her mind at the last moment. Too many cameras, and she couldn't use her Oyster card without risk. She had money in her bag – a giant roll of it – but all fifty-pound notes and no change.

OK, no problem. Just walk down to Euston Square or Warren Street, maybe a bit further. Buy a coffee to get the change on the way, ticket in cash, done. Maybe Billy would be caught up in traffic. Maybe something else would have come up and she would be able to get somewhere safe before he and Buster turned up. Maybe she would be lucky, and they would be late, and she could get away before they saw her.

No chance. Seminole Billy was parked in the bus zone, leaning against the bonnet of the Merc, squinting one eye against the smoke of his cigarette. She should have known he was as good as his word.

Billy reached into the stream of people and grabbed her elbow. 'Hey, nearly didn't recognise you there,' he grinned. He stood back and took in her full outfit. 'Good thing I can tell that walk anywhere. Didja go and convert on us while you was gone?'

Erykah shrugged as he led her to the car. 'What's that supposed to mean?' No going back now.

'Just saying it ain't your usual look, is all.'

'Oh?' Erykah said. 'What's my usual look?'

'Like you don't know,' Seminole Billy popped open the boot. 'Ten pounds of sugar in a five pound sack.' He reached for her bag. Erykah looked down and saw Buster's familiar legs, and also something that made her heart skip a beat.

A pile of sports bags with Union Jack prints. Crisp and unused, folded in plastic sleeves. Bags exactly like the one Schofield had been dumped in, according to the news.

She clutched her bag with her free arm. 'You know what? I think I'll keep this up front,' she said.

Billy slammed the boot shut. 'Suit yourself,' he said.

Erykah took a crumpled pack of cigarettes from the dashboard and lit up. She savoured the momentary sweet smell of tobacco after lighting, before it was replaced with smoke.

'Didn't know you smoked.' Seminole Billy merged into the queue of traffic, raising a scarred hand to a black cab that let him in.

'New phase of a bad old habit,' Erykah said. Maybe the cigarette would calm her nerves. Wasn't that why they always gave a last smoke to prisoners before they were executed? An ambulance zoomed the other way. She watched it in the rear view mirror until she was satisfied it wasn't heading for the station. 'This fucking week I've had.' She drew a deep lungful and coughed.

'That bad, huh,' Seminole Billy said. 'Did you not have a nice time in Cameron Bridge with the Major? I take it he and Heather are making their own way back.'

Erykah took a deep breath. 'Yeah.' She wondered how long she had before anyone found the body. 'I guess so.'

'Nice trip?'

'It was fine,' Erykah said. She slipped her hand into her bag to check everything was still there. For all she knew Billy was going to drive her off somewhere, slash her, and dump the corpse as he had with Damian Schofield's.

'Cool. We have a stop to make this morning,' he said. 'After that I'll take you home.'

The corners of her mouth turned up in a smirk. 'My knight in shining armour,' she said.

'Someone's gotta be,' he said, and gave her a sidelong glance. 'You don't think much of that husband of yours, do you?'

'No, I suppose I don't.'

'Why'd you marry that dude anyway?' he said. 'I don't know much about cactus but I know a prick when I see one.'

'Bad time of my life. We got married quickly. He seemed nice for a while, and when I came out of my trouble, well, that's where I was.'

'Bad time huh? What'd you do, knife someone?'

She laughed, smoke pluming from her nose. 'No, nothing like that. I was kicked off my degree.'

'Ooo, dreadful,' Seminole Billy said. 'How did you ever recover?'

'Shut up. It was bad at the time. There were drugs involved, someone got shot.'

'Yeah?' he said. 'I never figured you for a runner.'

She shook her head. 'Not even close. I was pretty uptight back then,' she said. 'Believed those scare stories they tell you about drugs at school, you know? Thought if I got downwind of a crack pipe or even a spliff – well. In retrospect, if I'd known the trouble I was getting into, let's say a toke here and there wouldn't have made a difference either way.'

'It was because of a man,' he said. 'Not your husband.'

Was it that obvious? 'Yeah.'

'Did you ever love him?' Billy said. 'Your husband, I mean.'

'I think I did,' she said. 'Maybe I loved the idea of who he said he was.' Fog burned off the city as they turned onto the Westway. She had got so used to seeing the sunrise from the water, she had trouble imagining it any other way. Now the city looked strange to her, the morning routines of London unfamiliar. A mass of people in their own bubbles, millions of them rising and leaving their houses to go about their lives, wrapped up in their little dramas, unaware of any of this.

'How about you?' Erykah asked. 'Love, I mean. There must be some great romance in your past.'

Seminole Billy shrugged. 'There was a woman. We weren't right for each other. I knew going in, she didn't.' He paused. 'About all there is to say on that.'

'If you knew it was wrong, why let that happen?' Erykah asked. 'Wouldn't it be better to not even start?'

'I couldn't help myself,' he said. 'The moth loves the lamp, even though it does neither of them any good.'

Erykah nodded. Love. She didn't know what to think any more. She had loved her husband, for a bit, in a way. She had been in love with Nicole or thought she had . . . well, who knew.

She leaned her head back on the rest and pretended to sleep as they came into Ladbroke Grove. Billy guided the car down a series of streets and to a deserted building site by a canal. The car slowed and the suspension creaked as he navigated the potholes in the hard standing drive. A hulking great gas works loomed over what had once been an industrial estate, cleared for planning a Crossrail station and high rise apartments that, as it turned out, no one was interested in building. The low arched bridges over the canal and towpath were empty save for a barge moored in the water on the far side. Across the canal was Kensal Rise Cemetery. Not much of what had been on the spot before was left, apart from a few shipping containers, broken glass, and pieces of twisted sheet metal strewn about. Behind the high brush and scrub that had grown up on the perimeter of the site, a few trains ran along the cluster of lines from Paddington to the rail depots. It was an eerily empty location for being so close to central London. You could get away with a lot of things in a spot like this.

She tried to remember the sequence of turns they had taken getting there, in order to escape later. It might be her only chance to run before they killed her.

Billy switched off the engine and went to the boot. Buster bounced out and sprinted off towards a shipping container.

Erykah gulped and opened her eyes as slightly as she could. She was in the same position, leaning against the head rest, her hand buried in her bag. There was a lump in her stomach, dread of what she was about to do. She eased her other hand onto the door handle and prepared to push it open. She listened, tried to figure out where he was without moving her head. His cowboy boots made a scratching noise on the dusty ground as he paced in the yard.

Billy leaned down and tapped slightly on the passenger window. Erykah suddenly opened her eyes, sat up and kicked the door open, knocking him backwards several feet. He doubled over, winded. She jumped out with the bag on her shoulder and the pistol from the Major's office held tightly in both hands in front of her.

'You keep backing up now,' she growled. She realised she had no idea whether the gun was loaded or not. Erykah's heart was pounding.

'Fuck's sake, woman, what has gotten into you?' Billy squinted up at her, clutching his middle.

'Shut up. Just shut up. I know what you came here to do. Get your hands up where I can see them.' Slowly, Billy raised his hands.

Buster jogged back towards them with a canvas bag rolled up in his hand. When he saw Erykah and Billy he started sprinting. 'Call him off!' Erykah shouted. Her voice bounced off the grimy brick sides of the canal and echoed back at her.

'Call what off?'

Erykah closed the gap between them to a few metres, aiming now at Seminole Billy's temple. 'I know Buster has a gun and you don't,' she said. 'Call him the fuck off.'

Billy raised his hand. 'Buster,' he said. 'Do what she says.'

'The fuck is this shit?' Buster said, but he did stop, hand still poised over his side. He looked from Billy to Erykah to the open car door and back again.

'I know you're here to kill me and dump me, like you did with Schofield,' Erykah said, 'And just so you know, that is not what I had planned for today.'

'Woman, listen—'

'Shut up! I know what you did. I read Schofield's notes. I know about Livia.'

'The hell are you talking about?' Billy said. He straightened up, keeping his eyes on the gun.

She dropped one hand from the gun and pulled out her mobile. She tapped at it with her thumb.

'Bitch, you better not be calling no police,' Buster said, but stayed planted where he stood. 'We don't know any Livia.'

Erykah dropped her phone on the ground and kicked it towards Billy. 'Go on, pick it up,' she said. He crouched down, hands raised until the phone was within reach, and plucked it off the ground. 'Now look at the screen. Tell me what that is.'

Billy shook his head slowly. 'It's a photo of a whiteboard,' he said. 'Meeting with LL?' He looked at Erykah. 'Sorry, but I got no idea who that is.'

'Liar,' Erykah said. 'Lady Livia. Knows the Major. Schofield's co-worker said she was a journalist working for LCC. Only I called the station and they've never heard of her. So who is she? I reckon she hired you to off him,' she said. 'Like you were going to do with me.'

'This is bullshit,' he said. 'Never met any Livia.'

'Bullshit yourself. I saw the bags in the boot. Exactly like the one he was dumped in.'

Billy nodded slowly. 'OK. OK.' He sighed. 'You're right, sort of. It's complicated. I can explain.' His voice was reedy. She could hear his age in his voice, the years he had spent inside. 'Buster gets those bags from his cousin. Used to run a market stall. Now he's got a shop in Clapham selling ironic junk at insane mark-ups to jerkoffs.' Buster murmured agreement. 'Come on,' Billy said. 'Put the gun down. You, me, Buster here, the Major – we're all on the same side.'

'Right,' Erykah said and licked her lips. 'Guess I should mention the Major's dead.'

Buster's eyes looked like they might pop out of his head. 'You killed him?' he said.

'I wish. He drank a bottle of water, poisoned. The water came from Schofield's office.' She shrugged. 'That was Plan A, right? You were going to poison him, and when it didn't work out, you cut him up and shoved him in a bag and threw it in the ocean.'

Billy offered his hands towards her. She snatched back her phone. 'You're not listening. It's not what you think,' he said.

Erykah took a step back so he couldn't grab the gun. 'I said keep those hands up,' she said. 'If it's not what I think then what is it?'

Billy frowned. 'It was back sometime after New Year, I guess,' he said. 'We got a call from the Major to get out to a house. The guy was in a bad way. Cut to the neck. Not quite dead, but not exactly alive either. This woman had made a hash job of it, she called the Major, Major called us. All we did was put him out of his misery and clean things up. No more, no less.'

'Jesus,' said Erykah. 'You said he was not quite dead – how close to not quite?'

'He was mostly still,' Billy said. 'And you would have thought he was dead, but as soon as we put the light on in the bathroom, he starts thrashing around on the floor.' Billy looked at the ground, as if seeing the scene right there in front of him. 'Like he was having a seizure. Blood everywhere. Fucking mess. Buster had to get on him and we tied him up. The woman who did it left a knife on the floor, and—'

Erykah gulped. 'OK, I think I get the picture,' she said. 'What about the Major? Why didn't he finish the job?'

'Cold feet, who knows,' Billy said. 'He looked in shock. PTSD maybe.'

'But if Schofield wasn't dead yet, why do it? Why not walk out of there and call the police?'

Billy pursed his lips. 'Is that what you would do?' he asked. 'As soon as we took the call we were involved whether we liked it or not. Might as well see it done right.'

'I guess,' she said. The sickening lump in her throat would not go away. She had known he was a killer, had even seen him inflict damage on her own husband, but the way he talked about it stunned her. Like a hunter talking about putting a stag out of its misery. 'What house was it? Whose?'

'I got no idea,' he said. 'We weren't introduced. The place was dark, and the woman didn't say nothing to us. I didn't get a photo ID, you know? Had other things to deal with.'

'Was it Livia?'

'I don't know,' Billy said. 'I never met any Livia before.'

'Where was the house?'

'Over in South Ken.'

'What was the woman like? Old, young? Did you get a look at her?'

He shook his head. 'Nope.'

'That seems uncharacteristically unobservant of you.'

'Half of my job is to notice things,' he said. 'The other half is to make sure I don't see nothing.' He looked up at her. 'Listen, woman, just so you know, this is between us. I got no interest in making you disappear.'

She wanted to trust him, or at least, trust that he was telling her the truth. 'No?'

She lowered the gun, but her finger was still on the trigger. 'Buster, you put yours on the ground,' he said. Buster unclipped his holster and threw it in the dirt. Billy turned back to her. 'I got no loyalty to that man that he ain't paying me for. If the Major's really dead then that's my work with him done.'

Erykah considered this. He had no reason to lie. Seminole Billy might have been a criminal, but as far as she had seen he was also a man of his word.

There was something else as well. She couldn't put her finger on it. The way he looked at her. No, not lust . . . something else. Like he – she didn't even want to think the word – cared about her. She shook the thought out of her head. But in her heart she knew he wasn't going to do anything to bring her to harm. 'Really?'

'Really. Now come on, drop that gun.'

Erykah threw the pistol into the dirt at his feet. Billy picked it up and examined the small grey handgun. He ran his fingers down the slide, stroking it like he might have been stroking skin.

'Is that thing real?' Buster said.

'Real? Sure,' Erykah said. 'It came from the Major's office. I guess it was his father's.'

'It's an old school Haenel Schmeisser. Point-two-five ACP,' Billy whistled. 'This brings back memories. Seen a few at gun shows back in Florida. Not for a long while.'

'In Florida? Really?'

Billy nodded. 'Not as many of these around as Brownings, so some guys'll try to pass it off to skinheads and rednecks as a Third Reich make. They'll get an eagle stamp, hammer it in the body there, rub some shoe polish in so it looks like a '40s mark. Worth a few hundred on its own, but scam the right Nazi fanboy and you might walk away with a cool two grand.'

'Sorry – I'm not following,' Erykah said.

'It's a pocket sidearm, not a service pistol,' he said. 'His dad would have been issued with an Enfield or a Webley, not one of these. This thing might even be older than Abbott Senior himself.' Billy moved the slide back. 'Fucking hell. Nothing in the chamber. Should have known.' He pulled the trigger to hear it snap and wagged the gun at Erykah. 'I oughta kill you for that, you know?' But he was smiling.

'Yeah, well,' she shrugged. 'Why was Schofield a target?'

'Beats me,' Billy said. 'Like I said, the shady lady didn't exactly welcome us with open arms. Whoever it is, once she hears about the Major though, we had all better start running.' Erykah nodded. 'Gimme your phone,' he said. 'Trade ya for the gun.'

'Are you sure? About the gun I mean.'

'Sure I'm sure,' he shrugged. 'What are you gonna do with an empty gun, pistol whip me? Nah, you probably got lipsticks in that bag of yours bigger'n this.'

She handed over her mobile, and he gave her the pistol. The Major's phone was still in her handbag. Probably best to keep that information to herself for now.

Billy looked back through her sent and received messages. 'This is the one I texted you on?' She nodded. He scrolled through the menu until he found the option to reset to the factory settings, erasing any stored data. 'Pay as you go or contract?'

'Pay as you go,' she said. 'I have a contract phone for talking to Rob, but I never use it. This is for things I don't need my husband to know about.' Like Nicole. Like the Major.

'Good girl,' he said, and slid the back of the phone off. He popped the SIM card into his pocket, dropped the handset onto the ground and crushed it under the heel of his snakeskin boot. Erykah gasped. Before she could object he kicked the bashed mobile into the canal. It sank fast into the murky water.

He took one look at her open mouth and winked. 'Cheer up, sunshine, we'll drop in somewhere and pick up a new burner on your way home.' Billy dusted his hands on the thighs of his black jeans. 'I'll even spring for an upgrade,' he said.

'That's coming out of my share of the money, isn't it?'

'If there even is any money,' he said. 'More like it's coming out of your pocket cash.'

Erykah hadn't thought of that. 'Shit. You two are not going to get paid, are you?' Billy shook his head. 'I'm sorry.'

Billy shrugged. 'It ain't my first time at the rodeo,' he said.

'Sometimes the jobs work out, sometimes they don't. Besides, we got bigger things to think about. Once the news about the Major hits the airwaves, we're both in for a world of hurt.'

'But who from?' Erykah asked.

'You guess is as good as mine,' he said. 'All I know is, it's someone who's got a good eye for distracting attention.' He chewed over the possibilities. 'Someone who knows how to keep the press looking at the piece of totty, not what's behind it.'

'You think I'm just a – a piece of distracting totty?' Erykah said.

'Could be worse,' Billy said. 'Imagine if you had to go through life looking like me.'

'Are you two done flirting yet?' Buster grumbled. 'I got somewhere to be, man.'

Billy flushed slightly. 'Gimme the stuff. Get outta here.' Buster threw the rolled canvas bag at Billy, scooped up his own gun and jogged away. 'You got the money we gave you?' he said to Erykah.

'Most of it,' she said.

'Enough to make things look normal for a while? Keep up your bills, so no one asks questions?'

She frowned, totting up the sums in her head. 'Yes. And I had a few grand in cash before that. I'm not sure how far it will go.'

'Have to do for now,' Billy said. He walked back to the Merc and stood with exaggerated formality at the passenger side door, still hanging wide open. 'Your chariot awaits.'

Billy turned the key and the car coughed and shuddered itself into life. The radio came on, loud. It was tuned to LCC, where the mid-morning call-in was well underway. 'Keep your ears glued to the news, OK?' he said. 'Odds are they'll break it as soon as someone finds the body.'

He drove out of the estate at the same slow speed he had driven in. She looked back at the canvas bag on the back seat, the one Buster had thrown at him. 'What's in there?' Erykah asked.

'What we came for in the first place,' he said. 'Have a look.'

She unrolled the bag. It was a thick waterproofed fabric with a seal and lock along the top edge. 'Key's in the magnetic box under your seat,' Billy said.

Inside the bag were wads of cash, three of them, thick bundles of fifty pound notes, Bank of Scotland. Much like the ones they had given her to look for Media Mouse. Sixty, maybe seventy-five grand in total. The money wasn't all. An Italian passport and national ID, a US Permanent Resident card and a driving license for the State of Florida. All of them with the Major's moustachioed face staring back at her. But an array different names: Jack Arsenal, Stephen Chelsea, Robert Fulham. 'Fake IDs?'

'In case he needed to disappear,' Billy said. He dug out the last cigarette from the pack and jammed it in his mouth. 'He called me yesterday. Said to be ready for when he got back to London.'

'But all the dates on these are old,' she said. 'If he only rang you yesterday, why is that?'

'Easier to fake,' Billy said. 'Before chips became standard. Most of the old style documents will be phased out or expire in the next few years, but for right now, and if you're only going one way? You got a window.'

'He must have thought time was up for him, too,' Erykah said. No wonder the Major hadn't wanted to talk about what happened in Cameron Bridge. She turned the pages of the Italian passport. The cover was the same colour and much the same as her own British one, apart from the lettering. The paper was thick and it felt legitimate. She would have been fooled. 'Did you do these?'

'Buster knows a guy who knows a guy,' he said. 'You meet all the best kinds in lockup.' He glanced at Erykah. 'It's not good enough to get into the States, but it'd do for Latin America,' he said. 'Panama, Belize, places like that. Maybe Bahamas.'

'Could you get one of these for me?'

'It's not cheap and it's not fast.' Seminole Billy shook his head. 'Not today. I'm taking you home.'

Home was the last place she wanted to go right now. 'Is it safe there?'

Billy shrugged. 'Is anywhere safe? Woman, if the police are headed your way, home is exactly where you want to be right now. I'll sweep the neighbourhood first if it makes you feel better. Tell that husband to cover your ass, and sit tight for a few days.'

'Fine,' Erykah said. The Merc cruised west in the light mid-morning traffic. Sitting tight was one option. But she had no intention of doing anything of the sort.

: **26** :

'Good God.' Arjun wrinkled his nose at the LCC green room with its sagging sofa and broken coffee machine. 'This is, like, where interns' dreams come to die.'

'The glamour of politics,' Morag said. 'This sofa? No fewer than a thousand Cabinet ministers' farts are trapped in there at any given time.'

'Look at that carpet. I'm getting emphysema just looking at it.'

'If you think it's bad now, you should have seen green rooms before the indoor smoking ban,' Morag said. 'Vile. Even smokers couldn't hack it. I once walked in on an anti-smoking campaigner – Royal College of Surgeons no less – sucking down Silk Cuts like a condemned man headed for the gallows.'

'No!' Arjun's eyes opened wide. 'Who?'

'Before your time,' Morag waved her hand. 'Turned out he was taking money from the industry to make the stop smoking campaign as unappealing to kids as possible. Surprise, surprise.'

A runner came in with two cappuccinos from a café around the corner. Morag noticed the girl's hands were shaking. She had the feeling she had seen the girl before, probably another studio somewhere. Morag's memory was good but she had long since given up trying to remember the names of runners, cameramen, and make-up ladies.

'I never hear any of the good gossip,' Arjun said. He patted his pocket. 'Hold on – I'll take this while you go over the briefing.' He thrust a folder in her direction.

Morag flipped through the notes Arjun had prepared. English regional devolution high on the list as ever. Immigration, as always. A ten-minute rule bill on sex education coming up later in the week that had about as much chance of going forward as the M25 at rush hour. Strict instructions to deflect any questioning about a challenge to the leadership, as per.

Arjun hovered in the far corner of the room. He kept the mobile on speaker, holding it horizontally a couple of inches from his mouth.

'No, no, yes, no . . . I'm not certain that's relevant . . . Is it breaking right now? Is this going to bounce us from the show?' He jabbed at the phone screen and marched over to the sofa. 'Morag, are you listening to this?' he said.

'Arjun, I have you on staff precisely so I don't have to listen to whatever this is,' she said. 'What's going on?'

'That old Marine, Major Abbott, has only gone and died on a train.' He rolled his eyes. 'They found him locked in a toilet on the Caledonian Sleeper at Euston.'

'Well, that's terrible,' Morag mumbled, turning back to her notes.

'The news channels are going nuts. Apparently he was picked up by the police for inciting a riot in Cameron Bridge yesterday, and they have all kinds of phone footage,' he said. 'BBC 24 is rolling the black bar under the headlines. *GONE BEFORE HIS TIME*, all caps, apparently.'

'Oh for fuck's—' Morag snorted. If anything, the Major had squeezed out more time than he was strictly entitled to. According to those who claimed to be in the know, had he really been the fearless leader his memoir claimed, he probably should have died on a Falklands' battlefield.

She wasn't sure if she believed the people who said that. Morag knew all too well that nasty rumours had a surprising affinity with envy. But there was no denying the haunted, hunted look in his eyes behind the handlebar moustache and genial sexist exterior. The look of a man waiting to be found out.

'I hate to be a pain,' Arjun said. He did not really hate to be a pain. Being a pain was what he was paid to do. 'But this is going huge. If he died at any other time, it wouldn't be a thing. After that press conference earlier this month, then the protest in Cameron Bridge . . . I'm saying, be prepared for the producers to cut you down. Or even bump you.'

Morag frowned. 'You think they're going to pre-empt me for some dead soldier?'

'A dead Royal Marines officer,' Arjun said. 'And yes, they are. Television is live at Euston right now. Radio won't be far behind.' He switched on a TV in the corner of the green room and turned it over to a 24-hour news channel. There wasn't much to see yet apart from a bit of the platform and some police in high-vis. The carriage where the body was found had been detached and rolled off to a maintenance shed where crime scene investigators waited for a pathologist to arrive.

'You told them no call-ins while I'm on, yes?' she said.

'I told them. No guarantee they'll listen.'

Morag pursed her lips. The fact that Jonathan had not tried to get in contact after their last argument concerned her. She had left the organ- ising of this interview to Arjun and hoped that sent the message that things were strictly professional now. On the one hand, it was good to have drawn a line under the relationship. What the hell had she been thinking? On the other hand, she had no idea what this meant in terms of news coverage.

Maybe he would take the high road and decide to be a gentleman about it.

And maybe pigs would be spotted in their customary migratory pattern over Westminster Palace this very afternoon.

The runner waved at them. 'Diana's ready for you in the tank,' she said.

Arjun peppered the runner with questions. 'Are we still on for the full twenty minutes?' he asked her. 'Are we cutting away to news while the Shadow Home Secretary is on? Is she going to be expected to make a statement on this?' The runner didn't know the answer to any of them.

'Morag, hi, good to see you,' Diana Stuebner raised herself halfway from her chair and held out her hand.

'Pleasure,' Morag murmured and put on a pair of headphones. Jon- athan's voice came over and counted them back in from the advert break.

'Welcome back,' Diana purred. 'In the next half hour we'll be talk- ing with Shadow Home Secretary Morag Munro. But first, a recap of breaking news. Police report the death of Major Whitney Abbott whose body was discovered on a train early this morning. They have yet to confirm a cause of death, though sources say foul play has not been ruled out. Welcome to the show, Morag.'

'Thank you,' Morag said. 'Although not quite the introduction I was expecting.'

'Did you know the Major?' Diana asked, crinkling her nose and leaning forward.

Morag paused. There was no point lying because the press would be scrambling to find out who he had been lobbying to and photo- graphed with over the years. 'Only slightly,' Morag said. 'We met once or twice; he was a regular at various fundraisers in Scotland, as I recall.'

'But he was one of your constituents,' Diana said.

'He had a house in the Highlands,' Morag said. 'I don't know if he was registered to vote there.'

'Still, given his association with your area . . .'

'You have to understand, Diana, the Highlands are not like London. My constituency is the size of Belgium.' Morag was trying not to be patronising, but it wasn't easy in the circumstances. 'I'm not on first name terms with everyone there.'

'Such a loss to Britain today,' Diana cooed. 'And of course the nation of Scotland. The Major was perhaps best known for his opposition to Scottish independence in later years, and most recently for his campaign to represent Scotland Liberal Unionists in Brussels. Did you agree with his party's policy to dissolve the Scottish Parliament?'

Morag smiled tightly. She despised these kinds of questions, the ones that came with an obvious agenda attached. In this case the agenda was getting a quote out of context that they could chop and run endlessly in a news loop for the next twenty-four hours. It didn't matter which way she answered as long as they got their yes or no. Either was spinnable. 'I am certain that irrespective of the outcome of the referendum, the people of Scotland can be assured of a positive future,' she said.

Yes, she knew their tricks well. It was a catch-22. Producers knew that the audience take their cues off of the presenter, not the guest. No matter how capably and truthfully you respond to questioning, all the listener hears is hostility from the host, and they assume there is a valid reason for that. Whether there was or not.

'That's not answering the question, is it?' Diana pressed. 'You said that you campaigned for the No side – and I quote –to preserve Scotland's prosperity. But, as a member of the Shadow Cabinet, were you not also worried that had the Yes won, it would have sent MPs home? Including yourself?'

Morag's face set in a tight line. Her right hand started drumming the table reflexively. 'As a politician I have no greater mandate than to respect the choice of the people, whatever that choice may be,' she said. 'I am confident that the results of the referendum and the general election are fair representations of our nation. The point now, surely, is to move forward and build our country and economy together.'

'Naturally,' Diana said. 'But you have to agree you have come very close to losing your job not just once but twice in the last eighteen months.' She moved on quickly, before Morag had a chance to object. 'Would you agree that the Scottish wing of your party was treated as a – again, I quote – branch office of the London party?'

Morag opened her mouth to object, but Diana was talking again before she could get a word in. 'Now, a break as we recap the headlines.' Diana read through a summary of the Major's career, from the Falklands to the recent appearance in Cameron Bridge when he'd been locked in a pub as Scottish nationalists rioted outside. The show cut away to audio clips from news pieces featuring Major Abbott.

Morag smiled stiffly as the minutes ticked by with no sign of returning to her. Diana announced an advert break. She saw Arjun in the corner waving his hands at Jonathan. 'Bring it round to her,' he was saying. 'Let her answer the questions, or I swear to you we are not coming back again.'

Jonathan came into the studio. 'Morag,' he nodded. His voice was perfectly neutral. As if there had never been anything between them. 'Diana, a quick chat outside.'

He pulled the presenter out into the hall. His voice was low. 'I know you're used to managing the beasts on call-in, of being the voice of reason. But this is in danger of going soft, especially with two women on. You need to go harder.'

'I need gravitas,' Diana said. 'A reason for listeners to take this interview seriously.'

'Exactly,' Jonathan said. 'Get her wound up enough that she cracks.'

Diana laughed. 'Morag Munro? Crack? She has a reputation as a bit of a bore, but I've never heard of her losing her cool.'

'Oh, it can be done,' Jonathan said. 'She has a temper under that cold exterior. I can vouch – I mean, I've heard.'

'If you say so,' Diana said. Her eyes sparkled. She had a feeling there was a lot more to this than he was telling.

'Trust me,' Jonathan said. 'Go hard after the break.' He pressed a printout into her hand. 'You wanted to bring social media into the station, well, here's your shot.' Diana unfolded the paper, looked at it, and nodded. 'Be the terrier.' Jonathan made a motion with his hand like a dog's jaw snapping shut. 'Get her.'

'Got it.'

'Good.'

Diana came back and gave Morag a smile. One that seemed to say, I'm so sorry about this. Morag suddenly felt stiff and sweaty. Something about that smile didn't sit right. Before she could finish the thought, though, the show had started again.

'We're back. For those just joining us, our guest today is Morag Munro, the Shadow Home Secretary, and we have been discussing the shock death of Major Whitney Abbott whose body was discovered on a train this morning.' Diana's deep voice was pitched even lower than usual, as befitted the solemn occasion. 'Thank you so much for coming on the show today, Morag.'

'No, thank you, Diana,' Morag said.

'Before the break we were discussing your stand on Scottish independence . . .' Diana said. 'And since the topic *du jour* is Major Abbott, that leads us obviously to the uproar over Media Mouse.'

'Um, I suppose so,' Morag said. 'To be honest, I haven't followed that story. My office maintains an official social media presence, but I never go on it myself. It's really for the younger generation.' Moisture started trickling down her back under her jacket.

Diana tilted her head, obviously listening to something from Jonathan that Morag couldn't hear. 'And would you like to comment on Media Mouse's latest scoop involving you?'

'Scoop?' Morag said. 'As I said, my office have already released an announcement denying the silly rumour –'

'Not about that,' Diana interrupted. 'About the photo posted today.' Diana unfolded a piece of paper and passed it across the desk to Morag.

It was a printout of a picture, a black-and-white photo of her from the side. She was smiling at someone whose face was turned away from the camera. The angle was odd, shot from below.

She looked more closely at the picture, but couldn't immediately remember what it was. When would she have been wearing a white jacket?

A shape in the corner of the picture caught her eye. It was a metal countertop, stainless steel. Just like the kind they used in the mortuary.

'It appears to show you watching an autopsy,' Diana explained for the radio audience. 'Morag Munro, can you explain what this is please?'

'I was on an official visit in my constituency, doing research for our planned response to natural disasters,' Morag said. 'I don't see what the scoop is here.'

'So you weren't there for a particular autopsy?' Diana asked.

The trickle of sweat down Morag's back was now a flood. 'As I recall, it was a routine day for them, nothing of interest,' she said.

'Our producer rang the facility. It turns out not only did you not sign in as a guest – they deny it was an official visit – the post-mortem was murdered scientist Professor Damian Schofield. And you had no particular interest in attending that? A murder victim turns up in your own constituency and this was routine?'

'I had no way of knowing the body – Professor Schofield – was there,' Morag snapped.

'And what would you say about Media Mouse's continued – I mean, sudden – interest in your activities?'

Morag's hand ached to drum the table, but she resisted. The pent up frustration seemed to build under her skin like sparks of power down a cable. So now Jonathan was going to have his attack dog push the line that she was the one who was having an affair, without mentioning the inconvenient fact that he happened to be the other party? She had no way of dropping him into it without confirming that the blind item was indeed about her. He gave Diana a double thumbs up through the glass.

'This is clearly an orchestrated smear campaign from someone with an axe to grind.' Morag caught Jonathan's eye through the window. Was he going to be man enough to look her in the eye when he stabbed her in the back? He flinched and looked down at the mixing board. Not only was he a weasel of a man, he couldn't even stab her in the back the right way. Morag felt the sparks of suppressed rage reach her chest, and for once she did not push it away. 'If they have something on me, they should show it. If they have something they want to say, they should have the courage to come out from behind the mask and say it to my face.'

Diana nodded. 'So you are saying that there would be something on you to find?'

'Will you shut up and listen!' Morag shouted. 'I came here to talk politics, not to answer baseless and defamatory claims about – about some anonymous troll. I've had enough of this.' Morag stood up and ripped the headphones off. She turned and stomped out of the tank, nearly tripping over a cable on the way.

Diana leaned in to her mic, unable to keep the wide smile from her face. Getting a guest to fly off the handle was hands-down the best thing that could possibly happen from a ratings standpoint. There had been many highlights in her career so far, but this? This was radio gold. 'You're listening to Daily Edition,' she purred. 'Coming up after the weather, what next for Britain's energy security? And what to make of the Government's new oil and gas licenses being awarded north of the border in Scotland?' She couldn't resist twisting the knife one last little bit. 'I had hoped the Shadow Home Secretary would stay with us after the break to comment on the issue, but I'm sure we'll hear more about – I mean *from* – her soon.'

'You're going to be fine.' Seminole Billy turned on to Erykah's street. 'Deep breath, style it out. Pretend nothing happened on that train. You weren't there, OK?'

'Thanks,' Erykah said. 'Can you drop me here and I'll walk the rest of the way? I need some fresh air. I have to figure out what I'm going to tell Rab.' She patted Billy's hand. A stroll on the towpath was the best medicine right now. Her old thinking space.

'Sure,' he said. 'You give me a ring if anything goes wrong with Him Indoors, yeah?'

'Meaning what, exactly?'

'Meaning, that husband of yours. I don't trust him at all.' Billy glanced at her wrists. The bruises were faded yellow now, nearly gone – you would have to know they were there to spot anything at all.

Erykah circled one narrow wrist with the other hand and nodded. 'When Rab said it was the first time, he was telling the truth,' she said. 'He's done a lot of terrible things to me in the past, but he's not in the habit of knocking women around.'

'They all say that,' Billy said. 'I watched my mother go through . . . anyway. I've seen how it starts.'

'Rab knows what's at stake,' she said. 'He knows we can't afford to let emotion get the better of us right now.'

Billy snorted. 'That's your first mistake, woman,' he said. 'Assuming men aren't the more emotional sex.'

'I think I can handle my husband for one night.'

Billy nodded. 'I can drive by later, check on you.'

She shrugged. 'Sure, if it makes you feel better. How about if you don't hear from me in a couple of hours, come past and make sure everything's good?'

'I'll do that,' Billy said. 'Be in touch, yeah?'

Erykah smiled and waved. She watched the Merc disappear then started down the towpath. The sun was already behind the trees and the sky going dark. A couple of scullers were out on the water – she could see the silhouetted shapes, about a quarter of a mile upstream – but apart from that the river was hers.

A waft of breeze rose wavelets like scales on the water. She buttoned up her coat and turned the collar against the wind. The air seemed to have something different in it this evening, though. A hint of green. The start of spring, maybe.

How many times had she been out on this stretch of the river? Five sessions a week, sometimes more. Hundreds of times a year. Thousands over the time she lived in Molesey. If she closed her eyes, she could play back the various training routes in her head, stroke by stroke, metre by metre. She knew what every house looked like from the level of the water, every boat, every tree. The way the current ebbed and changed with the tide, the right place to point a boat to get in the fastest part of the stream.

Already it felt like part of the past. She searched her heart for something more than that, some deep well of feeling. It had seemed like something else was going to happen, something good, something new – and then nothing turned out the way she had imagined it would. Nothing ever did.

She had walked away, changed and remade her life before. She could do it again.

But how many times? Erykah wondered how long it would be before she ran out of options. Before she ended up trapped in a dead-end existence, like her mother had done. She shook her head. No. She would not, could not, be like Rainbow. That wasn't a possibility. She refused to entertain it.

Leonie's words in Ardgour haunted her. *I wished you had come back.* Why did she never think going back was an option?

A sculler passed leaning deep into his catches, a woolly hat pulled low on his brow. Most likely he didn't even see her on the path, and if he did, well, what of it? The sport existed in its own self-contained bubble, everyone fully absorbed in the yearly treadmill of training and competition. Someone who wasn't in a boat was someone you didn't know – and therefore didn't need to know. Civilians. Muggles.

It was funny how fast you could go from being part of the group to being invisible. Not only to the rowers – to anyone. No one who had known her growing up would recognise her now. Right now Rab was the only person who knew about her life in any real way. For better or for worse, he knew her secrets, or most of them. Realising that was something she couldn't give a name to. She felt like she ought to know what it was, but she didn't.

She walked slowly, trying to put off the inevitable. How much should she tell Rab about what had happened? How much would he know already? The story about the Major's body being found on the train was everywhere. The only way he could have missed it would be if he hadn't turned on the TV. Given that most of his time these days was spent in glassy-eyed silence in front of the tube, that was unlikely.

Which meant she would have to tell him about her deal with the Major and the danger they were in. It would be stupid not to. If he didn't know Billy was on their side now, he might do something rash. If she kept Rab out of the loop it could be a disaster for them all.

She didn't know how to say it. 'Rab, those guys who broke your fingers? They're our only friends now.' Or 'Rab, we're going to have to pretend for a while longer – or we could end up in a bag in the North Sea.'

They had been listening to the radio in the car when Morag stormed off Diana Stuebner's show on LCC. So Kerry had decided to release the photo after all. Erykah hoped the girl was right, and that staying in the public eye was the best way for her to keep from getting into worse trouble. Maybe with the Major dead and Billy and Buster under control, it could even turn out to be true. Erykah hoped so.

As far as she had heard on the radio no one was looking for a woman in a headscarf. Not yet.

Morag's media faux pas might be enough to bring the press attention around to her illicit activities. Surely once that happened, she would have to step back from secretly pulling the strings of the SLU. Erykah could anonymously deliver the Schofield files to a newspaper – who knows, maybe even to Kerry? – and never have to think about any of this again.

With a little luck Erykah could find herself home free. Free enough to get away, in any case.

Maybe everything was going to be all right after all.

From the path she could see the corner of their back garden. Best get the talk with Rab over with, then. She unlatched the gate and crossed the garden to the French doors.

As she got closer she noticed the curtains were shut. Odd. Rab wouldn't have done that until it was bedtime, and that was still hours off. On the edge of the back deck, a plant pot of flowers left from the lottery photo shoot was tipped on its side, broken. One of the French doors was partly open. Something was not right here.

There were voices inside. Rab's, and another man's she didn't recognise. They were arguing. Then the voices stopped.

That was when she heard a muffled BANG.

It sounded like it could have been a gunshot from inside the house. Very much so. Erykah froze with her hand on the doorknob. Rab had never held a gun in his life. Maybe she was wrong. Maybe something had dropped, a glass off a table, perhaps. Don't be so silly. Erykah straightened her shoulders and started to open the door a bit further.

BANG. A pause. BANG. Then a fourth time, and twice more. A click, the sound of someone releasing a magazine to reload. No, that was definitely a gun.

So whoever was in there – however many of them there were – had just shot her husband. Most likely shot him dead.

She doubled over and stepped carefully back to the garden gate, closed and latched it behind her as softly as possible. She got on her hands and knees and crawled around the side of the house. The pulse in her neck thrummed hard.

She stopped and flattened her entire body on the ground. There was an unfamiliar saloon car parked on the street outside the house. Black, maybe dark blue. The windows were tinted like a limousine's. She tried to read the number plate but that angle wasn't right; she would have to go all the way to the street to see it.

The front door opened. Through the low branches of the hedge, she saw two pairs of shoes walk out into the front garden. Unfamiliar shoes, black lace-up, and suit turn-ups.

'I'm telling you, I heard something,' a man said. It was a deep voice, London accent, no one she knew.

'Maybe it was a cat.'

'Maybe.' The first pair of feet took a few steps towards the hedge. The sound of metal on metal.

'Hey, how did you get on with that new silencer?'

'Eh, not the worst. Loads of muzzle flash though. Might go back to the Hush Puppy. Listen, I'm going to do a check of the perimeter just in case.'

'What, and call more attention to the fact that we're here? Someone will see you for sure prowling around in the garden. Come on, let's get inside before the wife gets home.'

A chuckle. 'Yeah, all right. Wouldn't want to kill the mood when she gets in. Did you see the photos? I bet she's a goer.' He whistled low. 'Can't wait for a little romance.'

'Yeah, I saw the photos, mate. One thing at a time. Get her to hand over the files, then you can have your fun.'

'Lotta hassle over a few pieces of paper,' the second one said. 'Wonder what it's about?'

'Mate, if I ain't being paid to think, then I don't,' the first one said. 'We top the pair of them, make it look like a burglary gone wrong. Anything else is above my pay grade.'

'Guess you're right,' the other one said. 'It's funny, if I had won the lottery and was all over the papers I would have put in a security system by now.'

'People are stupid, that's why bad things happen to 'em,' the first one said. The two men laughed. Their footsteps went back inside and the door slammed shut.

Erykah held her breath until her lungs were screaming for air, and when she finally opened her mouth, stuffed a fist between her teeth and bit down hard. The hot drops rolling over her knuckles might have been tears or they might have been blood.

: **28** :

It was a couple of minutes before she could breathe properly again.

No one had come back outside that she could see. Erykah edged past the back of the house towards the towpath, keeping her eyes glued to the windows. Once it was out of sight she picked up speed. She ran as fast and hard as she could, past the cricket club and the park, all the way to the boat club.

The building was quiet. Anyone around at this time of day would be on the water. With most of the women's and vet's squads on training camp in Lucerne, there would be a handful of people coming in and out at most.

Her heart was beating hard. Ring the police? But what if the killers led back to the Major and they were all exposed? Call Billy? She tried his number, but it was switched off.

The motion detector lights in the corridors flickered to life one by one as she walked past. The blinds were drawn in the inner office. Rowing machines and workout equipment hulked in the shadows in the corners of the gym. She swept past them to the doors in the back.

Erykah wrinkled her nose as she entered the changing room. The familiar, musty smell of damp wellies lingered in the air. Sports bras and lycra one-pieces left hung from the radiators and dried to a crisp. Erykah spun the combination lock on her old locker and it popped open. She was relieved to find that nothing inside had been moved or touched since she walked out.

Maybe she could stay here, wait it out a few hours. Or even until the next morning, if she couldn't find Billy. But no, that was too dangerous. If the men at the house knew about her rowing, this was surely the first place they would think to look for her.

The envelope and card Nicole gave to her on Valentine's Day was still stuffed in the corner of the locker door. Erykah felt for the key, the impression it left in the paper. She stuck the envelope into her bag, grabbed a few bits and pieces of clothes she had left behind, and shut the door.

She sank down on the wooden bench and held her head in her hands. What was going on? She should have taken that key when Nicole gave it to her, packed her bag, left the house before Rab came home and never looked back. Maybe if she had, none of this would have happened. The Major wouldn't have died. Rab would still be alive. And she wouldn't be in an empty, horrible, stinking changing room, fearing for her life.

She heard a few people come in and out of the main doors. Veteran men, from the sound of it. Her backside grew numb and cold from the bench, but she didn't want to shift and risk anyone hearing her. Eventually, after a few hours, she finally heard the last one leave.

It was fully dark outside. It was a mile up the towpath, give or take, to Nicole's cottage. About fifteen minutes walking, ten at a jog, in the direction of the station.

At Nicole's cottage, everything was dark. She fumbled the key out of the envelope and tried it in the lock. The key rattled in the hole and felt like it started to turn, but something wasn't right – it wasn't catching. She found a cycling LED in her bag and shone the light on it for a better look.

The lock wasn't turning, because the hole was too big. Or the key was too small. She took the key out of the lock and examined it under the light, turning it over in her hands. There was some raised lettering on the side of the key, Erykah licked her thumb and rubbed at it.

Which is when she realised it wasn't even a real key.

Erykah's wounded cry echoed out over the water, sending a pair of startled geese flapping and honking down the river's edge.

She had got it wrong, entirely. It wasn't a copy of Nicole's house key. The lettering on the side had revealed the name of a chain of stationers. It wasn't a key at all, it was a trinket, a piece of junk jewellery, a cheap piece of metal painted to look vintage. The kind of thing teenagers up and down the country would have bought for their valentines and still have change from a five-pound note. She would probably have more luck trying to open the door with the underwire in her bra than with this stupid thing.

Why not? She had tried and failed to pick the lock at Damian Schofield's office, but the principle wasn't so difficult. And there was the book. Yes, there it was, buried under the piles of clothes and the Schofield folders, the dog-eared paperback of puzzles and mind games. Erykah sat on the ground and flipped to the page about locks. The

LED lit up a small white circle on the page and she read it twice over to make sure she understood.

The instructions were basic and the illustrations were only line drawings, but that was no problem. What other choice did she have? Billy was still not answering. Going home was not an option, not with what those two men had been talking about doing to her. Going back to the boat club was too dangerous, and ringing 999 – no. She could break a window, but someone might hear her or spot it and call the police.

It was picking the lock or nothing. She had been so close to getting it right at Professor Schofield's office, it might work this time. Erykah looked up and down the towpath. It was as quiet as a country lane. With any luck if the killers came along she would hear them coming long before they got to her.

According to the book picking a lock required two tools, one to put pressure and start turning the lock, and the other to feel for the moving parts inside. The lock at Schofield's had been a Yale lock with a tumbler and pins, but the mortice lock at Nicole's wasn't all that different in theory. In theory. The reality, as the book hinted, was that mortice locks were harder to pick.

Instead of the sprung pins of a Yale lock to feel around for, there were lever tumblers inside instead – a set of flat metal plates that, when pushed at the right depth, slid into alignment and allowed the lock to turn.

Erykah peeled off her coat. A sharp tang of body odour wafted up to her nose, the smell of concentration and anxiety. She unhooked her bra through the fabric of her dress and shrugged and wiggled her arms, sliding the straps over her shoulders as best she could without baring her skin to the cold breeze. The grey silk bra dropped off her body to the ground. She picked it up and felt the damp edges of the cups. Yes, the thin strip of metal would be perfect. She snipped through the fabric with the scissors of the multitool and pushed against the under-wire until it slid out.

She had a pick. Now she needed something for tension.

The fake key would do. It fitted into the lock a little bit, and was thicker than the underwire, so she could turn it more easily.

Erykah squatted down so her eyes were at lock level and stuck the LED light in her mouth. She slipped the fake key back in and stared to turn until she felt the lock resisting. With one hand on the key keeping the tension she used her other hand to slide the tip of the underwire next to the fake key, but she couldn't get purchase on anything with only the wire as it was. She slid it out again. Using the pliers on the multitool, she bent the tip at a right angle to the rest of the wire and then a second time, so the end looked like a P. She tensioned the fake key and tried again.

The light she held in her mouth wobbled unevenly. A trickle of drool ran out of the corner of her mouth. Erykah was aware that she was shaking, and yet, with all her concentration focused on the tiny spot in front of her, it was as if it was happening to another body.

But the lock would not budge. The book made it look tantalisingly easy, more of an intellectual challenge than a physical one. Her temperature was dropping fast, her fingers going numb in the chilly breeze. Erykah dropped her hands from the tools, blew on her fingers and rubbed her palms together to try to get circulation back up. The cold was seeping in, and experience told her that before long she would lose sensation in her hands altogether. Not a disaster if you happened to be out on the water in a rowing boat. Far worse if you were doing anything that required fine motor control.

She had no idea how long she had been there. Minutes? Hours? It felt like an eternity, screwing all her concentration into this one tiny space. Erykah drew deep breaths and held them as long as she could, trying to steady her hands and quiet the sobs that threatened to take over her body if she stopped what she was doing for even a second to think about anything else.

Still the lock would not move. She could feel the pins inside, feel the fake key start to bite, but her hand would slip or a tumbler would refuse to move and then . . . nothing.

Erykah's concentration was broken by a sound coming up the path behind her. Her shaking hands clutched at the improvised instruments. Were those footsteps? A light breeze swept the towpath. No, it was only the clattering of dead leaves on the dirt. In the panic her tenuous picking at the pins had slipped, so that she couldn't even feel the tumblers with the end of the bra wire now. And her fingers were cold and numbly unresponsive.

She sank down on the welcome mat, body shaking with cold, fear, and exhaustion. This was never going to work. Unless . . . Unless? With a finger she turned up the corner of the mat. Surely not. Nobody left their door key under the mat, not even in twee suburban Molesey.

Although, whether true or not, people liked to flatter themselves that the suburb was not the kind of place where crime happened.

Erykah's mouth twisted into a bitter smile. She had a feeling that by tomorrow morning that particular strain of smugness was about to be blown wide open. Still, surely Nicole would not be so stu—

And there, in the dust, was the key.

She scrambled frantically, pulled the tools out of the lock, and slid in the real key. The lock clicked and gave way, the door swung open. Erykah collapsed in a heap on the floor.

The tiles of the entryway were cold against her legs. Erykah closed the door, locked it from the inside, and pocketed the key. Outside on the path the noise started again. Not the wind. Footsteps. She was sure of it. The muffled sound grew closer.

Erykah was hit with a wave of paranoia. What if the killers had followed her here, waiting until they knew she was alone and indoors to strike? Then they would have a better chance of doing whatever they wanted to unobserved, just as they had to Rab back at home. She didn't want to risk being seen through the windows or stand up to close the curtains.

Erykah checked her watch – Billy would be expecting a call soon or else he would assume something had happened to her and go past the house himself. She considered whether it might not be better to let him do that, then rejected the idea. No. Letting someone else walk into an ambush would be wrong. Even if it was someone who could probably handle himself better than most people would have a chance of doing.

The noise started again. It sounded like only one person. Impossible to tell who it was without standing up and making herself known. Could be serious, could be nothing at all. Could be a neighbour. A jogger. Could be someone just out for a late walk with their dog.

Every one of her breaths seemed to her as loud as the puff of a steam engine. Surely if someone was outside, they could already hear her – or soon would.

The footsteps passed the door of Nicole's cottage, then stopped. A shuffle. Then they turned back in the direction they had come.

She crawled on her hands and knees to the bedroom, dragging her bag on her coat behind her. Her phone started buzzing, startling her. It was Billy. 'Where the hell have you been?' she whispered.

'Sorry about that, I was in a black spot,' he said. 'You sound stressed. I went by but all the lights are off at your house. Everything OK?'

'Yeah. No. I don't know.' A sob wrenched its way up to her throat. She choked it back, like a hiccup. 'Did you see any police?'

'If I did, would I be on the phone?' It was a question that did not especially need an answer. 'Why would there be police there? I've been listening to the radio, there's nothing about a woman at the train station. No one's looking for you.'

'Someone's at the house – or was. I don't know who. I didn't even get inside. I think Rab is d-dead.'

'Shit.' A pause. 'That didn't take long. Where are you now?'

'Not far from there. Where are you?'

'Fuck knows,' he growled. 'I went looking for you. Some damn houses by the river, about a mile from where I dropped you off.'

'Hold on.' Erykah opened the door and took a peek. At first it looked like there was no one there in the dark. Then a light from the moon caught the edge of a pair of silver-tipped boots and she saw him. The black-clad figure of Billy was only metres away from where she had heard the footsteps. 'Oi, look to your right,' she said.

He glanced round and caught sight of the open door. He walked over in three long strides and looked down at where she was huddled in the doorway. 'Fuck's sake, woman, what do you call this?'

'I call it a safe house, for now,' she said.

'All right,' he said. 'Let's go see what's back at yours.'

Erykah shook her head. He reached down and took her arm and led her into the kitchen. Her bag hung limply from one arm, her jacket still bunched in a ball. 'I don't know . . . I mean, I heard a gun. I heard . . . I heard them say . . .' She couldn't finish the sentence, couldn't put into words what she had heard them planning to do, what she feared they had already done. Her whole body shook, first silently, then a low, anguished moan.

Billy reached to switch on a light. Erykah grabbed at his arm. 'No – leave it off. In case they're still out there.'

'We can't stay here,' he said. 'Whoever's house this is, they could come back.'

Erykah shook her head. 'It's my girlfriend's. She's away, I should have been there with – with her . . .'

'Fine,' he said. 'Calm down. Now tell me what you saw.' Erykah opened her mouth to reply but started shaking again. 'Hey, hey, woman, deep breath.' Billy gripped her shoulders and manoeuvred her to a chair. 'You got to hold yourself together. You don't have to do it for ever. Just right now.' Erykah whimpered in response. 'It's fine. We'll stay here. We'll deal with it in the morning.' He reached into his leather jacket and pulled out a small glass bottle. 'Brought you something. Thought it might help.'

Erykah took the bottle and looked at the label. Grant's. 'I know it's not as nice as the stuff you usually drink,' he said.

'No, that's good, that's great,' she hiccuped. 'I could use a couple of Valium too, if you happen have any of those.'

'Do I look like a man who goes anywhere near a GP?'

'No, I don't suppose so,' she said. 'Thought you might know the sort of people who could get it.'

He shook his head. 'I stay far away from that business unless I got no choice,' he said. Erykah got up and took two glasses from the kitchen. 'Just water for me, thanks,' Billy said. 'I went clean my first turn in the joint and never looked back.'

'Is that why you don't deal with drugs?'

'Part of it,' he said. 'It's been long enough now that it's not a temptation any more. And what people do themselves, you know? That's their shout. I can't judge anyone for the choices they make. Went a long way down that road myself.' His eyes squinted, as if pushing back an unpleasant memory. 'But the people who take advantage of someone else's illness to make money?' He shook his head. 'Nah. That's where I draw the line.'

She poured a generous amount of the alcohol into her own glass, filled his with tap water, then dipped her long fingers in the water and flicked a few drops into her drink.

Seminole Billy watched her. 'Does that do anything?'

'Opens it up,' Erykah said, and buried the rim of the glass under her nose. She inhaled, then pulled it away and swirled the caramel liquid. 'Brings out the spice, a little bit of toffee.'

'You make it sound like a dessert.'

'I guess it is to me.' Erykah took a mouthful. The fire of the alcohol warmed her throat and made a lifeline right for her heart.

He didn't say anything after that. She was glad. He watched while she had a second glass of whisky, then a third. They sat in the kitchen, lit by the glimmer of the moon, its reflection on the river shifting as dawn grew nearer. 'There's something I have wanted to ask you,' she said.

'Ask it.'

'You really a Seminole?' she said. 'You don't look . . . you know.' She grimaced. How many times had people said the same thing to her, or something very like it? If he took offence, she would claim it was the whisky talking.

He didn't flinch. Billy reached in the front pocket of his jeans and pulled out a battered leather wallet. He passed a dog-eared identification card across the table.

Erykah looked at the black-and-white picture for a long time. A boy looked back at her, with rolled-up shirtsleeves and a clean-cut, old fashioned hairstyle. The teenaged Billy was just about recognisable, the close-set eyes especially, though time had changed his face a lot. 'Is that your name?' He nodded. 'Billy Billie,' she read aloud, and looked up at him. 'Really? Not William?'

'Family thing,' he shrugged. 'Dad ditched before I was born, Mama gave me a family name.'

'Were you close with her?'

'Was.' He frowned and ran his tongue over his teeth. 'Things didn't work out so good; I fucked up a lot when I was a kid,' he said. 'But Mama tried.'

'What's Florida like?'

'Like a good woman,' he said. 'Hot and wet.' He seemed to regret the flippant answer as soon as he said it. Billy turned his eyes towards the ceiling and sighed, digging deep for a memory. 'Sorry. I mean . . . It used to be mostly empty, now it's mostly not. Used to be all they wanted that cheap land for was orange groves and cattle farms. Now it's country clubs and sky-high condos on the beach. Lots more people too. Most of 'em not worth a damn. Retirees and drifters. A lot of 'em get down there with no idea what they want to do, and it sucks 'em in. Poor folks looking to make a dollar out of fifteen cents. The ones with money are even worse.'

'Not exactly what they put in the holiday brochures.'

'No, it ain't. Lot of lost people in Florida. Been like that for centuries. Lot of cons. Go on vacation, leave on probation,' he said. 'But it's still beautiful. The way the air feels, the way the wind smells coming off the beach, you can't take that away.'

'What did your family do?'

Seminole Billy shrugged. 'The usual. Truck stop, monkey farm and gator wrestling.' He looked at her raised eyebrow. 'I'm not joking.'

'It must be so different, living here.'

'Sure,' he said. 'The food's different. I miss a ripe tomato sometimes. And those things that get called grapefruit in your stores? Don't eat those. That's not what grapefruit is supposed to taste like. You have one picked fresh off the tree, it's as sweet as an orange.' He looked at her face and laughed. 'You think I'm lying. But that's the truth. And that's what I miss.'

'Do you go back much?'

'Haven't been in ten years,' he said. 'Didn't even want to go back that time, either. Nothing to go back for. Had enough of the place.' He put the card back in his wallet and the wallet in his jeans. 'Ask me again in a few years, though. Maybe I'll say the same. Maybe I'll say different.'

'What was it like in Scotland? I'm assuming you went up there to get rid of – of the bag.'

'I thought you only had one question? I counted seven so far.'

'Sorry, she said. 'But since all this started I can't help but wonder . . .'

'I drove it up,' he said. 'Just me. Buster was too much of a risk. If you think he's easy to spot in London, imagine how he'd stand out anywhere else. The Major gave me the keys to his place. It was being renovated or whatever, but the builders were off for the holidays. Place was full of plastic sheeting. I camped out there, cleaned the body up. Used to know a guy in Ullapool who ran drug boats all up that coast, so I figured that was as good as anywhere to dump him. Place was deserted. Everyone was sleeping off their Hogmanay hangovers. The tide did the rest.'

'But what about . . .'

'I know you have a lot of questions. Trying to make sense of it all,' Billy shook his head. 'But you gotta stop this. The less you know about it, the better.'

He was probably right. The more she found out about the whole situation, the less she wished she knew. It was enough having to walk away from the train at Euston and the Major's body as if nothing had happened. But now she was having to do the same to her own husband. Erykah wasn't sure what kind of a person that made her, but it probably wasn't a good one.

Billy reached across the table and slid the bottle back, capped it, and put it in her handbag. 'You need sleep. We'll figure out what to do in the morning.' She couldn't object.

They went to the bedroom with its one bed and Erykah paused. Billy pulled an armful of blankets from the cupboard and laid them on the floor. He took off his leather jacket and rolled it up as a pillow.

'There's a sofa – wouldn't you be more comfortable there than on the floor?'

He shook his head. 'I'm not leaving you. I did that already today, and you were right: it wasn't safe.'

Erykah crawled into bed. She was about to go to bed less than six feet from a man who had just admitted murder to her, and he was the only person right now that she trusted even a little bit. The pillow was dented with the shape of a head and the duvet smelled of Nicole. She had never felt so alone in her life. Erykah sobbed in the sheets until they were soaked. When the tears ran out eventually, the whisky did its work and she dropped into a deep, dreamless sleep.

: **29** :

The light came slowly and late. The sky was low with cloud but not raining. Diffuse light brightened the white walls of the bedroom. For a moment she did not remember where she was or why she was there. A few seconds of peace, of feeling both empty and complete, with no regrets, no grief. She reached out a hand to feel who might be next to her in bed only to find the sheets empty. Then the events of the last two days came rushing back, and she remembered why she was in Nicole's house, what she had seen and heard. She remembered why her throat was dry and cracked and her chest painful from heaving.

Billy must have risen early. The woollen blankets he had slept on were folded on a chair in the corner of the room. Erykah hauled herself to the bathroom, rinsed her mouth and looked in the mirror. Her bloodshot eyes were buried in a puffy face and her frizzy curls sprang out in all directions. She wrestled her hair back into a knot and turned the shower on full. Soon, steam billowed from the taps, filled the room and frosted the windows.

She lathered herself with a bar of soap and washed away days' worth of sweat and dirt. Underneath her skin felt taut, raw, like a sunburn. The scrapes and cuts across her knuckles stung where she had bit her hand. She turned the temperature up as hot as she could stand it. Maybe it would wash away the hollow feeling in her head and chest, help her figure out what to do.

The men who had been at her house last night were most likely long gone. She could go back, find Rab's body, and ring the police as if she had been out all night. But then what? Getting the cops involved would only alert whoever was after her to her whereabouts and maybe they were watching the house from a distance.

Or . . . she could go away. Disappear. Take the money and leave London. Billy could get her a passport. She could be halfway across the world in less than a day. Boston? India? It didn't matter. She would change her name, cut her hair, and fold into the rhythm of somewhere else. Frozen cocktails and fried fish sandwiches on the beach in Florida, sarongs and scuba diving in Thailand. Open a shop. Work in a market. Grow old and wrinkled. Never come back. No reason to. No need.

Tempting as it was, running away would not work. If the secret was big enough to be worth killing her husband over, it was big enough to follow her if she skipped town.

She tilted her face up to the ceiling and breathed the hot steam in deeply. There was no choice she could make that was the right one. Here was the rock. Here was the hard place.

When she was a girl, she had thought the saying was between a rock and a *hot* place. She imagined people crouching between the shadow of a boulder and the gates of hell, her imagination influenced by lurid Breugel prints in the front of a library book about Ancient Greek myths that she had pored over until Rainbow yelled at her that it was time to go to bed.

One time Rainbow and her friends were sitting around the flat, playing cribbage and smoking pot and talking gossip. Erykah hovered at the edge, hating the acrid smell of the smoke but fascinated by what it did, how it turned women who had once been suspicious of her hippy mother into old friends. Rainbow's feather and bead earrings fluttered as she laughed. One formidable lady called Joy with the voice of a chain smoker was lamenting her sixteen-year-old daughter, who was pregnant by her boyfriend and refused to discuss it. 'She's between a rock and a hot place,' Erykah piped up, and the women all broke into peals of laughter, like it was the punchline of the funniest joke ever told.

Joy laughed too, but she also rubbed Erykah's shoulder, seeing the confusion and hurt in her eyes when the grown-ups laughed at her. Joy was from Chicago, but that was a long time ago, and sometimes she brought round buttered grits that she simmered in a slow cooker. Erykah loved and hated the grits: they tasted nice but the texture was so weird, like something you weren't supposed to eat on purpose.

A rock and a hot place. Even now it made more sense to her than the real phrase. Anyway there was no way out of this situation that she could see.

Erykah sat on the bed and started digging through her bag. The Schofield files were still there. So was the Major's phone, which was out of power. But it was the same make as Nicole's and there was a spare charger next to the bed.

All she had to wear were the same clothes she had come in, the same ones she had been wearing since she got on the sleeper in Cameron Bridge. She couldn't go out in that. Erykah looked at the now ruined bra and decided to go without. She took a jumper, knickers and pair of jeans from Nicole's wardrobe, as well as the phone charger.

The smell of hot coffee and eggs wafted in from the kitchen. Erykah gathered up her things and shuffled to the kitchen. Billy was standing over the cooker, a blue and white checked tea towel tucked into his narrow waist for a makeshift apron.

In spite of herself, she smiled. 'You look ridiculous.'

'Yeah all right,' he said, and put a plate of eggs and a hot mug of coffee on the table. 'You need fuel. Eat.'

Erykah knew better than to disobey. She sat at the farmhouse table with her plate and the deciphered papers from Damian Schofield's office. She looked around at the cottage, the scrubbed pine and whitewashed lime walls as sparse as a showroom. It was mock Tudor outside, but mock Tudor of a vintage old enough to have its own charm. Inside it was middle-class-renovation chic, reclaimed boards and rose-sprigged vintage prints juxtaposed with recessed lighting and slick, polished stone. Nicole lived in the place as if it was a hotel, which Erykah supposed wasn't too far off the truth.

She cut the eggs and put each bite in her mouth without tasting it. The same few options spun around in her head until she couldn't make sense of any of it.

Right now no one knows where we are. I could stay here until Nicole comes back, Erykah thought. And then what? It wouldn't make a difference to what she would have to face the minute she stepped outside. And she couldn't take the chance that they might pull Nicole into it as well.

'Radio?' Billy said. Erykah nodded and he switched it on.

'Later this morning I'll be speaking to Heather Matthews from the Scotland Liberal Unionist Party,' Diana Stuebner purred through the radio speakers. 'With the shock death of Major Whitney Abbott this week, can the party survive the death of its highest profile – some would say only – political candidate?'

Billy snorted from the kitchen. Can it indeed? Erykah thought. Surely more troubling was the possibility that a police investigation of the death – not to mention Morag's on-air meltdown when confronted with the mortuary photos – would turn up facts they didn't want people to know about.

Yet, without any obvious connection to Schofield and Morag still denying involvement with the party, who would connect the dots? If she had walked into her own house last night, if those men, whoever they were, had killed her, who would know? Schofield had been so careful that the papers were all that was left. The irony was that the steps he had taken to avoid being detected were exactly the things that would probably see his killers walk away scot free.

Billy hovered over the sink, washing up plates, drying them and putting everything away exactly where he had found it. She considered for a moment telling him about the high efficiency, water-recycling dishwasher Nicole had just had installed where the vegetable pantry would once have been, but thought better of it. Leave no trace.

The kitchen window faced the towpath, towards the river. Erykah spotted a hard core of veteran men's squad rowing past with a coaching launch following close behind. A crackle from the cox box and the men came to a stop, listening for their next instruction.

The crew leaned over their oars again and started to move off. The men's faces were set in hard lines as they leaned deep into the catch of the oars, their eyes focused only on the back of the person in front of them.

In most other kinds of boats, people faced forward – kayaks, sailing, motor boats. In rowing you did not. You faced backwards and you had to trust. Trust the coxswain steering the craft, or if there was none, your own judgment. In the pair Nicole had been the one setting the pace, but it was Erykah who kept them on the course. Every time you swivelled around to have a look it risked throwing the boat off course, throwing the rhythm of the oars out of sync. You had to piece together your path from glances over your shoulder, from the feel of the water, the signs and sounds around you. There was no way to keep moving forward if you were always looking to see where you were going. The only thing you could see, for the most part, was the past.

'Billy,' she said. 'Can I ask you another question?'

'Shoot,' he said, and paused. 'Not literally.'

'If someone wanted to hire you, to find a couple of men, I mean . . .'

Billy wiped his soapy hands on a tea towel. 'Oh no. You're not thinking of going the eye-for-an-eye route, are you? Because what I cost for that kind of job, you can't afford.'

'Maybe,' Erykah said. 'I don't know. He was my husband. What am I supposed to do?'

'Sure, he was your husband,' Billy said and crossed his arms over his chest and leaned back against the counter. 'Just twenty-four hours ago you were telling me you weren't sure if you ever loved him.'

She looked away. It hurt to hear it laid out plainly like that. But it was true. How many times in the last weeks – the last years – had she wished Rab was gone? But this wasn't the way she'd wanted it to happen. Not like this.

'Hey, it's OK.' Billy said. 'It's normal to feel everything at once right now.'

Erykah nodded. 'Sure. Yeah.' Her fingers stretched and twisted the cuff of her sleeve. 'I feel as though I ought to be doing something,' she said. 'Instead of sitting here.'

Billy walked over and sat down in the chair next to hers. 'When someone hits you close to home it's easy to do something rash,' he said. 'I've never been much for quiet contemplation, but you need to take this one step at a time.'

'I don't even know what the first step is,' she said.

'A good offence is the best defence, you know? But what you're thinking about is base revenge.'

'You don't believe in revenge?'

'Not on a personal level, not unless I'm getting paid,' Billy said. 'You know what Marcus Aurelius said in *Meditations*? It is best to leave another man's mistake where it lies.'

'Marcus Aurelius, huh?' Erykah said. 'You make it sound like a Bible verse.'

'Well, it is a good book.'

She rubbed her fingertips on the smooth waxed wood of the table. 'I can't just let him lie there,' she whispered. 'I could phone the police and report it anonymously.'

'Woman, you know as well as I do there ain't no such thing as anonymous,' he said. 'Not when it comes to murder.'

Erykah nodded. The police were definitely better at tracking calls now than they had been when Grayson was arrested. And if that happened there was no way the press would ever leave her alone afterwards. She would be fair game for the rest of her life.

The Major's mobile buzzed and vibrated on the table, alerting her that it was now fully charged. Erykah picked it up and scrolled through the messages. A flurry of missed calls from the previous morning, then nothing.

'That your new burner?' Billy asked.

'Ah . . . no. It's the Major's phone.'

'You didn't tell me you had that,' he said. But it was appreciation, not accusation, in his voice.

'Can't go revealing all my secrets now can I.' The Major must not have used the mobile to contact many people. The list of numbers stored on the phone was short.

'Livia,' she said. She flipped through Schofield's notebook. 'Look, look here,' she pointed at a number scrawled on the paper in her own handwriting, where she had noted down the last person to ring his office phone. 'Same number. One of Schofield's colleagues said Livia was a radio journalist, but I rang LCC and they had never heard of her. I think it's the woman you met the night you got Schofield's body,' she said.

'You didn't call this number?'

Erykah shook her head. 'I didn't want to risk it until I had some idea what might be on the other end.'

'So do it now,' Billy said. 'Find out.'

'Are you joking?'

He reached across the table and punched the buttons. The phone rang a handful of times then went through to voicemail. Erykah leaned in, the better to hear if there was a personalised message.

'Sorry, I can't take your call right now,' a voice said. It was familiar . . . who was that? Erykah and Billy jumped back at the same time as they realised. He dropped the phone like it was hot and it clattered on the kitchen table. Erykah reached across and switched it off before the answerphone started recording.

'Is that who I think . . . ?'

'Yeah,' she said. 'It is.' And if that was the case, then Erykah wasn't the only one who was in immediate danger. But she was probably the only one who knew about it.

She had got it wrong. Completely wrong. But maybe – just maybe – there was a large enough window to make it right. She stood up from the table. 'Get your jacket and let's go.'

'What's up?' he asked.

'First, get Buster to meet us at the house,' she said. 'Tell him to bring cleaning supplies. You still have those Union Jack bags in the back of your car?'

'Sure do,' he nodded. 'If you're thinking what I think you're thinking – is that what you want?'

What did she want? Erykah couldn't have said, exactly. Things she thought she wanted a week ago were now long gone. Never mind the things she thought she had wanted twenty years ago. A simple answer might be to say she wanted a quiet life. But no matter what she did, trouble had a way of finding her. You can try for quiet all you like. The universe might just have other plans.

'Yes,' she said. 'Can't go to the police with this.'

'Let them think it was a robbery,' he said. 'Millionaires get knocked over all the time. And you two weren't exactly discreet about your home address.'

'Phone in a body at my own home? You know the first thing the police will do? Take me into custody until they decide what to charge me with. No way.'

'But you didn't do it,' Billy said. 'I'm playing devil's advocate here, you understand. I wouldn't ring them. But I'm not you. And you definitely don't wanna be me.'

Erykah shook her head. 'How do I tell them where I was? My alibi is either being on a train with a dead man, or being in a car with you. I'd be fucked either way. Can't leave him there, because . . .' She shuddered. 'I just can't. We do this now and I'll report him missing in a few days. After all the media interest and the state of our marriage it will look credible enough.'

'Yeah. Sure. I get that. But are you going to be OK with that?'

She paused. Was this it? Was this going to be the choice that changed her life forever?

No. Her life had already changed forever.

Dumping Rab's body was not what her twenty-year-old self would have advised. But maybe it was time to stop trying to make the decisions other people thought were right, and start making the ones she thought were right. 'I don't see we have much choice,' she said.

'Your wish is my command,' he said. 'Then what?'

'We're going to the radio station,' Erykah said. 'And you're going to finally meet Diana Stuebner.' She may not have known what she wanted, but for the first time in a long time, Erykah knew exactly what she needed to do.

30

Morag popped an antacid tablet in her mouth and chewed. The chalky mint taste kept down the bile in her throat for now. Her fingers beat a staccato rhythm on her desk.

The party whip had been round to see her. Morag knew what she was in for: a tongue lashing for the radio affair. Well, fuck it. It was an ambush. A man walking off would have been said to be standing up for himself. A woman? Already the tabloids were calling her hysterical.

That PR guru, Delphine, who had been chasing her down the hallway at Westminster last week now wasn't returning her calls. Morag had tried a couple of times during breaks from committee, but no answer. Delphine never let a call drop. Never. This was not good.

Outside her office door voices were arguing. Arjun seemed to be trying to prevent someone from getting into her office. 'No, I'm sorry, she's working right now, you'll have to make an appointment . . .'

Morag flung the door open to find her assistant scowling at two uniformed police. 'Is there a problem here?'

'The officers are here about a murder investigation, and I told them no way, no how, not without a warrant they're not,' Arjun said. 'If this is about that vile rumour – this is ridiculous. Show me a warrant or make an appointment.'

Morag laid a hand on her assistant's shoulder and smiled for the benefit of the police. One man and one woman, she noted. It could be random but didn't they usually send a woman if a female suspect was being taken into custody? 'Arj, it's fine. I'm so sorry about this,' she said. 'Arjun is looking out for my best interests. I'm sure this isn't anything to do with the radio interview yesterday,' she said. 'Is it?'

The police exchanged glances. 'Well, it is, in a way,' the woman said. 'I am Sergeant Okafor. Could we speak to you somewhere a bit more private?'

'Come in,' Morag said and stood aside. 'Arjun, get the two officers a cup of tea. And one for me as well. You know how I take it.'

Morag arranged herself behind the desk and crossed her legs at the knee. There was only one extra chair in the office. Neither officer would sit, so they were both left standing. Many thought that sitting down put you at a disadvantage, but in Morag's experience being comfortable while others shuffled and fidgeted on their feet was always a better option. 'To what do I owe the pleasure?'

Sergeant Okafor flipped open a notebook and clicked her pen. 'We are here regarding the ongoing investigation into the murder of Damian Schofield,' she said. 'After you were on the radio yesterday, we had a very interesting phone call.'

Morag stiffened, but her smile stayed in place. 'Do tell.'

'First, can I confirm that the photo revealed is, in fact of yourself, and that it was taken at the Cameron Bridge mortuary last week?' Sergeant Okafor laid a photocopy of a picture on the desk, the same one Diana Stuebner had revealed to her yesterday.

Morag looked at the picture. Her face was in profile, she was moving . . . it might have been someone else. But if she was caught out lying to the police, it wouldn't matter what she said afterwards. 'Well, it certainly appears to be me, doesn't it,' Morag said. 'Yes – I was there. I don't recall a photographer being there at the time.'

'And did you post a genetic sample to the mortuary, in case evidence was contaminated by your visit?'

'Yes, I did,' Morag said. She laced the fingers of her hands together and rested them on the desk. Her voice was slow, calm, deliberate. 'I sent the mortuary a cheek swab. My assistant Arjun will remember passing on the sample tube, and the phone call from – what was her name? – ah, Dr Hitchin, will be logged in our calls register.'

'Harriet Hitchin, yes,' Sergeant Okafor jotted down notes while her colleague scowled and tried to look tough. 'The pathologist at Cameron Bridge.'

'That's right.'

'And at the time you didn't know the identity of the deceased.'

Morag searched the sergeant face, but there was nothing to be read there. Even less in the face of the man with her. 'You know, I don't wish to be rude, but – should I be phoning a solicitor before this goes any further? Because if you wish to put questions to me in a, how shall we say, more formal fashion, I am more than happy to meet you at a nearby station.'

'No I don't think that will be necessary,' Sergeant Okafor said. 'We were contacted by Police Scotland late yesterday. They have processed your genetic sample, and apparently, there are links with a potential suspect.'

Arjun came back in the room with three mugs. He put them on the desk, eyes shooting daggers at the police. Morag shooed him away. The dark wood door clicked shut behind him, but she knew he was probably still there on the other side, listening.

She blew on the surface of her tea and took a tiny, experimental sip. The swallow clicked in her throat, like she had something to hide. 'Please continue,' Morag said.

Sergeant Okafor gestured to her partner, who produced a folded printout from inside his vest. She glanced over the paper, a printout of an email. 'Apparently they say your – what is this word, Barry?'

'Mitochondrial,' her partner murmured.

'Mitochondrial RNA is a match with material they extracted from under the deceased's fingernails.'

'I don't really understand what you're saying, but if you mean to imply that I could possibly be a suspect—'

'No, not that,' she said. 'You are not a person of interest. Not directly. Sorry, science is not my native language.' Sergeant Okafor laid the printout on the desk next to the mortuary picture.

'I mean, I'm sure my husband isn't involved in anything like this, we have no children, and my parents both died some years ago.'

'No, none of that. The mitochondrial RNA is maternally inherited, so it seems to be from someone you're related to, through your mother's side of the family. Can you tell us about your living relatives on that side of the family?'

Morag frowned. She had only fleeting contact with family since her mother's funeral. She was not like them. They were not like her. Her mam was the eldest of four, and the others, well . . . She hardly knew their families apart from the wedding and birth announcements that had come through over the years.

'The results have been run against the criminal database and match with no one else,' Sergeant Okafor said. 'Is there a possibility – I mean, even names would do, if you don't have addresses.'

Morag pursed her lips and thought. 'My uncles – as far as I know, neither had children. My mother's youngest sister, she had a daughter. Much younger than me. Lives in London I believe, though I've not seen the girl since she was knee-high.' Morag frowned and sipped her tea. 'No, even before that. The last time I saw her in the flesh was at her baptism.'

The policewoman scribbled in her notebook and nodded. 'Name? Age? What year would that have been?'

'Now let me think . . .' Morag closed her eyes and flipped back through her mental Rolodex. It had been a long time. 'Ninety-one, is when it was. It was quite something. Very glamorous. Very unlike having it in the local kirk, where the rest of the family were all brought into the church.'

Morag, who was still on the Cameron Bridge town council back then, had made the trip down by coach. It had been her first time in London save for a school trip years before. She had watched out the window at the last slow progress of the bus into Victoria coach station, past the grand façade of the Science Museum, the Victoria and Albert, the lights and crowds outside Harrods. The size and sprawl of the city was unlike anything she had ever seen. It was scary but also a little bit thrilling. She would never have imagined that she would be living there herself less than a decade later. Nor, for that matter, would any of her family imagined it of her.

'My aunt married money,' Morag went on. 'A Catholic man, but they all are in South America, aren't they?' She chuckled. 'He had some sort of Papal title and that set the cat amongst the pigeons – not that she cared. After that we were sure we would never see her again. She changed their name back after his suicide. Poor dears, they never wanted for anything, but her little girl growing up in boarding schools with a trust fund instead of a father? That can't have been nice.'

'I'm sure that's all very useful,' Sergeant Okafor said. 'But if you could give us a name . . .'

'Oh, it was – what was it – Castano-Perez. Their girl is called Heather.' A flicker of memory passed across Morag's face. The body on the slab in the Cameron Bridge mortuary, the horrible grin of the lipless, decomposing corpse, the cut throat. The body cavity splayed wide open, and the smell. The smell. Whoever had done that to a man would have to be crazy, or heartless, or likely both. Morag leaned on her elbows and looked up at the police. 'My God! You don't really believe Heather might have killed someone, do you? What was done to that man was awful.' She shivered.

The sergeant shook her head. 'At this point we can't know anything for certain until we speak to her,' she said. 'But we are taking this very seriously.'

'And you haven't had contact with her?' the man said.

'No. I heard some things because we have a few acquaintances in common. She went to work last year with the Scotland Liberal Unionists.' Morag said. 'Everyone who does the fundraising circuit knows everyone else. It's only about two degrees of separation. But she never contacted me and, to be frank,' Morag gestured at the office, 'I'm a very busy person.'

'Right, the SLU. That anti-devolution party,' the sergeant said. 'But you weren't backing them, or involved in any way? Maybe financially? You were on the same side of the referendum, is that right?'

'God, no,' Morag shook her head. 'I mean, yes, they also were against independence, but we never worked together. The SLU set out their stall to challenge the main parties. Even a hint of sympathy in that direction and I would be dumped from the front bench in no time.'

'No donors in common?'

'None that I know of.' Morag leaned back again and waved her hand. 'In any case, she comes from money; her father's family were loaded. Doubtless she picked up a few lucrative connections growing up in those social circles.'

'Mmm.' Sergeant Okafor raised her eyes from the notebook. 'You said you and Heather knew people in common,' she said. 'Anyone in particular?'

'You know how it is, lobbyists get around.' She sipped her tea. 'Come to think of it, there was something else. That Major, you know – Abbott?'

The man perked up now. 'Major Abbott? The one who was found dead on a train yesterday?' The police looked at each other, and Sergeant Okafor started scribbling again.

'The very same.' She swung the tip of one red shoe back and forth. 'He was there, at her baptism. If memory serves me correctly, and it usually does, he was one of her godfathers.'

'Wouldn't that be a bit odd, though,' the policeman said. 'To be a godparent to someone from Argentina. Isn't he famous for fighting against them in the Falklands?'

'Arguably, he's more famous for shagging his ghost writer,' Morag said. 'And these days, for being a social media liability. Old military links, I assume. Before the war – and this is well before your time – Britain was fairly chummy with the junta, back when we believed in the Red Menace and the threat of Communists taking over.'

'You mentioned her family have a lot of money,' Sergeant Okafor said.

'Had, in the past tense,' Morag said. 'I didn't keep up with them nor they with me. But you hear things. There was a deal that went wrong, a government contract they lost. The father killed himself. My aunt came back to Britain. She had to pull Heather out of boarding school.' She leaned back in her chair. The old leather and wood creaked. 'They weren't skint exactly, but most of what was left was tied up elsewhere. A pity. But perhaps a lesson to all of us not to count your chickens before they hatch.'

'So they had money and lost it,' Sergeant Okafor said. 'What was the business again?'

'Why, it was oil, of course.'

31

'Hey, lady!' The security guard leapt up from his chair. 'Where the hell do you think you're going?'

Erykah hurtled through the revolving glass doors and sprinted for the lifts. She stopped in her tracks and turned to face the guard whose burly arms were planted like tree trunks on the desk. His voice was familiar – it was the same man who'd answered the phone when she rang the station.

She glanced at her watch. The radio station had been trailing Heather's interview on air for the last two hours; she was probably in the studio right now. And only metres away from Kerry who was entirely unaware of the danger.

'Where's Kerry Wilder?' Erykah gasped.

Barrington remained exactly where he was. 'I'm s'posed to ask if you got an appointment,' he said.

She reached into her bag and pulled out the black and yellow scarf. 'No, no appointment, she left this at a coffee shop earlier. I thought I would drop it by, you know, say hello. Were, uh, we're friends.'

'Friends. Uh-huh,' Barrington said. 'You can leave it here and I'll make sure she gets it.'

She glanced over the security guard's shoulder at the CCTV monitors and flinched. On one screen it looked like a woman was stabbed and bleeding while a man on the other side of a glass wall tried to save her. What the hell? 'What's that?'

Barrington looked over his shoulder. 'Oh. Right,' he said, and switched it back to a sedate scene at the top of a stairwell. 'I was watching a film.'

'Instead of the CCTV?' Erykah raised her eyebrow. 'Uh-huh. I'm sure it's very edifying.'

'Watch your mouth, that's *Bird With the Crystal Plumage*,' Barrington said. 'It's a classic.' He looked at the scarf, then at her face, then at the scarf again. 'A'ight, I'll swipe you through. This time. Level four.'

'Thank you,' she breathed and hurried away.

The lift was old and seemed to be taking forever. Erykah tapped her foot on the floor. She should have come up the stairs. They had spent too much time at the house. Seminole Billy wouldn't let her go inside, said she didn't need to see that. Asked her what if the neighbours saw her, what if they talked to the police later? He was right, of course. Better to leave him and Buster to take care of Rab's body, do what they needed to do.

It wasn't only the gore. In the time while his death was still new, while she hadn't seen anything, it still existed in a not-quite-real space, one where she didn't have to think through what she was doing right now or admit that things would never be the same again. Maybe she had made the decision already, when she chose staying with him over leaving with Nicole. Or when she got more deeply involved with the Major. Or maybe she hadn't made the decision at all, maybe the decision was and had only ever been Rab's, and he chose for her.

And maybe, as with Grayson's trial, the situation had nothing to do with her after all. The tide just turned and you dealt with it. People did whatever they were going to do, with little or no thought of the effect on others, and only she could pick up the pieces of her own life.

The lift pinged open on the fourth floor – LCC was in front of her. Erykah strode into the corridor, looking left and right for a sign of Kerry. She poked her head in the green room – no one there, just a tired sofa and a collection of unwashed mugs. A row of offices was empty. She spotted, through a glass wall, the production team hovering over mixing boards. They gave the thumbs up to Diana through a window to the main studio.

Diana and Heather were inside, fiddling with the equipment. Diana adjusted her microphone, which was attached with a hinged mount from the ceiling. The she showed Heather the right distance to sit to get the best sound on the small, heavily weighted guest mics on the desk. Erykah noticed for the first time how Heather's eyes darted around the room, the way she ran her hand through her hair, which looked lank and unwashed. Her blouse was expensive but when she raised an arm to adjust the headphones, there was a tell-tale dark patch of sweat. The formerly confident young woman Erykah had met at the press conference was beginning to show the strain.

Erykah spun around on her heel before Heather could spot her and, in doing so, nearly knocked into Kerry, who was carrying two mugs of coffee.

'Watch it!' Kerry scowled and gripped the mugs. Her eyes met Erykah's. 'You! What are you doing here?'

'I need to talk to you.' She hauled Kerry into one of the empty offices and shut the door behind them. 'Listen to me, something bad is about to go down.'

'Yeah, like I'm gonna get a bollocking from my boss if I don't get in there right now,' Kerry said.

Diana's honeyed voiced poured out of the station speakers. 'Joining me live on air this afternoon is Heather Matthews, spokesperson for the Scotland Liberal Unionist Party. Heather, thank you for joining us. With the sudden death of Major Whitney Abbott, and post-referendum debates accusing both sides of misleading campaigns, is it fair to say your young party has had its worst week ever?'

'You don't understand,' Erykah hissed to Kerry. 'We got it wrong. It's not Morag behind this. It's her. It's *Heather*.'

Kerry's eyes widened. 'Are you sure?'

'I'm sure.' Erykah pulled the files out of her bag and laid the papers on top of the desk. 'Here,' she pointed at the notebook. 'That's the phone number of the last person to call Damian Schofield at his office before he disappeared. He had a meeting in his diary next to the initials LL. Lady Livia, I assumed – a contact of the Major's. One of Schofield's co-workers said she claimed to be a journalist here. But when I phoned the station no one had ever heard of her.'

'Go on.' Kerry set the mugs down and bent over the files, tucking her hair behind one ear.

'I thought it was unusual, but there was a lot else going on and it didn't seem important,' Erykah said. 'Then yesterday, I was going through Major Abbott's phone—'

'Wait!' Kerry said. 'You have the Major's phone?'

'Ah,' Erykah said. It was probably not a good idea tell anyone else about her presence on the sleeper train that night. Especially not someone with the habit of tweeting out every piece of gossip she heard. 'It's a long story. Anyway, I plugged in the phone and the same number I got off Schofield's office phone is in the Major's phone as Livia. So we ring it, and it's Heather's voice on the answerphone.'

'It's her pseudonym,' Kerry half-smiled.

'Sort of,' Erykah said. 'Heather Matthews isn't Heather's real name, or at least, not the one she was born with. I've done some checking and she was born in Argentina and her name is Castano-Perez. Olivia Heather Castano-Perez. She comes from an oil family. I did some digging on the way here – once you have the right name, guess whose family's old company turns up all over the applications for new oil and gas exploration sites in Scotland? Anyway, I believe she was trying to get close to Schofield and discover what he knew, and when she had her evidence—'

'That's when she decided to kill him,' Kerry said. She bit her lip. 'Do you think Schofield knew?'

'Maybe,' Erykah said. 'Maybe he tried to confront her. No way to tell for sure. That's why I'm here. She must know the leak is someone in this building.' If Erykah had figured out the location of Media Mouse so quickly, it wasn't hard to believe plenty of others would as well. 'Or else why raise her head above the parapet? She's here to take someone out – and that someone is you.'

Kerry started poking at the screen of her phone.

'Are you ringing the police?'

Kerry flashed Erykah a wicked smile. 'Are you fucking kidding? I'm tweeting this!'

Someone started pounding at the door. 'Come on, Kelly, we've been waiting for that coffee for almost five minutes!' Jonathan shouted. 'I'm going back in the tank and if you're not there in ten seconds you're toast.'

'It's my boss.' Kerry gave Erykah a see-what-I-have-to-deal-with look and put her phone back on the desk. 'I have to go or they'll know something's wrong.'

'Please,' Erykah whispered, a hand on Kerry's shoulder. 'Whatever you do—'

'I have to go.' The girl shrugged her off. 'It'll be fine. Heather can't do anything to me here, right? Not in front of all these people.'

Erykah slumped in the chair. Kerry still didn't understand. She hadn't heard that gunshot back at the house when Rab was killed. She hadn't listened to what the people who did it had planned to do to her, or to anyone else who got in their way. She had no sense that with just one wrong choice her entire life could fall apart.

The station switched over to a weather and traffic update and Diana and Heather left the tank for a few moments. Kerry was busy fetching Jonathan his drink, so the women were left to get their own in the green room. Heather smiled and picked up both mugs while Diana jogged down the hall for a quick loo break.

Erykah watched from the crack in the door. What was Heather doing?

She picked up Kerry's phone. Media Mouse was still logged on to Twitter. Erykah scrolled down the screen, flicking past mentions and messages, wheedling requests from students who wanted to interview her and journalists who wanted to trap her into revealing herself. But maybe . . .

If she did nothing, Heather could have Diana in her sights. But if she tweeted, Kerry would be at risk as well.

Jump before you're pushed.

Maybe Kerry wasn't entirely wrong. Twitter might not save her, but the phone lines could. Erykah's thumbs hovered over the screen, shaking. What to type? *'BREAKING Schofield murder. Last contact before disappearance Scotland Liberal Unionists sec Matthews, now on LCC.'* She followed it up with the station switchboard number, took a deep breath, and pressed send.

Then a follow-up message, in case the meaning wasn't clear. *'She is the killer. I know because I am in the station right now. I work here.'*

Within seconds, it had been retweeted ten times. That seemed a lot. Then thirty. Almost as many replies popped up to warn her of libel suits if she was wrong. But who cares about self-appointed Internet legal experts? Even more people started responding to the second message, the one saying where she was.

Erykah peeked back out at the studio. Sure enough, the lights on the switchboard were already going mad, with producers pointing and gesturing through the glass. Diana and Heather, unaware of what was happening, settled into their seats and the last seconds of the advert break ticked away.

'Welcome back. Today I'm talking to Heather Matthews, spokesperson for Scotland Liberal Unionists, the party that was until this week running Whitney Abbott as a candidate for European Parliament. With Major Abbott's tragic death, can the party struggle on – and what does this tell us about the landscape of Scottish politics, and Britain in general, post-referendum? We're taking your calls now at LCC. Our first caller, David in Putney, you're on the air.'

'Hey, hi,' the man's voice said. 'Long-time listener, first-time caller. I love your show, Diana.'

'Thank you, David. Do you have a question or comment for our guest?'

'Sure. Yeah. I was wondering if Heather could comment on the online rumour that she was involved in Professor Damian Schofield's death?'

Diana's eyes went wide. She signalled to the producers through the glass with a finger across her neck with one hand while she pounded the hang-up button with the other. 'Wow! That was unexpected. Ha ha. Huge apologies to our guest. I think,' Diana shot daggers at the team on the other side of the glass. 'It sounds like our call screening is not as sharp as it might be today. Next caller, you're on the air.'

'Hi, Jenny from Bedford. Same question. Also for Diana, did you know Media Mouse was someone who works at the station?'

Diana's finger came down again and cut the call. 'Ha ha, well as we all know just because something is online doesn't mean it's true,' she said. She looked at Heather, whose face had gone white with rage. 'I don't expect you to answer any of this, of course.' She gestured again to the producers. 'Guys, can you possibly find us a caller who isn't trying to accuse our guest of heinous crimes? You know I love the drama, but I can hear the legal department screeching from here.'

Jonathan made a spinning circular motion in the air with one finger. Fill the time, he was telling her. 'While our producers get on that, let's go over some of these headlines again.' Diana pressed a hand to her headphones, and listened for a moment. 'Wait, yes, I'm getting some confirmation from the producers. Apparently the Media Mouse account has been online today, making accusations about our guest and claiming she disguised herself as a journalist to get close to Schofield. Unconfirmed allegations, I have to emphasise. It also claims the account is run by someone who works right here at our LCC studio but, ah, we have no confirmation of the truth of any of these claims.' Erykah saw Kerry turn her head in the direction of the office, then quickly look away, then at the floor. 'Well, I'm sure you'll be giving your solicitors a call as soon as we're off the air,' Diana chuckled. 'Moving swiftly on—'

'No, by all means, let's talk about this,' Heather said. 'I've been meaning to pick a bone with you, Diana Stuebner,' she said.

Diana looked surprised, but spread her hands in invitation. 'Pick away,' she said.

'Don't you think it's a little odd that your station seems to be on top of anything negative that happens with regards to the SLU?'

'Bias, you mean? We are a news organisation,' Diana chuckled. 'Like most we have our ups and down when it comes to being the first to break stories. I mean, it's not as if the Scottish Liberal Unionist Party is all we cover—'

'And the fact that you specifically had a tip off from Media Mouse with photos of Morag Munro at the Cameron Bridge Mortuary is nothing to do with that.'

Diana smiled patiently. 'I'm sorry, Heather, but I don't see how that's related? Let's turn it back to our callers.'

'What I'm saying is, Diana, you are clearly the source. *You are.*' Heather pointed across the table. 'The manhunt for the real identity is a set-up, because the whole thing is a set-up. You are Media Mouse, and you're manipulating stories to make sure your station gets the best ratings,' she said. 'You've had it in for me – for the SLU – from the start. It's a vendetta, and it's time you were stopped.'

Diana's mouth dropped open but, ever the professional, she recovered quickly. 'Wow! I've been accused of many things over the years, but this has to be the first time anybody mistook someone else for me.' Diana started to laugh.

'It's funny to you, is it?'

'I'm sorry,' Diana said, waving her hands. 'I don't mean to make light of this. You have to admit, it's certainly an odd thing to be accused of. We're just having, I don't know, maybe silly season came early this year. Don't worry about those callers, I'm sure they'll be on to the next Twitter outrage in no time.' She shuffled a few papers on the table in front of her nervously. 'In the last few minutes you've been accused of a lot of frankly unbelievable things.'

'Right.' Heather nodded. 'But for the sake of argument – and your audience loves an argument, don't they? Let's say it was true. What would you do, Diana Stuebner?'

Diana looked to the production room where Jonathan was grinning and holding two thumbs up. She bared her teeth slightly, but he ignored her subtle indication that maybe the ratings spike they were having right now was secondary to her misgivings about the way the interview was going. 'I'm not sure,' she said. 'Ring the police, most likely.'

'Sure.' Heather nodded. 'Ring the police. Meanwhile you're locked in a room with someone you think very well could be a violent murderer.'

'Well, I haven't seen any evidence to indicate that, and so far . . .'

Heather waved her hand. 'I haven't seen, blah blah, blah whatever. So for the sake of argument you *are* Media Mouse.'

'I'm not, but for the sake of argument, let's say I am.'

'And let's say the supposed murderer in the room with you does . . . something rash.' Heather's steady voice hardly changed, but something in her face had. It looked more pointed, somehow. Feral. 'What would you do?'

Diana swirled coffee around the bottom of her mug. 'I suppose it would depend on what that something rash was.' She tipped the mug up to her mouth and swallowed.

Heather smirked and watched Diana. 'Let's say she'd put something in your coffee during the break,' she said. 'Let's say you were drinking it right now. For the sake of argument.'

Diana spat out the mouthful of coffee and stared at her mug. She brought her fingers to her mouth, to try to induce vomiting but Heather leaped over the oval table and grabbed her hand. Diana ripped off her headphones and backed into the corner of the studio, with Heather close behind, brandishing the heavy base of her guest microphone in one hand like a club.

Jonathan ran to the door separating the production staff from the studio, only to find that Heather had locked it from the inside. He pounded at the door, then ran back to the mixing board. The lights were off the charts now, flashing as hundreds of callers all tried to reach the station at once.

Kerry slipped out and ran back to the office where Erykah was hiding. Her eyes were wide, her breathing rapid. 'What the fuck just happened out there?'

'The poison,' Erykah said.

'What poison?' Kerry said.

'I'll explain later.' She should have seen this coming, after the Major and the bottle of water he drank from Schofield's office. Of course Heather would try it again. 'We have to get you out of here *now*.' She looked across at the studio. Heather and Diana were still inside. Jonathan was on the phone while the rest of the production staff cowered behind the mixing boards. Erykah and Kerry started towards the stairwell.

Kerry looked to the door, then back at Erykah. 'I don't understand. They were talking, right, and then Heather just . . . snapped. What the fuck?' she repeated.

'I don't know,' Erykah said. Heather had always come across as controlled, smooth. In front of the cameras anyway. There had to be more to the story than Erykah knew, something truly personal in it for Heather. Otherwise, why flip out like this?

A voice erupted on a loudhailer from three floors down. 'This is the police,' a deep voice boomed outside. 'Heather Matthews, release your hostages and come out with your hands raised.'

Heather's head whipped round towards the source of the noise. She lunged for the door to the production room and fumbled the lock. Jonathan threw his body across to try to keep her from getting out. 'Go on, go on, get out!' he shouted to anyone who would listen. 'Take the stairs!' About a dozen people ran out of the production booth and back offices, heading for the fire exit.

Suddenly, the lights went out. Someone screamed. The police must have cut the power to the building. Then a flicker as the emergency generators kicked in, bringing the studio back to life. The office lights were dim, but the studio and production room lit up again. The red On Air lights and stairwell Exit signs that came back to life glowed in the half dark, guiding everyone to the stairs.

Erykah and Kerry lingered at the back of the rush. 'Come on, there's no time!' someone shouted. Erykah turned her head back towards the studio for a glimpse of what was going on, but it was hard to see. As far as she could tell Diana was now crouched under the table in the studio, the station still on the air.

Police downstairs. Heather up here. Erykah felt a pinch of pain in her chest as if her lungs were being squeezed. She slowed her breath and tried to hold it for a count of three, feeling the flush of blood rising to her skin. Whatever she decided, it had to be done right now.

Her palms were sweaty. She wiped them on her thighs and reached in her bag for the Major's pistol. She tucked it in the front of her jeans waistband and Kerry's eyes went wide.

'Is that real?' Kerry squeaked. The heavy footsteps of the rest of her colleagues disappearing down the stairs started to fade away.

Erykah shook her head. 'No, it's not real.'

'It bloody looks real.'

'Well, it's real, but it doesn't work.' Erykah thrust her bag, with the sheaf of papers and notebooks at the girl. 'Take this.' Kerry wrapped her skinny arms around it like a kid holding a school bag. 'Guard it with your – um, just guard it. Make sure no one takes it off you until you see me again. And call an ambulance. If I'm right about what this is, Diana has about ten minutes. Fifteen at most.'

'What are you going to do?'

'Wait for me in the lobby.' Erykah pulled her jumper down to hide the bulge of the pistol stock sticking up from her jeans. 'I'll be close behind you.'

: 32 :

Erykah shut the door and turned to face the studio. Jonathan was alone in the production booth. He had dragged a heavy chair to the door between his room and the studio. On the other side, Heather had gone back to brandishing the microphone in Diana's direction.

The red On Air light was still on.

Erykah walked over to the production room and planted her hand on Jonathan's shoulder. He turned, panic in his eyes. Did he recognise her? Did it matter right now? 'Get this off the air,' she said. 'Now! Put a recording on – go to public service announcements. *Do it.*'

Jonathan looked as guilty as a child caught with a hand in the biscuit tin. Like most angry little men she had met in her life, all it took was a matronly air of authority to defuse him. Was that what had attracted him to Morag Munro? 'What if something happens?' he said. It was a baby's whine, a plea. 'What if she does something, and we miss it?'

Erykah was gobsmacked. How could he be thinking about broadcasting at a time like this? 'Do you really want to be the person responsible for broadcasting the assault and possible murder of your star presenter?' Erykah asked. Jonathan blinked and didn't answer. Jesus, he had to think what the right answer was? 'Fuck's sake,' she said. 'Get this off the air.'

'But what if the safest thing is to leave the mics—'

'Do it!' she said.

'Hold on, hold on.' Jonathan's fingers hovered over the mixing board, but he touched nothing. He chewed his thin lower lip. He seemed to be waiting for something else to happen first.

'Do it,' Erykah growled. 'Now. Or else.' She lifted the hem of her jumper and showed him the pistol sticking out from her jeans.

'Fine!' He slowly brought up the volume on a recording of station promos that looped through announcements of upcoming shows and brought the studio mics down. The red On Air sign flicked off. Erykah crouched behind the mixing board, just high enough so she could still look through to the studio. Heather was ranting and raving, facing away from the glass, and hadn't seen her. Jonathan got down to Erykah's level. 'Now what?' he said.

'Get her attention,' Erykah said. 'She doesn't know I'm here. Don't tell her.'

Jonathan looked over his shoulder. 'Why aren't the police up here yet?' he said.

'I don't know,' Erykah said. 'They're probably waiting to see what she does. Don't want to risk her hurting someone.'

Jonathan nodded. He stood up and started pounding again on the glass. 'Heather!' he yelled. 'The office is evacuated and you're off the air.'

Heather turned and looked at him. She came around the studio table, slowly, like a cat on the prowl. She stopped with her nose just inches from the glass and started to push against the door. Jonathan managed to brace himself and the chair, but was struggling. 'Turn it back on,' she said. She backed up a few paces, lowered her shoulder and pushed against the door again.

'Heather, be reasonable, the police are outside,' he said. 'They have the building surrounded.'

She backed up again a few feet further. 'Turn it back on.' The microphone stand swung from her arm like a club.

Jonathan ducked to one side. Suddenly there was a giant crash and he was bathed in a shower of broken glass as the microphone shattered the door. She climbed through the hole in the glass and over the chair. Jagged shards tore at her clothes and skin. Heather held the steel bottomed mic in one hand.

Jonathan cringed, his hands raised in front of his face. Tiny, grain-sized specks of blood started to appear where the tiny pieces of glass had hit his face and neck. 'Put it back on!' Heather shouted, but he only cowered in fright.

Erykah slid the pistol out of her waistband and wrapped one hand around the stock. She crawled towards them as quietly as she could. A piece of broken glass crunched under one of her knees. Heather looked around to see where the noise came from. Her crazed eyes were bright, the pupils pinpoints. They trained on Erykah.

Erykah stood and brushed the glass from her knees. She raised the pistol to her eye line, her arms out in front of her. Her breath was fast and shallow. She backed away from Jonathan and the mixing console, putting herself between them and the production room door. 'Leave it off, Jonathan,' she said.

Heather snarled at Erykah. 'You're supposed to be dead!'

'That what they told you, was it?' Erykah said. 'Sorry to disappoint. Looks like you need better hired help.'

'I told them to humiliate you,' Heather sneered. 'Did they blow the head off that stupid husband of yours? Did you watch his useless brains spatter all over the walls?'

'Fuck you,' Erykah said. She hadn't seen what they did to Rab and didn't want to imagine it. Not now, not while she was trying to hold herself together. She pulled back the slide of the small pistol. It clicked in what she hoped was a convincing way.

Heather broke into a hyena's laugh. 'Oh, that's rich,' she hooted. 'The trash is going to take me out. No offence, honey, but you haven't the balls.'

'Trash with enough on you to put you in jail, Heather Matthews.' Erykah's tongue darted in the corner of her mouth and tasted a drop of sweat there. 'Or should I say, Heather Castano-Perez?'

'Get you, girlfriend,' Heather mocked, swinging her head in an exaggerated motion. 'So you know how to use the Internet. It's not a secret. Go on then. Do your worst.'

'My worst,' Erykah said. She thought she heard a click and droning buzz from Jonathan's direction, but dared not turn her head for a second. Maybe she could get over to where he was, switch the board off again. No: better to keep Heather engaged, keep her talking. 'How about your money laundering plan for starters. The fake political party. The fraudulent lottery. The threats, not to mention the killings . . .'

Heather cocked her head and raised an eyebrow. Her damp, sweaty hair stuck to one side of her face. 'Killings? Dear me, I thought you of all people would know better than to believe everything you see online.'

At the edge of her vision Erykah spotted Jonathan's hand retreating from the mixing board. The On Air light was back on. She looked away quickly. 'I guess the ball's in your court now,' she said.

'Aren't you clever?' Heather said. 'Only you're too late to do anything.' Heather's face was streaked with make-up and sweat, the knuckles of her hands scraped raw from the glass and starting to drip blood. 'Story of your life, though, isn't it?'

'All this time I was looking for who was really behind the SLU,' Erykah said. 'With only your name and the Major's on any of the paperwork. It didn't make sense at all. I thought you were fronting for someone else. But you were right there all along, hiding in plain sight.'

'It's a little thing I like to call subtlety,' Heather said. She tossed her head, and a flash of that public schoolgirl, hockey captain control showed through for a moment. 'You might want to try it sometime.'

Erykah grimaced. The broken glass crunched under their feet. She felt the sticky sensation of blood seeping through from her cut knees to her jeans. 'In which case, nicely done,' Erykah said. 'This certainly is subtle.'

'Are you here for a social call or was there something you wanted to talk about?' Heather asked. 'Because if you don't mind, I have a very busy day planned.'

Erykah gulped. 'I'm here because of Damian Schofield. You're the one responsible for his murder.'

Heather shrugged. 'So? That's it? You came here to tell me something I already know?' She stepped forward, towards Erykah and the door out of the production room. 'Now get out of my way.'

Erykah stood her ground. 'That's not all.' Heather stopped a few feet from the gun and sighed. 'When he was going to break the silence on the fracking report, you disguised yourself as a journalist to find out what he knew. Only you couldn't finish the job. So you got someone else to knock him off and dump the body.'

'I'm sorry, what?' Heather's laughter rang through the room, loud. There was the slightest amount of feedback over the station monitor, but she didn't seem to have noticed. 'The fracking report?' she said, and took a step towards Erykah. 'You think this is about a *fracking* report?'

'Isn't it?' Erykah said. The notes and papers in Schofield's office. Apart from the harassment allegation, he seemed as straight as they come. What else could there have been to find?

'My God, woman, you really don't know?' Heather said. 'I've known – *knew* – Damian Schofield for a very long time.'

'This isn't about the oil?'

'Oh, it's about oil, but not in the way you think.' Heather flicked the dry, reptilian end of her tongue over her lips. Her glassy eyes seemed to be looking somewhere else. Out the window, maybe. 'He might not have remembered me, but I never forgot about him.'

The stock of the pistol slipped in Erykah's sweaty hands. She gripped the gun tighter. The longer she could keep Heather talking, the better. Maybe she could convince her not to do anything dangerous. Or maybe it would be long enough for the police to find a safe way in and get Jonathan and Diana out. At least with the radio on, they could hear what was happening. Jonathan was in the studio now, propping Diana up, slapping her pale cheeks so she stayed awake. But if the Major's death was any indication, Erykah knew she didn't have much longer. 'So tell me how you knew him,' she said.

'Do I have to do everything for you? In Argentina. The oil was denationalised in the '90s. My great-grandfather had managed to hold off the government when they forced control of the entire industry in the '20s. He buried the surveys that put million of tonnes under our property. We waited. We knew we were sitting on money and the political situation would change eventually.'

She paused. Erykah was entranced. The words had a strange, rehearsed quality; like a tale of lost pirate gold told to a little girl at the family dinner table and never questioned. 'When the YPF collapsed, that should have been when we made our move. But Schofield didn't cooperate. He said the old surveys were wrong, that the land, at least in terms of energy, was next to worthless. Father knew he must have been taking money from someone to skew the results. *Must* have. There was no other explanation. He sealed his fate when he put his name to the seabed surveys and wiped our family out overnight,' Heather said. 'He deserved it, you know. Signed his own death warrant.'

Erykah nodded slowly. Heather's picture of Schofield didn't accord at all with what little she knew of him. But she had to keep her talking. She clearly hadn't seen Jonathan's hand or realised the mic was back on.

'My father had offshore rights secured. He put the family fortune on it. All Schofield needed to do was make sure the fields landed in our area.' Heather swept her arm wide, the microphone stand in her hand like a baton, or a hammer. 'One kilometre east and we would have been billionaires. But he didn't. He ruined us, ruined my father. He deserved to die, and you know what?' Her pin dot pupils held Erykah's gaze, unblinking. 'I enjoyed it.'

The longer she talked, the more Erykah noticed how odd her accent was. She had thought Heather was just English, but she sounded Scottish when talking about Scotland, and different still when talking about her childhood. The product of having been moved around a lot when young, perhaps. Or of something else. 'And then what?' Erykah said. 'Once the police open a murder investigation they're not going to walk away.'

'They have nothing,' Heather smiled. Her arm kept going like a pendulum, weighted by the heavy microphone. 'No confession, no fingerprints, no real proof.'

'What about Media Mouse?'

'What about Media Mouse?' Heather said. 'What about the anonymous tweets planted by the media to try to libel me. Or at least, that's how the courts will see it.' Her white-knuckled hand kept swinging. 'There's no evidence. There are no witnesses.'

'Apart from those men you hired to kill me,' Erykah said.

'Sorry, what men?' Heather laughed. 'Try again.'

'The post-mortem, then.'

'Right, Harriet Hitchin,' Heather said. 'The least credible pathologist in Britain, and that's saying something. She should have been lost her license years ago.'

'They'll get a second pathologist, now that it's a murder. You won't be so lucky twice.' Erykah's arms started to shake. Her mind rattled through all kinds of possibilities, but there was not one that wasn't a disaster. If the cops came in, they might neutralise Heather, but they would also nail Erykah for the gun, and probably for the Major as well. And money laundering. She would have to face the horror of trial by media again. And if Heather got away? Nowhere would be safe.

'Aww, thinking about what to do now are we?' Heather taunted. 'Go on then, have-a-go-heroine. What are you going to do? Kill me?' Heather opened her arms wide, challenging. 'No, I think not. The tabloids would eat you for breakfast. Put the gun down like a good girl.'

'You won't hurt me,' Erykah said. Her voice was shaking, but she had to believe what she said was true. 'You're crazy, Heather, but you couldn't put the finishing touches on Damian and you're not going to kill me.'

'Oh really?' Heather started to laugh again. Her arms kept swinging, back and forth, further and further. The microphone, now dangling from her fingertips, passed under a monitor speaker mounted between the production room door and the outside hallway. The interference caused a sudden loud squawking sound, like a tuba being crushed.

Heather froze and looked up. She spotted the red On Air light, glowing in the dim room. The microphone in her hand was picking up everything.

She froze, and her manic grin reformed into a horrified rictus. She looked from Erykah to Jonathan and back again.

'How long has that been on,' she said.

'Long enough.' Erykah edged around Heather, putting herself and the gun between Heather and the studio. 'Put the microphone down and come downstairs with us. The police are waiting.'

Heather pulled the microphone, hard. Another loud screech as the audio lines disconnected. She backed out of the room and into the hallway. 'Calm down, no one has to get hurt,' Erykah said. She looked over her shoulder and nodded her head at Jonathan, who was propping up Diana's pale and weak form. He pulled her step by shaky step to the safety of the stairwell. 'That's it, now put your hands up and sit on the floor,' Erykah said to Heather.

'No,' Heather's gargoyle grin hardened. 'Never.'

'Heather, you have no other choice,' Erykah said. 'The police are downstairs. Put the microphone down. Just – just put it down, and come with me. We'll go together.'

'I'm not going anywhere,' Heather said.

'Just come downstairs. It's fine. It's not far,' Erykah said. She hoped to keep her talking, calm her down. Maybe not calm her, exactly, but enough to let someone else take over. What was it Heather wanted? She didn't know, but it might have been something like she had wanted, or thought she wanted, once upon a time. Someone to listen and feel her pain. 'You can talk to the police and tell them. What you told me. You can get your story out there. People will listen. They're listening to you right now. You don't have to hurt other people just because you're hurting.'

'Hurting.' A snort. Heather stepped back a few paces, and tensed her legs like a sprinter at the start line. Her eyes focused on a spot over Erykah's shoulder and she licked her lips. 'You don't even *know* about my hurt.'

'So tell me.'

Heather snorted again. 'I was in Switzerland when it happened,' she said. 'They didn't even . . . the police walked into one of my tutorials and told me my father was dead.'

'How did he die?' Erykah said.

Heather held the mic like a pistol, straight under her chin. 'There were two bullets,' she said. 'One he must have fired in the air as a test shot. Then the real shot. My mother was the one who found him.' Her eyes hardened again and sought Erykah's. 'Do you know what that's like?'

Erykah closed her eyes. She was sitting in the car outside her house, waiting for Buster and Billy to finish inside. They had told her not to come in, said it was because she might leave evidence, but it was her own house, her prints and hair were already all over the place. She knew they didn't want her to see.

And she resisted the urge to look, kept resisting, when they drove past the canal. She heard them take the bag with Rab's body out of the boot, heard the heavy steps to the water's edge, heard the splash of the bag in the water. She didn't open her eyes again until they got back in the Merc, until Billy told her it was safe to look, that they were going to the radio station now. 'How did your mother react?'

'The way she always did,' Heather said. 'It was a shock for her, but the money was always more important to her than he was. She was only there that day because she was waiting for her tennis coach. She didn't love him the way – she didn't love him any more.' Her voice went softer, childlike. 'She blamed him for everything that happened to us after that. Said he was selfish, said he had done it to ruin her social chances. He had life insurance, but it was a suicide, so it didn't pay out. She never stopped blaming him for her having to come back to this country. But I knew him. And I loved him. I knew it wasn't his fault.'

'How did you feel?'

'How did I feel,' Heather said. She let her arm with the mic fall by her side, swinging. Her eyes focused on the gun. 'How did I feel?' She said it as if it was a punchline she was struggling to comprehend. 'How do you think I felt?' She was average size, maybe even slight. She was smaller than Erykah, but Erykah knew that wouldn't matter much if she made a run at her armed with the microphone stand and the will to kill or be killed.

'I think you felt as though there was no one left in the world who cared about you,' Erykah said. 'As if you were powerless. And that there was no one who would listen to the truth. I haven't been through what you've been through, but I know what it feels like not to be heard.' She licked her dry lips. 'I'm listening to you. Whatever you have to say, you can tell me.'

Heather was silent. 'You are the one who can end this now,' Erykah continued as gently as she could. 'You have the power to turn this around. Imagine Diana's family having to go through what your family went through. Do you want to do that to someone else? Take someone else away from the people who love them?' Heather didn't answer. 'Do you want more people to die? It won't bring your father back. It won't replace the family you lost. At least tell us what the poison is, and we can get her medical treatment right now. She can live. You don't have to kill anyone else.' Erykah's arms started to shake violently. Her thoughts were flying. Was Heather going to try to get the gun? It wasn't loaded. Did she know that? Did she recognise it from the Major's office? Why weren't the police here yet? When the police did come, would they arrest her too? Should she run at Heather? Or turn and run?

Heather shook her head slowly, her eyes not leaving the pistol in Erykah's hands for a moment. 'A good try with the first year psychology. No offence, but you're more than a little out of your depth here.'

'You have to talk about it to someone. You don't have much choice. Maybe if someone hears your story, this won't – this won't end as badly as it could.'

Heather met her eyes and smiled. A cool, flippant smile that chilled Erykah to the bone. She flicked her hair over her shoulder as if they were two schoolgirls standing on the sports pitch, not two sweating and bleeding women about to be overcome by police. 'No choice? Now that is where you are wrong,' she said. 'There's always another choice.'

Suddenly, Heather sprang into motion and a bolt of fear travelled through Erykah's body like a wave. Maybe she had been wrong after all, maybe Heather really did have it in her to kill. She really was going to do it.

Erykah dove to one side and landed hard on her left shoulder. A pain shot down her arm, so sharp it felt metallic. She rolled out of the way, the gun still clutched in her right hand.

But it wasn't her that Heather was making a run for. Heather barrelled right past where Erykah had been standing and kept on going. She was heading straight towards the outside windows. Too late Erykah realised what she was about to do. It all seemed to be happening in slow motion: the leap, the mic stand held in front of her face, the last scream as Heather made a jump for it. She hit the huge single pane window at full speed. The sound of glass again, crinkling like cellophane, falling away from the rotten old window frames.

Jump before you're pushed.

The time between when Heather jumped and when she landed felt like the longest few seconds of Erykah's life. Her mind knew what she had just seen, but refused to process it.

There was a wet thump and crunch of bone on the pavement outside the LCC building, muffled from three floors away. Erykah hauled herself off the floor and tiptoed to the window, the gun hanging by her right side. People were crowded on the pavement and looking down at the body. The unnaturally twisted neck. A pool of dark blood started to spread from under Heather's head. They hadn't yet started to look up, to wonder where this strange and unexpected offering came from. One lone face was tilted to the sky. A pair of eyes met hers. His face lit up in recognition. It was the evangelist in the bad suit who spoke to her on the street outside the station the first time she met Kerry. 'God has sent us a message from above! Repent sinners! Satan shall be defeated!' he shouted. Erykah ducked back inside.

The pair ran out to find Diana and Jonathan still on the stairs. Diana had collapsed and Jonathan was unable to carry her. Erykah shoved the gun down the back of her jeans. She put her good shoulder under Diana's arm, heaved her to a standing position and together the three of them managed to walk her down. The shoulder where Erykah had landed felt weak and she dared not look down in case it was broken. Run now. Deal with it later.

Seminole Billy was waiting at the bottom of the stairwell with Barrington and Kerry. He propped the door open with one shiny leather boot. 'Jesus, woman, you know how to keep a man waiting. We have to dash. Like, fifteen minutes ago.'

A few dozen people were trapped in the foyer with them: the radio staff, the accountancy firm from the floor below, secretaries and a few irritated executives from other small offices. Their excited whispers hummed in the air. Nobody seemed to notice their small group emerging from the stairwell: they were looking at the glass front doors, pointing at the police trying to come inside. Some were even pointing their mobiles that way, filming something happening on the other side.

'I know,' she said, and nodded towards Diana. 'And she needs a doctor. But how do we get out of here?'

'Out the back,' Billy said.

'Door's broken,' Kerry shook her head.

'Not broken, just out of order.' Barrington produced a key chained to a large wooden stake from behind his back with a flourish. He caught the questioning look in Kerry's eyes. 'What? Vampire insurance,' he explained.

'We only got a few minutes before the police get in,' Billy said. 'Some weirdo chained himself to the front doors.'

'You're leaving?' Kerry turned to Erykah. 'Where are you going?'

'Anywhere but here,' she said. She was wired with adrenaline, short on sleep, and struggling to make sense of the last few days. But one thing was certain: she had no interest in being in front of the cameras again. Ever. The face of the evangelist looking up at her: had he recognised her? He must have done. Would he tell the police? She wasn't about to wait around and find out.

'You can't go,' Kerry said. 'I mean for one thing, someone's got to tell the police what happened.'

The girl had a point. With a crowd of several dozen people outside growing larger by the second, it was hardly likely that she would be able to slip out with a 'no comment' and a smile.

Erykah examined the few faces she could see through the doors. She saw a few of the evangelists, but not the man in the rumpled suit who had been looking up at the window when she was looking down. Was he out there? Maybe the crowd had ruined any chance of bringing people to Jesus today. Or maybe the sight of a real person falling from the sky for no reason had changed something in him. Death had a way of doing that.

'So you'll be me,' Erykah suddenly said.

'Excuse me?'

'Think about it. There's no reason why this can't be your scoop instead of mine.' She took the handbag back from Kerry and unloaded the papers and notebooks and shoving them her direction.

'But I can't do that!'

'Why not?' For all anyone knew it was Kerry in the studio with Heather, not Erykah, when the radio was on. Kerry worked there. She was the anonymous tweeter already, the insider. She had done no wrong in the eyes of the press. Why not be the hero who saved the day as well? It was a better story that way; it made more sense. 'Take the papers and go public. Show them what Media Mouse is made of.'

'No,' Kerry said. 'I don't know what most of this is.'

'Doesn't matter,' Erykah said. She looked at Jonathan and Diana. 'And you two – this never happened. You never saw me.' She hoped, in the hurry and the shock, that they would listen to her. Or if they didn't, that no one would believe them anyway.

Jonathan shook his head. 'Saw nothing,' Diana stammered, her arms and legs limp. She held the sleeve of her shirt against her forehead to stem the trickle of blood running down her face, but she needed more than basic first aid, and fast.

'Wait,' Kerry grabbed Erykah's shoulder. 'What about me? What am I supposed to do?' she said.

'Everything you need is in there.' She jabbed a finger in the stack of papers. 'Schofield wrote his notes in code, here's how it was decrypted. It looks like someone tweaked the government report on oil shale deposits, and he was going to blow their cover.' She didn't know what to make of what Heather said about her father and Schofield in Argentina, or whether it was even true. That would be somebody else's job to figure out.

'This is incredible,' Kerry said, flipping through the notebooks and photocopies. The look on her face went from horrified and frightened to ecstatic, and back again. 'And so fucked up. I mean, thank you . . .'

'Don't thank me,' Erykah said. 'Seriously, don't. Find a journalist you can trust.' She paused. 'On second thought, there are no journalists you can trust.' She nodded in the direction of Diana and Jonathan. 'Definitely not these two. Find someone who will give you the credit for this. Make sure they publish everything. Stand over their shoulder while they type if you have to.'

'Wait . . . are you sure? Don't you want to do it?'

'No way, no day,' Erykah shook her head. 'I've had enough of that treadmill to last the rest of my life. ' Even the crowd on the other side of the doors unnerved her, and they were at a safe distance, at least for now. 'Go on. Take it. Enjoy whatever this brings you.'

Billy was pulling at Erykah's arm now, with Barrington the security man unlocking the back exit. 'There's no police if we go across the alley and through the next building,' he said. 'Barrington has the keys. But we have to hurry – come on.'

'Where's Buster?'

'He's at the canal with the car. I don't want to keep him waiting.' The risk Buster would be spotted was too high otherwise, and with the bags and cleaning supplies in the back of the car he would almost certainly be nicked.

Erykah looked from his face to Barrington's. 'What about security cameras? They would have got us coming in and up in the studio.'

Barrington shook his head. 'Already taken care of. Power goes out, the system loses any data that wasn't backed up, and we only back up at the end of the day,' he said and nodded at Billy.

'So the power loss wasn't the police?' Erykah said.

'Hey, I didn't say that.' Barrington shook his head. 'All I'm saying is, it turns out I owed this man a favour from a long time back, and he collected on that debt today.'

'He's an old friend of Buster's cousin,' Billy said.

On the other side of the revolving doors, police had dropped a plastic sheet over the body on the pavement and were pushing back the crowd, waiting for scene of crime officers to arrive. An ambulance had mounted the kerb, and paramedics were rushing for the doors to take Diana to hospital. Photographers pushed through, trying to get as close as they could to the body. 'Now let's get out of here before one of those dumb fucks catches us in a shot.'

'Wait,' Kerry clutched at Erykah's jumper. 'Is there some way I can get in touch with you? In case there are questions?'

'You've been winging it fine so far,' Erykah said. She walked to the back door where Billy was waiting.

Kerry looked at the scene on the other side of the glass, then back at the open door leading into the alley. Her mouth turned down at the corners. 'I can't. I'm not ready for this.' Her voice wavered. 'I never intended for this to turn into anything, nothing like this.' Her thin arms wrapped tightly around the files. 'Can I come with you?'

Erykah put a hand on her back. She could feel Kerry's sharp shoulder blades through the cheap fabric of her shirt. The girl's heart was beating so hard and so fast, rattling the ribcage, it might as easily have been her own. 'I know you're frightened,' Erykah said. 'But people are rooting for you. They want a whistle-blower. They want the little guy to win and the conspiracies to be exposed. You've captured something. You would be a fool not to grab this.'

'They deserve better than just me,' Kerry said. 'I'm only an intern. Why me?'

'Why not you?' Erykah said. There was a tap of a truncheon on the glass. They had finally snapped through the chains and were about to come in through the barred doors. Barrington rushed over. 'No one deserves what they get. And no one gets what they deserve.' She pulled the scarf from her bag and wound the ends around the young woman's neck. 'Here, I forgot to give you this.'

Kerry dragged the end of a sleeve under her nose, took a deep breath, and nodded towards where a scrum of photographers was standing in a ring around Heather's shrouded corpse, scene of crime officers in white plastic suits pushing their way through the crowd. 'Any advice before I go out there?'

Billy pushed Erykah towards the open door into the alley. She started to go and then paused, counting off the fingers of one hand. 'Never trust the press,' she said. 'Never marry someone less than a year after you meet them. And never, ever accept a key to a lock you haven't tried.' She turned and followed Billy. They walked out the door into the back alley, and then they were gone.

: 34 :

They said little on the drive; there was little to say. Seminole Billy kept checking his mirrors but only out of habit. The police were not looking for them. Buster got in the boot without even a protest. The radio stayed off. Whatever the news was, they didn't need to hear about it now. They had been there.

Erykah's shoulder throbbed painfully from where she had hit the floor. But she was too dazed to do anything about it, even to look through her bag for painkillers.

She wasn't sure at first if she remembered how to get where they were going. To her surprise, even though the streets and shops had all changed, there was one thing you could never forget: the way home. There was the old crumbling picture house. The boarded-up nightclub where Grayson used to meet his associates. The bus shelter on the corner where they had their first kiss.

The truth of the story, or parts of it, were going to come out. The fake lottery, the laundered money. With neither Heather nor the Major there to keep the cameras distracted, surely it was only a matter of following the money back to – where? The lottery scam, of course. Scotland, maybe. Then? The Channel Islands? Argentina? Who knows? Who got to tell that story, and what kind of narrative emerged, was still to be decided. There was still all to play for. But not for Erykah. Not by her.

Kerry had questions. Well, Erykah had questions of her own. Such as what made Heather do what she had done? Oh, she told them all right – but what caused the switch to flip, caused someone to go from a simmering, long term resentment, to outright hatred, to . . . this? And then, having failed to achieve what she wanted, to end it all. An impulsive decision, maybe. But an impulse at the end of a long and deliberate plan of action. Most people, when faced with the failure of the one thing they had spent their whole lives building for, would take their lumps and go home. Bury the shame and sorrow under food and drink and long nights staring at whatever the television had to offer.

Back to their unsatisfying lives, their unsatisfying marriages. Heather must have imagined all that in the time they were standing there, and decided it wasn't for her. It was admirable in its own way.

At least Heather wouldn't have to see what the news cycle decided her story was going to be. Erykah knew that even the public's desire for a mystery to have a satisfying ending was no guarantee of an easy ride for the rest of them. As long as Media Mouse was anonymous people seemed happy to take her at her word, give or take the odd conspiracy theory. Would they feel the same way when presented with a flesh and blood person? Or would they take one look at Kerry with her crooked pigtail, the inexpensive, high street work clothes, and decide that she wasn't the symbol they wanted after all? How long before the snide columns appeared, tearing her down for being insufficiently feminine or feminist? How long before she became a where-are-they-now, a footnote to the story?

Soon it would turn from a juicy scoop into a feeding frenzy. Erykah had been in the middle of those before and if she had learned anything, it was that she never wanted to be inside of one again. But she wanted to believe it could turn out differently. Maybe someone younger would have a chance of surviving it. Someone who chose to get involved, rather than ending up there by accident. Maybe for people who grew up with celebrity culture and social media, where everyone was angling for their fifteen minutes of fame, things would be better.

It didn't seem likely, but it could happen.

As the Merc got closer to the flat, the cosmetic differences that had built up in the last twenty years fell away. Here were, if not the same people, the same kinds of people she had grown up with. They were standing on street corners, looking out of windows, waiting for something to happen. She remembered what it was like to be always waiting for something to happen. Had spent most of her life waiting, in fact. Now she was sure she had enough of whatever that something was for a lifetime. Maybe two.

'That's it there, pull in on the left,' she said. Seminole Billy brought the car to a stop under a row of cherry trees. They had been spindly seedlings twenty years ago. The first few pink blossoms were starting to show on the highest branches, now some thirty feet high. Things had been smartened up a little – a few new gates here and there, the short iron fences painted. The grass had recently been cut.

'You going to be safe here?' he asked.

Was she going to be safe? Was anyone? On the ride from Soho to the flat she had been trying to make sense of something. Of the story, as she uncovered it. She thought she had found the deep roots of a conspiracy, and for the most part, she wasn't wrong. What surprised her was Heather's bottomless hatred for Schofield. The wounded child who wanted revenge for something that had been done a long time ago in another country. It wasn't just politics. It had been personal for her.

'I'll be safer here than anywhere else,' she said. It hadn't been true in Molesey, quiet suburban Molesey, but for some reason she knew she would be fine here. She caught the look in his eye. 'Don't worry about me. If there's one thing I know it's that this place looks out for its own.'

'You could come with me,' he said.

Erykah snorted. 'That had better not be a double entendre,' she said.

'Only if you want it to be.'

She rolled her eyes and looked out the window. 'I was wondering if we were going to be able to finish things without you hitting on me,' she said. The engine of the Merc rattled and chugged in neutral, shaking the seats under them. 'Anyway, where do you guys even live? Don't answer that – I probably don't want to know.'

'No, probably not.' He looked out at the estate, with its crumbling low rises and patchy thin grass sprouting up between pavement blocks. 'Be in touch. I don't want to come hunting you down again.'

'Thanks.' She opened the door and started to get out, then on impulse, leaned across and planted a kiss on Billy's cheek. His skin felt older than she thought it would, thin and delicate like paper.

Billy gave a cockeyed salute and waited while she entered the front of the red brick building. She looked back outside and saw him set his mouth in a thin line and look away. The car disappeared around the corner, coughing and sputtering.

She walked up the three familiar flights of stairs. It still smelled the same, like industrial orange-scented cleaner, and underneath that, a smell of rubber and ashes.

Two dark, scuffed squares of linoleum outside the door marked the entrance to the flat. The key fitted in the lock and she pushed the door open. Dozens of old bills and junk mail envelopes were piled behind the post slot. She cleared it away with her foot.

Rab hadn't been the only one with secrets to keep. While he had been busy trying to hide his mistresses and juggle his lies all those years, Erykah had quietly made an offer and bought her mum's old flat when the council put it on the market. It had stayed empty most of the years since, gathering dust and spiders and the mildew smell of abandonment. Erykah had never changed the locks, in part hoping her mother would come back, in part afraid that she would. Rainbow stayed gone; whatever had happened to her remained a mystery.

Erykah bolted the door behind her and tossed her handbag on the sofa. It was musty, she heaved open a white-painted sash window to let in some air and light. She looked around. All of the old furniture was still there, sitting on the oddments of carpet that she had dragged piece by piece out of other flats and skips. In the corner of the front room was the television her mum had been paying twelve pounds fifty on every week for years. Those places were such a rip-off, Rainbow had probably paid for the thing in full several times over. Here was the worn spot where she used to sit, waiting for the lottery. Waiting for things to change.

The glass-topped round table in the corner was covered in a thin film of dust. In times when Rainbow had been doing well, that was where she had held court, chain smoking and cackling with neighbours as they played endless rounds of cribbage and spades, sometimes for money, sometimes for weed. When things were not so good, it was where Erykah often found her mother in the mornings, collapsed forehead first on the glass, usually with a smouldering fag butt or a cold cup of coffee in her hand.

She thought about Joy, the neighbour with the grits, and wondered if she was still alive.

Erykah rubbed her thumb across the surface of the table. It left a long clean streak on the top. Maybe the shop was open and she could get a bottle of ammonia and some rags and set about cleaning the place.

In the kitchen the fridge with its tiny freezer compartment was empty, open and unplugged. The walls were still tea coloured from cigarette smoke and cooking grease. She knelt down and opened the cupboard next to the sink. The old electric meter that took coins was gone; now everything was on cards. Erykah put the card in the slot and pressed a button. The lights flickered on. One bulb popped, but the rest were fine. The shower still worked: good. There was clean linen in the hall cupboard: even better.

She pulled her jumper off over her head. Gingerly, so as not to hurt her shoulder. In the mirror over the sink she saw a large bruise blooming on her left side, from where she had hit the ground when Heather started to run. She touched the tender flesh, stretched and rolled her shoulder to test the joint. Only bruised, nothing broken. She rooted in the cupboard but found only an empty blister pack of ibuprofen. There was still half a small bottle of whisky in her bag from Billy. That would have to do. The grimy mirror blurred her face. The woman looking back at her was not the same woman she had seen there a month ago. Or even this morning.

She went back to the front room. There was a cheap chipboard bookshelf with white veneer peeling off the sides. Once it had been in her bedroom, full of books; now it was empty. Well, that wouldn't do. She took the book of puzzles out of her bag and propped it on the empty shelf.

What was the saying? Home is the place that, when you have to go there, they have to take you in.

So this would be home, then.

Erykah Macdonald had a gun with no bullets, a change of clothes, two diamond rings and twenty thousand pounds in cash. She had no idea what she was going to do next.

ACKNOWLEDGEMENTS

Thanks are due to my former colleagues at the Medico Legal Centre who put up with a lot and taught me even more. I am especially grateful for the professional knowledge and generosity of Robert Forrest, Andrew Chamberlain, David Jarvis, Ian Newsome, and Steph Davy during those years. Thank you as well to Misha Laurents and anyone who shared a studio with me at WVFS, a lifetime ago now (Continuity and News keep the faith). A nod as well to old rowing chums at Sheffield and Imperial, especially Clarice Chung, Ben Anstiss and of course, to Nick Wilde. Much gratitude to Simon Singh for tips regarding ciphers. Uncle Jon, know that dragging me to all those gun shows meant something. This would be a very different book indeed without the input of Schuyler Towne and Nigel Tolley, locksport mavens. Aspasia Bonasera and Chris Nicholson also provided helpful advice. I couldn't have got through the past few years without the unwavering support of Maggie McNeill, Matthew Garner, Antoinette Cosgrave, and Paul Duane. To Peter Kenny, fellow colonial misfit and keeper of the Brain Soup flame, I hope you find the starter appetising! A certain Internet degu deserves a nod here, for donating the name of his owner to the cause, even though I didn't use it in the end (sorry, Rog). Much thanks as ever to Genevieve Pegg, Patrick Walsh, and Michael Burton – hands down the kindest and most trustworthy people in London. And thank you to my husband, a forgiving early reader and patient editor with a thing or two to add about the Royal Marines and war history.

Also how gracious is Professor Damian Schofield for allowing me to borrow his name for a corpse? It would be remiss of me not to mention he is neither a geologist nor is he, at the time of printing, dead.